A KISS BETWEEN THE RAINDROPS

Bella tipped her head back. Spiky, wet lashes framed his fathomless brown eyes. A raindrop slid down his cheek, and she reached up to catch it with her fingertip. Mesmerized, she traced the strong line of his jaw, the hint of his day's beard a mere gentle scrape. She let her hand drop past his shoulder to his upper arm.

Honey gold skin backed the wet, white lawn shirt, which molded to the contours of his biceps. There was absolutely no give to the solid muscles beneath her hand. Over the years she had come to associate strength in a man with unpleasantness, but Mr. Rosedale's well-honed body roused only passion and a pressing desire to see more.

He stood perfectly still, and she knew he was letting her do as she pleased. That he was giving his body up for her pleasure. She looked up into the face tilted down to hers and found patience, and delight at her exploration. And a bit of arrogance as well, judging from the faintly smug curve of his mouth. The man had to know he was put together perfectly.

Unable to resist the lure a moment longer, she placed her hands on his broad shoulders and lifted up onto her toes. She could taste the cool spring rain on his lips . . .

Her Ladyship's Companion

EVANGELINE COLLINS

BERKLEY SENSATION, NEW YORK

THE BERKLEY PUBLISHING GROUP
Published by the Penguin Group
Penguin Group (USA) Inc.
375 Hudson Street, New York, New York 10014, USA
Penguin Group (Canada), 90 Eglinton Avenue East, Suite 700, Toronto, Ontario M4P 2Y3, Canada
(a division of Pearson Penguin Canada Inc.)
Penguin Books Ltd., 80 Strand, London WC2R 0RL, England
Penguin Group Ireland, 25 St. Stephen's Green, Dublin 2, Ireland (a division of Penguin Books Ltd.)
Penguin Group (Australia), 250 Camberwell Road, Camberwell, Victoria 3124, Australia
(a division of Pearson Australia Group Pty. Ltd.)
Penguin Books India Pvt. Ltd., 11 Community Centre, Panchsheel Park, New Delhi—110 017, India
Penguin Group (NZ), 67 Apollo Drive, Rosedale, North Shore 0632, New Zealand
(a division of Pearson New Zealand Ltd.)
Penguin Books (South Africa) (Pty.) Ltd., 24 Sturdee Avenue, Rosebank, Johannesburg 2196,
South Africa

Penguin Books Ltd., Registered Offices: 80 Strand, London WC2R 0RL, England

This book is an original publication of The Berkley Publishing Group.

Cover illustration by Jim Griffin.
Cover design by George Long.
Interior text design by Kristin del Rosario.

PRINTING HISTORY
Berkley Sensation trade paperback edition / May 2009

Library of Congress Cataloging-in-Publication Data

Collins, Evangeline.
Her ladyship's companion / Evangeline Collins.—Berkley sensation trade paperback ed.
p. cm.
ISBN 978-0-425-22820-3
I. Title.

PS3603.O45423H47 2009
813'.6—dc22

2008054337

PRINTED IN THE UNITED STATES OF AMERICA

10 9 8 7 6 5 4 3 2 1

To Chris,
my wonderful and very supportive husband,
for always believing in me.

Prologue

MAY 1811
LONDON, ENGLAND

MIDNIGHT. The appointed time was so close Bella could almost taste the kiss waiting for her. Even the cool night air floating in through the open carriage window seemed to carry the scents of horses, hay, and leather. The scents she so closely linked to him.

"And her grandson returned from the war with a bride in tow. Can you believe it, Lady Isabella? Some chit from Italy, and he . . ."

Lips curved in a small smile and features schooled in polite attention, Bella found it was nothing at all to feign mild interest as her chaperone relayed the latest bit of gossip. It was the same expression she had worn all evening. The one she had spent the majority of her last eighteen years perfecting. And it effectively masked the very unladylike thoughts occupying her mind.

Midnight. The stables. The memory of Conor's voice drifted over her. The potent desire in the whispered words shivered down her spine. She hadn't been anticipating them, but the second before he lifted her onto her horse for her five o'clock ride through Hyde Park with today's bland lord, he whispered them in her ear. And those words stayed with her all evening. "Midnight," he said. Never before had seven hours passed so slowly.

Her perpetually straight shoulder brushed the wall of the carriage as the driver made the final left turn onto Grosvenor Street. The anticipation that had been tickling and teasing roared through her veins. Wicked and heady, it lit up every nerve in her body.

The edges of her lips twitched. Almost home.

After what felt like an eternity, the carriage stopped outside of Mayburn House, the London residence of her brother, the new Earl of Mayburn. Through sheer force of will Bella remained seated on the black leather bench, her hands folded demurely on her lap, waiting for the footman to open the door.

"I do so hope you feel better on the morrow." The light from a nearby street lamp illuminated her chaperone's wrinkled face, etched with genuine concern. "Lady Knolwood is hosting a musicale tomorrow evening and everyone will be there."

The pang of guilt at deceiving her indulgent chaperone could not compete with the prospect of Conor. A passing comment about a headache brought on by the overheated ballroom was all it had taken to ensure their prompt departure at the necessary time.

"I am sure a bit of rest is all I need. Good evening, your ladyship." With a tip of her head, Bella exited the carriage. The front door of the stately townhome swung open as she approached. The house was empty save for the servants. Still, she did her best to walk serenely up the stairs, the almost unstoppable impulse to bolt straight to him, to run into his arms, winding tighter and tighter with each measured step.

When she reached the landing, she glanced over her shoulder. Her brother's butler had his back to her as he locked the door. Seizing the opportunity, she lifted her skirts with one hand and raced along the hall and down the narrow servants' stairs.

Her pulse pounding, her breaths light and fast, she threw open the door to the stables and stopped just inside. Her hand fluttered to her chest, her heart beating high and hard against her ribs. The golden glow from a small lantern along the aisle barely penetrated the darkness. Except for the sounds of the horses moving about in their stalls, the stable appeared empty.

"Conor?" she whispered, hoping she was not too late yet at the same time suddenly tentative. A cool breeze blew in through the open door, wrapping her silk skirt about her calves and rustling the leaves on the tree in the courtyard. She glanced over her shoulder, toward the white stucco walls of Mayburn House. Perhaps she should turn back and—

"Lady Isabella." Low and rich, and with a deliciously lyrical Irish accent, his voice drifted from the darkness, vanquishing the apprehension that had begun to settle in her belly. "I am here."

A sob of relief shook her chest. She darted forward, the soles of her slippers tapping swiftly on the bricks, the sound of his voice pulling her into an open stall and straight to him.

The moonlight seeping in from a window at the back of the stall outlined the broad line of his shoulders and gave his black hair a bluish tint. Tall and rugged, he had the build of a laborer, of a man who spent his days putting his muscles to good use.

"What brings the lady to the stables at such a late hour?" Head tilted down slightly and with his dark blue gaze locked with hers, he advanced. Straw crunched beneath his dusty boots with each slow, predatory step.

She didn't take issue with his teasing question. If not for his arrogance, for that cocky self-assurance, she'd still be fantasizing about what it would be like to kiss a man rather than having experienced it. And more than anything, she wanted to experience it again tonight.

"You," she said, lifting her chin while she backed up, keeping the distance between them and stopping only when her back encountered the wall.

He continued to advance, coming closer than any gentleman had ever dared. He braced a hand against the wall, about level with her shoulder. With his other hand, he trailed his fingertips up her bare arm, leaving a trail of gooseflesh in his wake. A tremble wracked her body.

His lips curved in a devilish smirk. "I am honored," he said, pressing so close her breasts brushed his shirt with each rapid rise and fall of her chest.

Then he claimed her mouth as only he could, as only he had. Bold and aggressive, he took what he wanted, and she eagerly gave it to him. Every bit of restraint left her as she threw her arms around Conor's neck, reveling in the urgent demand of his kiss. His tongue tangling with hers, his mouth slanting harshly over hers, the hard bulk of his body surrounding her as an incredible, intoxicating rush of passion overtook her.

Growling low in his throat, he tugged at the low neckline of her bodice. Cool air hit her breasts, drawing the tips into hard buds. She closed her eyes as a pinch of modesty threatened to infiltrate the luscious haze of sensations. Then he dragged his lips from hers, his breath scorching her neck, his teeth nipping her skin, sending desire clamoring full force once again through her veins.

He dropped his head to her chest, his day's growth of beard an unexpected tickle on the soft underside of her breasts. She gasped for breath, threaded her fingers into his thick black hair, and shifted beneath him, wanting more. The next instant she felt him gathering her skirt, reaching beneath, work-roughened fingertips trailing up her thigh. He captured a nipple between his lips and suckled, pulling the hard tip into his hot mouth.

At the sharp lance of pleasure, her eyes fluttered open and her gaze fell on a figure standing just outside the open stall door. The black greatcoat broadened his already impressive frame, making him appear that much more imposing. A leather saddlebag was clutched tightly in one fist, the ends of his horse's reins in the other.

The light from the sole lantern three stalls down provided enough illumination for Bella to make out her elder brother's face, slack jawed with horror. Then the horror abruptly faded, replaced with such outrage it doused every trace of desire coursing through her body, leaving her once heated and flushed skin icy cold.

For a moment, she could do nothing but stare in pure disbelief into Phillip's narrowed eyes. *What was he doing here? He had said he would be gone for a week and he left but a handful of days prior.*

"Get off of her."

The low, vengeful rumble snapped her to her senses, and Conor apparently as well. With a curse, her groom untangled himself from her. Hands shaking with a near-paralyzing mixture of humiliation and panic, she tugged up her bodice to cover her breasts and straightened her skirts.

Conor hastily turned to face Phillip. "Your lordship . . . I-I—"

"You. In my study. Isabella, go to your room." The words were a growl.

Horrid, heavy guilt descended. Unable to think of anything to say to him, for no words could excuse her conduct, she darted past Conor and Phillip, past the burly black hunter standing patiently in the aisle, out of the stables, and into the house.

LADY Isabella Riley paused before the oak door. Phillip had not said a word to her for two long days. Bella had not even laid eyes on him. She had stayed ensconced in her room, alone save for the servants who delivered her trays and returned to take away the untouched dishes. She had already missed one musicale and an afternoon tea, but had not received a note from her chaperone inquiring about her absence. Which meant Phillip had spoken to the old dowager or somehow word had gotten out about her indiscretion. And if that happened, she was absolutely ruined, no use to Phillip at all.

All the years she spent perfecting the ladylike veneer, polishing that image of what everyone wanted and expected her to be, were for naught. She had always known that wickedness was inside of her, and she had done everything to fight it, stifle it, deny it the light of day. But when the test came, when it truly counted, she failed. Failed

Phillip. Failed her younger sisters, Kitty and Liv. Failed her mischievous little brother, Jules. She had failed.

If word had truly gotten out, there was no way she could repair the damage. Gossip and rumor ruled a lady's reputation. The virginity she had managed to keep intact had lost all value. No respectable gentleman would ever wed her. Phillip had been fully confident she'd succeed in bringing the needed husband to heel by the end of her first Season. Together, they would right the earldom and secure their younger siblings' futures. But the massive debts their father left behind would now continue to go unpaid. They could lose everything, all because she hadn't been strong enough to resist.

Conor was the first man who had not been fooled by the icy façade, by the defenses she raised against herself. The first man bold enough to test it, to steal a kiss. And that kiss, on that fateful morning when she ventured innocently into the stables, had been her downfall. With him, she had been able to be, for the first time in her life, simply herself. And her mind had not been able to focus on anything else but him—not even the consequences of getting caught with one of her brother's grooms.

Heart clenching in despair, Bella pushed aside the threat of tears pricking the corners of her eyes. Phillip expected her—his terse note requested her presence. Her arm felt like it weighed ten stone as she slowly raised it to rap her knuckles on the solid oak.

"Enter."

She opened the door and walked serenely across her late father's study. The fact that Phillip did not look at her cut to the quick. Inwardly shaking, she paused before the large oak desk, clasped her hands in front of her, lifted her chin, and waited.

When he finished the letter he was writing, he slipped his pen into the silver penholder. His short brown hair looked as though he had recently run his fingers through it in frustration. Frustration brought on by her reckless actions. He was only twenty years old, yet since he inherited a few short months ago, the heavy weight of the earldom had aged him beyond his years. Instead of being able to bring him a reprieve, she'd brought him yet another defeat against the constant battle to keep them afloat.

The thick silence pressed in on her, a physical force compressing her lungs. "Phillip, I—"

"You will wed Lord Stirling." There was absolutely no inflection, not a trace of his usual brotherly warmth in those cold, flat words.

Bella swallowed past the lump in her throat. "Yes, Phillip."

When his blue green eyes met hers, she truly wished he would go back to staring at his letter. Anger she could take, but his disappointment she could not. It was too much for the practiced calm to hold up against. Before she crumpled to the floor, before she wept for his forgiveness, she fled the room.

The coldness in his eyes said she could never make it up to him—the bond they once shared had been irrevocably shattered, never to be repaired. The only hope she had was to wed a stranger, this Lord Stirling, this husband Phillip had found for her, and somehow through it, perhaps, someday, become worthy of being Phillip's sister again.

One

APRIL 1816
BOWHILL PARK, SELKIRK, SCOTLAND

LIPS pursed, Bella cocked her head and debated the stretched white linen on her lap. *Not another red one.* She had too many of those already. Over the last five years almost every towel, napkin, and pillowcase at Bowhill Park had been gifted with a red rose. Her fingers hovered over the tin box next to her hip on the settee before selecting the yellow silk thread and slipping the end through the eye of a needle.

The logs in the hearth crackled. The fire chased the spring evening chill from the small parlor. The soft flick of a page of a book being turned barely penetrated her concentration as she focused on her embroidery. Drawing the needle through the linen, stretching the thread taut, carefully placing the next stitch. Slow and meticulous, with absolutely no reason to hurry.

It was a ritual she knew well, one she repeated most every evening, but at least she wasn't alone tonight. Her cousin's presence, infrequent though it may be, was a treasured respite from the usually long, lonely days.

"You need a man."

"Pardon?" Her hands stilled. She glanced to her cousin, Madame Esmé Marceau, who sat across from her.

Reclined elegantly in a floral chintz armchair, Esmé closed the small leather-bound book of poetry—*The Works of Anacreon and Sappho*—and placed it on the end table next to her half-filled glass of wine. "You need a man, Isabella."

Amusement tickled Bella's chest. Esmé definitely did not fit the mold of demure English propriety. Widowed at nineteen and long accustomed to arranging her life as she pleased, the Frenchwoman thought nothing of speaking her mind. Clothed in the latest fashions and backed by her husband's wealth, the striking brunette found few who dared to match wits with her. Bella just happened to be one of the few.

"Do I, now?" Actually, Bella did need a man, but she wasn't about to admit it, let alone the reason why.

"You're in need of a flirtation. You have become much too maudlin. It's just the thing to raise your spirits."

Her violet eyes, an exact match to Bella's own, were devoid of their usual impish spark—that look that made others feel as though Esmé knew their most scandalous secrets. The amusement seeped out of Bella, leaving behind a very faint tremble in her hands as she tucked the needle into the linen. Esmé was not teasing her. She was not being her usual bold, playful self. She was deadly serious, and that fact alone concerned Bella far more than her perceptive suggestion.

"Esmé." She forced a firm note into her voice to cover the alarm tightening the straight line of her spine. "I do not need a flirtation and I am not maudlin."

"You are significantly more subdued than when last I visited. I have only been able to coax but a handful of smiles out of you this past fortnight."

Unwilling to risk revealing the source of her malaise, Bella dropped her gaze and studied the partially embroidered yellow rose. "The weather has been so dreary of late. I do not believe the sun has shown itself for days. And it did nothing but rain yesterday."

"The weather?" Esmé gave her a look of patent disappointment. "Do you truly believe that will work on me? My dear Isabella, surely you can conjure a better excuse than that."

She should have known her attempt at nonchalance would not fool her cousin.

Esmé let out a soft sigh and reached for the glass of Bordeaux. "I have extended the invitation countless times, yet you refuse to come to France to see me." The hint of her native French accent gave her voice a sophisticated lilt. "If it's the long journey that has put you off, why not go to London instead? Though you have yet to use it, I can attest to the quality of your traveling carriage."

"I am more than content to accept your word on the quality of my carriage." Shipping a traveling carriage across the Channel was a cumbersome affair. Not that Bella had ever endured the process, but that was what Esmé gave as the reason she hired a carriage at the docks to take her to Scotland and borrowed Bella's when her visit was over. But the long journey was not the cause of Bella's reluctance to leave Bowhill.

"I heard Julien's in Town. Your brother would be happy to see you."

Jules probably had the entire female population of London at his feet. At the thought of her mischievous little brother, a smile teased Bella's lips, and then vanished. "But Phillip would not be happy to see me."

A scowl marred Esmé's brow, but thankfully she did not argue the point. "Then don't stay at Mayburn House. Rent a suite at the Pulteney and go to the theatre. While you're there, select one of the many gentlemen who will undoubtedly be vying for your attention and spend a few days with him."

"I have no desire to go to Town. I prefer to stay at Bowhill." It was so much easier to be good, to resist temptation, if she stayed where her husband had put her.

"But you're much too isolated up here. All you have are your servants to keep you company."

"I have callers," Bella said, doing her best to sound indignant.

Esmé's amethyst silk dress rustled as she pulled herself up from her elegant slouch to lean slightly forward. "Who?"

"The neighbors, Mr. and Mrs. Tavisham, come to dine on occasion."

"They're an old married couple." Esmé dismissed them with a wave of her hand. "You need someone your own age. Someone other than those roses to entertain you."

"I enjoy the gardens. Tending the roses is very peaceful and rewarding," Bella said, repeating the words she told herself on too many occasions to count, when the isolation and loneliness threatened to overwhelm her. "I do not need a man. In any case, I am married. I have a husband." She lifted her chin.

Esmé took up the challenge, just as she always did. "When was the last time you saw him?"

Fighting to keep her shoulders from rounding against the jagged shudder skipping down her spine, Bella paused for the space of two heartbeats. "Before Christmas."

"And how long did this husband of yours stay?"

"A day," Bella confessed, dropping her chin. It had been a day much too long.

Esmé's expression hardened, her full lips thinning into a straight line. "He is not a husband to you. We both know your marriage is not a love match. And before you even say it, any man who abandons his wife in the country for years cannot expect fidelity. Lord knows he certainly has not been a monk."

Unnerved by her words, Bella did not contradict her. "Even if I wanted to indulge in a flirtation, I could not. I cannot very well enlist any man from around here. Men talk, they brag about their exploits, and word could get back to Stirling."

Esmé's eyes twinkled with mischievous intent. "Since you won't leave Bowhill, if you agree, I will hire you a man and have him sent to you."

Bella sucked in a swift, startled breath.

Esmé let out a soft tsk of annoyance. "Don't presume to be scandalized. You're not some innocent young miss."

She caught the correction before it could leave her lips. "But Esmé, how could you possibly suggest—"

Esmé cut off her protests. "Most of the married gentlemen of the *ton* visit brothels and a few of the married ladies do as well. You are a woman and you are my cousin, Isabella. We share the same blood. And I am telling you, you need a man." She spoke the last words very clearly and deliberately.

Esmé did know her. She knew Bella better than her siblings, even better than Phillip. Knew her well enough to know what lay beneath the well-schooled façade. As such, her cousin was the only person who had not been shocked and appalled at the reason behind her exile from London. Her only comment on the whole affair had been—*Maybe the stables weren't the best choice of venue. I myself have always been partial to the comfort of the indoors, though the feel of sun-warmed grass beneath bare skin does hold a certain appeal.*

Bella should be brimming with outrage. She should look Esmé in the eye and tell her she had gone too far this time. Yet she could not deny how Esmé's wicked suggestion simmered and sparked, igniting that part of her she had kept firmly locked away for so very long.

"But I cannot have a man come up here. The servants will talk and then . . ." Her mouth tightened with worry. She was married, as she had recently reminded Esmé.

Esmé shook her head, dismissing her concerns. "The servants adore you. They wouldn't say a word to Stirling. But if it concerns you, I will simply mention to your housekeeper that I will soon lose the distinction of being your sole family relation to call upon you at Bowhill. That I have finally managed to convince another of your cousins to pay you a visit."

"But the whole notion of having some strange man come to my home, and pay him?"

"Therein lies the beauty of it, my dear. Why do you think so many men pay women? It's neat, simple, no ulterior motives, no expectations beyond the obvious. Trust me. I will find you one who will suit. And he doesn't have to stay here. You can install him at Garden House. If you don't like him, send him back to London. But if he does appeal . . ." She let her voice trail off, one fine dark eyebrow raised, her lips quirking. "You don't even have to take him to your bed. You just need a man. A deliciously handsome man. Someone to give you a bit of attention, to remind you that you are a beautiful woman. And you needn't worry the man would not be attracted to you."

Bella's mouth twisted in a grimace. "Of course he'd act as if he were attracted to me. That's what you'd be paying him for."

"It wouldn't matter. With you, he'd have to be made of stone not to be."

Closing her eyes, Bella shook her head. She should not agree. She really shouldn't. But it had been so very, *very* long since a man had looked at her. Looked beyond the lady and seen the woman within. It had been too long since she felt the brush of warm lips against her own, the admiring caress of a strong hand and the answering fire that could burn so quickly through her veins. Burn so hot and so bright it consumed her.

Her pulse quickened, her breaths turned shallow, as the vintage memories seized hold. For a brief moment she savored the flush of arousal. The way her head went light, the way her thighs begged to clamp together to deliver some hint of pressure to the region between her legs that needed, more than anything—

"Isabella."

Her eyes snapped open. The lady instantly masked the wanton.

"You needn't give your answer tonight. I don't leave until tomorrow." Esmé set her now empty wineglass on the pedestal tea table beside her chair, picked up her slim volume of poetry, and stood. "But don't think on it too long or you will convince yourself not to go through with it. And you should. You need to do something for yourself, just because it is what you want. There's no need to keep punishing yourself, Isabella. Five years have been quite long enough."

She did not immediately rise after Esmé left the room, but remained still as a statue on the settee, her mind locked with indecision. After many long moments, she carefully set down her embroidery and entered her bedchamber, which adjoined the sitting room. The deep rose coverlet on her four-poster bed was folded back, revealing the white sheet. A fully stoked fire burned in the marble fireplace. Her young ginger-haired lady's maid, Maisie, stood by the vanity and bobbed a short curtsey.

At the plain white nightgown folded over the girl's arm, Bella said, "Not that one. The ivory." She sat on the vanity stool as Maisie crossed to the nearby dresser and selected the requested garment.

One by one, Maisie removed the many pins until the heavy weight of Bella's pale blonde hair tumbled down her back. She closed her eyes as the long, mesmerizing strokes of the brush and the gentle scrape of the stiff bristles against her scalp coaxed her spine to relax. Not enough to be noticeable, but just enough to ease the constant tension. At the light click of the silver-backed brush being placed on the vanity, she reluctantly opened her eyes and stood so Maisie could help her undress. Then she donned the ivory nightgown.

Within an instant the heat of her body warmed the cool silk. Narrow ribbons tied at her shoulders held up the plunging bodice. The intricate lace-edged hem skimmed her bare ankles. The thin silk revealed the outline of her body. It was the type of garment designed with a man's tastes in mind. Provocative, tantalizing, and easy to remove. But no man's hands had ever touched this nightgown, and no man's eyes had ever seen it. Still, she did so adore it. And there were certain nights, like this one, when she could not resist the urge to wear it.

With a tip of her head, she dismissed her maid and slipped under the blankets of her solitary bed.

SUN poured through the tall arched windows, bathing the breakfast room in rich golden light. Small spirals of steam rose from the ivory cup beside her plate. With a start, Bella blinked, pulling herself from the mesmerizing sight, her eyelids heavy from a sleepless night that had been for naught.

Morning had come and she still had not reached a decision. For endless hours she had lain awake in bed, alternating between chastising herself and fantasizing about the type of man Esmé would send her. Would he be a fair-haired Adonis or a dark-eyed devil? Every man her eye had ever paused on flashed before her mind. Would he be like him? Or him? Or him?

Just when she would linger over one, when her nerve endings would awaken, she'd wipe the tempting image from her mind with a firm and painful reminder of what happened the last time she let that wicked part of her rule. She was a lady, and ladies did not contemplate paying a man to do things to them, be they wonderful things, decadent things, wicked things. Things that fed that part of her she tried so hard to deny.

She shook the thought aside. The last five years had been hard enough. But if word reached Phillip's ears, or if her husband found out she had an unrelated gentleman at Bowhill . . . she did not know how she would endure if the next five proved worse than the last.

But it was *oh*, so tempting. She had been so good, done her best to be so perfect. Had not said a word of complaint about Stirling to anyone, not even to Esmé. Surely she had earned a bit of a reward. Just one glimpse. A few days out of her life to be herself. To indulge, to luxuriate, to fully experience passion, and then, then no more.

Scowling slightly, Bella moved the fluffy yellow bits of egg around her breakfast plate with the silver tines of her fork. The decision should not be so hard as it was something she very much wanted. No, needed. The prospect of spending the rest of her life a virgin had at first been more painful than the results of Stirling's rage. To never again be kissed, be touched by a man—her soul had screamed in agony. Time had dulled the pain to an ignorable ache, one she had long reconciled herself to. Yet Esmé's scandalous offer . . .

If she hadn't mentioned it, Bella would never have known the possibility existed. Now that she did know, she could not ignore it. Could not blithely dismiss it as ridiculous, unheard of, outside the realm of any conceivable, plausible notion.

"I prefer to stop in Langholm for the night, Porter." Bella heard Esmé's voice a second before the woman appeared. "The inn there is far more suitable." Dressed in a smart blue carriage dress trimmed in pale yellow, Esmé walked into the room, her manservant beside her.

"Yes, madame," Porter replied in the calm, neutral tone of a proper servant. Tall, broad of shoulder, and a man of few words, he had accompanied Esmé on every one of her visits to Bowhill Park, seeing to the travel arrangements and ensuring her safety. Yet there was something about the way the Englishman moved when he was near Esmé that made Bella wonder if there was more to their relationship than met the eye.

"*Bon matin*, Isabella," Esmé said with a smile as she approached the dining table.

Bella set her fork beside her plate. "Good morning."

Porter pulled out the adjacent chair and Esmé sat down. "I will inform the driver of your wishes, madame," he murmured, bowing over her shoulder, his neatly trimmed chestnut hair falling over one eye as he spoke close to her ear. With a sharp tug on the end of his plain brown jacket, he left the room, his long strides hindered by the slightest of limps.

The footman who had been stationed along the wall poured Esmé a cup of coffee and added a splash of cream, just enough to turn the black liquid to a rich chocolate. With an absent flick of her fingers, Esmé dismissed the servant, leaving the two of them alone. She had done it on purpose to ask for her answer, and Bella still did not know. Anxiety and trepidation coiled low in her belly as Esmé brought the ivory cup to her lips, her gaze on Bella.

"I must be going. The carriage is ready. I wish I could stay longer, but . . ." She lifted one slim shoulder.

Esmé never stayed longer than a handful of weeks, but the fact that she made the long journey to see Bella meant the world. Her infrequent visits were the only thing Bella ever looked forward to, and the only physical link she had left to her family.

"Do I have a reason to stop over in London?"

With one hand, Bella worried the corner of the linen napkin on her lap. "Esmé, I . . ."

"Say yes. Trust me. Don't deny it—you know I'm right. You need a man, Isabella," she said with a teasing glint in her violet eyes, her lips twisting in a knowing smirk.

"How long would he stay?" Bella asked, stalling.

"A fortnight."

She raised her eyebrows. "So long?"

"It will take you a few days just to get comfortable with him, and he will be traveling all the way from London. Should keep him long enough to cover the time there and back." Esmé spoke so casually, as if hiring a man for one's pleasure was a simple, easy decision. For her, it probably would be. Bella could well imagine her cousin perusing a line of handsome men and making a selection like one would choose a pair of new slippers. *The blond. And have him delivered today.*

"Oh, I—"

"Say yes," Esmé said softly, tempting her. She laid a hand on Bella's resting on the white linen tablecloth and gave it a squeeze. "Let me do this for you. Let me give you a reason to smile. No one will know besides you and me and your guest. I will take care of all the arrangements. You just have to be here, at Bowhill, where you always are."

Bella closed her eyes against the battle raging within. She pressed her lips tight together to keep the word inside. It was right there on the tip of her tongue, demanding voice. Esmé had countered every one of her arguments, leaving the path clear, offering her this one chance. The chance she never thought would present itself.

But she couldn't take it. It went against the very person she worked so hard to be. It mocked all the promises she made to herself to never give in to temptation again. To never be reckless again. Above all, it could mean the end of any hope she had left of ever earning Phillip's forgiveness.

So she swallowed the word she desperately wanted to utter and spoke another that caused her starved soul to cry out in agony.

"No."

THE tall clock in the corner of the room struck three. The echo of the last chime lingered before fading to nothingness. Stretching out his long legs, Gideon Rosedale settled in the leather armchair. He lifted the newspaper to catch the daylight from the window behind him.

Manor house, land with income of £4,000, 5 miles east of Reading . . .

"Too close to London," he muttered.

Manor house, land with income of £1,000, north of Brighton . . .

Scowling, he shook his head. Definitely not near Brighton. Too many ladies went there on holiday. In any case, the property would not bring in enough income. He skimmed down the front page of the *Times* and paused on the last advertisement.

House with 6 best bedrooms and 70 acres, Derbyshire, South of Hartington. Lease hold—

He was not even aware he had held his breath until the last two words caused him to release it in a dejected *whoosh.*

No. Not that one either. He would have a hell of a time convincing anyone to lease a property to him. An outright purchase was his only option, one that would cost significantly more than a mere lease, and one he should not contemplate at this point in time. There was no use taunting himself with something that could not be, at least not yet.

He picked up a heavy, cut-crystal glass from the end table and took a large swallow. The fine aged whisky burned a pleasing trail down his throat and effectively aided his effort to turn his mind to other, less disheartening matters. He set the glass down and opened the newspaper.

A sharp double knock reverberated in the quiet parlor, pulling his attention from the latest parliamentary debates. He folded the newspaper, stood, and laid it on the brown leather armchair. A note was thrust at him the second he opened the front door.

Rosedale—your immediate presence is required at my office to greet a potential new client.

The note wasn't signed but the scarlet and black liveried servant standing in the doorway identified the sender well enough.

Suppressing a resigned sigh, he set the note on the console table next to the door. When had the prospect of a new client become a chore? No, that wasn't entirely correct. It was only a chore when he had to see *her.* "I'll be but a moment."

"Better hurry," the manservant said with a surly twist of his mouth.

Ignoring the comment, Gideon crossed his comfortable and well-appointed front parlor, went through the small formal dining room and into his bedchamber. He took but a minute to pull on the navy jacket his Bond Street tailor delivered yesterday. It fit perfectly to his specification, with simple, clean lines and was cut just loose enough so he could don it himself. He didn't stop to glance in the oval mirror above the dresser, but simply picked up the silver pocket watch and affixed it to his iron gray waistcoat.

He locked the door to his apartment, slipped the brass key in a pocket, and followed the servant down the stairs leading from the top floor suite. A weak afternoon sun greeted him as he walked out the front door of the exclusive bachelor residence.

She had not used the word *immediate* lightly. A black town coach with scarlet trim stood at the ready. The coal black coats of the four horses in the traces held the same shine as the heavily lacquered coach. He could not remember the last time she put herself out to the extent of sending her carriage for him. This new client must be someone worth impressing and someone in a hurry if she was unwilling to wait the extra ten minutes it would take him to travel the distance on foot.

The arrogant manservant did not bother opening the door for

him, nor had Gideon expected it. The interior of the carriage was lush opulence, just like its owner. The soft cushioned benches were upholstered in scarlet velvet. Rich satinwood lined the walls, and all the fittings were crafted of highly polished brass. He pulled down the shade, cloaking the interior in cool semidarkness, and within minutes the carriage stopped in a small back courtyard.

He took the usual route to the private office, up the back stairs and down the servants' corridor, but stopped when he rounded the corner. A man stood in front of the office door, shoulders squared, hands clasped behind his back, and legs slightly spread. The brown coat and tan breeches signified he was not one of the brothel's employees. Nor was he a client. The coat was too plain, his expression too detached, his entire bearing too . . .

An ex-soldier. Gideon had seen enough about Town since the war ended. This one must be in the employ of Gideon's potential new client.

Wonderful. A client with an overprotective servant.

The man caught his gaze and held it. Unflinching and steady gray eyes bored into his.

The hairs on Gideon's nape pricked. He squared his shoulders and was just about to demand the man move aside—not ask, that stare did not warrant the courtesy—when the man opened the door.

Without a word, Gideon strode into the room, the door closing behind him. A woman with dark brown hair pulled back in an elaborate knot sat in one of the scarlet leather chairs facing the teakwood desk, her back to Gideon. He stopped a few paces behind her and slightly to her left.

She didn't turn to look at him but merely lifted one small pale hand and flicked her fingers. "Come around so I can see you."

A Frenchwoman. Interesting. Though in his experience, they tended to be rather haughty. He rounded the chair and stopped next to the side of the desk.

His potential new client lounged casually in the chair with an ease that indicated she was comfortable in her own skin and confident of her appeal. Telling this woman she was beautiful would simply be repeating the obvious and the aloof, slightly bored expression on her face said she would not welcome gratuitous flattery.

Her gaze traced the length of Gideon's body. He had no doubt her violet eyes took in every detail of his person.

He looked to the other woman seated behind the desk, silently asking for the required introduction.

Clad in one of her standard figure-hugging scarlet silk gowns, Madam Rubicon merely arched one eyebrow. The yellow blonde hair piled high on her head fully exposed the jewels draped around her neck, which he knew to be paste. The few errant strands pulled from their pins had been purposefully arranged to draw the eye to the ample, barely covered bosom. She was the very picture of a purveyor of costly flesh, and unfortunately, she was also his employer.

Rubicon brought a plain, short glass to her lips and finished off the remaining gin in one swallow. "This is Mr. Gideon Rosedale. As you can see, he is simply perfect."

Christ, how he hated it when she made those gloating comments. He did his best not to visibly bristle, but knew he failed by the sharpening of the Frenchwoman's violet eyes.

"Madame has some very specific requirements and I, of course, thought immediately of you, Gideon."

Her rouged mouth smiled but her kohl-rimmed eyes did not. He heeded her warning and waited to hear what the woman had to say.

"Before we go any further, are you available for the next few weeks?" the Frenchwoman asked.

A few weeks? Gideon hesitated. "Yes."

"What is your opinion of ladies?"

The question took him aback but still he replied truthfully. "I hold women in the utmost regard. They deserve nothing less than my full respect."

His answer got him an interested raise of a fine dark eyebrow. "And what is your opinion of gentlemen?"

Why would she ask him that? He furrowed his brow, his mind

jumping to the ex-soldier outside the door, the man's protective stance, the hard stare. A ménage? How did one say no without saying no? "I do not have one." It was the most neutral response he could think to give.

The violet eyes flared. The woman had not expected that answer, yet Gideon could understand her ill-concealed surprise. Gideon was a rarity in a world where those of his kind earned the bulk of their income from servicing men. And his exclusivity had earned him a fair share of animosity from Rubicon's other employees. Jealousy and spite had long ago severed the old friendships of his youth, but he didn't mind. Not much, at least.

She quickly recovered and continued with her inquisition. "What do you do with your clients when you pay them a visit?"

"Whatever they wish. Within reason. I'd never hurt a woman, even if she asked me to."

This time Gideon got a single tip of the perfectly coifed dark head. "And what measures do you employ to avoid conception?"

"French letters," Gideon replied matter-of-factly. That question, at least, was one he was accustomed to answering.

"Always?"

"Always and without fail."

Eyes narrowed and full lips slightly pursed, the woman studied him. Hands clasped behind him, Gideon waited for her to render judgment. He never yet had one refuse him; still, these moments always proved most uncomfortable.

"Before you make your decision, I must tell you," Rubicon said into the silence, "he does have one eccentricity. He requires his own accommodations. She should not expect him to play the besotted husband, but the traditional one."

Must she speak of me as though I'm not in the room?

The woman waved a hand. "There is a guest cottage on the estate which should prove suitable. Private but within walking distance of the manor house." She paused, her gaze sweeping up and down Gideon's body. "How much?"

Even though the woman was looking at him, Gideon knew the blunt question was not directed at him. Rubicon pulled a neat square of white paper from her desk drawer, scrawled out a figure, and pushed the note across her desk. "You will find the price for perfection to be . . . within reason."

The woman picked up the paper and took in the figure. Then she flicked the note back to Rubicon. The white paper slid across the highly polished surface of the desk. Gideon caught the scowl that pulled Rubicon's mouth at the dismissive gesture.

"When can you be ready to depart?" the woman asked.

"Within the half hour." Gideon kept his trunk packed, just for such an occasion.

"He will do," she said to Rubicon as she dropped a hefty stack of pound notes pulled from her reticule onto Rubicon's desk. "Porter." She didn't speak any louder than she had during their rather odd exchange, yet the door opened as soon as the name left her lips.

"Yes, madame."

"Take Mr. Rosedale to the carriage and give him his instructions."

His instructions?

"Yes, madame." Without so much as a glance to Gideon, he turned on his heel and left the room.

Feeling distinctly wary, Gideon took up pursuit. The man didn't turn left toward the back stairs Gideon always used, but continued straight ahead and down the main stairs leading into the receiving room. The sound of low grunts and feminine moans hit his ears before his feet touched the plush carpet. Two beauties flanked a young buck sprawled on a red velvet settee. The diaphanous, jewel-toned silk wraps did nothing to hide the girls' charms. The man groped the honey blonde's quim as he kissed the raven-haired girl who had her hand down the front of his unbuttoned breeches. Another young man, obviously the other's acquaintance judging by the similarity in afternoon merriment, occupied the opposite settee.

Gideon's lip curled. Impatient whelps. Rubicon had plenty of rooms. There was no need to indulge here.

One other beauty lounged on a nearby divan waiting for her next customer. At the sight of the ex-soldier entering the receiving room, her languid pose took on a provocative cant. She flicked her auburn locks over her slim shoulder, exposing rouged nipples straining against a sheer ivory wrap.

"Sir." She rose and intercepted the man.

Gideon suppressed a groan and stopped one pace behind him.

She placed a pale hand on the man's forearm and batted her eyelashes. "Surely you are not leaving so soon?" Her purred words grated down Gideon's spine. Her gaze flickered to Gideon and the lustful gleam took on a mocking edge. "I can offer you any pleasure *he* can, and more."

Gideon kept his chin up and did his best to ignore her, and the spectacles on either side of him. The distinctive scent of male arousal hung heavy in the air. An unmistakable suckling noise was added to the low grunts. His cock twitched with envy. He hadn't been sucked off in ages.

The man removed the girl's hand from his arm. "No, thank you, miss."

With an affronted pout, the girl stepped aside. The man continued out of the receiving room. The pout turned nasty as Gideon passed the girl.

"Do let me know how his cock tastes."

Gideon gritted his teeth. The spoiled creature's softly hissed barb was the perfect accent to what was turning into an entirely unpleasant day. Within minutes, word of who she believed to be his new client would spread throughout the house. If the next few weeks were anything like the last twenty minutes, then they would prove to be very long.

He received a quick double take from the two massive ex-pugilists guarding the entrance to the decadent West End brothel and continued out to a traveling coach stationed just down from the scarlet front double doors. A burly man with a shock of untidy red hair jumped down from his perch on the driver's bench to open the carriage door.

Gideon followed the ex-soldier into the carriage and sat on the opposite bench.

"This carriage will take you to Selkirk, Scotland, where you will meet Isabella, Lady Stirling. You will stay at Bowhill Park for a fortnight unless the countess chooses to send you back to London earlier. Lady Stirling's household is preparing for a visit from her cousin. The driver is in her employ, but his silence has already been assured. He will see to any expenses incurred on the way to Scotland and back to London." The tone was brisk and no-nonsense, as if they were discussing the details of a mundane business transaction. "Any questions?"

It took a full second for the man's words to solidify in Gideon's mind. The woman in Rubicon's office wasn't his client. She was acting in another's stead, sending Gideon to another. A Lady Stirling. Goddamn Rubicon! That bitch knew all along. She had only wanted to watch him squirm.

"No," Gideon replied, a tad sourly.

Though the man moved not a muscle, the air in the closed carriage shifted subtly, causing the hairs on the nape of Gideon's neck to prick with unease, just as they had done when the man had stared him down earlier.

"If word should reach my ears that you displeased Lady Stirling in any fashion, you will be most sorry. You have one half hour. Alert the driver when you are ready to depart."

After a hard, piercing stare, the man alighted from the carriage.

The slam of the door unleashed a wave of bristling indignation, twisting Gideon's mouth into a hard sneer. He didn't need the man's damn warning and it would not change the way he behaved with Lady Stirling one bit. But instead of shouting a rash reply, the prospect of receiving half of the large stack of pound notes on Rubicon's desk kept him silent. He could not deny he could do with a new client, for it would put him one small step closer to leaving all of this behind.

Two

SOMEHOW Bella kept the shocked screech from making its way past her lips.

No. She couldn't have. No, no, she couldn't.

Bella sent her mind frantically back over their last two conversations, searching for anything she might have said that could have been misinterpreted as approval. But found nothing.

Nothing.

She must have read it wrong. There was no way Esmé could have. She couldn't. She didn't.

Isabella—

If my timing proves correct, then Bowhill Park will receive a guest on the afternoon of your receipt of this letter. Mr. Gideon Rosedale will be situated at Garden House. He is prepared to remain at Bowhill for the fortnight. Please be so kind as to inform your housekeeper of the imminent arrival of your dear cousin. I promised to find you one who would suit, and I do believe this one will suit.

Regardless of how displeased you may be with me, I do hope you at least invite your guest to dinner before dispensing with him. If not for yourself, then do it for me, because I love you and only wish for your happiness. S'il vous plaît, take a holiday from your penance.

—Esmé

She did.

The note fluttered from Bella's limp fingers to the neat surface of her writing desk. For the past week she had fought with herself, in the way one only could with regret. She had bemoaned her decision and convinced herself she should have said yes. It was so much easier to say yes in hindsight, when she did not have to live with the consequences. The complications were lessened, the risks easily ignored. Bella had even indulged in a daydream yesterday afternoon when she had been in the hothouse cutting a few new blooms, and her musings had been most pleasant indeed.

But it had been just an idle daydream. A fantasy.

It was not supposed to actually happen.

But now it *was* going to happen. Esmé had found her a man. A man who was currently en route to Bowhill. The timing of Esmé's note was not lost on her. She could have easily sent the note via express post and it would have arrived before today.

"Damn her," Bella muttered.

Esmé had succeeded in flustering her to the point of cursing and she wasn't even here to witness the event. If Bella knew where to reach her, she would pen her a scathing reply. But Esmé never stayed long in one place. She could be anywhere in England or on the continent. Esmé could send her letters, but she did not have the luxury of doing the same. Bella wrote her notes, but they were never sent, nor placed in her hand. There were moments when she simply found solace in the act of writing words, which were never to be read by another.

She allowed herself a brief slump in her desk chair and let out a deep, unladylike sigh. Well, there was nothing to be done for it. Cursing her high-handed cousin would not remedy the situation, and Bella could not take her ire out on Mr. Gideon Rosedale. It would be the height of rudeness to turn the man away without at least inviting him to dinner, especially after such a long journey from London.

Her glance fell onto the small porcelain clock on the corner of her desk. She abruptly straightened in her chair. It was ten o'clock. As the roads to Selkirk from London had proved, a few hours could easily be gained or lost. Her guest could arrive momentarily or late tonight or even tomorrow. And Bowhill was not prepared in the least.

She rang for a servant and requested her housekeeper. As she waited for the woman to arrive, she folded Esmé's note and slipped it into the top desk drawer, pushing it to the far right corner. As she was sliding the drawer closed, the door opened and Mrs. Cooley walked into the sitting room.

With her black hair streaked with silver and her tall, sturdy frame, the woman brought to mind the image of a headmistress of an orphanage. *Stern* was an understatement. When Bella first came to Bowhill, she had not known what to make of the woman. Over the years she came to realize the ironlike countenance was just the woman's way. The two women had never been close, but Bella had caught the usually hard gray eyes soften with what could have been compassion, or even pity, on more than one occasion.

"Yes, your ladyship?"

"I have received word from Madame Marceau that she has convinced another of my cousins to pay me a visit. Mr. Rosedale is traveling from London and is due to arrive this afternoon. Please see that Garden House is aired out and made ready." Esmé's explanation flowed smoothly off her tongue.

Bella received a questioning look from Mrs. Cooley at the mention of Garden House. Esmé always stayed at the manor house, in the yellow bedchamber, and as she was Bella's only guest, she never had a use for the cottage.

Her chin remained up and her composure in place. The small

staff at Bowhill saw to her comfort, but was paid by Stirling. Even if she only allowed Mr. Rosedale to stay one night, it was critical they never know he was not what she led them to believe.

"Yes, your ladyship. I will see to it immediately."

"Alert the kitchen we will have a guest for dinner." Bella picked up the previously approved menu from her desk. She kept a scowl from marring her brow. The simple, light fare would not do. She picked up her pen, dipped it into the silver inkwell, and paused, the black tip an inch from the paper.

What would he prefer? She had not the faintest notion. All she knew about him was his name and that he was traveling from London. Keeping her attention on the menu, she spoke with a dismissive casualness that belied the butterflies in her stomach. "Dinner will be at six this evening. Please see to Garden House. I will have the menu sent down to the kitchen."

"Yes, your ladyship."

The moment Mrs. Cooley left the room she dropped her pen and pressed a sweat-dampened palm to her forehead. Bella still could not believe she had done it.

Esmé had sent her a man.

GIDEON contemplated the manor house at Bowhill Park as he walked up the front steps. The home was modest by country terms. Not a sprawling many-winged structure built upon over the decades designed as a showplace to impress callers. Rather, it was a square Georgian mansion with two sets of Ionic columns carved in relief into the stone walls flanking the arched portico. The sort of house he imagined himself owning many years from now. Neat and understated, he doubted it was the Stirling family seat. Earls preferred much grander homes to tout their status over lowly viscounts and barons. If that were the case, then what kind of woman would he find waiting for him if her husband found her unworthy of the Stirling estate?

With that question lingering in his mind, the front door swung open a second after he knocked. The dour-faced butler didn't ask his name, but simply gave Gideon one long look down his hooked nose and motioned for him to enter. The man led him to a drawing room and, with a barely audible yet purposeful little huff of displeasure, closed the door with a smart snap.

Long accustomed to dealing with a client's servants, the butler's slight didn't even prick Gideon's pride. But clearly that one already doubted the ruse. Experience taught Gideon that as long as he kept up the oft-employed guise of a visiting relative any suspicious servants would hold their tongues. The veil of propriety was what mattered to them, not the truth hidden behind it.

He paused in the center of the room and glanced about. A home could reveal a lot about a woman, and this one spoke volumes. An ivory silk brocade settee, two chairs, and a low table formed a sitting arrangement between a pair of tall windows. A fire burned invitingly in the white marble-mantled fireplace. Gilt-framed paintings featuring lush gardens and flowers in full bloom dotted the walls covered in chinoiserie paper.

Not a single object was out of place. The formal drawing room was clean, without a speck of dust. The housekeeper he spotted on the way to this room, lurking midway along a long corridor leading to the back of the house, certainly had the capable, efficient look of one who did not tolerate lazy maids.

But it was more than that. This room spoke of sophistication, refinement, and attention to detail. The Ming vase on the sideboard told of wealth, the red roses arranged within told of an appreciation of things beautiful. He doubted Lady Stirling was past her prime. The furniture was not gently aged, but less than a decade old. The English ambience, the absence of anything remotely Scottish, said she was not a native but imported by her husband.

The woman who decorated this room would not flout convention. She would be constrained, the typical English lady. And she would want him to be . . . Gideon glanced about the room again. A gentleman. One of her kind.

He strode to a window, clasped his hands behind his back, and took in the view of the grounds surrounding the side of the house. The sun hung low on the horizon, streaking magenta across a sky that faded to deepest midnight. One could see nothing but open acres framed in the distance by thick woods. It was pleasing to the eye but felt secluded from the world. Now he knew why he was here.

Lady Stirling was lonely.

Well, at least we have something in common, he thought sardonically. But he had long ago realized physical acts could not fill the void where a family should reside. If anything, it made the emptiness reverberate with a painful echo that drove home just how alone he was in the world.

Gideon shook his head, dismissing the thought. He was here for Lady Stirling. And she wanted a gentleman, not a maudlin fool. Taking a deep breath, he righted himself to his current task.

The sound of a door opening reached his ears. With a welcoming smile, he turned from the window.

He blinked. Then remembered to take a breath.

Refined and sophisticated, without a button or hair out of place. She was everything this room had foretold. But he had not been prepared to find this.

Lady Stirling was . . . *exquisite.* An ethereal beauty with alabaster skin and white blonde hair pulled up in an expert chignon. The gown draping her graceful willowy body told him something else about her. The rich cranberry silk said she did as she dared. She was not as conventional as she would like one to believe.

He quickly recovered his wits and walked forward to greet her. “Good evening, Lady Stirling. Mr. Gideon Rosedale.”

“Good evening.” She offered her hand.

He executed a smooth bow, bringing her hand up to his lips but not quite brushing the back. “It is a pleasure to make your acquaintance.”

“Would you care for a glass of wine before dinner, Mr. Rosedale?”

"Yes, thank you." He held up a hand when she took a step toward a table laden with a bottle of wine and two goblets on a silver tray. "Allow me, and would you like a glass as well?" Though she appeared outwardly calm, he had been conscious of a faint tremor during the brief moment when she had laid her hand in his.

She tipped her splendid head a fraction to indicate acceptance.

Gideon poured two glasses of Madeira and delivered one to her. She sat on the settee, her delicate hand curved just so around the fragile goblet, and took a long sip, downing half the glass's contents. With her other hand, she motioned to the green and ivory striped chair angled toward the settee. He dropped into the chair. After tasting the sweet wine, he set his glass on a nearby table. He needed to keep his wits about him. It would require a fair share of charm to soothe the nerves she attempted to conceal.

She turned her straight shoulders to him, the sleek indent of her waist evident by the curve of her upper body. "I hope the journey from London found you well?" Her voice carried smoothly on the air. Soft, melodic, and definitively feminine.

"Yes. It only rained a bit through Carlisle. The roads were in as good a shape as can be expected in the spring. All in all, a pleasant ride."

She brought the wineglass to her lips for another long sip. "And how do you find Garden House?"

"Charming." When the driver had deposited him at the quaint cottage this afternoon, his initial assumption had been that she would visit him there in an effort to keep their liaison as discreet as possible. He had been pleasantly surprised to find a note on the small dining table written in flowing feminine script requesting the pleasure of his company for dinner. "The roses"—he gestured to the bouquet—"were grown in the hothouse?" He had passed the stone and glass walled structure on the walk to the manor, its many windows misted against the crisp evening air.

"Yes." The smile of an angel spread across her face, softening the almost unapproachably elegant features. He barely kept his jaw from dropping in awe. *Christ*, she was beautiful. "It is a small hobby of mine. The hothouse allows the less hearty varieties to thrive even through the frigid Scottish winters."

"I would be honored if you would show it to me." There was no teasing lilt to his voice. He employed no suave charm. It was simply a request, infused with enough honest interest to take it past the purely polite.

Her long lashes swept down, hiding her exotic violet eyes, as she tipped her head. Then she set her empty glass on an end table and gracefully rose to her feet. Instinctively, he stood as well. The silence was broken only by the soft *swoosh* of her silk skirts as she glided across the room. One lean arm reached out to lightly, lovingly brush a red bloom with the tips of her fingers as she passed the sideboard before stopping in front of the same window he had gazed out of earlier.

Twilight was full upon them. The sun's rich amber rays no longer made their way into the room. The light from a nearby lamp flickered across her aristocratic profile. The smile was gone. She was a study in elegance.

He clasped his hands behind his back and waited patiently for her to speak.

"Mr. Rosedale, your presence is only required for dinner this evening. After that you are here by choice, free to take your leave anytime you choose. You needn't provide a reason. Just as I am free to request your departure from this estate. I wish our time together to be a consensual flirtation."

THE rapid beat of her heart filled her ears. Bella kept her gaze straight ahead, fighting the impulse to glance to Mr. Rosedale, his presence a physical force that demanded her complete attention.

But Mr. Rosedale's reason for being in this room was a double-edged sword. It pricked her interest, but also pricked at her conscience. The thought of him kissing her, touching her, all for the lure of money . . . it struck a chord deep within her. A chord that did not sit well at all. She knew before even meeting Mr. Rosedale that she could not match Esmé's blasé attitude about such financial arrangements, and therefore, she had devised her terms. A flirtation was something she could possibly engage in. A paid servant was not.

But how would he react to her terms? She still could not believe she had laid them out like that. Cool. Impersonal. Her voice had not wavered the slightest bit. Remarkable, given her nerves were drawn tighter than an archer's bow.

"Your ladyship, dinner is served."

She whirled from the window at McGreevy's words. The butler had opened the double doors leading to the dining room. Mr. Rosedale walked to her side and offered his arm. Bella laid her hand on the fine black wool, and the second before he took a step he caught her eye and gave her a small smile. If it were meant to put her at her ease, it worked. The tension slipped away and in its place settled a definitive, undeniable spark of attraction.

He led her into the dining hall and to the far end of the long mahogany table where two places were set. The light from the silver candelabras stationed at regular intervals along the table danced on the gold bands encircling the crystal goblets. The table was set with her finest Limoges china, stark white linens, and heavy silver flatware. Velvety darkness backed the three tall, arched windows on one wall, acting as a curtain closing out the rest of the world.

Lowering into the chair Mr. Rosedale pulled out at the head of the table, Bella watched as he settled himself with complete ease into the adjacent chair, as if his presence at such a formal dinner was a natural and frequent occurrence.

The footman poured the wine and placed a bowl of leek soup before each of them. Though she had tried not to stray from her usual routine with Esmé, she had taken great care in the selection of the dishes for this evening's meal. As she waited for Mr. Rosedale's approval, she reached for her glass. The full-bodied Bordeaux did little to calm the butterflies infiltrating her stomach.

His silver spoon skimmed the surface of the sage green liquid then he brought it to his lips. The man had the most beautiful mouth. Firm. Sensual. Made to bestow kisses.

"My compliments to your cook."

She let out a small sigh of relief and picked up her spoon. "I'm pleased you approve."

His whisky brown eyes locked with hers. The edges of his lips quirked. "Most assuredly."

His deep voice wrapped around her like a gentle caress, leaving her with the impression he wasn't just referring to the soup.

"You have a beautiful home, your ladyship. Yet it pales in comparison to you."

The heat of his gaze seared her skin. A flush rose from her chest, pricking her neck, her cheeks. She smiled and tipped her chin, her shoulders rounding before she caught herself and straightened her spine. "Thank you." She licked her lips, struggling to find a topic to discuss. "Do you travel often?"

"On occasion."

He brought his spoon to his lips again. She silently cursed the stark white cravat for hiding his throat. How she would love to watch the strong lines of his neck work as he swallowed. "Have your travels taken you to Scotland before?"

"No. This is a first. I rarely stray beyond a couple of days' ride from London." He leaned back as the footman removed the first course and laid out the second. Mr. Rosedale's shoulders were so broad the wooden back of the chair was completely hidden. "And what of you? Do you stay close to Bowhill, or do you dare to venture beyond?"

Her fingers tightened around her fork. "I haven't traveled to England in years."

His smile soothed the knot forming in her belly. "How fortunate for Scotland to be given such a gift. London is prized for its diversions, but most grow bland after a short time. There is one, however, that never loses its appeal."

"And what would that be?"

"The British Museum. Just when I think I've explored every one of its treasures, I discover a new find."

Fortunately, he kept the conversation flowing, for she knew she was failing miserably in her role as hostess. It took considerable effort to simply refrain from studying him too closely. Time and again her naughty mind attempted to wander down paths that included such musings as if the body beneath his strict black evening attire matched the classic angles and planes of his face.

His features were those of the marble statues she had once glimpsed on a long-ago visit to the very museum of which he spoke. But even the Italian masters would have been hard-pressed to achieve such flowing symmetrical precision in their works. He was not overly masculine—there was nothing rugged or blunt about him. Nor was any angle too sharp, or plane too flat. He was the ideal brought to life—a timeless image of man in his prime. His freshly shaven, chiseled jaw held not a hint of his dark brown hair, the color of deepest sable, which was just a snip from being too short. And those eyes . . . she could definitely lose herself in the rich golden-flecked depths.

I believe this one will suit, Esmé wrote. And Mr. Rosedale did suit. Bella could feel her spirits rising with each admiring glance and each word from his lips. She had forgotten what it felt like to be the object of a man's attentions. It was infinitely pleasing and gave the evening a rosy glow. Whether she would be brave enough to seize the opportunity and take him to her bed in the coming days . . . of that she wasn't yet certain.

So when dinner was completed, she instructed the footmen to clear the table. As her guest partook of a glass of port and she of a cup of tea, she allowed herself a few more minutes to bask in his attention. Then she set her empty cup on the barren white linen and moved to stand. He drew out her chair before the footman stationed along the wall could move a muscle, and led her out of the dining room to the foot of the staircase leading to the second floor.

Her hand drifted off his arm as she turned to stand before him. Then she let her gaze travel down his body once more. He was tall, even taller than she. A rarity, given the number of gentlemen she had met who were on eye level or less. And he carried the height very well. Not lanky or bullish, but broad shouldered and with a fitness that spoke of frequent exercise. Yet his imposing presence did not intimidate her. Maybe it was the overwhelming totality of his perfection that prevented, until now, her noticing the magnitude of his height.

"Thank you for dinner, Lady Stirling. I had a very enjoyable evening."

She swallowed to moisten her suddenly dry mouth. "As did I. Would you care for a carriage to be brought round to see you back to Garden House?"

"Thank you, but it's a pleasant evening and the walk will do me good."

His mouth curved in the most divine little smile. Heady warmth washed over her, lulling her senses. Breeching the line of polite distance, he took one small step toward her and slowly reached out to rest his hand on her waist. The heat of his palm penetrated her silk gown, sending a bolt of lush sensation through her.

"Dinner is over. Our flirtation begins," he said, his voice a deep, suggestive rumble.

In his fathomless half-lidded gaze, she glimpsed carnal pleasures beyond her most scandalous dreams. A flush of arousal swept up from her belly. Her breaths turned short and heavy. The air crackled between them.

The moment stretched on, growing taut, pulling tighter . . .

He lowered his head then paused, his mouth an inch from hers. Unable to resist the offer, she swayed into him, her eyes fluttering closed.

Warm lips brushed hers. Once. Twice. The lightest of touches.

Blindly seeking more, she lifted up onto her toes and flicked her tongue against the seam of his lips. Large hands grabbed her backside, jerking her tight against his muscular body. He slanted his mouth harshly over hers. An intense wave of desire saturated her senses. She opened her mouth eagerly, her kiss strong and full of unleashed, unbridled passion. Passion that had been locked away for too long. Passion that reveled in this small gift of freedom.

A moan of pure, unadulterated longing shook her throat. She clutched his broad shoulders, the muscles hard beneath her hands. The rich, masculine scent of him filled her every breath. The hot brush of his tongue against hers fed the flames burning white-hot inside her, until they threatened to consume her.

And then he was gone, so abruptly a light breeze brushed across her parted lips. Her senses reeling, she blinked open her eyes to find him staring at her.

His dark eyebrows pinched together. The next instant, he took a quick step back, reached for her hand hanging limp at her side, and executed a smart bow. "Good night, Lady Stirling."

He turned on his heel.

Why is he walking away? Closing her eyes tight, Bella struggled to calm her racing pulse. She could still taste his port-sweetened tongue.

The click of the door closing reverberated in the marble-floored entrance hall, hitting her like a splash of cold water.

Breath catching, her eyes flared. Her heart stumbled.

She had let him kiss her in the entrance hall. Anyone could have walked by and seen with one glance that Mr. Rosedale was not at all what she led them to believe. The narrowly avoided ramifications passed through her, quick and familiar, and did nothing to aid the effort to slow her pulse.

A sudden weakness gripped her. Her legs trembled. Bella locked her knees, resisting the urge to crumble onto the step and hold her head in her shaking hands. She was so very close to sending Mr. Rosedale packing, to calling for her butler and letting the request for the traveling coach tumble out of her mouth. With one kiss he had pulled such an extreme reaction from her—if he had but given the word, she would have let him take her virginity right there on the steps.

The lithe grace of his every movement, the inherent power in his impressive frame, the easy confidence of his smile . . . everything about him spoke to her on a deep, sensual level. Never before had a man's mere presence roused passion on this scale. She wanted what Mr. Rosedale could offer. God help her, she wanted it desperately to the point where she did not trust herself.

Turning, she placed a hand on the smooth wooden banister and walked up the stairs on still-weak legs. She placed her other hand on the bare expanse of chest below her collarbone. Her heart beat mouse-quick beneath her palm. By the time she arrived at her bedchamber the lingering traces of heady arousal had dissipated, her pulse had slowed, and her breathing had returned to something approaching normal, so when her lady's maid asked which nightgown she would prefer, she was able to answer in her usual calm tones.

As Maisie unbuttoned her gown and unlaced her stays, Bella couldn't help but question if this flirtation had been a wise choice. This afternoon as her household had prepared for Mr. Rosedale's visit, she had convinced herself the best course of action was to leave the fortnight open, to let it unfold as it may. It was too unique, too unprecedented an opportunity to blithely push aside. In any case, it would have been rude to dismiss Esmé's offering so succinctly.

Rude? She suppressed a sardonic snort and pulled her nightgown over her head. The cool silk flowed over her bare curves until the lace-edged hem settled at her ankles. That had been one of her reasons—a fear of being rude to her cousin. A cousin who thought it perfectly acceptable to hire her a man. What a poor excuse, and a blatant show of how desperate she had become. Grasping for anything to give her a reason to allow her guest to stay longer than one evening.

Her mind too wrapped in itself to do anything but react on routine, she sat on the cushioned stool before the vanity and closed her eyes as Maisie pulled the pins from her hair. If she had sent him home the moment he had arrived, as she should have done, as a proper lady would have done, then she would not be in this predicament, this war with herself. Fighting temptation, yet at the same time wanting more than anything to give in.

But she hadn't been able to resist the lure of him. And not merely the obvious lure, but of a companion. Someone to spend a day with. Someone to talk to other than her roses.

"Is there anything else I can do for you this evening?"

With a start, Bella glanced to the oval mirror above the vanity, barely registering the concern on her maid's face. "No. That will be all."

The girl curtseyed and left the bedchamber. Bella doused the candle on the vanity. The newly stoked fire in the hearth created a pool of golden light that touched the black legs of the nearby Egyptian armchair, the rest of the room cloaked in darkness. On bare feet, she strode to the window next to her bed and held aside the heavy damask curtain.

The stars provided enough light to make out the curved gravel paths cutting through the dark mounds of the rosebushes. She strained her eyes, trying to see past the grass clearing beyond the garden, and could just make out the jut of a chimney and the straight lines of a roof among the surrounding trees. Garden House. And Mr. Rosedale.

She worried her bottom lip between her teeth. She knew the sincerity of every word from his beautiful mouth should be doubted—the man was a prostitute and surely an expert at making a woman feel cherished, desired, wanted. Yet . . . he had made her smile when she had almost forgotten how.

Bella learned long ago the days passed by a bit quicker and did not blend together to form a monotonous, single entity if she seized the simple pleasures in life. Treasured them, cherished them, siphoned what joy could be had from them. An evening spent with Mr. Rosedale was indeed a pleasure. A pleasure she could quickly grow accustomed to.

Therein lay another worry. Even if their flirtation never went beyond a pleasant evening's meal, she already knew watching him leave Bowhill would be difficult. And more time spent with him would simply make it harder to return to her isolated existence.

On a long shaky sigh, she released the curtain, covering the window and blocking out the view of Garden House. She pressed her palms to her closed eyes.

"One day." The pleading tone in her whisper echoed in the quiet room. "I'll let him stay one more day, and then . . ."

She shook her head, unable to give voice to the words she did not want to speak. Slipping beneath the blankets, she did her best to push aside the worries and allow sleep to overtake her.

Three

A knock at the door pulled Gideon from his morning routine. With the long length of his cravat loose around his neck and his newly shaven jaw still damp, he left the back bedchamber, went down the short hall to the parlor, and opened the front door, revealing a young maid with a wicker basket in hand.

Her freckled face blanked with the sort of awe natural wonders usually inspired. He gave her five seconds to gather her wits and then raised both eyebrows in expectation.

She bobbed an abbreviated curtsey and lifted the basket, offering the purpose for her visit. "Good morning, Mr. Rosedale." The brogue could not disguise the hoarseness of her voice.

He opened the door fully and allowed her inside. She set the basket on the small dining table in the adjacent kitchen as he finished tying his cravat.

"Is there anything you require, sir?"

"Does Bowhill receive the *Times*?"

"No, I don't think so. But I can check down at the village if ye'd like," she said with a mixture of nervousness and an obvious desire to please.

"Thank you." He might be in a different country but he did still need to keep current on the comings and goings of London.

She lingered by the table, fiddling with the end of the embroidered towel covering the basket's contents. Before she could work up the courage to ask if he "required" anything else, he sent her politely on her way. Nestled inside the basket with the warm bread, sausages, and fresh fruit was a note requesting his company for an afternoon stroll. It wasn't signed but the flowing feminine script could only belong to her.

Contemplating her note, he picked up a piece of bread and took a bite. Lady Stirling had not changed her mind come morning. That was always a risk, but one he had yet to have the misfortune of experiencing. Those terms of hers though . . . was she serious, or were they just a means to ease her conscience? Being free to leave was an unaccustomed-to concept, and one he was not planning to familiarize himself with. Unless she requested otherwise, his next thirteen days and twelve nights would be spent at Bowhill Park catering to the beautiful lady's every whim and desire.

Those little smiles she cast him during dinner . . . each one had made a bolt prod his nerve endings. He had not felt that in, well he didn't know how long, but the sensation was almost as pleasurable as the short time spent in her presence. And that kiss. The first kiss revealed a woman's true nature.

And that kiss . . .

One glimpse. All it had taken was one glimpse of the passion hidden beneath the cool, contained exterior, and he had momentarily forgotten where he was and whom he was with.

Very uncharacteristic.

He furrowed his brow, still not pleased with how abruptly he had left her last night. Should he have accepted the invitation in her kiss? *No, no.* She had made it quite clear she wanted him to return to the cottage alone. Yet . . .

With a quick shake of his head, he dismissed the question forming in the back of his mind. Grabbing another piece of bread, he went back to the bedchamber. After he finished dressing, he cleared the contents of the wicker basket and passed the solitary morning hours in the comfortable front parlor rereading the *Times* he had brought with him. When afternoon approached, he donned his navy jacket, pulled on his kidskin gloves, and set out for the manor house.

The butler didn't show him to the drawing room but left Gideon to cool his heels in the entrance hall.

The wait was not long. She emerged from down the long hall. The Kashmir shawl about her shoulders exactly matched her brilliant Prussian blue walking dress. The housekeeper, trailing two steps behind her, was a somber figure in black.

"Good afternoon, Lady Stirling," he said with a tip of the head.

"Good afternoon, Mr. Rosedale."

She was all polite distance, her posture strict and her tone impersonal. He did not take it to heart—their audience required a performance.

He ignored the hard stare from the housekeeper. "Shall we be on our way, cousin?"

"By all means." She laid her gloved hand on his proffered arm.

The butler shut the front door behind them with a smart click. She paused at the foot of the stone steps, outside the shadow of the portico, and tilted her face up to the sun to catch the golden rays under the brim of her bonnet. Long satiny lashes caressed her high cheekbones. A hint of yesterday's angelic smile pulled on the edges of her mouth.

With her icy cool beauty, Gideon had taken her as a winter queen. But in that moment Lady Stirling was a sun goddess, soaking up its rays, feeding off the warmth, infusing it into the deep recesses of her being as if she needed it to draw breath. Yet her skin was a flawless alabaster. There was not one freckle on the bridge of her straight nose, not even a brush of pink on her cheeks. He held silent and still, aware he was witnessing a rare event.

"It is so kind of the sun to come out again today. I feared it would go back into hiding after yesterday's brief appearance."

"I take it Scotland's springs are like London's?" He spoke quietly, not wanting to break the spell.

"Yes," she said on a regretful sigh, her eyes still closed against the sun. Her lashes swept up and she looked at him. "But colder." The polite distance returned, the winter queen regaining her dominance.

Gideon discovered a newfound interest in the weather. It had always been a bland topic of conversation, something to discuss to fill a void. Yet now he was rather hoping the coming days would be devoid of the usual gray clouds and rain showers. Not for himself, but simply because it would give her pleasure. Because it was something she needed.

"If you are not averse, we can begin with a short tour of the garden," she said.

"If it would please you, Lady Stirling, then it pleases me." Her wishes, her desires, were his command.

Side by side, with him matching his stride to hers, they made their way around to the back of the house. He had passed the rose garden a total of three times since he had come to Bowhill, but on each instance he had not breached the garden's boundary. It was not lack of interest but rather fear of intruding. The large rectangular space, though outdoors and not formally enclosed by stone walls, had an air of sanctuary. Before he even had the pleasure of meeting Lady Stirling, he'd known this was not merely a bit of landscaping to complement the manor house. It was a part of her.

They passed between a break in the bushes bordering the garden and traveled along a path wide enough for two. With each matched stride, the sounds of the gravel crunching beneath the heels of his black boots drowned out her lighter steps. He knew it to be a rose garden by the foliage but could spot not a single bloom. It was a vast sea of green.

She must have sensed his thoughts for she broke her silence. "The garden is at its best in the summer. None of the roses here bloom as early as April. The Cerisette la Jolies are the earliest and should begin to form buds by the end of the month." She waved a hand, indicating the roses on either side. "By May a few blooms will show themselves and by June everything will be in bloom. The Great Maiden's Blush will grow tall, forming a six-foot-high border of double blush pink blooms. Inside, crimson pink from the Jolies will give way to a thick line of red from the Duchess of Portlands, which will flow to the pink of the Celsianas at the center and end with the pink-kissed white of the Shailers White Moss. And the scent . . . strong and sweet upon first entering the garden, then you will be enveloped by an exquisite deep, potent fragrance."

He closed his eyes, picturing her words, then opened his eyes again and saw the garden in a new light. There were no physical boundaries between the bushes, but the shifts in the green tones of the foliage marked the different varieties. It would be a truly spectacular sight come summer and he felt a twinge of regret knowing he would not be here to witness it. "Do you care for the garden yourself?"

"I do what I can. The majority of the initial planting was done by the small staff of gardeners who come up from the village to see to the grounds. Since there are so many plants they also manage cutting them back. Now that the roses have matured they do not require constant care. Just a watchful eye."

"You do yourself a disservice. The garden is breathtaking and it is clear it thrives under a woman's touch."

The small gloved hand on his arm tightened. She tilted her head, hiding her face under the brim of her bonnet. If he didn't have the hamper in his free hand, he would have captured her chin to view the blush he was certain warmed her cheeks.

When they reached a fork in the path, he followed her lead and headed to the right. The gravel gave way to a grass clearing. A large stone statue marked the center of the garden. A single ring of short green bushes encircled the statue's marble pedestal. Three weathered wooden benches were stationed at intervals around the clearing.

Lady Stirling walked a few steps from him to inspect one of the roses bordering the outer center of the garden. He almost snatched her hand back when her hand left his arm. He had grown accustomed to the light, warm weight and now the spring breeze cooled the space where her hand had rested.

Cocking his head to one side, he studied the statue. If he wasn't mistaken, he knew whom she had chosen as the centerpiece for her garden. Oddly, he wasn't surprised by her choice but rather intrigued. "Why is the goddess of love presiding over your rose garden?"

She glanced over her shoulder. An amazed smile curved her lips. "You recognize her?"

He tipped his head. "The museum has a similar statue of the goddess Aphrodite."

"Are you a student of Greek Mythology?" she asked with patent interest.

"No. Never studied it. I read a book on mythology once, but that was years ago."

Lady Stirling walked to the statue, her gaze on the lush, nude female form of the goddess, whose pose was a bit more than slightly provocative. "It was actually Chloris, the goddess of flowers, who created the rose. Though it was Aphrodite who gave the rose its beauty and its name."

"Who made the rose smell so sweet?"

A little chuckle, light and airy, and so short it would have been missed if his attention were not fully focused on her, bubbled from her lips. "Dionysus."

"Ah. The god of wine. Capital chap, Dionysus."

"And do you worship at his altar?"

Was she teasing him or questioning him? Gideon wasn't certain. "No. No worshipping." He decided to go with the former and gave his head a playful shake, his lips quirking. "Merely appreciate his gifts."

Violet eyes searched his face. She turned on her heel and headed back toward the path. "Come. I have something else you may appreciate."

His naturally longer stride brought him to her side before she reached the fork in the path. She turned right instead of going back the way they had come. His gaze followed the winding path and a jolt of pleasure bounced off his chest when he realized where she was taking him.

The door swung silently open on well-oiled hinges and he was greeted with a profusion of red. The contrast with the green of the outdoors was shocking. Before his eyes had a chance to adjust, a strong scent hit his nose. *Lemons?*

"They don't smell like roses," he said, speaking the thought passing through his head.

She hung her shawl on a hook beside the door and donned a plain white apron. "No. They are unique in many ways. These are the Chinas, Slater's Crimson Chinas to be specific, the first China brought to Britain, and they bloom almost year-round. They are from the East and would not survive one year in Scotland if not for the shelter of the hothouse. Come, have a closer look," she said, pulling on a pair of leather work gloves.

He followed her down the straight dirt path. The dark green bushes weren't the typical thick and full, but spindly and sparse, yet covered in red flowers. A true rich, brilliant red. The same red that graced the Ming vase in the drawing room. The majority of the hothouse was given over to the Chinas, as she proudly called them, but not the entire space. The dense, pure green of the bushes along the walls marked them as a different variety. He felt like he had just walked into a summer day. Sunlight streamed from the tall windows along the stone walls and from lean windows in the steep roof. The air was noticeably warmer and more humid than the outdoors, and held that lemony scent in addition to the scent one associated with newly turned fields. "And you called this a small hobby?"

"It passes the time," she said with a little lift of one slim shoulder.

The time she must have to herself to be able to produce this result . . . It was a staggering view of how truly lonely she was up here in Scotland. But he didn't need the hothouse to tell him that. The simple fact that a woman as beautiful as Lady Stirling had called on the services of one such as him was testament enough.

She paused next to a wooden bench stationed along the path and leaned down to gently cup a fully open red blossom with her palm. "What do you do to pass the time, Mr. Rosedale? Do you have any hobbies, any subjects that interest you?"

"Nothing as grand as yours."

A smile tugged her mouth. "It is not grand."

She did not speak the words with a coy bat of the eyes, begging to be contradicted. She spoke with the self-consciousness of a woman unaccustomed to receiving compliments. But Lady Stirling was too lovely to have never been told so by a man. She had that rare combination of beauty and bearing that turned most men into fools. Could it be she had never had a man compliment her on something other than her appearance? If that were so, then he would gladly be the first. "You are a rose breeder."

"Oh no," she denied, straightening. "I would never bestow such a lofty title on myself, nor should others. I enjoy my roses, that is all."

He gave her a smile, one that said he knew otherwise, but was indulging her refusal. She held his gaze for a moment then continued down the path. This time he was able to view the blush rising over her high aristocratic cheekbones before she turned her back to him, hiding the proof of her modesty.

The path ended at what must be her work area. A large stone hearth, made of the same gray stone as the hothouse, dominated the far wall. To the left were a white wicker settee and a small round table. To the right, three long, aged wooden tables stood in parallel, laden with young plants, mature plants, and others covered with glass domes.

Stepping into a sunbeam streaming from a window in the roof, she stopped before the closest table to check on her charges. The golden light gently caressed every inch of her willowy body, giving her an angelic radiance that caused his stride to falter. It felt as though time slowed down. He could see the tiny dust particles shimmering in the bright rectangle of light surrounding her. The sound of distant birdsong reached his ears.

An irresistible urge seized hold. To feel her sun-warmed skin beneath his hands, his lips. To touch her, kiss her, to take her here in the hothouse amidst the roses with the scent of fragrant blooms heavy in the air.

Before he was aware of it, he had pulled off his gloves, baring his hands. With both leather gloves clutched in one fist, he strode to her. Slow and predatory, his steps made nary a sound in the compact dirt beneath his feet.

He was within three strides of her when he stopped in his tracks.

Too soon. He was certain of it. The questioning glances, the rigidity of her posture, the physical distance she kept between them—her reticence was a tangible force. She wasn't ready to go the next step, let alone skip ahead to the final one. The last thing he wanted to do was rush her. Women moved at their own pace, each unique unto themselves. He needed to continue to follow. To keep things light, flirtatious, while fanning her desire for more.

Patience, he reminded himself, as he shoved his gloves into his coat pocket. After all, thirteen days remained, and ladies did not invite a man such as himself to their home without an agenda in mind.

Not wanting to crowd her, he took up a spot a few paces from where she stood. Orange brown clay pots were arranged in two neat lines on the table. Small and dense, the young plants looked like miniature bushes. Except for one. "That one doesn't look like it's doing very well."

"No." She pulled off a glove to check the soil. "Not too wet. Not too dry. Perfect, yet she is most unhappy. I've tried everything, even changed her soil and moved her from the other side of the hothouse."

He moved a step closer. Her skirt brushed his leg. The skin beneath his breeches tingled. He flexed his hand by his side, resisting the impulse to reach up and trace the delicate curve of her cheek. "Perhaps she just needs to be out in the sun."

"But there's plenty of sun in here and this table will soon have full sunlight."

"You misunderstand. Out in the sun, experiencing the elements. Perhaps it's too sheltered in here. The little rose may yearn for the full force of the sun, not merely that which comes through the windows." *Like you*, he was tempted to add.

She wiped her hand on her apron and replaced her glove. "She *is* a Celsiana and can take the Scottish weather," she murmured, brow furrowed, clearly contemplating his suggestion. With a gentle touch, Lady Stirling examined a thin, spindly branch covered with few leaves. "Perhaps that is the answer, but the gardeners aren't due until tomorrow. She'll have to wait another day. Hopefully it won't rain. It's been so lovely of late that we are past overdue for a few days of clouds and showers."

At the disappointment on her beautiful face, he said, "I can do it for you."

His offer was greeted with three seconds of silence.

"Do you have experience with gardening?" she asked, her tone a combination of doubt and expectation.

"No, but I'm fairly confident I can dig a hole and I can follow instructions, so just tell me what to do. I am at your service, Lady Stirling." He took a step back and gave her a bow.

Her chuckle filled the hothouse. "All right then. Since I am loath to wait another day, I accept your kind offer. Thank you."

When she moved to pick up the plant, he stopped her. "Allow me. And do you have a shovel?"

"Thank you, and yes. In the cabinet by the door."

With the clay pot cradled in one arm, he followed her to the door. He waited for her to place the shawl about her shoulders then he picked up the shovel on his way out of the hothouse.

Gideon had grown accustomed to the warmth of the hothouse and the breeze that ruffled his hair seemed cooler than it had been before he had gone inside. She adjusted the shawl, pulling it tighter around her. The bottom edge ended above the neat bow at the small of her back. The gentle sway of her hips as she walked along the path leading to the break in the rosebushes made the white ties of her apron brush ever so faintly against her backside.

"She needs to go in the middle, with the others of her kind." Lady Stirling's voice drifted back to him.

His attention fixed elsewhere, he merely stopped when she did and only looked up when she turned to face him.

Standing in the grass clearing, framed by springtime green bushes and with the contrast of the nude statue of Aphrodite behind her, she was the very picture of innocence. The shawl softened the straight line of her shoulders. The wide brim of her hat cast a shadow on her face, masking the elegant features, but could not hide the pure delight in her eyes. She quite simply took his breath away and for a split second he questioned the real purpose behind his stay at Bowhill. Then he wiped away the nudge of uncertainty. She was a married woman, one whose kiss contained raw passion the likes of which he had never before encountered. No, she couldn't truly be *that* innocent.

BELLA indicated one of the weathered wooden benches lining the perimeter of the center of the garden. "You can set her down. It will take me a moment to find a home for her."

With a nod, Mr. Rosedale complied. She turned, her gaze sweeping the surrounding area. If she recalled correctly, there was a large enough space beyond the statue where the gardeners had removed a diseased rose last fall. She walked to the spot in question. The bushes on both sides and the one behind had not yet encroached to fill the vacancy. Crouching, she carefully poked in the soil, checking to see if the neighboring plants had grown offshoots. All was clear. The space would do nicely. "Over here. And bring the shovel."

She picked up a few dead leaves from the ground and slipped

them into her apron pocket. At the sound of Mr. Rosedale's approaching footsteps, she straightened and turned. Her breath caught on a little gasp. She glanced past him, craning her neck to see around the statue. A neatly folded dark blue coat graced the back of the bench.

He stopped, the shovel in one bare hand. A hint of a smug, devilish smile pulled one corner of his mouth. "You want me to work, don't you?"

The man had to know he was throwing her senses into a riot. Standing casually before her in a state of semi-undress, he appeared somehow more virile, more masculine. Not one button on his white shirt or pin-striped waistcoat was undone, and his cravat remained tied in a simple knot. Yet the removal of his coat made her insides quiver.

"My lady, I await your instructions."

Take something else off. "I need you to dig a hole. Here." She pointed to the patch of dirt with a finger that shook only slightly.

"How deep?"

"Not quite two feet, but almost. And be careful of the surrounding bushes."

"I will," he said with deliberate patience.

Her shoulders tightened, dousing the arousal coiling inside her. "My apologies."

"There's no need to go that far," he replied in a wry tone. "So how wide do you want it?"

"About the same."

Bella stepped aside to linger by the statue. Mr. Rosedale took up her previous place and started digging. Her lips parted as she soaked up the view he presented. He had quite a nice backside, the buff breeches stretching taut each time he placed a booted foot on the flat edge of the blade. The soft sheen of his silk waistcoat seemed to attract the sunlight, yet it did nothing to hide the bunch and play of his muscled back as he lifted the shovel to deposit the dirt in a neat little mound.

Her pulse picked up. Burgeoning arousal sparked anew. She wondered how he would look without the shirt and waistcoat. His upper body bared, the sun kissing his honey gold skin. Liquid warmth pooled between her thighs and she fought to keep from shifting against the sensation.

"Done." He turned to her.

"Oh. Ah . . ." She struggled to recall exactly why they were out in the garden. "You need to plant her next."

"Of course." He smiled. "The purpose for my labor."

He crossed to the bench, returning with the Celsiana. Dropping to one knee before the newly dug hole, he had the clay pot in one hand, the other reaching for the base of the rose, when she scurried forward, then stopped. Her mouth worked soundlessly.

How did one say "be careful" without actually saying it? She was loath to deliver an insult, especially given his willingness to help her, yet he did mention he had never gardened.

He glanced over his shoulder, his whisky brown eyes alight with expectation. "Yes? Am I doing something wrong to cause that look of concern?"

"No." *Not yet.* "Just give the pot a couple of taps to loosen the soil. She should come out easily. And put some of the loose soil in the bottom of the hole first."

He set the pot down and moved to grab a handful of dirt.

"Wait."

His bare hands stilled over the mound of dark earth.

"You're not wearing gloves. You'll get your hands dirty. Why don't I transplant her? I still have my work gloves on, and she is delicate." Bella shifted her weight, suddenly conscious of how ridiculous it was to get this anxious over something as mundane as putting a plant into the ground. If the remainder of the fortnight unfolded as it possibly could then she would be trusting him with something more important than the young rose.

"My lady. Dirt washes off."

He seemed to have infinite patience, even when she was certain she was trying it. And she found it to be . . . settling. Soothing, offering a sense of steadiness. Something she could depend upon. Mr. Rosedale would not raise his voice at her if she pushed him too far. Her ears would not ring from the force of his screams. And he wasn't holding back. He wasn't masking his true nature.

"Yes, dirt has been known to wash off."

Her flippant statement got her a quizzical look. He shook his head, a rueful grin on his lips. "Am I allowed to proceed?"

She gave a dramatic sigh but spoke the word *yes* with a wide smile. Not wanting him to think she was watching him over his shoulder, she wandered off to check the surrounding plants—though she did sneak a few peeks from the corner of her eye. His large hands were infinitely gentle as he coaxed the young rose from her pot and set her into the ground.

"I believe I'm finished here, that is if my work passes your inspection."

At his confident words, Bella turned from the other roses. Suppressing a grin, she slanted him a "we'll see" look and flicked her fingers. He stepped aside. Already the little Celsiana appeared stronger in her new home. He had done an expert job. Not one leaf lay lost on the fresh, dark soil under her branches.

"Well done, Mr. Rosedale. You make an admirable gardener."

He tipped his head. "I try, ma'am."

Bella chuckled at his failed attempt at humility. She turned on her heel. "Come along. We're done here."

"Yes, ma'am," he replied, the grin clear in his voice.

He stepped ahead of her when they reached the hothouse. The shovel and empty pot held in one arm and his coat slung over one shoulder, he opened the door.

"Thank you," she murmured as she walked passed him, untying the ribbons of her bonnet.

He replaced the shovel inside the cabinet. "Where does the pot go?"

"You can set it next to the worktables by the other empty pots. There's a bucket of water by the hearth if you wish to wash up." She pulled off her bonnet and ran a hand over her head, smoothing any stray hairs.

The grin just wouldn't leave her lips. If all days could be like this one . . .

Water splashed as Mr. Rosedale washed off the dirt from the garden. He wiped his hands on an old embroidered towel. Bella walked to the left and set her bonnet on the settee, removed her gloves, dropping them atop her discarded shawl, and reached around to untie her apron.

"Allow me."

His deep male voice washed over her, so close it tickled her ear. Slightly damp, cool hands stilled hers. Gooseflesh rose up her arms. She took a quick breath against the sensation and dropped her arms to her sides.

Slowly, lazily, he pulled one apron tie. It was so quiet she could hear the fabric unravel. She felt the instant the bow released. His fingers brushed the small of her back as he pulled the tie loose. He reached around to take hold of the top center of the apron. Instead of removing it, he pressed his palm to her waist, holding it in place. He leaned closer. Heat scorched her back. Her derrière tingled where the top of his thighs brushed the sensitive flesh. She was still fully clothed, but felt exposed. As if she stood bare before him.

The scandalous image formed in her mind. He exactly as he was—in buff breeches, black boots, white lawn shirt, and a proper pin-striped waistcoat. And she . . . naked, the warm air in the hothouse caressing every inch of her skin. A quiver seized her body.

Held within his light embrace, she could do nothing but close her eyes against the heavy flush of raw need. She knew all it would take was one movement, one word and he would release her. But she stayed still as a statue, fighting the impulse to rock back against him, to feel the long length of his body pressed fully to hers.

His other hand coasted up her side, grazing the sensitive outer swell of her breast to settle on her shoulder. A gasp expanded her lungs as his warm lips met her neck. Shamelessly, she arched, granting him access. He caressed the point of her racing pulse with the tip of his hot, wet tongue before laying openmouthed kisses on her neck. The brush of teeth grazing her skin incited her passion. Her hand clutched over his at her waist. Unable to resist a moment longer, she thrust her hips back and encountered the unmistakable evidence of his arousal. A low groan shook her throat.

"Dinner tonight?"

The soft, husky words shot to her core, his deep voice a potent source of lust. She shifted, needing to ease the ache. "Pardon?"

He nuzzled the small cove behind her ear. "Dinner. Tonight. Am I to be your guest?"

"Oh," she gasped, trying to right her mind and focus on his question. "Yes." *Always. Forever.*

He laid a light kiss on her neck then stepped back, his hand sliding out from under hers. "What time?"

She blinked her eyes open and turned, her mouth jealous of the attention her neck had received. "Ah . . ." Time didn't matter. She wanted him to kiss her, to feel his lips upon hers, to taste the hot recesses of his mouth. "Six," she heard herself say.

He stepped around her to drop the apron on the settee. "Six it is."

Discomposed, Bella smoothed her hands down the front of her dress, her senses still in a riot. Yet he spoke so casually. Mild irritation clashed with thwarted desire. She looked through the windows until she found the sun. "I should go."

"Why?"

"It's getting late and I need to dress for dinner."

"You needn't stand on formality with me."

"But it's dinner." She rarely had guests and going through the feminine ritual of dressing for dinner was one she was loath to skip.

"Surely you can stay a bit longer," he cajoled. "You've only shown me a few of your young roses."

He sounded earnest, as if he truly wanted her to stay and wasn't just being polite. "Another time," she said with a smile.

"All right then. Six." He sketched a short bow. "I shall count the hours, my lady."

Four

Bella scanned the menu on her desk and made a few necessary adjustments for tonight's dinner. The light scratch of her pen was quick and deliberate. Then she slipped her pen into its holder and lifted an ivory cup to her lips. The crisp, tart Earl Grey tea exactly matched her mood. She had awoken this morning with a new sense of purpose, of confidence in the coming days. It was as if her sleeping mind had worked over all her worries, casting aside the frivolous and leaving the remaining neat and organized.

She was glad she had not sent Mr. Rosedale packing after their first dinner together—that would have been foolish, beyond impetuous. She was a grown woman, fully in control of herself, and if she wanted to indulge in a harmless flirtation then she would. Her eyes were open. The situation understood. The ramifications known.

Mr. Rosedale earned his living pleasuring women. Many men employed the services of whores and thought nothing of it. Surely she could do the same, or at least something similar. She would simply look at the situation as Esmé suggested—see it as a practical arrangement, with very nice benefits. As Esmé had pointed out, she was under no obligation to him. She did not have to take him to her bed. In fact, the way he turned from her last night indicated he was the gentleman he appeared to be.

Last night's dinner had been a thoroughly enjoyable affair, yet it had not ended with a kiss. *Oh*, she had wanted one, especially after being teased to distraction in the hothouse. But he had been more aware of her butler's hovering presence by the front door than she. Mr. Rosedale ended the evening with only a sincere "Good night, Lady Stirling."

Tonight she would again be denied the opportunity for a kiss. She had extended a dinner invitation to her neighbors weeks ago. While she would prefer to cry off and spend the evening with him, it would be most impolite. In any case, she had no excuse at the ready, at least none that wouldn't rouse suspicions or get back to the wrong ears. But today . . .

Dragging a fingertip over her impatient lips, she glanced out the window of her sitting room. The curtains were drawn back, exposing the tops of trees in the distance and a clear sky. A grin curved her lips as the answer came to her—a carriage ride. They wouldn't be alone, but the driver's attention would be on the horses. Surely there'd be an opportunity or two, or more, for Mr. Rosedale to steal a kiss as they toured the estate.

A quick word with a servant was all that was needed to have the landau readied and sent to Garden House to pick up her guest. She left the last of the household matters completed on her desk and entered her bedchamber. After donning a short amber spencer over her cornflower blue walking dress and tying the ribbons of her bonnet in a neat bow, she went down to await the landau in the entrance hall. The crunch of gravel under horses' hooves and carriage wheels made its way to her ears as she descended the staircase. McGreevy opened the front door, his expression more sour than usual. Ignoring him, Bella stepped out of the house and into the sun.

A smile tugged Mr. Rosedale's mouth. He stood beside the carriage dressed in buff breeches and a dark brown jacket that was the exact same shade as the hair currently hidden beneath a proper black top hat. He was the very image of an afternoon gentleman, arrived to take his lady on a drive through Hyde Park.

"Good morning, Lady Stirling."

"Good morning, Mr. Rosedale." The smile at the prospect of spending another day with him could not be suppressed. A short gust of wind ruffled her bonnet ribbons, the bow tickling her cheek as she descended the stone steps.

Setting her hand in his, she stepped into the open carriage. He settled beside her on the black leather bench. The driver snapped the lines and the carriage lurched forward.

He leaned close, his broad shoulder grazing hers. "Where are you taking me this morning?" His conspiratorial whisper tickled her ear.

She kept her gaze straight ahead and on the driver's back, resisting the urge to turn and brush her lips against his which were *oh* so close. It wouldn't do to behave like a tart while within easy view of the manor. "You had mentioned you'd never been to Scotland before. As your hostess, it is my duty to show you the beautiful countryside."

"How thoughtful of you. Thank you." He gently tugged on the amber ribbon of her bonnet, releasing the neat bow. "The sun is shining today. You should enjoy it before it goes back into hiding."

She didn't dare think to protest when he removed her bonnet, and simply passed a quick hand over her head to smooth her hair. Setting the bonnet on the opposite bench, he picked up the folded blanket.

"Though it is still April," he said. "Wouldn't wish for you to catch a chill. The wind is rather brisk." With a snap of his wrists, the navy tartan billowed before them as he settled it over their legs.

"Thank you," she murmured, a blush warming her cheeks at the thoughtful gesture.

"My pleasure," he replied, his voice a shade lower than normal.

Bella took a deep breath against the new intimacy of being under a blanket with a man and a scent hit her nostrils. It wasn't thick or sweet like cologne, rather a light fragrance that rode over the brisk outdoor air, hinting of cloves, lemons, and clean male skin.

She continued to take deep, even breaths, taking in the scent of him as the driver guided the team of four along the lane. The horses' chestnut coats gleamed like newly hammered copper. Their hooves beat the ground in steady cadence. The blanket effectively trapped the heat rolling off the male body next to her, and it warmed more than her legs.

The trees blocked the sun as they traveled under the thick canopy arching over the path; it reappeared once they reached the north entrance to the estate. The driver turned the team to the right, onto the dirt road that bordered Bowhill.

"That's Moorehead, the Tavisham estate." Bella indicated the Tudor-style, modest mansion that could be seen in the distance to her left. Mr. Rosedale leaned forward to view the house around her. His thigh pressed against hers. The hard long muscles were evident through the layers of clothing. Her deep breaths stuttered. "They're a delightful, if eccentric old couple. Mrs. Tavisham shares my affinity for roses and recently imported a new variety from the continent. I have not seen them as yet, but once the plants have acclimated to her conservatory she's promised to make a gift of a cutting. In fact, she is to bring news of her new additions this evening."

"You will have guests this evening?" he asked, his attention on Moorehead.

"Yes," she said with a trace of unease, hoping he would not see it as a slight against him.

He tilted his head to look at her from the corner of his eye. "Well then, I insist you extract all the details of your forthcoming gift and relay them to me on the morrow." His tone was casual, as if he understood and accepted the delicacy of the situation.

Seemingly satisfied with the view of Moorehead, Mr. Rosedale righted himself, resting against the bench, but his thigh stayed pressed against hers: one long continual line from her hip to her knee. She turned to him and expected to meet whisky brown eyes, for he always seemed to be looking at her, but his gaze was downcast. The sunlight just made its way past the short brim of his top hat to bathe the ends of his dark lashes.

"Is the plaid doing its duty, or shall we head back to the manor house?" he asked.

"The blanket is sufficient, thank you. We needn't turn back on my account."

"A lady's account is the only one that matters."

She tipped her head. "Ever the gentleman."

"Of course," he said with a teasing smirk. "Would you care to fill our carriage ride with a parlor game?"

His question gained her full attention. "What sort of game?"

"It's more of an old gypsy's trick than a game. Shall I show you?"

Her curiosity piqued, she nodded.

He removed his black leather gloves and set them on the bench. Turning his broad shoulders toward her, he held out a hand, palm up. "If you please," he murmured.

She eagerly placed her right hand in his. He rubbed his thumb over the back of her gloved hand. Once, twice, three times. The caress slow and decadent, as if he were touching a different part of her body. He turned her hand over. The small mother-of-pearl button holding the glove closed posed no difficulty. With a deft flick of his fingertips the button was undone, exposing her wrist. She swore she could see her pulse beat lightning-quick though the lattice of thin blue veins. One finger at a time, he pulled on the leather, loosening the cream kidskin, until with a final tug the glove slipped off her hand.

The spring breeze cooled her skin, but did nothing to cool the blood drumming through her veins. Caught on the hook of suspense, she could only stare at their hands. His dwarfed hers, her skin palest ivory against his honey gold.

With the back of her hand cradled in his left palm, he passed his right hand over hers, the simple weight of his hand drawing her cupped fingers flat. In that brief moment her hand was pressed between both of his, surrounded by strong warmth and the unique feel of his skin. Velvety soft, yet her suddenly highly sensitized nerves could feel the ridges on his fingertips. Heat radiated up her arm and across her chest until she was so warm she welcomed the chill wind brushing across her flushed cheeks.

"It is said the hands reveal the most about a person." Slow and light, he traced the creases in her palm with the tip of his index finger. A tremble seized her body. "Every feature is significant. The length of the fingers. The shape of the palm. The strength and intersection of the lines."

"Palmistry," she said with wonder, guessing his game. Her gaze left the infinitely appealing sight of their joined hands to meet his eyes.

"Yes. But I am only a novice."

"Where did you learn it?"

"From a woman whose grandmother was a gypsy. I simply learned palmistry because . . ." He gave a little huff of self-directed amusement. His voice lowered, as if he were divulging a scandalous confidence. "I was thirteen and had a certain fondness for my instructor. The lessons gave me an excuse to spend time with her. The naivety of youth. She was more than double my age."

She smiled at the thought of him as a boy. Lanky, eager, and without the smooth polish of charm and experience.

The broad line of his shoulders tightened. His composure vanished for a brief moment, a blink of an eye. The way he startled himself with the admission of a youthful infatuation gave him a vulnerability she had not sensed in him before.

He regained his composure in the next instant, once again the charming suitor. "And I haven't tested those particular skills in years, so I beg your forgiveness in advance if I am a bit out of practice."

"There's no reason to beg, Mr. Rosedale. A simple request will suffice."

"Yes, ma'am," he replied, with a tip of his head. The same one he had given her yesterday. And as before, the confidence of his posture destroyed any attempt at humility. "May I proceed?"

She squared her shoulders. "Please," she said, using her haughtiest tone.

A faint chuckle rumbled his chest as he bowed his head and focused on her hand. "These are the heart and head lines." He traced the two lines crossing the upper portion of her palm. "This is the life line," he said, indicating the faint creases curving around the pad at the base of her thumb. "And this one is the fate line."

Her breaths stuttered as he drew his fingertip down the center of her palm. The sway of the carriage made his broad shoulder brush against hers. The continual press of his thigh branded her skin. The intoxicating scent of him filled her every breath. It was all she could do to sit still and not launch herself at him, wrap her arms around his neck, and demand he kiss her.

"We shall start at the top and work our way down." A toying lilt entered his voice, adding one more layer to the arousing sensations threatening to overpower her. "The heart line reveals responses of an emotional nature." He lifted one dark eyebrow. "Ah, a curved heart line, and steeply curved at that. Passion, in abundance."

She slanted him a sly, questioning glance. "Abundance? Are you certain?"

Those beautiful, kissable lips quirked. "Most assuredly." The soft tease of his fingertip moved down to trace another line. "And here is your head line. This one is forked, indicating creative talents. Your hothouse and garden are certainly stunning examples of your creative talents, Lady Stirling."

"Thank you," she demurred.

"My pleasure," he said softly before continuing. "Your fate line starts at the life line. Ever the proper Englishwoman, you have a strong sense of duty toward your family." He indicated three creases on the lower left side of her palm. "These little lines here . . ." His fingertip lingered on the highest line, which was longer and stronger than the other two and ended on her fate line. He leaned back just enough to fully hold her gaze under the brim of his hat. "Which do you think I am?"

The heavy tone in the question gave her pause. She glanced at her palm, looking for the answer, though she didn't understand his question. She replayed everything he told her in her mind, everything he divined, which had been surprisingly accurate. She shook her head and posed her own question. "What do the lines signify?"

Serious and searching brown eyes swept her face. Just when she did not think he would answer, he spoke, the word almost too low to hear. "Affairs."

Her entire body went rigid. *Three.* The number reverberated in her head. *One, two . . . where was the third?* Would there be a third in her future? Anxiety coiled low in her belly. "Does a marriage count?"

His gaze took on a concerned aspect, his dark eyebrows lowering. "Yes."

Three. Him, him—she fought the cringe—and *him.* The tight beats of her heart slackened. The tension left her limbs. Mr. Rosedale was rubbing his thumb over her palm. Large, slow circles that had nothing to do with any intention of arousal and everything to do with comfort. His expression was so intent she wasn't sure he was aware of the way he soothed her.

Then everything shifted. It was subtle, for neither of them moved, but she felt it down to her bones. His brown eyes darkened; the amber flecks glowing gold bright. Her breaths turned heavy and short. His eyes never leaving her rapt gaze, he removed his top hat and set it on the bench beside him. The horses moved at a brisk canter, their harnesses jangling with each rhythmic stride. The wind tickled the ends of his hair. The short locks shone a rich, deep sable under the sun.

He slowly leaned toward her, his head tilting to one side. She felt herself sway, an involuntary feminine reaction. He reached up his free hand to gently cup her cheek. His long fingers curved around her neck, tickling the fine hairs at her nape. The warmth of his hand seared her skin. Lust crashed over her, flooding her senses. A thick, potent, undiluted wave. Her head went light, her eyelids fluttering against the sheer overwhelming force.

"Kiss me," she whispered hoarsely, needing more than anything to feel his lips against hers.

"My pleasure," he murmured.

He closed the last remaining distance, his sinfully dark eyes locked with hers. Her lashes swept down the instant before the soft brush of his warm lips.

THE intensity of her response caught Gideon off guard. Given their first kiss, he should have been expecting it. But nothing could have prepared him for the full force of Lady Stirling's honest and uninhibited kiss. It bowled him over, momentarily stealing his wits and leaving him feeling like a green lad, struggling to keep up as she took each sweep of his tongue and gave back threefold.

She arched into him, her perpetually rigid spine supple as a blade of tall grass in the wind. One breast pressed against his chest and he swore he could feel the hard tip of her nipple even through the many layers of clothing. Heat lanced to his groin and he shifted to accommodate his rapidly hardening cock.

She kissed him with complete abandon. A mixture of untutored eagerness and raw need that demanded he respond in kind.

A primitive need to mate, to possess, one he thought long ago forever tamped down, surged from deep within. His kiss turned fierce as he plundered the hot depths of her delectable mouth. He grabbed her waist, the sleek indent made for his hand. He was but a moment from wrapping his arm around her, hauling her to him and settling her astride his lap, when the snap of leather lines broke through the haze of lust.

They were in an open carriage. The driver's black-coated back not five feet from them.

He suppressed a groan. *Not here.* When she came to her senses, she would be mortified. In any case, gentlemen did not make love to proper ladies in open carriages traveling on Scottish country roads.

Through conditioned force of will, he ignored the demands of his own body, ignored the hard cock crammed in his breeches, dismissed the ballocks drawn up tight begging for release, and took control, reining the kiss in to gently nip her full lower lip.

On a breathless mewl of protest, she pressed closer to him, seeking his lips. In less than a second, his mind raced through his vast catalog of sensual experience and quickly selected an acceptable compromise. At least that was how he rationalized it—a compromise for *her.* Inwardly, he could not deny the impulse to take this elegant creature over the edge, to watch the passion shatter the poise.

He trailed openmouthed kisses down the column of her long swan's neck. Her skin was fire hot and rose petal smooth, and the scent of her . . . Not a hint of perfume. Inhaling deeply, he flared his nostrils. Clean, fresh as a spring morning, the distinct note of feminine arousal, and something else, something indefinable that made him want to taste every inch of her skin.

The image slammed into his mind—her lithe nude body offered up on white sheets, his face buried between her lean thighs, as he tasted the most enticing part of her.

Focus!

On that harsh reminder he mentally shook off the image. Righted to his current task, he delved a hand beneath the woolen blanket. Caressing the point of her hammering pulse with the tip of his tongue, he slowly gathered her skirt, bringing the hem up past her stocking-covered knee, his senses attuned for any sign of refusal, no matter how small, that she was not an eager participant. With her skirt bunched over his forearm, he reached up, fingertips whispering over the line of her garter to the soft warm skin of her inner thigh. Then he paused, hand splayed, his index finger curving over the taut tendon at the very top of her thigh.

Back bowing, a tremor shook her entire body. "*Please.*"

The word was so low, so soft, a mere tremble of sound, yet it was as clear to him as if she shouted.

Permission granted.

He smiled against her neck. "Shh, Isabella."

He brushed his fingertips over her thatch of curls. Gossamer soft, and he knew without looking it was as pale as the hair on her head. Supplicant and eager, her legs parted at his gentle request, bathing his hand in scalding heat. He thought the appeal of such a benign act had been blunted long ago, no longer the titillating play of his youth. Yet his heart pounded in anticipation, as though he was on the verge of opening a great treasure. He knew he would not find relief this afternoon, but the prospect of touching her added another inch to his already painful arousal. On a deep breath of self-restraint, he slipped one finger between the silken folds of her sex. He swallowed hard, finding her drenched.

Her breath hitched on a whimper.

"Quiet now. Quiet, Isabella, and I'll give you what you need." He looked into her face, intent on watching every minute, committing every sigh, every gasp, her every reaction to memory.

Long satiny lashes rested on her high cheekbones. Her lips, still damp from their kisses, parted on short, quick breaths. Her chest heaved, luscious breasts straining against the expertly tailored spencer. One small hand clutched his free hand so tightly her nails bit into his skin. With her other hand, she grabbed the blanket, fingers clenched tight in the tartan. She tilted her head down and to the side, hiding her flushed cheeks from view of all but Gideon.

In an effort to keep her from coming too quickly, he worked her carefully. Not too swift, not too hard, with just enough teasing pressure to keep her at the point of maximum pleasure. Playing at the soaked entrance of her body, giving her just the merest hint of penetration before sweeping up to graze her clit. He wanted her to savor, to take from this a taste of the pleasures he could offer, to prompt the invitation he needed her to extend.

But it was no use. Once it was tapped even *he* could not check her passion. Within a very small handful of minutes she came violently. Back arching, thighs clamping tight around his hand, shudders wracking her body. Exquisite bliss reflected on her beautiful face.

Gideon silenced her eminent cries with a kiss as he petted her, calmed her, gently easing her back to the present. He pulled his lips from hers and trailed light kisses across her silken cheek to nuzzle at the fragile shell of her ear. He slipped his hand from between her now lax thighs and out from under the blanket.

He gazed into her eyes and found them heavy-lidded and glazed with desire, glittering like precious gems. Her lips were plumped from their kisses. Her cheeks flushed rose pink. The winter queen looked utterly debauched and more beautiful than ever. The vision prompted a surge of triumph, victory, and pure male pride.

She gave a start. Her supple body went rigid. Her breath hitched sharply. She released his hand so quickly one would have thought his touch burned.

Damn. The smug grin vanished from his lips. Had he taken her too far, too soon? He was certain she had been ready, but now . . .

Her eyes darted left and right then fixed directly over his shoulder

"It's all right," he murmured, relieved, at what he hoped was the true source of her distress.

"But—?"

He shook his head, cutting off her words. "It's all right. Your driver picked me up in London. His silence has been assured."

Needing to erase the concern pulling her fine eyebrows, he cupped her cheek again. His thumb caressed the corner of her mouth, drawn in a straight line. Her body relaxed under his touch but the worry still invaded her eyes. The same worry his impetuous question had produced.

What had made him even entertain the notion that the long, sweeping line on her palm could have anything to do with him? His time with her so short, so insignificant, it would not even manifest itself. It had been meant to be a game. A light, flirtatious game. And all it had done was make her anxious as his amateur fortune-telling had inadvertently hit a very raw nerve.

He would have to carefully choose what games he played with her. She wasn't merely a lonely woman who had been left too long without the pleasures of a man. The worry, the concern, that damn flash of true fear that had flickered across her face . . . it made him want to wrap his arms around her, hold her close, and—

A sharp lance of longing pierced his chest, stopping the unprecedented thought before it could go any further.

This was the third time she had managed to slip under his skin. He really did need to be careful with her. And right now what *she* needed was to forget their last game.

"Truly. It's all right," he said, leaning closer to whisper the words against her lips.

He stole one quick kiss. Soft and light, but with enough intent to distract her from her worries.

When next he pulled back to gaze at her beautiful face, he found a delightful little sparkle in her violet eyes.

He smiled as he pulled on his gloves and replaced his hat on his head. "It's a beautiful day for a drive, is it not?"

"Yes," she replied on a bashful chuckle.

Rose du Roi."

Bella forced her mind to her current dinner guests and processed Mrs. Tavisham's words. "All the way from France?"

"Yes, from Dupont's own garden. Of the three plants, two are doing very well but one is struggling. Most distressing. I talk to her for endless hours, but maybe she simply misses the sound of a French voice," said Mrs. Tavisham in all seriousness.

Bella could empathize with the little Rose du Roi, but the voice she missed at the moment was an English one. *Quiet, Isabella, and I'll give you what you need.* The memory of Mr. Rosedale's soft croon flowed over her, bringing to mind his tantalizing caress. Oh, he had most definitely given her what she needed. The residual hum from the orgasm he'd given her had yet to leave her senses. Conscious of Mrs. Tavisham's rapt gaze, she took a deep breath and was quite pleased with the way the exhale flowed smoothly and without even one telltale hitch. "Being uprooted from one's home is never pleasant but at least there are two others of her kind to keep her company."

Mrs. Tavisham replied with a solemn nod. "I moved one of the young Cuisse de Nymphs next to her pot and this morning she seemed a bit more cheerful. Perhaps I will have a new variety come fall." Her hazel eyes twinkled at the thought of playing matchmaker. "While we are on the subject of love matches, I must tell ye, the butcher's youngest daughter is to marry, and she'll be wed before the eldest."

"That gel's a tart," Mr. Tavisham declared in his harsh brogue. He speared a green bean onto his fork and popped it into his mouth.

"Walter!" His wife shot him a remonstrating glare from across the table.

Bella kept the startled chuckle from making its way past her lips. The Tavishams were an odd pair, yet Bella adored them. They were truly the only two people in Scotland she enjoyed socializing with.

Well, there was a third—her own new addition to Scotland. What was he doing at this very moment? Her wicked mind jumped significantly past the mundane. To Mr. Rosedale, his large hand wrapped around his cock, pursuing the orgasm he had denied himself earlier. Her pulse quickened. She squeezed her legs tight together in an effort to ease the ache building between her thighs.

"And what of you, Lady Stirling? Do you have any news?" Mrs. Tavisham asked.

Yes, an impossibly gorgeous man ravished me in my carriage. Quite a most delightful afternoon. Bella resisted the urge to lick her lips and instead smiled politely. "No, nothing of interest."

"You aren't planning a visit to London?"

"No. Why do you ask?"

"I thought that was why you have developed a taste for the news. I myself prefer the scandal sheets. Though Tavisham is in accord with you and takes the *Times* on occasion."

Bella furrowed her brow. The *Times*? Then her heart stumbled.

Mr. Rosedale.

Feeling the color leech from her face, she picked up her knife and fork and cut the squares of tenderloin on her plate into smaller pieces. She cast her mind desperately for some excuse, some plausible explanation to divert Mrs. Tavisham from discovering she had a man staying at Garden House who apparently had a preference for the *Times*.

And why did it not surprise her to find out Mr. Rosedale read the daily paper?

She looked to Mrs. Tavisham. "No, I'm not planning to visit London. I am most content here at Bowhill. I merely asked for the *Times* to be delivered in the event it would please Lord Stirling."

"Is Lord Stirling due to arrive soon?" Mrs. Tavisham's look of innocent inquiry couldn't cover the eagerness at the possibility of a new piece of gossip to share with the village.

Bella dropped her gaze to her plate. Why had she mentioned Stirling? She hated to admit her husband did not keep her abreast of his comings and goings. It made her feel so unimportant, so trivial, as if her continual presence at Bowhill was not even worthy of an afterthought. She swallowed to ease the tightness in her throat, and unable to lie about everything to the one woman she called friend, said, "I do not know the exact date of his lordship's arrival, but I arranged for the paper so it would be here when he does arrive."

"You have family in London, do you not?"

"Yes, Mrs. Tavisham. My elder brother divides his time between Mayfair and Norfolk, the family seat." Her appetite completely gone, Bella unclenched her fingers from her knife and fork and set them with deliberate purpose on either side of her plate. When had the thought of Phillip become worse than Stirling? Probably when she had given up that last drop of hope of receiving even a note from him, let alone a visit.

"That's right. Your brother is the Earl of Mayburn. I often forget, as you rarely speak of him. A shame his responsibilities keep him from visiting Bowhill, but it would not do for a peer to be away from Town when Parliament is in session."

Phillip did not need the excuse of Parliament to keep him from Scotland. Her presence kept him away well enough. "Yes, he is a most busy man who takes his many responsibilities very seriously."

"Good to hear," declared Mr. Tavisham with a gruff nod. "Nothing worse than a lord who doesn't take his seat. Some of those young lords should be ashamed of themselves. Gambling away their fortunes, bleeding their estates dry, leaving their families with nothing. Appalling!"

No, Phillip would never be so irresponsible as to forget his duty. She alone bore that distinction.

"Walter." A mulish frown creased Mrs. Tavisham's pudgy face. She selected another slice of tenderloin from the large silver platter stationed conveniently close to her place at the dining table. Then she let out a gasp that caused her large bosom to quiver. "I almost neglected to tell you. Our old mare had a filly on Saturday. All long, spindly legs and with the softest little nose. Such a curious thing. You must stop by to see her."

Bella nodded and did her best to hide her sigh of relief. It had simply been a matter of time before the older woman tired of the subject of Bella's family.

They retired to the drawing room, where Mr. Tavisham indulged in a glass of port and she and Mrs. Tavisham partook of tea. As the evening wore on, as the conversation returned to the comings and goings of the inhabitants of the village, Bella found it increasingly difficult to keep her mind on the present company. Her thoughts skittered past the distressing topics of Stirling and Phillip to settle eagerly on Mr. Rosedale. To all the wonderful things he had done to her that afternoon, and to all the decadent things he had not yet done.

But when at last the Tavishams took their leave, Bella tamped down the impulse to run straight to Mr. Rosedale, and instead forced her legs to take her up to her bedchamber.

Passion did not rule her—she ruled it.

Five

GIDEON absently reached out a hand. The edges of the leaves gently scraped his bare fingertips as he walked along the line of bushes bordering the rose garden.

He had received no note from Lady Stirling last night, nor this morning. Left to his own devices, he had used the *Times* and a few games of patience to pass the morning hours. Lady Stirling's servants were as attentive to detail as she. All it took was one request for the London newspaper to become a standard part of the breakfast basket delivered to the cottage every morning.

But as the morning had turned to afternoon, he found himself growing oddly restless. The only sounds in the cottage were the rapid tap of his boot heel against the floorboards and the flick of cards as he sat at the dining table and uncharacteristically lost one game of patience after another. Frustrated, he laid the blame on being unaccustomed to having so many hours to himself when at a lady's home. Visits to the country were typically only a handful of days and therefore his clients rarely allowed too many hours to pass without calling on his services, be they sociable or other more pleasurable activities. Proximity was also a factor. His accommodations usually consisted of a guest room, one conveniently close to theirs, in the main house. Evenings, as well as every meal, were spent with them. A simple walk down a hall could bring him face-to-face with the lady of the manor.

Having the use of a guest cottage was therefore a luxury. Or Gideon had considered it a luxury before the solitary hours got the better of him.

It wasn't that he needed the constant companionship of another. When his schedule was open, he enjoyed spending a day or two alone at his apartment before stopping in at his tailor or testing his luck at a West End gentlemen's gambling hell. But it was different here. He felt like a racehorse confined in its stall too long. He knew his purpose for being at Bowhill and the suspense of when he would be called to the track kept him from being able to relax.

Outright worry had not set in yet—there were still many days ahead of him. The outcome of yesterday's carriage ride kept away any concern he was losing his vaunted touch with the fairer sex. She would come around. It was simply taking longer than usual for her to get comfortable with him. Still, the "when" had begun to nudge at the back of his mind. So instead of being reduced to pacing the front parlor, he had set out for a walk.

"Mr. Rosedale."

Glancing up from his study of the lush grass, he saw a maid walking toward him. He stopped. "Yes?"

"For you, sir."

He took the proffered note. "Thank you."

He waited until she took her leave before opening the note. An invitation to an afternoon tea. A smile curved his mouth. He pulled out his pocket watch and scowled at the small black hands. Three hours until he could present himself at her front door.

He let out an impatient huff, turned on his heel, and strode back to the cottage.

GIDEON set his empty teacup in the saucer on the nearby end table. "Would you care for more tea?"

"No, thank you."

"How about a tart? They're delicious."

He made the attempt, but somehow knew what Lady Stirling's answer would be. She had taken precisely three bites of the scone on her plate, and they had been small bites. Very ladylike. Given her lean figure, she wasn't holding back on his account. Her hunger for food apparently was not an indication of her hunger for other things.

"No, thank you," she said.

"You're in need of nothing?" He leaned forward in the chair to rest his elbows on his knees. "Nothing?"

Her lashes swept down and a slow smile spread across her mouth.

That was a new smile. He hadn't seen that one yet. He'd give just about anything to know what was going through that beautiful head of hers. Perched on the edge of the ivory settee, her emerald skirts arranged just so over her long legs, her shoulders and spine perfectly straight, she appeared so regal, so unapproachable, almost cold. But he knew better.

Lady Stirling glanced up. "A walk. I've been in the house all day and could use a walk."

That had not been what had caused the wicked curve of her lips. Oh well, it wasn't as if she would tell him yet. At least not while they were having tea in the formal drawing room, the door open, revealing occasional glimpses of servants going about their day. Too many glimpses. Her housekeeper must have walked by at least five times in the past twenty minutes. "Well then, if you're finished, we can depart."

She declined his offer to have her bonnet or shawl fetched, insisting the long sleeves of her cambric day dress would be sufficient. Side by side they stepped out of the house. She glanced up to the gray sky as they walked across the gravel drive, which curved in front of the manor.

"If I could, I would summon the sun for you."

Her step faltered and she looked slowly over to him with a smile full of unexpected joy. "Thank you, but I don't need the sun today."

"And why is that?"

"You're here," she said simply, as if that were answer enough.

It was the finest compliment anyone had ever given him. Tongue-tied and feeling strangely exposed, Gideon swiftly averted his eyes to the expanse of lawn before them and studied the trees in the distance. He had only given her one orgasm in the four days he'd been at Bowhill, so there was no reason for her to believe he rivaled the sun. With a mental shake of admonishment, he threw off the discomposure. He was looking for a meaning that wasn't there. Her words had been playful lover's banter and nothing more.

Reassured, he glanced to her, his confidence back in place. "Where shall we walk today?"

"The gardeners are around back, so why don't I show you the grounds in the front of the house?"

"We shouldn't wander far. The clouds look like they're holding some rain."

She passed a dismissive eye over the iron gray clouds on the horizon. "No. It will hold off. We have hours before those clouds move in."

Gideon tipped his head. "I concede to your greater knowledge. I am but a recent guest to your country."

"We are only four hundred miles from London, Mr. Rosedale," she said dryly. "It's not as if we are in Egypt. That cloud will make its way to England by nightfall."

"My, my. Aren't we a tad cheeky today?"

"Does my cheek offend your gentleman's sensibilities?"

"Oh no, not at all. I quite like your cheek." His roguish wink cracked her purposefully haughty face and got him a chuckle.

"Good. I'm glad." The laugh lingering in her voice rippled down his spine.

How he liked her smiles. Not the polite ones—the real ones. The rare ones. But they were becoming less rare as their days together wore on. "You never did tell me about your morning."

She smoothed a hand down the front of her dress. "Nothing of any real interest."

"I beg to differ. You are infinitely interesting."

She gave him a disbelieving shake of the head. "You exaggerate. I am nothing of the sort. But if you must know, I met with my secretary."

"And what did you discuss, if you don't mind me asking?"

"The estate, which isn't very large, so Mr. Leighton doesn't need to come up to the house often. Today he wanted to give me an update and needed to check an old account ledger. He's technically an estate manager, but he's more comfortable with the term *secretary* as that was his position before he agreed to postpone his retirement and work for Bowhill."

She spoke as if the secretary reported to her and not her husband. Gideon looked down to her ungloved hands folded casually before her. No ring. Though it was a rare occurrence when one of them wore a wedding ring during a visit from him. He had her features memorized and therefore didn't need to look at her beautiful face to confirm she was in her midtwenties. Too young to be a widow. No—she was married, else there would be no reason for him to play the visiting relative.

So what sort of man installed such an exquisite creature in the country?

A foolish one. Most likely an old, foolish one. A man who couldn't recognize the treasure he had been gifted with. An uncomfortable sensation tightened Gideon's gut, recalling him to his present surrounds and vanquishing any more unwanted thoughts of the man who had come before, and would come after him, from his mind.

"Do you have tenants?" he asked, in an effort to pick up the conversation where he had let it drop.

Lady Stirling looked up from her study of the grass, which brushed the bottom edge of her emerald green skirt. "Yes. Bowhill is comprised of three separate properties. There's this," she gestured to the surrounding grounds, "and two other, more productive properties closer to the village. One's a farm and the other is a large pasture for the sheep."

"You have sheep," he said, amused by the notion. "How very . . . Scottish of you."

She slanted him an arch glance. "They were not my choice, Mr. Rosedale. They were there when I arrived."

"Did Mr. Leighton's update include the incumbent beasts? Did they make it through the winter to see the spring?"

"Yes. They all made it through the winter. There are even a few new lambs, with more due later this spring."

"Congratulations on the additions to your flock. You must be most proud." His comment got him a condescending raise of her eyebrows, one worthy of a queen. "What? You don't take interest in your sheep? Think of how they would thrive if they received the same attention as your roses."

"And what sort of interest should I take in them?"

"Oh well, why not do it properly? You'd make a wonderful lady shepherdess standing amidst the flock with your long staff and a large white bonnet. A vision of loveliness," he said grandly.

She shook her head as though the idea was beyond ridiculous. "No, thank you, Mr. Rosedale."

"No? And why not?"

"They smell," she replied pertly.

"And how can you be certain?"

"How can you not?"

Gideon laughed as she threw his question right back at him. "I can't. The closest I've been to a live sheep has been while in a carriage, passing the wee beasts in a distant field."

"Since I am more knowledgeable about said beasts, being that they are on the property and all, I say they smell." She lifted her chin, daring him to challenge her. Her lips quirked from the grin she suppressed.

"Who am I to contradict a lady? I again concede to your greater knowledge," he said with an exaggerated tip of the head. At the divot in the lush grass ahead of them, he reached behind her to lay a hand on her trim waist and pull her close. "Rabbit hole," he murmured.

She tipped her face up to him. "Thank you." Her soft words barely reached his ears.

"My pleasure. Wouldn't want you to turn your ankle. Then you'd be stuck in the house for much longer than a mere morning." His fingertips skimmed the curve of her derriere as he reluctantly released her.

A short gust of wind loosened a few of her long, white blonde hairs from their pins. With a slight scowl, Lady Stirling tucked them back in place. "And what of you? How did you spend your morning?"

"Nothing of any real interest."

"Since that answer did not work for me, it will not work for you." She gave him a superior little tilt of her head, clearly pleased with herself.

Dull. His morning had been extremely dull. Gideon passed a hand across the back of his neck. "Truly, it was very uninteresting. I read the paper."

"That was all? You spent the entire morning with the *Times*?"

How did she know which paper he read? Then he dismissed the question. A servant, obviously. "I also played a few hands of cards."

"Oh, and do you gamble, Mr. Rosedale?" she asked with sharpened interest.

Conscious of the hours he did spend at the gaming tables, he evaded her question. "It is rather difficult to gamble with one's self. A win is a loss."

"Not this morning. In general."

"What English gentleman doesn't gamble from time to time?" He glanced over his shoulder. They had traveled farther than he realized. "We should head back."

"Not yet. A little bit farther," Bella pleaded.

A frown worried Mr. Rosedale's brow as he assessed the sky. "We really should head back. The wind is picking up and you didn't bring your shawl."

His concern would have touched her if she wasn't so focused on remaining outdoors with him. Alone. Away from prying eyes and ears. "I'm not cold in the slightest." His stride slowed. Impulsively she reached for his hand and gripped it tightly, keeping him with her. "Honestly. I'm fine."

"All right," he said, as if against his better judgment. "A little farther."

She smiled in thanks. It felt nice to have a man indulge her whims. Then she chanced a glance over her shoulder. The house was too far in the distance for anyone to be able to make out their joined hands. So she didn't release her hold on him, and instead moved closer so her shoulder grazed his bicep with each step.

A pressing need to know more about him prompted her to ask, "So you like to gamble and read the paper. What else interests you, Mr. Rosedale?"

At length, he simply looked at her. His mouth quirked, as if he found something unexpected. "You."

A warm blush crept up her cheeks but she didn't divert her gaze from his. The honesty in his whisky brown eyes tempted her to believe him. The large hand wrapped around hers loosened, and for a moment she feared he meant to let go, branding her a fool for daring to believe he could be truly interested in her. Not the body or the face that had drawn men's interest in the past, nor the money Esmé paid him to come to Scotland, but simply her.

Then his palm shifted, turned, until her fingers slid between his. Long fingers wrapped over her knuckles, resting lightly on the delicate bones and veins on the back of her hand. Bella had never held hands with a man like this before. It was simple, quiet, almost common, yet brought such a feeling of reassurance, of togetherness, that she felt closer to him now than when they had kissed in her carriage.

A drop of cold water hit her forehead, pulling her attention from their interlocked hands. Wiping it from her brow with her free hand, she glanced up. The dark clouds that had been on the horizon were moving closer, aided by a quickening wind that held the distinct scent of an imminent storm.

No. No. Not yet! "So we can add women to your short list of interests." The words rushed out of her mouth, falling over each other in her need to keep him from noticing the threatening sky.

"No. That's not correct. I didn't say *women.* I said *you.*" He punctuated the last word with a tightening of his grip.

"Oh." She opened her mouth, though she didn't have a clue as to what she should say. A part of her warned he spoke words she wanted to hear, and yet the words didn't feel false. The tingle spreading through her body gave them the weight of truth.

She didn't notice he slowed his steps, or that she slowed hers with his, until they were stopped. He turned to stand before her, blocking the direct force of the wind, but those stubborn hairs whipped across her cheek. Before she could tuck them back in their pin, he reached up. His fingertips were a mere whisper as he tucked the strands behind her ear.

The intimate gesture struck her as nothing else ever had.

And that empty part of her heart, the one that echoed with loneliness, that needed to be wanted again, that needed to feel loved, began to beat anew. Bella wasn't so far gone as to mistake his kindness for genuine love, but the mere brush of it, the echo of it, was more than she had felt in ages. She hadn't realized how much she missed it, until the glance of it made tears prick the corners of her eyes.

The tumult of emotion must have shown itself on her face, for

Mr. Rosedale spoke her name with true concern. "Isabella? Are you—" Three raindrops hit his face in quick succession. His head snapped up. "Bloody hell." He winced. "Pardon, Lady Stirling."

"It's quite all right," she said, taken aback by the swiftness of his apology.

He looked past her, his mouth opening then closing on what she was certain was a suppressed curse. The intermittent raindrops swiftly shifted to a steady downfall. Cold water soaked through the bodice and sleeves of her dress, chilling her skin and turning the once bright emerald cambric dark.

His gaze swept the grounds. He growled low in frustration. "Here." He unbuttoned his coat, shrugged it off, and held it out to her. "Put this on."

Bella stared at his offer. No man had ever done anything so chivalrous as to give her the coat off his back. Then she snapped to her senses and turned to slip her arms into the silk-lined sleeves. He settled the coat on her shoulders, turned her around, and slipped two of the buttons through their holes. The ends of the sleeves hung to her fingertips and the coattails grazed the backs of her knees, but to her it fit perfectly. She felt surrounded by him. The black wool retained the warmth of his body and his unique masculine scent.

Before she could luxuriate in the scent of cloves, lemons, and Mr. Rosedale, he held out a hand. "Are you up for a run?"

Smiling eagerly, she nodded and placed her hand in his wet palm.

With that, they were off. It wasn't a true sprint, more of a jog, one she was certain he kept slow enough to accommodate her. Their footsteps squished in the wet grass. The giggle bubbling in her chest could not be contained. Squinting against the driving rain smacking her face, she saw he was taking her toward the group of trees farther up along the drive. The wind gusted so fiercely it exposed the sage green backs of the leaves.

He passed the closest tree and stopped at the one behind it whose branches were high enough for them to stand underneath. The spring canopy wasn't thick enough to completely block out the rain, but it was enough to shelter them against the full force of it. Fat drops fell from the branches, but for the most part it was comparatively dry. The dirt surrounding the thick tree trunk had yet to get wet.

Releasing her hand, he turned to stand before her. He ran both hands through his dark hair, pushing the wet strands off his forehead. "We should be all right under here. As long as it doesn't lightning, that is."

He wasn't the least out of breath, whereas she panted lightly from their short run. "No, I don't think it will. It's just a usual rain shower."

"More of a deluge." His face tightened with remorse. "I'm sorry. We should have stayed closer to the house."

"It's not your fault. I'm the one who insisted on going out and staying out. You were merely obliging me, as I am finding you are apt to do."

He gave a short huff. "That doesn't excuse my lack of common sense."

She wanted to kiss the self-reprimanding wince off his mouth. He shouldn't be the one to feel guilty. It should be her, for getting them caught in the rain, for even being with him today. For where she wanted her fortnight with Mr. Rosedale to go. But oddly, she did not feel even a brush of guilt.

Shifting her weight, Bella pulled his coat tighter around her trying to find the last bit of warmth from his body that had not seeped out of the fine wool. The damp, chill air penetrated to her bones. Her hair was soaked, as if she had just washed it. Her skin pricked with gooseflesh as a gust of wind wrapped her cold, wet skirts around her legs.

"You're cold," he stated.

"No, I'm—"

"Yes, you are. Your teeth are starting to chatter."

She fought to keep the tremble from her limbs. "No."

"Isabella," he admonished.

"Bella," she corrected. No one had called her Bella for years, yet for some unknown reason it was now important Mr. Rosedale did.

He looked taken aback for an instant then shook his head, as if dismissing a thought. "You're going to catch your death," he muttered gruffly. "Come here, Bella."

Without a glimmer of hesitation she stepped into his open arms. Wrapping her arms around his waist she leaned into him, the copper silk waistcoat slick and wet against her cheek. The strong steady beats of his heart drowned out the hum of the driving rain. She could stay here, in the twilight darkness under the tree, in the comfort of his embrace, forever. Taking in the scent of him with each breath. Soaking up the heat from his powerful male body. Feeling her heart slip ever faster to his.

"Better?" His warm breath tickled her ear.

"A bit." She snuggled closer, loath to say anything to cause him to release her.

"Just a bit? That's all?" he asked, with teasing twist.

Bella tipped her head back. Spiky wet lashes framed his fathomless brown eyes. A raindrop slid down his cheek, and she reached up to catch it with a fingertip. His skin was cool, yet at the same time warm to the touch. Mesmerized, she traced the strong line of his jaw, the hint of his day's beard a mere gentle scrape. She let her hand drop past his shoulder to his upper arm.

Honey gold skin backed the wet, white lawn shirt, which molded to the contours of his biceps. There was absolutely no give to the solid muscles beneath her hand. Over the years she had come to associate strength in a man with unpleasantness, but Mr. Rosedale's well-honed body roused only passion and a pressing desire to see more.

He stood perfectly still, and she knew he was letting her do as she pleased. That he was giving his body up for her pleasure. She looked up into the face tilted down to hers and found patience, and delight at her exploration. And a bit of arrogance as well, judging from the faintly smug curve of his mouth. The man had to know he was put together perfectly.

Unable to resist the lure a moment longer, she placed her hands on his broad shoulders and lifted up onto her toes. She could taste the cool spring rain on his lips. Unsatisfied by the simple chaste kiss, she slanted her mouth over his and moaned as his tongue twined with hers. Outside was cold driving rain, but inside a tropical summer blazed. It heated her up from within and pushed her closer to him, seeking more. Unwilling to stop for even a second, she continued to kiss him as she pulled at his cravat. But her cold fingers struggled against it. The simple knot seemed to have seized from the rain.

The possessive weight of his large hands left the small of her back. His fingers settled over hers, stilling her anxious movements. He lifted his head just enough to break the kiss. "Allow me," he whispered.

Panting lightly, she nodded. Too impatient to stand idle, she slipped her hands from under his and kneaded his rock hard upper arms. Muscles flexed as he deftly managed the knot, unwound the cravat, and unbuttoned the top button of his shirt. Biting the edge of her lip, she watched his Adam's apple bob under the taunt skin as he swallowed. Then she kissed his throat, her tongue slipping out to taste the heat of his skin between quick little nips of her teeth.

Wrapping her arms around his neck, she dragged her mouth back to his lips and kissed him with complete abandon, reveling in the pure decadence of his mouth. It must surely be a sin for a man to taste this good. It was like kissing the summer sun, hot and luxurious, with a very faint hint of tart Earl Grey tea.

His hands roved up and down her sides and she wished she wasn't wearing his coat, or her dress. That his hands were gliding over her bare skin. As one large hand coasted up from her hip, it diverged from its path, curving in between their bodies. Bella trembled in anticipation. He cupped her breast, molding the weight in his palm. She sighed into his mouth as he brushed the pad of his thumb across the tip. Her nipple tightened into a hard bud, sending shivers down her spine. But his whisper-light touch didn't satisfy in the slightest. It served only to torment her; increasing the urgency drumming through her body.

He shifted his stance, putting one leg between both of hers. Instinctively she arched into him and rubbed along the long muscle of his thigh, trying to ease the ache centered between her legs. Sensation sparked through her, but it wasn't enough. Not even close.

Beyond desperate, beyond any thoughts of proper, ladylike behavior, she reached down. The length and breadth and sheer magnitude of his arousal made her breath catch sharply. But the moan that followed had nothing to do with any reservations. Her insides fluttered and her head went so light she swayed on her feet.

Leaning closer, she tightened her grip, trying to convey her need without words. A short grunt issued from his throat. The iron-hard length twitched, and somehow, unbelievably, swelled even further. The silken sweep of his tongue faulted. His hand settled over hers, pulling her fingers away from the object of her desire. He slipped his hand under hers to clasp it.

His kiss shifted, slowed, softened. *No, no, no!* With her other hand, she threaded her fingers in the short, wet hair at the nape of his neck, and gripped tightly, refusing to allow him to stop. The moment she thrust her hips against his thigh, he moved his leg to bracket hers. A groan of pure frustration rattled her throat.

He lifted his head, effortlessly breaking the kiss against her wishes. "*Shh*, Bella-Bella. *Shh*."

His soft croon only served to further her agitation. "No. I-I . . ." She closed her eyes, dropped her arm to her side, and ducked her chin, suddenly mortified by her overwrought passion. The desire that beat so swiftly and fiercely through her veins withered and died, and in its place dropped the cold, crippling weight of abject humiliation. It never occurred to her that he would not want her. *Oh*, but it should have. If she had learned nothing else from her marriage, it was that not all men jumped at the chance to bed every woman who crossed their path. With a jagged roll of her shoulder, she tried to take a step back, but Mr. Rosedale held tight to her hand.

"Bella, don't." He cupped her cheek, lifting her face to his. His dark eyebrows were lowered, his mouth set. Tension gripped the strong lines of his body. "It's not—"

She gazed desperately into his eyes, willing—no—needing him to finish the sentence. But he took a deep breath and rested his forehead against hers. His hand coasted down her arm to take hold of hers. With both of her hands now held in his, he gave them a squeeze. He let out a long sigh, his warm breath tickling her lips.

For a moment, neither of them moved. The rain tapped a steady beat against the sodden ground beyond the shelter of the tree. Eyes closed tight, Bella simply stood there, battling to make sense of what had happened this afternoon. She had felt the bond between them, she had been sure of it. Then his refusal had evaporated even the tiniest trace of confidence she had in her own judgment. And now she didn't know what to think. She needed something from him, some sign, something more than a couple of words. Words so open to interpretation. Words her mind rapidly completed. "It's not . . ." *you.* "It's not . . ." *what I want.* "It's not . . ."

His head snapped up. "Your carriage."

She blinked her eyes open. "Pardon?"

He let go of her hands. The efficient way he did up the buttons on her, well his, coat was so familiar. Then she remembered—he had already buttoned the coat once. When had it become unbuttoned? His cravat was managed just as quickly. At the sound of wheels on gravel, she looked to the right to see her carriage pulling to a stop not twenty paces away.

"Lady Stirling!" Her driver sat hunched within his black greatcoat, the leather lines held tight in his hands. Water dripped off the brim of his hat, pulled low over his eyes. One of the horses stamped an impatient hoof, splashing in a puddle on the gravel drive. With a jangle of harness, the other of the pair tossed its head.

Mr. Rosedale held out his arm with the distant air of a proper gentleman. Instinctively, she pulled her spine straight, lifted her chin, and placed her hand on his arm. The wet lawn shirt was surprisingly warm, as if he had donned it right after it had been washed in hot water.

Without a word, he led her to the carriage and opened the door. The storm had abated, the gusting winds gone, but the rain still fell in a steady, unyielding pattern that marked the Scottish spring. Eager to be out of the rain, she stepped quickly inside and sat on the black leather bench. With tight motions, she arranged her sodden skirt about her legs. A large hand settled over hers, stilling them for the second time this day.

One hand on the door, he leaned into the carriage. "Come to me."

His hoarse words swirled around her. His gaze stayed locked with hers, intent, serious, and almost, almost uncertain.

He shut the door and rapped once on the carriage. "Order a hot bath drawn for Lady Stirling the moment she arrives at the house," he called to the driver, his voice crisp and sure.

"Don't you want a ride back to Garden House?" the driver asked.

"Thank you, but no. The walk will do me good."

Bella reached for the small brass lever, intent on opening the door and demanding he ride back with her, when the carriage lurched forward. She was left to merely stare out the window and watch his retreating back as he walked across the lawn.

Six

MAY I take . . . your coat, m'lady?"

"No, McGreevy," Bella said using her coldest tone. She sailed across the entrance hall without a glance back to the butler at the open front door.

"McGreevy, tell Cooley to have a bath drawn for her ladyship. Mr. Rosedale ordered it."

Her driver's raised voice easily reached her ears as she ascended the main staircase, as did McGreevy's answering condescending huff. She stiffened her spine. The man would have been dismissed long ago if she did not fear Stirling's reaction, and the smug butler knew it.

Upon entering her bedchamber, she found the large claw-foot tub positioned in front of the fireplace. Efficient as ever, her housekeeper had anticipated the need before the request could be made. The warmth from the fully stoked fire filled the room and was a welcome change from the chill damp of the outdoors.

"Oh, m'lady, you're soaked through," exclaimed Maisie, a worried expression on her young face. "Come. We'll get you out of those wet clothes in a thrice."

Bella allowed her maid, the lone household servant she had personally hired, to do her job. Fairly vibrating with eagerness to help, Maisie reached for the buttons on Mr. Rosedale's coat. Bella tamped down the impulse to swat the girl's hands away and instead forced her arms to remain at her sides. *It's simply a coat*, she reminded herself. She wasn't truly giving him up.

The maid folded the coat over the back of the nearby Egyptian armchair and ran a hand over the black wool. " 'Tis very fine. Hope the rain hasn't ruined it. 'Twas thoughtful of him to lend it to you."

Afraid one wrong word would give away her wanton conduct with Mr. Rosedale, Bella kept her expression blank and merely tipped her head. Maisie quickly removed Bella's wet clothes then held out a quilted alabaster dressing gown. Bella tied the cloth belt at her waist and sat on the vanity stool. Maisie set to the task of removing the pins from her hair. The maid was combing the wet length when the bedroom door opened. Bella glanced into the oval mirror above the vanity.

Mrs. Cooley strode into the room, followed by two servants. "Into the tub," her housekeeper commanded. "Then run down and get the rest."

Water splashed as the servants emptied the buckets then scurried to do Mrs. Cooley's bidding. At her housekeeper's soft *tsk*, Bella turned her head.

Mrs. Cooley stood at the Egyptian armchair. "Is this *his* coat?"

"Yes," Bella said, a surge of possessiveness turning the word into a challenge.

Mrs. Cooley's thin mouth pursed in distaste as she examined the garment. "A mess."

It was nothing compared to the mess Bella had made of this afternoon. Marshalling her rank, she lifted her chin. "Have it cleaned and pressed then returned to me."

Assessing hard gray eyes held Bella's for a long moment. Only her maid broke the silence as she dropped the comb onto the vanity and picked up a silver-backed brush. The usually long, relaxing strokes of the brush were short and tight.

Bella felt as though Mrs. Cooley could see every place where Mr. Rosedale's hands had branded her skin. Her cheek. Her waist. The small of her back. Her breast. Her skin pricked with awareness, with the memory of those strong hands, but she managed to keep her composure in place and not avert her gaze.

Mrs. Cooley nodded. "Yes, your ladyship."

"Alert the kitchen I will be dining in my room. Have a tray sent up at six, and another sent to Garden House."

The housekeeper's eyes flared slightly upon word there would be no dinner for two this evening. But Bella needed time. Time away from him. Time to think. To ensure the mistake from years ago was not repeated. She could not allow passion to rule her completely, for when that happened, in its wake came regret. And regret was the last emotion she wanted to associate with Mr. Rosedale.

"Yes, your ladyship." Her housekeeper turned on her heel and left the room.

Maisie set the brush on the vanity and collected the wet clothes from where she had dropped them on the floor in her haste to remove them. Bella stood and walked to the window beside the four-poster bed. She didn't glance about the garden or to the gray sky. Her gaze went immediately to him, as if some part of her had known exactly where he would be.

The sounds of the servants coming and going from her room, filling the white porcelain tub with bucket after bucket of water, faded away. Mr. Rosedale walked across the back lawn, his head bowed and shoulders hunched against the light rain. A wince pulled her brow. Poor man. It looked as though he just took a bath but neglected to remove his clothes. He must be freezing. Even with the luxury of being indoors and out of her sodden dress, she had yet to warm up.

She curled her toes against the cold floorboards and crossed her arms, wrapping the dressing gown tighter around her body. Why hadn't he ridden back to the house with her? Why had he insisted on walking to Garden House, alone? On the short ride in the carriage, she had ceased the endless questions on why he refused her only to contradict himself and ask for her to come to him. She would never be able to determine the true answer herself, nor would she ever have the courage to ask him. Some questions were better left without answers—of that she knew well.

He walked between the break in the bushes bordering the garden. His long strides slowed to a stop. He looked so very alone standing amidst the roses, their many green leaves glistening from the rain. Mr. Rosedale ran both hands through his hair, disheveling the short, dark locks plastered to his head. The gesture reminded her acutely of her brother. It was one Phillip had employed frequently in the few short days before her wedding.

She let out a soft sigh that only hinted at the fierce war waging within. It was so terribly bittersweet to know the man standing in her rose garden, the man who had the power to make her feel so much more than blind passion, was in direct opposition to the hope she had held for so long. Phillip would never look on her as a sister again if he found out she had had a male prostitute at Bowhill. And one who had been there explicitly for her pleasure.

She had convinced herself if only she was really good, then her elder brother would forgive her. If only she could show him she wasn't the trollop he believed her to be. That she did care about duty and responsibility. Cared enough to do her best to be a good wife, even to a man like Stirling, though it would not gain Phillip one extra guinea to pay off the debts their father left behind. Debts which could have been gone, if only she had not turned her back on her family and acted recklessly so many years ago.

Yet how would Phillip know if she was good when she hadn't seen him in five years, nor even received a note from him? He wouldn't. He had passed judgment, rendered his verdict, and did not care to be swayed. She should let it go, this need to get back into Phillip's good graces, but she could not release it completely.

She lifted one eyebrow. Though maybe she could for the next ten days.

Phillip would never know, she reasoned. And Stirling . . . She let out a contemptuous breath, one she would never dare indulge in while in her husband's presence. No man who treated his wife the way he did deserved even the appearance of fidelity.

Her life stretched out before her, bleak and lonely. Unchanged from the last five years. Her gaze fixed again on Mr. Rosedale. Did she have the courage to seize the opportunity? To trust in herself? To do what her newly awakened heart begged?

Come to me.

"M'lady, your bath is ready," Maisie called from behind her.

A smile curved Bella's lips. She turned from the window, no longer the slightest bit cold.

GIDEON kicked a small stone, sending it skidding down the gravel path. Had his actions been that of a selfish man? He gave a sardonic snort. *No.* If he had been truly selfish, then he would not have needed a long walk in the cold rain to cool down. Christ, there was no way her driver would believe he and Bella were having a polite conversation under the tree, just innocently waiting for the rain to let up. Hopefully the silence the ex-soldier had secured would continue to hold up. But at least he had been able to get himself somewhat under control before the carriage arrived. In that, his perplexing behavior was well timed.

But what the long walk had not done was reveal the cause of the inherent distaste that had sprung out of nowhere overtaking her there under the tree. On the cold, damp grass, or up against the rough tree trunk. He had done it many times without a second thought, and in more challenging situations. It would have been nothing at all to wrap her long legs around his waist, brace one hand against the tree trunk, hold her tight with his other arm, and give the lady exactly what she wanted.

But for some reason he had not been able to do it. For the first time in his life, his body had been willing but his mind had not. Labeling the experience *unpleasant* would be a severe understatement.

Gideon thought himself so adept at keeping them out, at guarding the boundaries where true emotion crossed with physical pleasure. For it would be the height of folly to be swept up in the very fantasy he carefully constructed for them. Yet somehow she kept slipping beneath his defenses. There was something about her—

No! He gave his head a hard shake. It was simple arrogance to believe he would never meet a woman who truly intrigued him. He should be thankful he had been able to go ten years before this happened, and very thankful he recognized it before it turned into something more.

Something that could not be.

Gideon raked both hands through his wet hair. He should leave. She had given him permission to do so and he needn't provide a reason. But he couldn't. He had extended the invitation and could not back out now.

There was "leave the lady wanting more" and there was crossing the line into displeasure, annoyance, irritation. He very much feared he had crossed that line. But Lady Stirling hadn't been displeased. He upset her. She had the look of a woman stripped of all self-confidence. Exposed and raw. Afraid she was not desired. And that he could not tolerate. No woman should ever be made to feel that way, and especially not by him.

Therein lay the reason for extending the invitation. To erase the hurt in her beautiful violet eyes. It had nothing to do with any desire on his part to spend more time with her.

For nothing should ever have anything to do with his desires, his wishes, his needs. Only theirs.

If she did not come to him though . . .

He pinched the bridge of his nose, trying to distract from the incredible pressure inside his head. "She must," he muttered through clenched teeth. It was exactly what needed to happen. It would put him back on steady ground. Allow their time together to proceed, as it should have many days before. Then he would be in familiar territory and no longer feel this . . . He grunted in frustration. Whatever it was, it left him completely unsettled.

Gideon took a deep breath and continued on his way to Garden House. Lingering in her rose garden would not solve his problems. She had until tomorrow evening and if she did not come to him by then, he would need to leave.

THE next morning, a light, rapid tap broke through Bella's thoughts. With a start, she stilled her hand. She hadn't realized she was tapping the end of her pen against the silver inkwell. Glancing to the folded letter on her desk, it took her a moment to remember what she had been doing. *Oh, yes.* She received a letter from Liv, her baby sister, the prior week. What with Mr. Rosedale's appearance at Bowhill, the reply had completely slipped her mind until this morning when she had been looking for something to fill the hours.

After writing out the address of Liv's finishing school, she set down her pen and looked over to the porcelain clock on the corner of the desk. It was almost time for luncheon. An odd mixture of nerves and anticipation kept away any trace of hunger, but perhaps *he* did not suffer from the same affliction. Bella nibbled at the edge of her bottom lip. It wouldn't be at all well-done of her to make her guest eat alone for three meals in a row. A proper hostess would join her guest for luncheon, and, well, he may have need of his coat. Since he was kind enough to lend it to her, she should return it to him personally.

It wasn't that she needed to see him, and she certainly was not running to him. *No, no*, she told herself as she called for a servant and requested a light luncheon for two to be packed. It would simply be the right thing to do.

She walked quickly into her bedchamber to check her reflection in the oval mirror above the vanity. Pursing her lips, she tugged on her bodice and smoothed her hair. Then she looked out the window beside the bed. Yesterday's thick gray clouds had yet to dissipate. The tops of trees in the distance swayed under the breeze. On the way out of the bedchamber, she grabbed her navy woolen cloak and settled it about her shoulders.

With a wicker basket loaded with food and drink in one hand and his black coat folded over her arm, Bella set out for Garden House. This afternoon she did not linger over even one of the older, heartier rose bushes growing in abundance in the garden or pause to inspect the health of a green leaf. She traveled purposefully along the gravel path, her attention not straying to the hothouse to the left of the garden. She passed the statue of the goddess Aphrodite, passed through the yew bushes marking the perimeter of the garden, crossed the expanse of lush lawn dotted with large maples, opened the gate of the white picket fence surrounding the stone cottage, and stopped at the brown wooden door.

With the sound of her double knock ringing in her ears, it occurred to her—she could be intruding. *Should I have sent a note first?* Eyes flaring, she was a heartbeat from turning and walking briskly back to the manor house when the door opened.

"Lady Stirling," he said with a welcoming smile.

He stepped aside on a short bow and she entered the cottage. Mr. Rosedale was dressed casually. No jacket or cravat, only dark brown loose trousers and a powder blue waistcoat. The top of his white linen shirt was undone, exposing a hint of the hollow of his masculine throat. She captured her bottom lip between her teeth, as she recalled the feel of the smooth, taut skin beneath her lips.

"I have come with luncheon and to return your coat," she said, forcing an even note into her voice.

His mouth pulled in a half smile as he took the proffered garment and hung it on one of the pegs lining the wall by the door. "Thank you."

"No. Thank you."

She stood perfectly still as he reached for the metal clasp on her cloak. A little surge of satisfaction shot through her at the way his gaze dropped to the expanse of bare skin above her bodice.

"It was nothing." His whispered words were soft and light, like a reverent caress. He unfastened the clasp. Her breath stuttered as his warm fingertips brushed her collarbone. He pulled the cloak off her shoulders, draping it neatly over his arm before relieving her of the burden of the wicker basket.

She smoothed a hand over the front of her dress. Nervousness kept her from recalling anything on the topic of polite conversation. Just seeing him again, being in his presence . . . Her pulse raced with a mix of anticipation, arousal, and anxiety. She was here, at his request. He knew the true purpose of her afternoon call. Yet he seemed so casual, so at his ease, whereas she did not know what to do with herself.

With an awkward roll of her shoulders, she glanced about the parlor in an effort to find some subject to discuss.

A fire in the stone hearth warmed the room. A thick-cushioned brown couch took up one wall with two armchairs opposite. A series of three landscapes hung above the couch. A leather bound volume, most likely selected from the squat bookcase beneath the large front window, was on the square table between the armchairs.

The cottage had been designed as a guest retreat. A comfortable place to escape the formality of the manor house. But at the moment, she was anything but comfortable.

GIDEON hung up her cloak and set the basket on the dining table. Lady Stirling had finally fallen in line, done the expected. He was again in familiar territory. He could still taste the relief that washed over him at the sight of her on his doorstep. Hell, he had been a wreck since yesterday afternoon. But she had come to him, and now he could slip into the role he had perfected over so many years. Ignore the disconcerting foreign emotions she sparked within him and react purely on a physical level.

After removing the cork from the bottle, he selected one of the glasses from the basket and filled it with a generous amount of Bordeaux, all the while studying her from the corner of his eye. The pale blonde hair was pulled back in the usual tight knot at the nape of her neck. An empire-waist lilac day dress, the exact shade of her eyes, obscured the sleek curve of her waist and the long length of her legs, yet received his wholehearted approval, the bodice so wonderfully low her luscious breasts were a deep breath from spilling free. But she was visibly nervous and it clashed with the cool elegance.

Only the very bold and seasoned could take a paid lover to their bed without a bat of an eye. But he knew exactly what to do to ease Lady Stirling, to calm her. This past week had been nothing but a lead-up to this moment. He would take all he had learned of her and use it to strip away the edge behind her uncharacteristic fidgeting and replace it with a sharp hunger that would have her begging for more. The charming gentleman had done his job. It was time for the calculated seducer to take over.

Gideon picked up the wineglass then loosened his grip. This *was* the reason why he had been hired, proving her no different than all the rest. No matter the hours spent in pleasant conversation or playful flirtation, it always came down to this. That was all they truly wanted of him, and all he needed from them. Nothing more.

Definitely nothing more.

A woman like Lady Stirling would never want more from a man like him than a blissfully mind-numbing orgasm. And he was quite looking forward to receiving one himself. By the way she responded to his kisses, he knew she would be a very enjoyable bed partner.

Focusing on that goal, he closed his eyes for a brief moment and blocked out everything, leaving a calming sense of single-minded purpose. Then he turned from the table.

FOR the lady," Mr. Rosedale said with a charming smile.

"Thank you." Bella took the proffered glass and drained half the contents in a few unladylike swallows.

"Come." He strode past her with a flick of his head and settled on the couch, casually resting his elbow on the tufted arm. "Tell me about your morning. And I warn you now, 'nothing of any real interest' is not a satisfactory answer."

She chuckled. He was impossible to resist, his teasing mood infectious. She took another long sip of wine. "If you must know," she said, sighing dramatically as she sat down beside him, "I caught up on my correspondences."

"Are you a diligent correspondent?"

"Of course," she said with mock affront. "What proper English lady doesn't write from time to time?"

"Such an admirable trait."

She lifted one shoulder. "I try."

"So, you spent the morning with a pen in hand. That was all?"

"I also met with my housekeeper."

"Ah, the woman in black."

He made Mrs. Cooley sound so sinister. Bella threw him a playful, reprimanding scowl as she brought the glass to her lips. "Yes, she does wear black often. In fact, I don't believe I've seen her in anything but."

He took her empty glass and set it on the floor by his feet. "She doesn't put your castoffs to use then?"

"No." Bella grinned at the absurd thought of stern Mrs. Cooley in one of her own vibrant silk gowns.

"A shame." He shook his head. "Would liven up the house. Myself, I've always been partial to a spot of color. Very nice, by the way," he added in a silken tone, his gaze raking the length of her body.

"I'm pleased you approve," she whispered, hoarsened by a sudden infusion of lust.

"Very much so."

He turned his broad shoulders to her, the long length of his thigh pressing against hers, and slowly ran a fingertip along the ribbon trim of her bodice. A shiver gripped her spine at the faint brush of his skin against the swells of her breasts. Her gaze locked with his, she licked her lips.

The edges of his mouth quirked with a hint of a smile. Everything seemed infinitely right, as if it was always meant to be, when he leaned in for a kiss. A corner of her mind marveled at this man's ability to make her so comfortable. She had not noticed when it happened or how he had done it, but the stifling nervousness and awkwardness were blessedly gone. *Because he's done it so many times before.* She quickly shoved the unpleasant reminder of his profession aside and focused only on Mr. Rosedale and his wonderful kisses.

Just when she became fully immersed in his kiss, in the sublime delicacy of his mouth, he broke it to whisper in her ear. "Come with me."

He nipped at her earlobe and stood, extending a hand, palm up. The amber flecks in his eyes mesmerized her. They glowed golden bright, making the surrounding brown appear as black as a starless midnight. But beneath the lust she sensed a never-ending well of patience. His words were not a demand. She did not feel even a glance of pressure.

Gazing up at him through the veil of her lashes, she smiled softly and placed her hand in his.

Hand in hers and ahead of her by one step, he led her out of the parlor, down the narrow hall, and into the bedchamber. She immediately identified the scent in the air. Cloves, lemons, and the man who would make her complete.

He released her hand to close the door. Glancing about, she stepped further into the room. Like the rest of the cottage, the room was small, yet had a distinctly cozy atmosphere. Hazy daylight seeped through the gauzy white curtain covering the window. Flanked by spindly legged side tables, a bed, the one he slept in, dominated the room. A fire burned in the small hearth. A silver-banded wooden trunk stood on the floor next to a mahogany dresser. The various male accoutrements on the washstand caught her eye. An ivory comb. A wood-handled brush. A leather shaving kit. Each object personal. Each one his.

At the click of the lock turning, she started, whirling around to face the door. She clasped her hands before her.

Hand on the brass key, he lowered his head a fraction. "No?"

"It's all right."

"Are you sure?"

She had a feeling he wasn't referring to the locked door. "Yes." *I want you to be my first, my only.* Yet she kept the words inside, hoping he would not be able to discern the full truth. The last thing she wanted was to answer any questions regarding her marriage.

"Good." His heart-stopping smile melted away the last lingering bit of nervousness.

He stepped from the door and cupped her cheek. She closed her eyes and tipped her face up, lips parted and eager for him to pick up the kiss exactly where he left it in the parlor. Instead he pressed his lips to her temple, the arch of one eyebrow, her closed lashes, the crest of one cheekbone. Slowly worked his way down her features, blessing each one with a soft, playful kiss. All the while, he teased the corner of her mouth with the pad of his thumb.

Frustrated by his languid pace, she nipped at his thumb. The trail of kisses on her face ceased. She sneaked a peek at him from beneath her lashes. He gazed down at her with a most satisfied expression, as if it had been his intent all along to goad a response from her.

"Kiss me," she whispered, not caring in the slightest if he thought her bold.

The corners of his mouth curved in a devilish smirk. "It would be my pleasure."

She sagged against him in gratitude when his mouth met hers. The kiss was more than the one in the parlor. The strong, possessive sweep of his tongue infused a shot of desire into her already thrumming veins, quickening her pulse.

Large hands moved up and down her back, deftly working the buttons of her dress and the laces of her stays. She shifted her weight, impatient to be free of the confines of her clothes. Then he brought his hands up to her shoulders and dragged them down her arms. Nipping at his lower lip, she quickly shook her wrists free of the sleeves and reached for him again. Fabric *whooshed* to her feet. Cool air hit her heated skin. Tangling her fingers in his hair, she slanted her mouth full over his and writhed against him.

The sensation of bare skin against his fully clothed body intoxicated her. The tantalizing slip of smooth silk against her bare breasts. The press of small fabric-covered buttons along her chest. The brush of soft wool trousers against her stocking-covered legs. Her head swam as if she had drank three glasses of wine instead of one.

She was vaguely aware he was pulling the pins from her hair. The heavy weight of it tumbled down, the ends grazing her lower back. Lifting up onto her toes, she hitched a leg about his hip and encountered the hard arch of his arousal.

Large hands grasped her backside, jerking her closer, pressing them intimately together. On a low grunt, he thrust, grinding his trouser-covered cock against her sex in a seductive rhythm. The deliciously rough caress made lust blaze, fierce and hot. Clutching his broad shoulders, she moaned into his mouth, wanting more.

Then she felt herself being lifted. Urgently kissing him, she held on tight, more than eager to move to the bed. To have the solid weight of his male body cover her. To have him inside her.

Her derriere pressed against cool, smooth wood. His lips left hers. Panting heavily, she blinked open her eyes. She was perched on the edge of the mahogany dresser. He stood between her legs that were still wrapped loosely about his waist.

"This isn't the bed."

A low chuckle vibrated his chest. "No, it's not," he said with a smirk, as he toyed with the violet ribbons on her garters. "On or off?"

For a moment she couldn't decide. The question was one she never before contemplated, even in her most scandalous fantasy. And the thought of wrapping silk-covered legs around his bare waist was tempting indeed. The height of decadence. Yet—

"Off." Her answer came out on a shaky whisper.

"Excellent choice," he said, giving her a smile steeped in sin.

Kneading her hips, he bowed low, his tousled dark hair brushing her lower belly. The powder blue waistcoat stretched taut across his broad back. Warm breath fanned the pale blonde triangle of hair between her legs, teasing her sensitive flesh. A tremor shook her body, her pulse clamoring through her veins. Turning his head, he nuzzled her inner thigh then dragged his lips down to the garter above her knee. Holding the ribbon in his teeth, he pulled, releasing the bow. Straightening, he lifted her leg to slowly peel off the silk stocking. The position opened her, fully exposing her sex. His dark lashes swept down. His even breaths hitched. The heat of his regard sent a burning jolt of sensation through her.

"So pretty," he said in a husky murmur that flowed like rich velvet over her skin.

Perched naked on the dresser and with one leg lifted to his shoulder, she arched one eyebrow. "Thank you."

That got her a chuckle. He tipped his head. "You're very welcome, my lady."

Lips curved in a confident smile, she trailed her fingertips along his jaw, marveling at her boldness. This was the side of herself she had tried to deny for so long—the tart. Wicked and shameless. Bold and demanding. Ruled solely by lust.

That impulse to tamp it all down, to lock the lust away, to hide it from prying, judging eyes, was absent. Completely nonexistent. For the first time in her life she felt truly free, and it was all due to him.

He removed her other stocking in a thrice. Flicking it to the floor, he stepped closer, coasting his hands up from her knees to cup her breasts. "And these are very pretty as well."

Holding the weight of each, he pinched her nipples and drew out the tips. She groaned as a sharp lance of pleasure shot from his clever fingers to her core. The apex of her pleasure throbbed with an undeniable need for his touch.

He dropped his head to her chest and suckled on one breast and then the other. Throwing her head back, she lifted her chest, offering herself up to him. He delivered a sharp teasing nip then blew lightly over the tip. Her nipple hardened, tightened. Shivers gripped her spine. Lashes fluttering, she let out a shaky moan and clutched his broad shoulder.

Her hand slipped on smooth silk, reminding her he was still fully clothed. She tugged on his waistcoat. "Take this off," she said, more demand than request.

He dragged his lips up her chest. "As my lady wishes," he murmured against her neck.

She arched, granting him access. He alternated between open-mouthed kisses and short little nips as he removed his waistcoat. Impatient, she pulled his shirt from his trousers and slipped her hands underneath. Muscles rippled beneath her questing fingers. He pulled back to whisk the white shirt over his head, revealing a torso that perfectly matched the classical lines of his face.

Leaning close, she ran her fingers through the light sprinkling of dark hair on his chest and down the defined ridges of his abdomen that she had so recently explored. She pulled eagerly on the waistband of his trousers. "These, too."

With a flick of his wrist, the buttons on his falls were undone. Dark brown trousers whispered down his long legs.

Bella sucked in a short breath. Didn't men wear drawers? Obviously not *all* men. His manhood freed, it jutted proudly from his body. Long and thick and beautifully formed. The sight both impressed and intimidated her. God, the man was perfection.

Squaring his shoulders, he lifted his chin. "Do I meet with your satisfaction?"

The piercing look he gave her indicated he had absolutely no doubt what her answer would be, but she gave it nonetheless. "Oh, *yes.*"

"I'm pleased you approve."

He did not give her another moment to soak up the image of his gloriously nude male body, or allow the implications of his magnificent, splendid arousal to settle in her mind. For his arms wrapped around her, his lips found hers, and her passion careened out of control.

Writhing against him, she reveled in the unique feel of bare skin against bare skin. The velvety smoothness of his hips as she wrapped her legs around him. The hot press of the hard arch of his arousal against her inner thigh. The soft chest hair lightly abrading her nipples. One hand clutching the nape of his neck, she held him close, frantically kissing him, unable to get enough.

One of his roving hands paused to pull her leg from his waist. Hooking her knee over his elbow, he braced his arm on the dresser. His other hand followed her thigh up to brush the thatch of hair between her legs. A long finger slipped over the slick folds of her sex, teasing lightly, tormenting her, before finding that point of amazing sensitivity. Her entire body jerked against the sharp lance of pleasure. "*Yes.*"

He grunted, the sound pure masculine satisfaction. "So wet, my lady. So ready for me."

Needing more than the light pressure, she ground her hips against his hand. Imminent bliss coiled tighter and tighter. The release she needed more than anything in the world was right there, almost within reach, almost, almost—

"Oh, so impatient." His drawling voice both reprimand and encouragement. Lowering his head to her shoulder, he removed his hand.

"No!" she cried, frustrated close to the point of tears at being left in this tortured state. Agitation rode over every nerve in her body.

"Ah-ah. Not yet." She could feel him smile against her neck as he spoke. "I want to be inside of you when you come. Now hold on." Grabbing hold of her backside, he effortlessly lifted her and carried her the short distance to the bed.

And she was on her back, the mattress soft beneath her; he crouched over her. His mouth left hers to trail kisses down her chest. Strung tight to the point of desperation, Bella wrapped a leg around the back of his hair-dusted thigh and pulled his head up before his lips could reach her nipples.

When his whisky brown eyes met hers, she gasped, "No, I need—" With a thrust of her hips she attempted to fill in the unspoken words.

He shifted off to the side, reaching toward the small bedside table.

Panting heavily, she was a hair's breath from pushing him onto his back and straddling him. She needed him. *Now.* To fill the aching emptiness inside of her. "What are you—?"

His mouth was at her ear. "*Shh*, Bella-Bella, just a moment and I'll give you what you need." His hands moved between their bodies.

Perplexed, she glanced down. He was tying a ribbon at the base of his cock to secure a thin sheath. "What is—?"

One dark eyebrow lifted. "To protect against any unwanted guests."

His lips were on hers before she could process his words. Bracing his weight on one arm, he settled full between her spread thighs. Using his other hand, he teased her sex with the blunt head of his cock, kept her teetering precariously on the brink. She wiggled her hips, trying to get him where she needed him.

His heavy-lidded eyes locked with hers. "Yes?" he queried.

"*Please!*"

The smug arrogance in his grin should have earned him a slap, but her overwhelming need masked all dignity. Instead, a sob of undiluted gratitude shook her chest as he paused at the entrance of her body.

Finally, he eased inside the tiniest bit. Torn between intense pleasure and stretching pain, she shifted beneath him, struggling to take all of him. She wanted all of him. Needed all of him. But that flicker of fear settled in her mind. He was *much* too large.

Closing her eyes, she gripped his shoulders, fingernails biting into the smooth skin.

"Relax. I won't hurt you," he murmured, nuzzling her cheek.

She opened her eyes to find him nose to nose with her. Her tight breaths mingled with his steady ones. No, this man would never physically harm her.

"Here. Allow me."

He stole a quick kiss then began to move, but *oh* so slowly, easing a short distance in and almost completely out, giving her just the head of his cock, just a taste of his full penetration. In no time at all her body turned liquid. Every sense heightened. The intense pleasure wiped away any trace of discomfort.

Until she craved more.

Until the hard bite of impatience made her thrust up sharply into his next short downward glide, fully impaling herself on his cock.

The discomfort returned. A quick stab, like a prick of a needle.

There and then gone. On a surprised "Oh," every muscle in her body tightened.

And so did his.

His once half-lidded eyes flared wide, shock written all over his handsome face and in every line of the powerful body crouched over hers.

Oh no.

Before he could take issue with her virginity, she grabbed his head and slanted her mouth over his.

Her delicate flesh stretched taut by his thick length, she quivered on the knife-edge of bliss. He felt so amazing, so incredible, beyond anything she could have ever imagined, that with the first hesitant sweep of his tongue against hers, an orgasm rushed upon her, sending her senses reeling. She gasped into his mouth, the heavy tide of sensation rushing from her core out to her fingers and toes.

He started to thrust. Short, slow strokes through her climax. But she didn't want slow. She didn't want consideration. That release had been so quick, so hard, it only served to heighten her appetite for more. Bella rocked her hips, bumping against him, lengthening the strokes, increasing the pace.

Bracing his forearms on either side of her shoulders, he drove into her. Throwing back her head, she arched beneath him, a slave to the voluptuous sensation of his possession. Each controlled slam of his hips brought her closer, closer, and in no time at all she came again.

With the thick, heady pleasure still washing her nerves, he slipped a hand under the small of her back. He gathered himself, as if to change positions.

But she wanted none of that. No disruption in the rapturous rhythm. She grabbed his buttocks, the hard muscles flexing in time to his thrusts, and wrapped her legs around his. "No. Don't stop. *More.*"

Her breaths turned labored. Hard, heavy pants through parted lips. Her skin heated with sweat. Her strength dwindled, but she simply could not get enough of him.

He dropped his head to her shoulder. His thrusts quickened,

hard and demanding, pushing the all-encompassing pleasure swamping her nerves to new heights. She was right there, on the verge of another orgasm.

A tremor wracked his body as he let out a low groan she feared could only mean one thing.

"Not yet!" Though she knew her protest came too late. He had just found his release.

"Yes, Bella," he whispered, only slightly out of breath. He kissed her gently. Soft, light comfort kisses. When he made to pull back, she tightened her legs wrapped around his in an effort to keep him inside. "Bella-Bella," he crooned, brushing the tip of his nose against hers. "We have days ahead of us and I don't want to make you sore."

She didn't protest further when he moved off to lay on his side. With his head propped up on a bent arm, he trailed his fingertips up and down from the center of her chest to her navel. Rather than tickling, his light touch lulled her overwrought senses.

Bella smoothed his tousled hair. The short dark locks were warm silk between her fingers. A sense of utter relaxation stole over her. She let out a soft sigh of contentment. Not a whisper of regret passed through her. Not even a brush of guilt settled on her shoulders. She was infinitely thankful it had been him, for no other could have been able to take his place.

He grinned down at her.

Was it her imagination, or did his grin seem tight, taunt, almost forced?

"Hungry?" he asked.

She meant to say no, but the word *yes* came out of her mouth. A soft rumble echoed in the quiet room. Bella clamped a hand over her stomach and tucked her chin to her chest. "Sorry."

"Don't be." He dropped a kiss on her forehead, swung his legs over the side of the bed, and walked to the washstand.

Bella levered up onto her elbows to leisurely soak up the sight her impatience had denied her earlier. He was, quite simply, perfect. Sublime. A feast for her greedy eyes. His broad shoulders tapered to a hard waist. The sight of his back completely captivated her. All rippling male muscle and solid, strong bone beneath honey gold skin that looked as soft and smooth as the finest kidskin. She could still feel the memory of those lean hips between her thighs. She shifted, rubbing the arch of her foot up her calf. And his firmly muscled backside . . . She sighed. How was it that after he had given her so much, she could still want more?

After donning his trousers, he returned to the side of the bed. "Need assistance?"

Her gaze darted to his inquiring face and then to the damp towel in his hand. Oh, *that* had been what he washed up. A rush of modesty heated her cheeks. She snatched the towel. "No. I can manage."

He tipped his head. "I'll be right back."

A tight knot of trepidation infiltrated her stomach. What with the way he was practically racing to the door, she wasn't at all sure he spoke the truth.

Eight

GIDEON pulled the bedroom door shut and pinched the bridge of his nose so hard his arm shook.

Holy Mother . . . bloody fucking hell!

He had not been expecting that. He had not been prepared for that.

She was not supposed to have been a virgin.

And she had been a virgin. If nothing else, the faint crimson smear on the sheath proved it well enough.

Why had she given her innocence to him of all people? He was the last man who deserved it. Gently bred ladies did not choose him. Gideon had half a mind to turn around and demand to know why. Why him? Why the hell had she been a virgin? She was supposed to be married!

And how dare she not say anything, or at least give him a hint? Here he had toyed with her, taunted her, tormented her, taken perverse satisfaction in the sight of her laid out before him, her lithe body writhing in unfulfilled ecstasy. But that moment when everything clicked sharply into place, when his stomach dropped to the floor—quite frankly, he was amazed he hadn't gone limp from the shock. And he probably would have, if not for the fact he had been buried hilt-deep, her tight heat gripping his cock like a fist. Hell, he was lucky he hadn't come right then and there, before he gave her one orgasm.

He shook his head, short, hard, and utterly frustrated, and then removed his other hand from the doorknob lest he give into temptation. Forcing his feet to move, he walked down the short hall to the dining room. He should have known. Five days was an unprecedented length of time before they took him to bed. This appointment had been different from the start. The fortnight should have been the first clue. For country visits, a few days were standard. A week within the realm of the usual. Fourteen days were unheard of.

And what had driven her to procure the services of a man to relieve her of her virginity? Lady Stirling was beauty personified, body and soul. Men would sell all they owned for a chance to be with her. She needn't stoop so low as to pay one. It was pure chance Rubicon had thrown her to him. That heartless bitch could have easily chosen any one of the other three men in her employ. A cold shudder gripped him at the thought of Bella at the mercy of one of those three. Whores, the lot of them. Utterly without discrimination, willing to do anything for money, anything Rubicon commanded of them. None of them had the patience this appointment demanded. Focused solely on their own pleasure, they would have pressed their attentions on Bella, forced her hand before she was ready. And she would have gifted her innocence to a man who cared nothing for her and cared only for the gold in his pockets.

Gideon's stomach turned. A wave of imminent bile filled his throat. He grabbed the bottle of wine and brought it to his lips, took two long swallows, then slammed it on the table with a derisive snort. Bordeaux should be savored, not poured down one's throat.

He needed a real drink but there was no liquor in this damn cottage. He knew, for he'd already scoured the place last night after the servant delivered his solitary dinner. He should have given into his frayed nerves, gone up to the house, and requested a bottle of scotch. Then at least he'd have something stronger than wine to throw back. Christ, gin would be acceptable at this point.

But he had not left the cottage for fear of word reaching her ears that her "cousin" was a drunkard. In any case, he never presented himself at their doors, be it bedchamber or front, without an express invitation.

Cringing, he glanced swiftly down the hall. He never lingered overlong in bed with a woman, but he had never bolted like that. That look in her eyes, the one that bespoke a bone-deep trust, had scared the daylights out of him. The control he had fought so hard to keep in place was dangerously close to shattering. It was not the height of tact, but leaving, and quickly, had been his only option.

Resting his hands on the table, he hung his head, suddenly weary and defeated, as if facing a battle he could not come out of unscathed. One deep breath. And another. Focusing on the air filling his lungs and whooshing out his nose.

He righted himself, pushing the heels of his palms to his closed eyes. "Pull it together," he muttered.

She had been a virgin. He accepted the fact. He was bound to come across one sooner or later, so it was his own fault for not letting the possibility enter his head. Walking out the door and returning to London today was not an acceptable option. His shock behind him, his frustrations vented, he could face her again. He knew what he was dealing with now, and he was confident he could handle it like he handled all his other appointments. Their long walks, their conversations, that indefinable "something" he had sensed from her had nothing to do with him. It had all been the product of her untried state.

As for why him? He pushed the question from his mind. The answer did not matter. He would be leaving in ten days, so it was best if he kept it all in perspective.

Gideon chuckled, the sound cutting self-mockery. Well, he had been wrong—Bella was not *exactly* like all the rest.

A clock sounded in his head, ticking off the time remaining before her curiosity seized hold and she came out of the bedchamber. She deserved an extra measure of consideration given what she had lost today, and to whom. So he should get back in there and play the charming gentleman.

Grabbing the wicker basket, he returned to the bedchamber and found her standing before the dresser tucking a pin into her hair. *Damn.* He wished she had left it unbound a bit longer.

Arms bent up to her head, Bella glanced over her shoulder. Her white zephyr silk chemise was so thin it revealed the long, slim lines and graceful curves of her body. Why was it he felt like a thief, as if he had stolen something that did not belong to him?

Her lips curved in a failed attempt at a smile. "Hello."

"Need help?" he asked, doing his best with an open, friendly tone, while inwardly hoping she wasn't already regretting their afternoon.

"No, I can manage."

He smoothed the rumpled coverlet and set the basket on the bed. "Shall we have our picnic in bed?"

She hesitated. "All right."

He was unpacking the food when she bent to pick up her dress from the floor.

"Don't bother with that, or you'll make me feel woefully underdressed." Gideon climbed onto the bed, laying on his side and stretching out his legs. "Come on. Into bed with you."

His mock-gruff command got the response he was hoping for. She shook her head ruefully, a genuine smile curving her lips. Dropping the dress to the floor, she joined him on the bed. Bella smoothed her chemise to cover the long legs folded elegantly beside her and selected the smallest chicken leg from the silver bowl.

They sat in silence for a few short moments; he focused solely on her, while her attention never strayed from her plate.

"I thought you were married?" His careful tone begged to be confided in, even when it was the last thing she should do.

"I am," she said quietly, not meeting his gaze.

"How long have you been married?"

"Five years."

"But then, how could you have been . . . ?"

Ducking her chin, a wince flittered across her brow. "H-he can't. He's incapable."

How could such a beautiful, passionate young woman be married to an impotent old man? Fate could not have been crueler. He reached out, intent on lifting her chin, on not letting her hide, but stopped at the tension gripping her posture. Rigid to the point of brittleness. He should not feel this compassion, but he couldn't help himself.

Glancing down, he furrowed his brow. "Bella. The knife and fork are not necessary."

Her hands stilled over her plate.

"It's a chicken leg, designed to be picked up with your bare hand."

With a self-conscious lift of her shoulders, she set down the knife and fork and hesitantly reached for the leg on her plate, as if fearing a reprimand.

"Now take a bite. Your stomach will thank you." He took a generous bite of his own chicken leg and winked.

Her chuckle eased the rigidity of her body. She mimicked him, right down to the roguish wink. If she could laugh, then everything would be just fine between them, he assured himself.

After their picnic, he helped her to dress, deftly doing up the row of neat buttons down her back. He pulled on his shirt and waistcoat before seeing her to the door. Gideon draped the cloak about her shoulders, fastened the clasp, and pulled up the hood.

Bella smiled in thanks. "Mr. Rosedale, I would greatly enjoy your company for dinner this evening."

"It would be my pleasure."

She turned to leave.

"And Bella . . ."

She looked over her shoulder. The navy hood framed her features.

Her fine eyebrows were raised in question. The crests of her high cheekbones were still flushed a faint pink from the orgasms he had given her.

"It's Gideon, if it pleases you."

She gave him a small nod and he caught a glimpse of an abashed grin before she headed out the door.

He and Bella repeated their dinner ritual that evening, but things were more intimate than they had been on previous occasions. There was a certain softness about her, a languid ease to her movements, a look in her eyes. It was obvious to him now that next to him sat a woman secure in her sensuality, a woman without regrets, whereas two days ago he dined with an innocent.

When dinner was completed he was there to walk her to the staircase. Bella made to ascend the stairs but he stayed at the foot. She turned on the first step and looked at him askance. She was tall for a woman, about five foot eight, and the height of the step put her a hair above his six one.

"Would you care to retire to the sitting room for a glass of whisky or a cup of tea?"

The intention behind her invitation was crystal clear. But Gideon had never been with a virgin before and had decided it would be best to take the conservative approach. The last thing he wanted to do was hurt her. "Thank you, but I believe I shall retire early this evening."

She gave her head a tiny shake.

"Tomorrow," he whispered, holding her gaze. At the uncertainty flickering across her face, he added, "It's not that I don't want to. It's not that I'm unable"—he couldn't keep the smug smirk from his lips—"but you need to rest."

"No. Tonight," she replied, so softly he more read the words on her lips than heard them.

"Yes. Trust me. Tomorrow."

Mindful of the maid he spied entering the nearby drawing room, Gideon only bowed, bringing her hand up to his lips. A shiver wracked her body as he traced the lattice of light blue veins on her exposed wrist with the tip of his tongue. Then he left her on the stairs and returned to Garden House.

The next evening he accepted the invitation and ascended the stairs with her. He did not pause in the sitting room, but confidently went straight through to her bedchamber, shutting the doors and turning the locks behind him. And this time, there were no jarring surprises.

Bella was urgent, demanding, impatient, ever-greedy in her passion. Like an addict who had been denied for far too long, she couldn't seem to get enough. How she managed to go so long without a lover, to keep all of this contained beneath the usual cool exterior, was beyond his comprehension. She was a completely different woman in bed than out. And he found he liked this side of her, liked the dichotomy, and was *almost* too fond of the fact he was the only one to see her throw off the chains of propriety.

She was amazingly responsive—arching and writhing beneath him. It took hardly any effort on his part to make her come. Her orgasms were quick, many, and hard. But while Bella had enthusiasm in abundance, she was definitely lacking in patience. There was more to the act than her lying on her back, and the prospect of introducing her to the full spectrum of sensual delights was very, very appealing indeed.

The first night in her bed he acceded to her wishes for a while. Well, a long while. Then he gave her a taste of what she was missing.

When he shifted to pull out, he refused to heed her command to stay put, refused to heed the hands on his back, the long legs wrapping around his hips, and made his way down her body. He didn't stop to pay tribute to her luscious breasts, but went straight for his target. He settled his shoulders between her lean thighs and the moment his tongue touched her clit, she whimpered in comprehension.

Since he had a fair idea of how Bella's mind worked, at least in bed, the moment her little gasping moans began to crescendo, he crawled swiftly up her body and slid back into her tight heat, thrusting hard through her climax.

He gave her one more orgasm, then another, because well, she was Bella. And this time after Gideon allowed his release he did not practically jump from the bed, but remained beside her for many long moments, holding her close, before giving her one last kiss and returning to Garden House. Alone.

Nine

THE next few days passed by in a blur for Bella. The afternoons were spent taking long walks with Gideon, stopping here and there to steal kisses, and evenings . . . those were her favorite. Behind closed doors, in the sanctuary of her bedchamber, where clothes were not a requirement. Where bare skin was the preferred attire. And where Gideon took her to new heights of passion.

Instead of another walk, this afternoon she had suggested a drive. Just she and Gideon, no driver to accompany them. A quick stop in the stables was all it had taken to have a horse harnessed and put in the traces. After helping her into the carriage, Gideon had taken up the lines, driving the horse at an easy trot down the dirt lane bordered by neat lines of fences on either side.

She twisted around on the bench to look behind her. The two-wheeled gig left a small cloud of dust in its wake. She saw one of the grooms leading a black horse toward the open door of the stables, but could not make out which groom it was. Deeming them far enough down the road, she turned around and tugged on the end of the ribbon tickling her cheek, undoing the bow. After removing her bonnet, she tied the amber ribbons in a loose knot and slipped it over her arm.

She tipped up her face, savoring the sun's warmth. The Scottish spring weather was being remarkably cooperative. In fact, it had rained only once since Gideon came to Bowhill. Two days of gray clouds in the last ten. All it had taken to chase away those clouds was the loss of her innocence. The beginnings of a laugh teased her belly. If she had known that was the way to appease the sun, then perhaps she would have . . . *No.* She chuckled for being foolish enough to let the thought begin to form in her head. It could only have been him.

"Does my driving amuse?"

"No. I was just thinking." She turned slightly to Gideon. One could never find fault with his skill. He drove with the expertise of a gentleman, the leather lines held with an easy confidence in his strong hands.

He clucked and the horse obediently lengthened its stride to a smart trot. "About what, may I ask?"

She did not want to tell him the truth. Her husband, and why he had not consummated their marriage, was the last topic she wanted to discuss with Gideon. Instead, she told him what had been on her mind a few minutes ago. "I was thinking about yesterday. And the day prior. And the day before that."

"What about them prompted the chuckle?"

"You."

He slanted her a look. The sun bathed the classic angles and planes of his face. The wind ruffled his short dark hair. The teasing twist of his mouth could not hide the genuine male affront. "Me? Should I be relieved you didn't burst out in full-blown laughter?"

Bella rolled her eyes skyward. Silly man. "I wasn't laughing *at* you. It was more . . ." She shook her head, struggling for the words to describe how perfect the last few days had been. She could not remember ever being so happy, and so at peace with herself. It was as if by giving herself to him something inside had shifted, settled, finally slipping into balance. And it was not just their evenings, or instances like yesterday's stopover in the hothouse when she had not been able to wait until later. It was Gideon. "They were wonderful days, as today is sure to be."

"Such confidence. I shall have to do my best to ensure today lives up to your expectations."

"You needn't sound so grave. I'm not hard to please."

His gaze raked the length of her body. He smiled, slow and sinful. She pressed her thighs together to fight the tide of lust rising within, heating her skin. Her body half-primed, poised for arousal, whenever he was near.

He looked ahead and guided the horse around a bend in the road. "No. You are not at all hard to please."

Slow and smooth like warmed honey, his deep voice flowed down her spine. She took a quick breath and swallowed to moisten her suddenly dry mouth.

"Is my lady impatient?" His attention was on the road, yet somehow he knew without looking which direction her thoughts had turned.

"A bit," she confessed, trying to match his casual tone, but the hitch in her breath gave her away.

"Well then, I'll have to see what I can do about that. Which way? Left or right?"

Bella pulled her gaze from his handsome profile. The road forked up ahead. Open fields to either side dotted with the occasional tree. They must be well beyond the stables, for the wooden fences marking the pastures were behind them. "Left. Stay on the property. The road will take us through a small forest."

He nodded. "Good choice. Do we need to hurry?"

"Yes." The word rushed out of her mouth, the thought of having him now foremost in her mind.

"Your wish is my command." He snapped the lines and the chestnut mare broke from a trot to a ground-covering canter. "Hold on."

She grabbed the side of the carriage. She was glad she had slipped her bonnet ribbons over her arm, for at the pace they were traveling it would have flown out of the carriage if she had merely set it beside her. The gig clattered along the dirt road. Wind whistled past her ears. Exhilaration and lust sang through her veins. She tipped her head back and laughed, full and straight from her belly.

They hit a particularly hard bump and she grabbed his thigh, but did not release him once she regained her balance. His legs were slightly spread, booted feet braced against the floorboards. The muscles of his thigh were hard beneath her hand. She adored touching him, running her hands over the hard contours of his body, and what she adored most of all was just a little bit higher.

A mischievous smirk curved her lips as her hand crept up until she encountered a prominent bump under the fawn breeches. He twitched, his already hard cock lengthening, swelling. She had taken him in her hands and into her body many times in the last few days, yet his dimensions never ceased to amaze. And he was always so *ready*, whenever she wanted him. The experience was novel—having a man so willing, and able, to accede to her every whim. She shifted closer, pressing her thigh against his, her shoulder against his biceps, and swirled her fingertips over the head of his cock.

"Are you trying to distract me?"

"No, I wouldn't want to do that," she said coyly, rubbing her cheek against the soft wool of his jacket sleeve, breathing in the enticing scent of him. Cloves and lemons and fresh outdoor air. And *him*. Gasping, she closed her eyes against a heavy flush of raw need. She rotated her hips, seeking the friction of the cushioned bench. Her silk shift rubbed maddeningly against her sex, teasing her innermost flesh.

"Faster?" he asked.

"Yes!"

He snapped the lines over the horse's back. The gig lurched forward. She closed her hand around his manhood as much as the breeches would allow, and squeezed. He pulsed beneath her hand, solid as iron. Leaning into him, she reached farther up his thigh, lightly grazing her nails along the thick length. She gently cupped the heavy weight of his ballocks. On a throat-scraping grunt, he flexed his hips, his long legs falling open, granting her greater access to touch, to play. A low moan escaped her lips. Just touching him, the anticipation of what was to come, had her on the brink of orgasm.

He slowed the horse's pace as the road narrowed, leading them into the forest. Tall trees blocked out the sun, cloaking them in cool dark shadows, but it did nothing to cool the blood pounding though her veins. He pulled the brake and looped the lines around the rail. "Now then, what was on your mind?"

She pulled urgently at the buttons on his falls.

"Oh. That." All casual nonchalance, he lifted one arrogant eyebrow while fevered desire rode over every inch of her skin.

"Stop teasing me, and . . . and . . ." *Fuck me.* She clenched her jaw to keep the coarse words from being uttered. Abandoning the half-opened placket of his breeches, she shook her bonnet ribbons free from her wrist and leaned full over him, grabbing his head, seeking his lips. His tongue tangled with hers, his mouth hot and delicious. She levered up onto her knees, slanted her mouth full over his and threaded her fingers into his hair, his scalp warm, the silken strands cool from the wind.

He leaned back against the bench and she moved with him, unwilling to give him up. A draught of air hit her stocking-covered legs as he gathered her skirt, bringing it up to her thighs. She quickly straddled his lap, her knees on either side of his lean hips. He had showed her this position in the hothouse yesterday afternoon. She would have never guessed her wicker settee could be put to such a scandalous use, or that the removal of clothes was not an integral component of making love. Now she knew better.

He twisted his head, breaking the contact of their lips. "Sit back," he urged, low and hoarse.

Nodding, she complied, resting her bottom on his knees.

Lifting his hips, he undid the remaining buttons on his breeches.

A grimace tightened his lips as he reached inside to pull out his cock. It sprang up at attention, pointing straight to the canopy of leaves and branches overhead. A drop of fluid seeped from the small slit in the head. Her innermost muscles clenched, liquid warmth pooling between her thighs. She could almost feel him buried deep within her, stretching, filling, invading her. Her breaths coming hard and fast, she licked her lips and reached toward the object of her desire.

"Just a moment," he said, intercepting her hand and placing it on back onto her thigh.

She scowled, wanting to feel the hot silken skin, to trace the prominent vein running up to the head and marvel anew at the iron-like rigidity. But it did no good as his attention was trained on his jacket as he pulled a waxed paper envelope from an inside pocket. The next instant his magnificent arousal was sheathed, a rather untidy bow tied at the substantial base.

With one hand he gathered her skirt at her waist, baring her upper thighs and her sex, and took himself in hand. She could not explain it, but the sight of his large hand on his cock was infinitely arousing, wickedly so. Long fingers wrapped fully around it, his grip sure. Eager to feel him inside of her, she braced her hands on his shoulders and lifted up onto her knees. The blunt head brushed the apex of her pleasure. Sharp sensation jolted through her body. Wincing, she flinched. Nerves coiled so tight, the light contact was almost painful.

"Sorry," he said quickly.

She shook her head. She did not want an apology, she wanted—

"Yes." The word came out on a shaky moan, her insides fluttering, as he positioned himself at her core.

Biting the edge of her lip against the onslaught of undiluted pleasure, she sank slowly down. She was drenched with desire, yet still, she had to wiggle her hips and spread her thighs wider to accommodate his cock. He stretched her perfectly to her limits. Rapture flooded her brain.

A climax crashed over her, assaulting her senses, before she even took all of him. Her cry echoed off the surrounding trees.

Head thrown back, eyes closed tight, hands gripping his shoulders, she rode his cock, ravenous for more. The soft wool of his breeches gently abraded her inner thighs. Her silk-covered knees slipped a bit on the leather bench with each downward slam of her hips. It was wicked, it was scandalous, making love like this in a carriage. And it was spectacular, adding a tantalizing forbidden layer to the passion drenching her senses. No one would stumble upon them—they were on Bowhill property, and there was no reason for any of the servants to wander out here. Yet still, urgency nipped at her heels. She wanted to bare her breasts, feel his mouth, his teeth scoring her hard nipples, but there wasn't time.

Another orgasm. Then another. Hard. Fast. Sapping her strength. Hands spanning her waist, he aided her efforts when her muscles began to tire from her frenzied movements. But she did not stop.

One more. Just one more was all she needed. Head bowed, she gasped for breath. Sweat pricked between her shoulder blades.

"Bella. Come for me. *Now*," he urged.

Her head snapped up. Intent and heated, his dark eyes blazed, searing a path to her soul, sparking the orgasm hovering just out of reach. As the ecstasy claimed her, stealing the last of her strength, he thrust up on a groan, his cock pulsing within her, climaxing with her.

Bella slumped against him. Drained and satiated. Reveling in the languor relaxing every muscle in her body. Her pulse pounded thickly through her veins. Her fingers and toes tingled delightfully. She was suddenly aware of the sounds of the forest, as if a door had just opened, letting in the outdoors. A bird chirped overhead. Leaves rustled in the breeze. Harness jangled softly as the horse shifted in the traces.

"Where to now?" he asked, his breath tickling the hair on her head.

"Ummm." She smiled against his chest that rose and fell beneath

her cheek. She wanted to stay here like this with him. Her arms slung around his neck. Her skirt bunched at her waist. His hands skimming up and down her back. Content and drowsy, she arched like a cat. "The lake," she mumbled. "See the swans. They're beautiful."

Levering up, she cupped his jaw and pressed a light kiss to his lips. Then she ran her fingers through his hair, carefully smoothing the sable locks that had been disheveled by her hands. She smiled, feeling like an infatuated young girl, wanting only to be with him, to savor this moment in all its perfection.

He gave her bottom a playful smack. "Up with you. The swans are waiting."

"All right," she conceded on a sigh, knowing they truly could not stay here all day.

He lifted her and settled her gently on the bench. As she straightened her skirt, he removed the French letter, tucking it back into the envelope and into his pocket. So considerate, she thought, not to toss it to the ground. Then he buttoned his breeches. Her dress was wrinkled beyond all hope from their hasty coupling, yet there was not one crease in his dark brown jacket. He looked, as always, like a privileged London gentleman, the same variety she had encountered many years ago. Her lips pursed then she shrugged, practicality descending, soothing the feminine vanity that threatened to object. Her rumpled appearance would not rouse any suspicions from her servants when they arrived back at the house, at least not when paired with his.

Gideon gathered the lines and drove out of the small forest, through a wide field and stopped before the lake where three snow-white swans glided peacefully along the surface, their long necks bowed in a graceful arch, occasionally dipping their heads underwater in search of a meal. After a long walk, she and Gideon returned to the carriage and set off for the stables at a leisurely pace.

Her lust briefly appeased, she simply sat beside him and soaked up just being with him. The way his arm brushed hers as he guided the horse. The way he glanced at her every now and then, his gaze warm and filled with masculine appreciation. Living alone for so many years, she was accustomed to quiet. So one would have thought she'd have been eager to talk with another person, to fill every possible moment with words. Yet she stayed silent, lost in him.

When she had initially received Esmé's note, she had never imaged a man like Gideon would appear at her home. Well, she had never met a man of his kind before, so she honestly hadn't known what to expect. Regardless, she would have never allowed herself to hope for someone like him—a man who gave her the confidence, the courage, to simply be herself. A man who made her feel truly alive for the first time in her life. He was the ideal companion, so much so it was easy to forget Esmé had hired him.

She closed her eyes and pushed the unwelcome thought away, as she did every time the reminder tried to intrude on her happiness.

There were little pokes and nudges, of course, ever since she had muffled her conscience with her terms. Gideon never stayed the entire night in her bed, always leaving well before midnight and before any servants could wonder too long or hard over why it took so long for their mistress and her "cousin" to partake of a nightcap. But she and Esmé often talked for hours before retiring for the evening, so she did not put much worry into her servants' musings and did her best to ignore the creeping desire for Gideon to remain with her.

And they of course could not engage in any open flirtation when in view of the servants. There were no passionate kisses when he arrived at the manor house for tea or to escort her on a walk. But even though her lips tingled with the need for his whenever he was near, one could not so easily push aside a lifetime of proper English decorum. So it didn't feel out of place to have to wait until they were alone. If anything, the anticipation made his kisses sweeter.

After dinner that evening they retired to her bedchamber. Gideon had quite opened her eyes over the last few days. Quick trysts in carriages were one thing, but when they were in bed . . . *Oh*, the things he did to her. He maneuvered her, flipping and turning and arranging limbs as though she weighed nothing. The rhythm never lost, each change in position finding some new sublime spot.

But as he moved on top of her, under her, and behind her that night, the passion-soaked haze lifted just enough, like dense fog rising under the force of the morning sun, for her to realize that while she was always mindless and fully absorbed in him, he never seemed to lose control. And once she became aware of it, it stayed with her, keeping her from dropping back into the sensual fog.

The first tingle of ache pinched her wrists from the strain of holding her upper body up on all fours. The next moment, before the tingle in her wrists could turn into the slightest bite, the large hands grasping her hips shifted. One hand coasted up to splay across her chest, the other glided down to her lower belly. The thick length of his cock left her on the next stroke as he leaned full over her to nip at her shoulder, teeth grazing her skin in a playful lover's bite. Cradling her in his arms, he turned her onto her back. Her arms and legs wrapped around him in welcome when he settled between her spread thighs and braced his weight on his forearms, but her eyelids did not even flutter when he glided back into her.

It had not been quite calculated or orchestrated, but the effortless ease with which he moved, the way he always seemed to know a second before she did what she wanted, began to disturb her. It was a practiced ease, born of countless repetition, speaking much louder than words that this was his profession. While she knew men his age were rarely without experience, her own long-ago groom probably had scores of lovers before and after her, it was the knowledge Gideon got paid for this which kept her from losing herself in him. It tugged on the back of her mind, harder and harder. A mild irritant that rubbed until it became a full-blown wound, demanding the undivided force of her attention.

Closing her eyes, she tried to push it away, to ignore it. But the knot forming in her stomach refused to unravel. They were as close as a man and woman could be, yet he felt so very far away. She was strangely conscious of his every move, as if she were a mere spectator.

He must have sensed her distraction for his rhythm changed. He gave deep long thrusts, pausing at the end of each downstroke to grind his hips, rubbing his groin against her clit. It should have sparked an immediate orgasm on her part, but it did not spark anything pleasurable at all.

"Come for me." His words were a plea, whispered hotly in her ear.

He dropped his head and grazed his teeth across the hard tip of her nipple. Instead of arching beneath him, moaning her approval, coming for him, all she could think was—*Does he do that with all of them? Is he thinking about me, or is he thinking about the hundreds of pounds Esmé surely paid him?*

Her stomach dropped, like a lead weight thrown into the sea, plummeting to her feet. She needed him to stop. *Now.* Each decadent thrust drove home the fact she was just one of many, one more job, one more set of wages.

Before Gideon could claim her lips again, she pushed hard on his shoulders. Perspiration slicked the hollows behind her knees, but the velvety skin beneath her hands was warm and dry.

The word building in her throat pushed with such incredible pressure, finally working itself free. "Stop."

Lifting his head, he went still. Whisky brown eyes met hers, his lips wet from their kisses, his gaze questioning. She swiftly broke eye contact. Without a word, he shifted off to lie on his side.

She wanted to pound on his chest, demand to know if he felt anything at all. But she could not bring herself to speak. Thick tension filled the room, constricting her throat. Her heart beat a tight, rapid rhythm against her ribs. Her gaze was fixed unseeing on the dark canopy above. She could not even look at him.

Regardless of her terms, she was nothing but a fold of pound notes in his pocket. She had been a fool. A fool to try to turn their fortnight into something it could never be. A consensual flirtation? No, he had simply been working all along. She was just another woman in a long line of many. One month from now, he likely would not be able to distinguish her from all the rest.

Her heart felt like it was trapped in a vise—crushing, twisting, wrenching in agony. Tears pricked the corners of her eyes. She swallowed hard, fighting them down.

She meant nothing to him.

The past had repeated itself.

No, it was worse than that. For this time she had given her virginity to a prostitute, and had naively fallen in love with the man.

Ten

HAD he done something wrong? Gideon wracked his brain, quickly replaying the prior few minutes. No—he had done nothing new, nothing out of the ordinary to warrant *this*.

"Bella?"

He laid a hand on her hip, a silent request for an answer. But the instant he touched her silken skin, she flinched. Startled, he removed his hand.

"Bella. What's—?"

Cutting off his words, she rolled onto her side, showing him the lean lines of her back and the rigid set of her shoulder blades. The sweet musky scent of her recently aroused body filled his every breath, a primitive mating signal his body refused to ignore. He clenched his jaw, his ballocks aching with the need to come. Starting and not finishing was never a pleasant experience, but tonight . . .

Mentally floundering, he groped for anything to explain her odd behavior.

"Do you feel anything for me at all?" Bella asked, in the barest of whispers.

Fuck.

The breath whooshed out of him. His erection withered to embarrassing proportions.

He knew exactly why she had told him to stop. He opened his mouth, knowing she needed him to reply now and not hesitate. Yet the reassuring words refused to flow smoothly off his tongue. "Of-of course, I-I—"

"Stop. Please." The tremble in her quiet voice cut right through him.

He wanted to take her in his arms, to kiss her lush mouth until she went lax with passion, to tell her . . . Hell, he didn't know what to tell her to make it better.

Women were so very different than men. He had seen countless men walk into Rubicon's, selecting a different beauty on each visit. The only differences in their appearances when they left were slightly rumpled clothes and a sated, smug expression. But women . . . he had lived with enough as a boy to know how easily the inexperienced could confuse physical acts with true intimacy.

No matter his client, they were still women and he never wanted to cause them pain, in any form. As such, he long ago learned how to keep his appointments on a strictly physical level. Any conversations were kept on the surface. Any time he felt one of them begin to soften, he took a step back, creating the necessary distance.

He had done his best over the last few days. Kept his guard up and tried to keep her focused on the pleasures he offered. But it had obviously all been in vain, and well, one could not get more inexperienced than a virgin. Christ, she had even chosen to give her innocence to him. At the time, it had been a question he did not want answered. Yet now, the answer lay right next to him. Still, quiet once again, and clearly in pain.

Oh, Bella. Gideon took a deep breath, expanding his chest that felt unnaturally constricted.

There truly was nothing to be done for it, and he could not stay in her bed when she no longer wanted him.

He let out a shoulder-slumping sigh and swung his feet over the edge of the bed. After quickly gathering his clothes and boots from the floor, he made to leave the room. Hand on the brass knob, he glanced over his shoulder.

Please, please look at me.

The moonlight caressed the gently rounded curves of her backside and the graceful length of her legs. Her long tresses were fanned behind her and shone silvery white against the tousled sheets.

But he did not stay. He could not, should not stay.

He went into the sitting room and closed the door to Bella's bedchamber behind him. The soft click reverberated with a heavy finality. As he pulled on his clothes in the near-dark room, he told himself it was better this way. Better she remembered their respective roles. Better she remember now who and what he was before the lines that needed to remain clear and unmarred became too tangled to separate. She was still new to this concept. She needed to harden her heart. Remember he was not a man she should lose herself to.

Gideon sat in a chair by the window to pull on his boots, then buttoned his coat and left the room. He walked down the empty hall, down the stairs, out the front door and back to Garden House. Alone. Not bothering to light a candle, he went to the back bedchamber, stripped off his just-donned clothes, and laid on the bed.

When the first rays of dawn lit the white curtain on the bedroom widow, he gave up sleep as a lost cause. After a quick shave, he dressed, packed his trunk, and sat in an armchair in the front parlor. And waited.

He had a strong feeling a carriage would show up at the door to take him back to London. But he did not want that carriage to appear. They still had four more days left. He wanted Bella to knock on the door, but he knew she would not.

She had never been comfortable with his reason for being here. If nothing else, her terms screamed loud and clear she was not the type of woman who indulged herself with someone of his ilk. There were those who could and those who could not, and Bella was in the latter group. She had not even written to Rubicon herself but sent another in her stead.

As Gideon waited, as the rising sun filled the small parlor with bright golden light, he told himself firmly it should not matter if she sent him home now. He shouldn't worry about it, or dwell on it, or even let it pass through his head. The only thing that should matter was he would still get paid in full, and therefore Rubicon would not get pissed if word reached her ears he returned early. And, he reasoned, he would have a few more days to relax before his next appointment.

The thought of "that" did not sit well, so he very quickly pushed it from his mind. Resting his elbows on his knees, he hung his head in his hands and instead did his best to not think of anything, especially not the long-limbed ethereal beauty who was most likely, at this very moment, requesting a carriage to be readied for London.

THE blue or the rose, m'lady?"

Bella was aware of her maid speaking behind her, but Maisie's words were not significant enough to stand out amongst the clutter already filling her mind.

"Or perhaps the emerald cambric?"

What must he think of me? She closed her eyes, blocking out the view beyond her bedchamber window, but could not block out the crisp clear light of the morning sun. It bathed her closed eyelids in a warm deep orange glow, mocking her, taunting her, reminding her anew she could not escape her actions. It was morning, and with it had come the crushing weight of humiliation. She could not believe she had done *that* last night. On a wince, she rolled one shoulder. The pop and creak of her joints seemed unnaturally loud.

"No? Perhaps the amber muslin? Though it may be a bit light for spring. Are you planning a walk with Mr. Rosedale today? You'll need a shawl. The light blue cashmere would do nicely."

What must he think of me? Those words kept bouncing off her skull, refusing to leave. The very concept of Gideon negated a faithful relationship, or a relationship of any kind. And he was free to leave whenever he chose. He did not have to be intimate with her. He could have left after their first dinner. Yes, he got paid for this. Yes, she knew this, had known it all along. Had convinced herself a week ago she understood the terms of their flirtation. That she could treat it as a practical arrangement. Yet she had acted the part of a novice last night. A foolish young girl, shocked out of her wits when she had finally seen her starry-eyed fantasy for what it was.

"M'lady? Lady Stirling?"

"What do you want, Maisie?" Sharp and quick, the words rebounded off the window before her.

"I-I . . . Which day dress do you prefer, m'lady?"

Bella took a deep breath and forced her fingers to unclench from the drapes, the damask wrinkled and dampened from her anxious hand. She should not take her frustration out on her maid. The girl sounded downright cowed, her voice a tiny little squeak. Maisie was an ally of sorts, and Bella did not want to turn the maid against her. Ever since she began bringing Gideon to her room, Maisie had conveniently stopped tending to her in the evenings. The fire lit, the drapes drawn, the coverlet pulled back, but Maisie absent by the time they reached the bedchamber.

She took another deep breath, pulled her dressing gown tighter around her body, and turned from the window, the calm façade back in place. "The Prussian blue will do fine."

Standing beside the open door to Bella's dressing room, Maisie wrung her hands, her blue green eyes huge in her pale face. "Would you care for some tea? I can ring for a tray."

"No, and alert the kitchen that I will not be down for breakfast." There was no way her stomach could tolerate food this morning.

Maisie nodded, disappeared into the dressing room, and reappeared a moment later with the chosen dress in her arms. Chemise, stays, and stockings were already folded over the back of the Egyptian armchair.

Neither said a word as the girl helped her to dress and pin back her hair. Bella simply went through the motions, standing, turning, and sitting as required.

"Is there anything else I can do for you?"

She looked into the oval mirror above the vanity. The maid's ginger eyebrows were lowered with obvious concern. Bella opened her mouth then closed it, shying away from the request. It would be horribly awkward to have one of the servants report back that Mr. Rosedale was no longer at Garden House. She would have to determine that information for herself. "No. There is nothing else."

Maisie nodded. Her mouth thinned into a determined line. "Shall I order the kitchen to burn his breakfast?"

It took Bella a moment to realize what the girl was asking. "No," she replied with a poor attempt at a chuckle. "If there are any sausages to be burned, they should be my own." She tipped her head, excusing her maid before the girl could ask the imminent question twisting her young face.

As soon as the door closed, Bella went back to the window. The sun shined brightly, her roses soaking up its nourishing rays. The overabundance of pleasant days would coax buds to form earlier than usual. Her gaze strayed to the view she could not ignore. The leaves on the trees surrounding Garden House swayed in the breeze. The small stone cottage looked so very idyllic, as if it had been taken straight out of a fairy tale.

If that was not ironic, she did not know what was.

Closing her eyes, she pressed her fingertips to her temples. Their fortnight could not end so soon, could not end this way. Fully aware she had fallen in love with him regardless of his profession, she decided it could not get much worse. When he left she would be alone again, and she would rather have him for a few more days than not at all. The prospect of going this one day without seeing him, of allowing the sun to set without feeling the brush of his lips against hers, was unbearable. And almost frightening.

Turning from the window, she left her bedchamber and set out to walk in the garden with the express purpose of wandering upon Garden House. After stalling in the rose garden for a good half hour, she finally worked up the courage to knock on the door.

The first thing she noticed when Gideon opened the door was that he was fully dressed in a dark blue jacket and cream silk waistcoat, complete with leather gloves and a black top hat held loosely in one hand. The next thing she noticed was that he looked tired, as if he had not slept well last night.

"Good morning, Mr. Rosedale. Would you care to take a turn about the garden?"

His tight nod left her with the impression he had been expecting someone else, or some other question.

He hung the hat on one of the pegs lining the wall by the door and stepped from the house. She laid her hand lightly on his proffered arm. Ever the gentleman, he swung open the gate of the white picket fence surrounding the cottage and gave her a slight bow as she passed. They walked side by side along the path winding through the garden. The air was thick with the scent of spring. Their usual companionable silence stretched tight. There was a tangible distance between them. She no longer felt free to reach for his hand or lift onto her toes and capture his lips with hers.

The need to say something, anything to breech the distance, pressed in on her. She wanted, *needed* everything to go back to the way it had been before she had gone and acted the novice.

She chanced a glance at his profile. *Oh,* he was so handsome it almost hurt her eyes. His dark hair was much shorter than fashion dictated, just a tad from being so short it was cropped, with just enough left on the ends to give it some movement in the late morning breeze. If his hair were longer it would have distracted from his features. As it was the shortness drew her eye to the perfect symmetry of his face—the defined jaw, the straight nose, the smooth contours of his cheekbones, and the dark eyebrows which were currently the tiniest bit pinched. She doubted he spent much time under the sun, so the warm honey tone of his skin must be natural. Plus, she had the distinct pleasure of seeing him completely bare and knew every muscular inch of him bore the same smooth, honey-kissed skin.

He must have felt her regard for he glanced to her. She should say it now before she lost the nerve.

"My apologies."

He slowed to a stop. "For what?"

She stopped and shrugged uncomfortably, feeling like a child who didn't want to confess to her crime. "For last night."

The slight pinch between his dark eyebrows strengthened. "You don't need to apologize, Bella."

"Yes, I do. It was not well done of me." Clasping her hands in front of her, she twisted and untwisted her fingers together. "I behaved like a . . . a . . ." *Fool. An inexperienced fool.* "I don't know what came over me." That wasn't quite the truth. She knew exactly what came over her, but there was no way she could admit she had fallen in love with him.

He covered her hands with his, stilling her nervous motions. "It's quite all right. There's no reason to fret. Don't think on it a moment longer."

His words were calm and reassuring, yet his eyes held such uncertainty. She glanced to their hands, his covered in soft black leather. He had answered the door with his gloves on and hat in hand. Had he intended to leave? Did he still intend to leave? Did he believe she wanted him to leave?

Oh, Lord, no. If he believed that, then she needed to rectify his misconception straight away.

She took a deep breath, gathering the words. "I would very much enjoy your company for dinner this evening, Mr. Rosedale."

The pinch between his eyebrows immediately disappeared and a charming, almost relieved smile stole across his mouth. "It would be my pleasure. But . . ."

Bracing herself for the worst, she looked at him askance.

"Only if you call me Gideon."

A surge of giddy happiness tingled through her body. Chin tipping down on a nod, Bella gave him an abashed grin, fully relieved she had not done something irreparable last night. "Dinner will be at six, Gideon. If you will excuse me, I must see to the arrangements."

She turned to leave but he held her back with a hand on her wrist. A gentle tug brought her around. Before she knew it, his lips were on hers, his silken tongue sweeping into her mouth, tangling bolding with hers.

For the first time the kiss was completely unexpected and she sensed in it a quality she had never felt from him before. But before she could identify it he took a step back, leaving her dazed. Her hand fluttered up to her mouth, fingertips brushing her lips, as if touching could somehow reveal the answer.

"I shall be counting the hours, my lady." He executed a short bow and strode back to Garden House.

Dinner that evening was a pleasant affair. The distance from the morning was gone, but neither was the comfortable ease they once had shared present. She felt as though Gideon was watching her more closely than usual, gauging her, assessing her. He did not seem quite as sure of himself as he had been in the past.

So when dinner was completed and he led her to the foot of the stairs, she took his hand in hers and led him up to her bedchamber.

And like that, everything went back to the way it once had been.

WHY did it have to rain today, of all days? A steady hum tapped against the tall arched windows of the formal drawing room. Scowling, Gideon glanced out a window. Rain blurred the view of the grounds on the side of the house. "A walk is out of the question, unless you'd like to get wet."

"No. I don't have a pressing desire to get drenched today. Perhaps tomorrow." Her expression one of patent aristocratic hauteur, Bella brought her teacup to her lips.

He chuckled, amused as always by her dry wit. "We could take a closed carriage and tour the countryside."

"No. Then the driver would get drenched."

"Such consideration."

"I try." Seated on the settee, she leaned forward to place her teacup on the short table before them. He took the opportunity to admire the low neckline of her bodice.

"*Hmm*," he mulled, forcing his mind from her luscious breasts and back to the topic at hand. How to fill the remainder of their last afternoon together? He did not want to waste it, as he'd be leaving on the morrow. He scratched his jaw. There was the obvious answer, but—

"What would you like to do, Gideon?"

He went utterly still. Had he ever heard that question before? *No.* None of them had cared to ask. But Bella had.

"Gideon?"

He gave his head a short shake and met her inquiring gaze.

"What would you like to do?" she repeated slowly, as if speaking to a young child.

"*Ahh* . . ." The prospect of so many options was intimidating, to the point where he did not know how to choose. Maybe he could get her to help by narrowing them down. "Do you have a particular preference I should be aware of?"

"No." She clasped her hands on her lap and raised her eyebrows, expectant and willing to accede to *his* every whim.

He shifted in the chair, completely tongue-tied, and he had done nothing today to tire that particular muscle, at least not yet. Desperate, he searched her face for some hint of a leading question or of an ulterior motive for putting him so bluntly on the spot, but found only a small smile curving her lips.

She was the most beautiful woman he had ever met.

"I want to sketch you."

The way the words popped out of his mouth startled him. They rang in his ears as if not his own. And once out, he could not take them back.

"You're an artist?"

"No, no. Not at all."

She cocked her head, furrowing her brow.

"We don't have to if you don't want to. We can do anything you want. Anything." Was she disappointed because he had suggested something so benign? Had she expected him to suggest an afternoon tryst? Women always liked to hear that they were wanted.

"No. I want to be your model. I'm interested to see how you'd draw me."

"Well, don't expect a masterpiece. I'm not very good," he mumbled. He leaned forward to caress her knee through her skirt and lowered his voice, needing to test the sincerity of her response. "There are other things I'm much better at."

Her breath hitched, just as he knew it would. He ignored the rising disappointment, the sinking sense of misplaced hope, and gave her a slow sinful smile.

She swatted off his hand creeping up her thigh. "You aren't getting out of it that easily. Come along." She rose to her feet. "We'll need to go to my sitting room."

In a *swish* of turquoise silk, she turned and walked from the room.

BENT over at the waist, Bella searched her desk drawer. Was he coming or not? At the sound of approaching footsteps in the hall, she smiled. She knew the moment he entered the room. The air changed, charged with his presence.

"I see you remembered where my sitting room is located." She did not wait for Gideon to respond. "Pencil or pen? Sorry, I don't have any charcoals. Watercolors are the preferred medium for ladies, but you said sketch, not paint."

"Never used charcoals. Never had 'em."

She glanced over her shoulder. Hands clasped behind his back, face absolutely without expression, he stood just inside the room, the door still open. It had been his idea, so why did he look like he was waiting for a dressing-down from his father? Well, as she had told him already, he was not getting out of it. She had grabbed hold the moment he offered up the suggestion and was not about to let go.

"Pencil or pen?" she asked again.

"A pencil will do."

With a nod she glanced back down and found a pencil mixed in with her letters at the back of the drawer. Shutting the drawer, she placed the pencil on the desk atop two sheets of white paper. "Here, or would you prefer to go back to the drawing room?"

He glanced about the room, as if just realizing where he was. "Here is fine."

"Where do you want me?"

He glanced about the room again. "The settee."

"Shall I sit? What do you want me to do?" This was getting ridiculous. Almost comical. But she was not as adept as him at making one feel comfortable. If they went on like this much longer, then she would be placing the pencil in his hand and asking him if he wanted to draw a line or a circle.

"What would you normally do if you were just sitting here?"

Asking a question was a start in the right direction. "Usually I embroider."

The edges of his lips quirked. "The roses are yours. The pillowcase on my bed, the towel on the washstand, and the one in the basket that carries my breakfast. They are all adorned with embroidered roses."

She smiled self-consciously. "One must pass the evening hours."

"I like the ones on the pillowcase in particular. They look like the roses in your hothouse. Chinas." He shut the door and stepped further into the room, his strides comfortable and easy. "Gather your things and have a seat on the settee."

"All right." She went into her bedchamber and collected her embroidery hoop and tin of thread. When she returned she found him settled on the chintz chair opposite the lime green settee, pencil in hand, one leg crossed, booted ankle resting on his knee to prop up a thick volume upon which laid a sheet of paper.

Bella sat and arranged her skirts to drape neatly over her legs. She folded her hands over the hoop on her lap. "How should I sit?"

Mouth pursed, Gideon contemplated her. She resisted the urge to fidget under his intense scrutiny.

He stood and set down the book and pencil. He pulled a few blonde hairs from their pins, his fingers brushing her ear. Gooseflesh rose on her arms. "You were too perfect."

His low words made her breath catch. She fought back the lust that threatened to spark just minutes ago in the drawing room. He was doing it on purpose again, she was certain of it. "Is there such a thing as too perfect?" she asked, raising one eyebrow in defiance.

He held her gaze. He seemed even taller, standing while she sat with her head tipped slightly back. Yet, as always with him, she did not feel even a brush of intimidation.

"Yes. But in art, you do not want perfect." With that very artist-like response, he settled back in the chair.

"What should I do?"

"Embroider."

"But how can you sketch if I'm moving?"

"Don't worry. I have the image in my head. Just do what you normally would. Pretend I'm not here."

That was impossible. There was no way she could block him from her mind. His broad shoulders overpowered the feminine armchair, just as his presence overpowered her. But doing her best to heed his request, she picked up the hoop, removed the needle that had been tucked into the stretched linen, and resumed work on the partially embroidered pink rose.

The soft scratch of pencil on paper lulled her senses. Her fingers worked, pushing the needle through the linen and drawing the thread taut before placing the next stitch, while her mind wandered.

When she had awoken this morning, she had initially cursed the rain, wanting to spend their last afternoon together walking through the rose garden. She wanted to absorb every minute with him, not let any moment go wasted, and feared he would return to Garden House after their tea. Thus, she jumped at his request to sketch her. A request she had not expected from him. She should have, though. He certainly possessed the hands of an artist—long-fingered, strong yet elegant, nimble and wonderfully deft.

Their fortnight had slipped by too quickly, passing in a whirl of blazing passion and comfortable companionship. Why couldn't those days have been like all the others in the last five years? Stretching infinitely long. Seconds feeling like minutes. Minutes like hours. She should have stopped and savored them. But they were gone, and now all she could do was soak up their remaining hours, commit them to memory, and never let them fade.

She glanced up to find him studying her. His legs were stretched out before him, the book on his lap, elbows resting casually on the arms of the chair, the pencil held loosely in his long fingers. "Are you done?"

He flashed her a grin. "That's not a question a man likes to hear from a woman's lips. But yes, I'm done."

"So soon?" Five minutes could not have passed. She was sure of it.

He chuckled, a low rumble she felt in her bones. "Again, not a question a man wants to ever hear. But in my defense, I took at least twenty minutes. And yes, I'm done."

Suddenly impatient, she dropped the hoop on the settee. "I want to see it."

When she stood, he tipped the book up, shielding his work.

"Please. Show me."

"I warned you once. I'm not very good. Haven't sketched in ages. It was more of a childhood hobby than anything."

Poor man, he looked so very uncertain. She wanted to reassure him, to tell him she was certain it was wonderful. But she sensed in the tight line of his broad shoulders that such a straightforward approach would not be welcome. Instead she feathered her fingertips over his lips trying to erase the mulish frown. "Please."

His gaze testing, he glared up at her. Bella waited, hoping she had earned at least a bit of his trust at some point over the last thirteen days. At that moment, it was more important to her than anything that he trust her enough to show her the picture, to share something more of himself than his body and his conversation skills.

His broad chest rose and fell on a deep breath. He let the book fall onto his lap.

She did not know what she had expected, but the sketch took her breath away, his raw talent evident by the sweeping, purposeful lines. He had drawn her not seated in the sitting room, but in the garden on one of the weathered benches that lined the center. The bushes behind her were dotted with roses in full bloom. Her expression serene, yet the look in her eyes was one of burgeoning passion. She could imagine herself there in his picture. It was exactly how she would look if he was walking toward her.

"It's . . . it's . . . remarkable."

A faint blush stained the crests of his cheekbones. Her heart swelled, seeming to fill her entire being. She blinked, trying to keep the tears pricking her eyes from falling.

"Dinner tonight?" he asked.

"Pardon?"

"Am I to be your guest?" He looked up at her inquiringly. Every trace of discomposure, of self-consciousness, gone.

"Oh, yes." Bella shook her head, rattled more by his abrupt change in demeanor than by the change of topic. "Six. As usual."

"Well then, I shall leave you to dress." He stood, tipped his head, and strode from the room.

She bent to pick up the book, intending to place it back on the bookshelf beside her desk. She frowned. The sketch was gone. He must have taken it with him.

Even though she had wanted to keep it, she smiled, very willing to relinquish her claim on it to the artist himself.

THE fire in the hearth had burned down to embers. A single candle on the bedside table was all that lit the room. Deep shadows obscured everything beyond her four-poster bed, cloaking her and Gideon in a world she did not want to leave.

Impatient lust sated, Bella could simply luxuriate in being with him, spooned together, her back pressed against the hard wall of his chest. One arm draped over her waist, he held her close. Her hand rested over his, their fingers lightly intertwined. The tips of her toes grazed his calves. Wrapped in velvety warm comfort, she let out a small sigh, wanting to remain in his embrace forever.

He slipped his hand out from under hers to slowly caress her thigh. The strong body behind her shifted to move in for the final kiss he would lay on her exposed neck.

Trepidation shortened her breaths. She stiffened. The moment had arrived. The moment when he left her bed. Maybe it was because he would be leaving on the morrow, but tonight, more than any night, she wanted him to stay. And tonight, she found the courage to say the word.

"Stay."

Gideon pressed his lips to her neck, his answer in the infinitesimal shake of his head.

She persisted. "Stay."

"No." The word was the faintest of whispers, more breath than sound.

Reaching out a hand, she turned to face him. "Yes. Stay."

He pulled back. Not enough to be out of reach, but enough for her hand to drop to the rumpled sheet. "I cannot."

His response gave her pause. She pushed up onto a straight arm and tilted her head. "Cannot or will not?" There was a critical difference. "Cannot" implied forces beyond his control. "Will not" meant he was choosing to leave her.

He levered up onto an elbow. "Bella. Don't."

"Yes. Stay."

"You don't know what you're asking."

The frustrated edge tightening his words doused the last lingering bit of postorgasmic languor infusing her limbs. "Yes, I do. I want you to stay. Don't leave."

Regret flashed briefly across his face before hardening with conviction. "I must."

"Why? I want you to stay, Gideon," she pleaded, sounding like the most desperate of women to her own ears. The need for him to remain with her wiped away every worry she ever had about his profession and his visit. Stirling and Phillip no longer mattered. They no longer occupied even a tiny space in her mind. All that mattered was to convince Gideon to stay.

His brow furrowed. Whisky brown eyes sharpened. "For how long, Bella?"

She swallowed hard. "You don't need to leave. Remain with me." *I love you. Don't leave.* Somehow she kept the full truth from tumbling from her lips

"What do you plan to do when your husband returns? Shall I hide in Garden House and sneak up to your bedchamber at night? Will you keep me like one of your horses, just waiting to be trotted out of the stables whenever you deign to take me for a ride?"

"No!" she said, shocked he would think such a thing.

"Then what are you asking?"

"I want you to stay with me. You don't need to leave." She didn't want to think about the consequences. She just needed him to stay.

"I. Must."

She sensed she was within a word's space of discovering the limit of his patience. His unyielding stance hit like a mighty hammer to her fragile heart. "Don't you want to stay?" She gasped, left breathless from voicing the question.

The look he gave her clearly said she did not understand. The patronizing edge unleashed her anger. Hot and swift, it rushed unchecked through her veins, mixing violently with the desolation, turning her into someone she did not recognize. "You're leaving me for someone else, aren't you? You can't stay because you have some other woman's bed to crawl into."

A muscle ticked along his clenched jaw. "Bella, don't."

"That's it, isn't it?"

"Bella." His tone was low, a warning to stop.

But she couldn't. She knew she was getting hysterical, but she could not stop herself. Shaking with uncontrollable jealousy, she sat up and glared at him. "Who is she?"

Sitting up, he swung his legs over the edge of the bed.

"What will it take, Gideon? What will it take for you to choose me over her? Name your price," she demanded to the tight lines of his sculpted back.

There was a short, tense, thick pause, filled only by the soft thump of one of the burnt logs shifting in the fireplace.

He bowed his head, exposing the taut tendons of his neck. His fists clenched into the rumpled sheet. "Goddamn you, Bella."

The tone of the softly spoken curse startled her. The anger was easily detected, but beneath it she sensed genuine hurt. "Gideon?"

She reached out to the hard bulk of his bicep. The tips of her fingers grazed silken skin.

He strode swiftly across the room, his clothes and boots in hand.

Oh, dear Lord, what have I done? She scrambled to the edge of the bed. "Gideon, wait!"

He did not pause, but continued out.

The sharp slam of the door shattered what was left of her heart.

Eleven

DONNING his clothes quickly was a skill Gideon had mastered long ago, but tonight he did it in an exceptionally short amount of time.

She should count herself fortunate I even dressed. He pulled the door shut. The slam echoed in the empty corridor. It was tempting indeed to stalk out of the house naked as the day he was born. There was an unholy need burning in the pit of his stomach to flaunt the truth behind his stay at Bowhill. Yet through sheer ingrained habit, he had found himself tugging on his trousers. From there, it had been only a matter of seconds to throw on the remainder of his clothes.

His strides harsh, he descended the stairs. His hands shook with barely suppressed anger as he tied his cravat in a poor excuse for a knot.

Didn't she understand? Even if they did not have a husband, even if they were widows, he never spent the entire night in their bed and *never* slept beside them. It would be too much intimacy. They would be too easily confused.

He gave a snort of derision. Like sleeping beside Bella would have made matters any worse. That she had asked him to stay screamed loud and clear she did not understand the basic rules of their liaison. No sleeping together, no personal conversations, French letters were not an option but a requirement, and the length of the appointment was decided in advance. They were the rules, damn it, and they had to be preserved. Could not be broken, not for anyone.

And he could not believe she had stooped that low. To throw money at him, as if it alone could buy his complete submission. *Damn her!*

At the distant sound of footfalls mingling with his own on the marble floor of the entrance hall, Gideon glanced over his shoulder. A tall, sturdy woman clad entirely in black walked down the hall leading to the back of the house. He turned on his heel. "Mrs. Cooley."

Bella's housekeeper stopped and turned. Her eyes flared, obviously shocked at his state of undress. He had made it down the stairs before he could attack the buttons on his waistcoat and jacket. Her mouth thinned.

Servants never failed to pass up an opportunity to let him know, no matter how subtle or obvious, what they truly thought of him when their mistress was out of sight. He believed himself long immune. Yet the condescension on her face, the sneer of distaste twisting her mouth, cut sharper and deeper than a decade ago when a butler had shown him into a lady's home for his first appointment outside of Rubicon's brothel.

She could not know for certain he was a prostitute, and likely only assumed he was a gentleman, an acquaintance of some sort of her ladyship's. The "cousin" ruse was now totally up. Yet it was enough that *he* knew the truth. He wished he had taken the time to put himself together before leaving the sitting room. He was acutely aware that his hair was likely standing on end, disheveled by Bella's greedy fingers.

Gideon shoved aside the impulse to offer up an excuse for his hasty appearance and called upon the anger still pounding hard and fast through his veins, directing it at this haughty servant. "Have a carriage readied for London and sent to Garden House. Immediately."

She glared at him. Then she nodded once, curt and short.

He yanked open the door. But instead of walking out, he paused to glance over his shoulder, up the stairs, toward Bella's bedchamber. And the anger vanished. Gone. Leaving only . . .

He winced against the unidentifiable force gnawing at his chest.

It was over. This appointment was done. And his parting words assured she would never seek him out again.

His shoulders slumped as he let out a heavy exhale. Closing the front door carefully, he left Bella's house.

THE news her traveling carriage had returned from London jolted Bella from the painful indecision that gripped her for the past week. After turning the lock on her sitting room door, she sat at her writing desk, pulled out two sheets of crisp white paper, dipped her pen in the inkwell, and began writing. The first letter was easy—it contained a thank-you to Esmé.

The second letter was more difficult.

With the black tip of her pen poised half an inch from the unmarred white paper, she sat still as a statue for half an hour before writing out the three-line missive. Then she folded Esmé's note and tucked it away at the back of a drawer. The second letter was folded as well, but left just inside the drawer, for it was not ready to be sent yet.

Focusing on her goal, she went down to the first floor. She wrinkled her nose at the musky scent as she entered the study. The room was rarely used, and when inhabited, it was usually by Bowhill's secretary, Mr. Leighton. As she locked the door, she shook her head at the papers and account ledgers littering the surface of the large walnut desk. Mr. Leighton's previous piques of temper over any attempts at organization had prompted the servants to leave this room off their regular cleaning schedule. Bella had witnessed the man's last fit and had had to fight back the laughter that had threatened at the sight of the short, rotund older man, gesturing wildly, huffing in indignation, and mumbling under his breath about how he would never find what he needed in the recently tidied stacks of paper.

Stepping through the narrow beams of sunlight streaming through the breaks in the closed curtains, Bella crossed the room and rounded the desk. Purposefully averting her gaze from the portrait, she tugged on the corner of the heavy gilt frame. The portrait swung on its concealed hinges, revealing a small steel door. After unlocking the door, she opened it. Various documents, some rolled up and others in neat stacks, filled the majority of the space. Careful not to disturb the loaded dueling pistol at the back of the safe, she pushed aside the documents and after many long minutes of debate, counted out a large stack of pound notes.

Her quarry in hand, she shut the door and swung the portrait back against the wall, hiding the safe. She grabbed a blank sheet of paper from the disorder on the desk and wrapped it around the pound notes. She made to leave the study, but a prickle on the back of her neck turned her around when she was only halfway to the door.

A middle-aged man with dark blue eyes stared back at her from the portrait. His auburn hair was combed back, revealing features that could shift from passably handsome to downright ugly in a heartbeat. He was seated in a leather armchair, yet the sheer breadth of his shoulders told one he possessed the substantial frame of a pugilist.

Her pulse quickened, short beats filling her ears. Her breaths turned shallow, little pulls that did not quite reach her lungs. He was not even here, and she was infinitely thankful for that, yet just looking at him had the most disturbing effect on her. She swore he had the portrait hung over the wall safe deliberately—a constant reminder of whose money lay beyond the steel door. He had never specifically forbid her anything. Setting rules, expectations, was a kindness he did not bestow upon her. But she knew. Knew without a glimmer of uncertainty if he ever learned of what she planned to do, never mind what she had already done, his reaction would be most unpleasant indeed.

Paper crinkled as she tightened her grip on the stack of pound notes, drawing strength from the proof of her defiance. She met the dark blue stare, her gaze now hard and steady.

"I hate you," she whispered, her mouth twisting with the need to shout, to scream, to unleash all the pent-up hate she had forced herself not to acknowledge for so long.

She turned on her heel, dismissing her husband in a way she would never dare to do in his presence, and marched out of the study. She passed her housekeeper in the entrance hall.

"Mrs. Cooley, send Seamus to my sitting room," Bella said as she ascended the stairs.

A burly young man with a forever-untidy shock of red hair appeared in her sitting room minutes later.

"Yes, your ladyship?"

"I need you to take the traveling coach and return to London, to where Madame Marceau located Mr. Rosedale." She held out her carefully written letter made thick by the pound notes enclosed within. "Give this to the proprietor, await a response, and return with Mr. Rosedale posthaste."

"Yes, your ladyship."

To Bella's great relief, Seamus did not question her, nor did he hesitate to take the letter. The rebellion that had seized hold in the study, gifting her with the strength she needed to see this task through, started to wane, and it took considerable effort to keep her composure in place.

Seamus tipped his head and left the room.

Then she waited two very long weeks.

IT was midafternoon when Gideon entered his employer's office, his mood already soured from having been summoned by one of her minions.

"Do come in and have a seat, Mr. Rosedale," Rubicon purred. She waved a hand to one of the scarlet leather chairs facing her desk.

His senses sharpened. She never called him Mr. Rosedale. It was usually *Rosedale* or *Gideon*, depending on her mood, and *Mr. Gideon Rosedale* when she was flaunting him in front of clients. His only greeting was a tip of his head before settling in the chair.

She appraised him for a long moment, the look shrewd and cunning. A look that made his skin crawl. "You have quite the admirer, Mr. Rosedale."

His face purposefully blank, he said nothing.

"Pack your trunk."

"Excuse me?"

"You have an appointment and, judging by the driver who delivered the *request*, you are headed back to Scotland."

She waived a sheet of folded white paper. He leaned forward and snatched it from her. The sight of the flowing feminine script made his heart leap. Then he read the words.

Mr. Rosedale's company is requested for the space of a fortnight. Inform the driver when Mr. Rosedale will be available to depart. If the enclosed is not sufficient, send word back with the driver.

He swore he felt something inside of him rip in two. "How much?" he asked, hating the hollow tone.

A slow, satisfied smile spread across Rubicon's rouged lips. "I do so love how you leave them wanting more. But really, Mr. Rosedale, you haven't even been gone three weeks."

"How much?" He balled his hand into a fist, the crisp edges of the paper scoring his palm.

"It makes me wonder if I should raise your price. I hope I haven't been giving you away all these years."

His tolerance of her constant games was running extremely thin. "How much?" he said through clenched teeth.

She tossed a thick envelope across the desk. "That's for you."

Gideon quickly looked inside. Rubicon took half off the top, but what was in that envelope . . .

He tossed it back with a sharp snap of the wrist. "Send someone else. I already have arrangements and they can't be broken."

"Not to worry. I've already broken them for you. Markus is, at this moment, traveling to Devon to give her ladyship your regrets."

"What?" The word snapped out of his mouth on an affronted bark. How dare she rearrange his schedule without his consent? And how the hell had she known where he was headed?

"You can see her some other time as you will be in Scotland until the end of the month."

"No."

Her eyes narrowed to thin slits. Her face hardened, revealing the lines around her mouth and on her forehead she tried so hard to conceal with artfully applied makeup. "Yes. Go pack. You are leaving today. The carriage is waiting to depart posthaste." The teasing, toying lilt was gone. The words held an edge sharpened with unyielding command.

The game had ended and he had not come out the victor. A low, defensive growl shook his throat. He snatched the envelope off Rubicon's desk and stalked from the room.

"Oh, and Mr. Rosedale, do be so kind as to leave her wanting more again," she called to his retreating back, a noticeable chuckle of triumph in her voice.

THE light scratch of a knife and the soft click of a fork against porcelain were the only sounds that broke the silence. *Is he still upset with me?* Bella brought the glass of wine to her lips. Should she have waited longer to have Gideon return?

No. She had needed to see him, needed to be with him again. The prior four weeks had passed by slower than the previous five years. The stark contrast of her life without him had physically hurt. And the way he had left, the things she had said. Mrs. Cooley reported he had left that night, not even waiting until morning. He had not been able to get away from her fast enough.

But he had come back, so he could not be too displeased with her. Still, he was much more distant than he had been at previous dinners. His eyes had only met hers a handful of times and his conversation was so stilted and impersonal she had given up any attempts before they walked into the dining room. He gave the distinct impression of a man going through the motions. The warmth that had once radiated from him was frighteningly gone.

She needed to talk with him, apologize, assure him she would never make such demands again. That she understood she should not make such demands. But even though silence reigned, his impassive face did not give her the opening she so desperately needed.

The neat slices of roasted pheasant on her plate looked divine, but the tension knotting her stomach made it impossible for her to bring a small square to her lips. Gideon's appetite was not much better. The little mound of peas on his plate had yet to be disturbed and only one of the three slices of pheasant had been cut into.

The footman picked up the silent cue and cleared the last course. With a tight flick of his fingers and a sharp glance, Gideon dismissed the servant. The dining room door clicked shut, and before the sound could fade into nothingness, he spoke. "Is dinner over?"

"Yes," she responded, perplexed by the obvious.

He nodded once. "Have the carriage readied. I wish to depart for London tonight."

She went utterly still. Her pulse pounded swiftly in her ears. "Pardon?"

"Your terms still hold, do they not?" The nasty edge in the challenge chilled the surrounding air.

A shiver gripped her shoulders. Eyes wide, she nodded.

"Dinner is over. My obligation has been fulfilled. I wish to leave."

"But-but why did you come all the way up here if you had no intention of staying?"

"Why? There was no choice involved. Your *request* was a very thinly veiled command that I drop everything and hop in your waiting carriage."

"But—?"

"For Christ's sake, Bella, five hundred pounds? What were you thinking?"

Oh no. It had not been enough. The bottom dropped out of her stomach. "But Seamus never said a word," she said, leaning forward in the chair. "I wrote to have the driver notified if it wasn't sufficient."

"Not sufficient? It was too much," he said, incredulous and indignant, as though she had delivered the highest insult.

"What?" The word was an exhale that slumped her spine. The blood drained from her face.

"And I can't believe you wrote directly to Rubicon." Disappointment layered with sharp disdain pulled his beautiful mouth into an ugly sneer.

"But, who—?" Her mouth worked soundlessly, her mind seized with shock. She dropped her gaze to the barren white linen tablecloth. Forcing each breath, she struggled to project a calm façade, to erect a safe wall behind which she could hide.

She had gone and done it again. But this time it had not been in a fit of anger and jealousy. Somehow she had deeply offended him. And the way he looked at her . . . The pain of being separated from him was nothing compared to this agony lancing her chest. She tried to swallow down the threat of tears, but it felt as if there were thorns lodged in her throat. Nothing had ever hurt like this before. She would take Stirling over this any day. Those were wounds that healed, but this one . . .

It hurt too much, too much to bear.

With as much poise as she could manage, she stood and left the dining room while she still had the strength to do it.

GIDEON stewed in a noxious mixture of indignation, anger, and wounded male pride. He heard the light tap of footsteps quicken and fade as Bella walked down the hall. The sound muffled once she reached the stairs. The faint sound of a door clicking shut snapped him to his senses.

"Holy Mother . . . Bloody hell!" Had he absolutely no tact? He could not believe he had just yelled at her—Bella. The woman who never raised her voice above polite levels unless she was demanding more or pleading with him to stay in her bed. And that parting glance she had given him—he had pierced her very soul.

Gideon pushed back from the table and darted after her. Senses focused on her, he did not give a glance to the maid in the hall or the butler standing guard at the front door. The stairs were devoured in seconds and he was skidding to a halt outside her sitting room. He turned the knob but the door would not open.

He jangled the knob in frustration. "Bella? Bella?"

A quick press of his ear to the door revealed nothing. She must be in her bedchamber, most likely behind another locked door. He quickly appraised the brass knob but he had never learned to pick a lock and did not think it best to attempt his first try tonight.

His looked to the right and left, and glanced over his shoulder. Then he surveyed the corridor again, studying the doors, the distance between each and their relative positions. If Bowhill was anything like every other country house he had been in, then there was another way into her bedchamber. Gideon crossed to the door directly opposite Bella's and found it unlocked. Focused only on the doors he needed to pass through to get to Bella, he did not glance about but walked quickly through first one door then another.

After opening a third narrower door, he went straight forward though a dark room. One hand out to the side to guide his way. Silk, cashmere, and fine wool folded on shelves tickled his fingertips. The other hand stretched out in front until it encountered cool wood and a smooth round knob. He turned the knob and pushed open the unlocked door.

Compared to the pitch darkness of the dressing room, the moonlit bedchamber was quite bright. He spotted her crumpled on the floor a few paces from the ornate four-poster bed with its tapestry hangings. Her amethyst skirt looked like black silk pooled around her. Her bowed pale blonde head glowed silvery blue in the moonlight streaming in from the tall windows. Her quiet sobs struck him straight in the heart.

The thick rugs silenced his footsteps as he slowly approached. Dropping to his knees, he crooned, "Oh, Bella, please, Bella, don't cry."

She gave a start when his hand settled on her back. "Gideon, I'm sorry. I didn't mean . . . I didn't know." The soft words caught on her sobs.

"Please don't be upset," he begged, rubbing her back in large soothing circles.

"I just needed . . . I'm so sorry, Gideon."

"No, don't be. You needn't be. Oh, Bella, I shouldn't have railed at you. It's not your fault."

She pushed up onto her knees and turned to face him. Her violet eyes were thick with tears. Her beautiful face a canvas of sorrow. "I just needed—"

"Shh." An unexpected, indefinable burst shot through his body the moment he wrapped his arms around her thin frame. She leaned into him, pressing her cheek against his waistcoat, hiding her face. "I know. I understand. Please, please don't cry. I should have told you how to contact me, where to write. I shouldn't have been angry with you," he whispered into her ear.

Gideon had been in such a state when he had left her that he had forgotten to leave a note with the address. He never had them go through Rubicon. He had earned the right, the privilege, many years ago to manage his own affairs. There would always be a discreet envelope awaiting him in his separate room when he arrived at a client's home. And when the appointment was over, he would take half to Rubicon. Well, more often, send her half. The less he saw of her the better. The less he walked into that establishment the better.

But Bella had been unique. She hadn't originally written to Rubicon or visited. A close friend had not referred her to him either. And the French woman who'd secured his services had paid Rubicon. Bella had been left out of the specifics. Everything had been arranged for her. She would have had no idea how to contact him directly, or how much was insultingly too much, what all the niceties were, the etiquette as it may, for hiring a male prostitute.

Heavy guilt pulled at his chest. None of it had been her fault. He had directed his anger at the wrong source, and hurt her, Bella, in the process.

He leaned back to wipe the tears from her pale cheeks with the pads of his thumbs. Christ, she was beautiful even when she cried. With tears usually came red, runny noses and puffy, swollen eyes. But not Bella. He lowered his lips to hers and begged for her forgiveness the only way he knew how.

She instantly deepened the light kiss and brought her arms around his neck to hold him tight. Gideon felt the instant when her passion ignited. The deep kisses turned greedy, her movements became tight, jerky, and demanding as she nestled closer to him, straddling his hips.

He gave her a moment. A moment for her to kiss him as she wanted. To do with him as she pleased. A moment for him not to be the one in control. To simply experience the full force of Bella's ardent kiss.

Then with his lips never leaving hers, he gathered her in his arms, stood, set her down on the edge of the bed, and dropped to his knees. This was Bella—there was no gentleness as he shoved her skirt up to her waist, pushed her thighs wider, and settled his mouth on her pink, wet flesh. He plied her with light flicks of his tongue, soft presses of his lips, and teasing grazes of his teeth, as he slipped first one finger inside her, and then another. Her body gripped his fingers tightly and he grunted against her clit, his cock swelling to painful proportions.

Within no time at all she came on a rapturous moan. Her back arching, fingers tangling in his hair, legs spreading wider. But he did not crawl up her body. He stayed right were he was, pleasuring her until he threw her over the edge again.

Those fingers in his hair turned rough, pulling almost to the point of yanking. "Gideon, please. I need—"

She groaned, then sucked in a swift breath as he eased yet another finger into her, alternating between thrusting and wiggling, hitting those perfect spots deep inside her. She rocked her hips in counterpoint, an urgent rhythm his cock knew only too well.

"Gideon." The word was ripped from her throat on another climax. She pulled his hair again, hard. Her silk-clad legs wrapped around his back, heels pressing upward on his shoulder blades. "Please."

But he ignored the demand, refused the request—determined to make her come again and again and again, until she could take no more. To give to her the one thing that was in his power to offer her.

"Gideon. Please. *Fuck me.*"

This time it was he who shuddered, he who groaned. That crude command from her lips—it almost, almost, *almost* made him break the unbreakable rule. He tore at the falls of his trousers, one button undone, before he regained his senses.

He cursed himself, cursed the spite that had made him bring not even one French letter with him. He had absolutely no intention of bedding her when he went to the manor house, had every intention of leaving immediately after dinner. His trunk hadn't even been unpacked, but still stood inside the door of Garden House. That spite was now keeping him from the one thing he wanted, from the one thing he needed.

He knew the raw desire consuming him had nothing to do with the past four weeks of celibacy. It had everything to do with *her*. He needed to feel her lithe body writhe against his own, her nails score his back, her long legs wrap around his hips. But, damn it!

He wanted to howl at the injustice of it all, but also could not allow her to suffer for his misplaced spite. So he intensified his efforts, using all the skills he had acquired over the past thirteen years, since he had lost his virginity at age fourteen, to wring every last orgasm from her body.

Bella did not want to be denied. She persisted, repeating those two words again and again, until it was all he could hear, even above the pounding rhythm of his heart and his labored breaths, pushing him to a point he did not know he had, until he could take no more. Until he had to silence her lest the next "fuck me" drove him beyond rational thought and beyond control.

He lifted his head. "No." The refusal was harsh, guttural, abrupt.

She went still. Startled violet eyes met his.

"I can't," he added at the injured look finding its way onto her face.

"Why not? I need you, Gideon."

Her heavy pants filled the room. He was so close every breath he took was filled with the sweet scent of her body. The taste of her fresh on his tongue, his lips wet from her.

"I can't. Not tonight, Bella. Just let me pleasure you."

He could tell she did not understand, could tell she was starting to see this as some sort of punishment, retribution, revenge for her summons. The lean muscles of her thighs went rigid under his splayed hands. On a wince, she averted her gaze.

"I didn't bring . . . I don't have with me . . ." He took a deep breath, struggling to gather his thoughts, to gather the words. "I left them at Garden House."

She looked back at him. "Left what?"

"Sheaths. French letters. I won't take you without one."

"I don't care, Gideon. I need you." With one arm braced behind her, she reached out to cup his jaw.

He soaked up her caress. Her small, warm hand. Her fingers resting gently on his pounding pulse. Then denied her again. "No, Bella."

This was what he had tried to avoid. He had wanted to wring so many orgasms out of her she would be too lax and sated to do anything but fall asleep in her bed. Bella was inherently spoiled. A beautiful woman was not accustomed to refusal. And he almost gave in again. But not for his own needs, but to stem the fight, the test of wills, he knew would ensue.

"Please, Gideon. It doesn't matter. I want you. I want to feel you, skin against skin, just once. Please." Even in the darkness he could read the plea in her stark and honest gaze.

Sex without protection was unthinkable—the risks were too high. There were other methods to prevent conception, but the lust and need drumming though his veins warned now was not the time to attempt his first try at a well-timed withdrawal. And he knew at that moment he could not risk it just to avoid the possibility of getting her with child, but because he could not risk the intimacy. And not just the risk of her confusing their respective roles, but of him as well.

"No, Bella," he repeated before she could tempt him anew. There was a definite note of regret in his low tone, and he did not try to disguise it. "Please don't insist. I can't. I won't. Tonight let me give you pleasure, and tomorrow you can have it all."

On his knees and completely at her mercy, he held his breath, fearful she would persist. Or worse yet, take his refusal the wrong way. Or even worse, dismiss him.

Holding his wary gaze, she nodded. "Tomorrow," she whispered.

A relieved smile spread across his face. "Tomorrow."

Then he made good on his promise.

Twelve

LEAN over."

Gideon's words tickled her ear. The heat of him warmed her back. Gooseflesh rose up her arms. Her insides quivered. Keeping her face purposefully blank, Bella complied.

"More." When she did not immediately heed his command, he added, "It was your suggestion to fill the afternoon. If you don't want to play . . ."

Resting her forearms on the green felt, she bent over at the waist. "Like this?" She glanced over her shoulder, eyebrows raised in mock hauteur.

His sinfully dark gaze lingered on her derrière. His lips curved in an appreciative half smile. "Perfect."

She wanted to arch her back, rotate her hips, invite him to play a different game. Instead she looked ahead before her impulses got the better of her.

He leaned over her, resting a hand beside her elbow. She closed her eyes and took a slow breath. Just the scent of him made her pulse race, but to have him behind her like this . . . Bella swallowed.

"Now then, take this." Wrapping an arm around her, he held out a long wooden stick.

She shifted her weight, pushing up onto one hand and pushing back into his broad chest, to take the cue stick. The highly polished wood was cool to the touch.

"Not like that. Like this." He reached full around her, his arms bracketing hers. His hair brushed her ear. She let her hands go slack, allowing him to reposition them. "One at the end to provide the thrust. The other at the middle to guide. No, no. Don't grab it. Curl your index finger and thumb around the stick, but loosely. You need to be able to freely slide it between your fingers. See."

Placing his hands over hers, he moved the stick back and forth a few times. The smooth wood slid between her fingers, bringing to mind the way *he* slid between her fingers, though she would never be able to hold him between two fingers like this. Gideon put the thin cue stick to shame. The image of his magnificent cock sprang into her head. She suppressed a moan as a wave of lust washed over her. Her innermost muscles tightened, recalling how perfect it felt to be impaled upon his cock. The impressive length. The substantial width. The hard, heavy thrusts that sparked orgasm after orgasm. Yesterday evening he had made good on his promise of two nights ago, and then some. She had been so exhausted she could not even remember his last kiss before he slipped out of her bed.

But she had awoken this morning invigorated and wanting more. The masculine billiard room with its heavy velvet curtains drawn closed to keep in the warmth of the fire blazing in the hearth provided an ideal indoor location for an afternoon tryst. But first, she really did want to learn how to play the game.

With that thought in mind, she did her best to ignore the way the hard muscles of Gideon's body surrounded her. The buttons of his navy coat grazed her lower back. His long legs bracketed hers.

"I think I've got it now," she said, trying to project the manner of a proper student.

Air cooled the backs of her hands as he released them. Bracing his weight on a straight arm, he positioned the ivory ball a hand's space in front of her stick. "All right then. Next step. Slide the cue stick back and forth a few times as you aim for one of the red balls at the end of the table. Then, with a good snap of your elbow, strike the ball."

He rested his other hand on her hip. Sensation rippled through her body. She wanted him to grab her hips with both hands, to hold her steady for his powerful thrusts. To slam into her with all the force of his lower body. On a short indrawn breath, she squeezed her eyes shut to regain her composure. But as she focused again on the path between the two balls, a draught of air hit her lower legs, pulling her mind from the game and to Gideon as he slowly gathered her skirt.

"Remember, don't grab the stick so tightly. You need it to slide easily toward its target."

She forced her fingers to unclench then gripped the cue stick anew as his fingertips brushed her outer thigh and curved in to tickle the sensitive skin of her inner thigh. An anticipatory jolt shook her body, lust spiking her senses.

"Relax," he said softly.

The way he was nuzzling her neck was not helping her efforts. A mix of chills and desire chased over her skin and rushed down to settle at her core. With the lightest of touches, he brushed the damp hair covering her mound. Reflexively, she went up onto her toes then sank slowly down. His finger parted the folds of her sex. She let out a low moan.

"Are you going to hit the ball or not?" he asked, as casual as could be, as if he did not have his hand up her skirt, teasing her drenched core.

Forcing deep, even breaths, she lined up the shot and drew the stick back. As soon as the smack of the felt-covered tip against the ivory ball rent the air, she planted her palms on the billiard table and hung her head.

"Damn, you're wet. How long have you been like this?"

His blunt words added to the decadent sensations coiling tight in her belly. "Since you walked in the front door," she managed to get out between short panting breaths. "And you know it."

He chuckled, full of smug male pride. He might sound unaffected, but from the corner of her eye she could see his biceps bulge beneath his coat sleeve. The tendons on the back of the large hand splayed on the green felt were taut. He nipped at her exposed neck, his heavy breaths scorching her skin.

Rounding her shoulders, she rocked into his caress, increasing the pressure on her clit to a maddening level. An orgasm tickled the edge of her mind. She rotated her hips, rubbing against his groin, pressing the hard arch of his manhood erotically between the two halves of her bottom. The sensations gathered. Her nerves tightened to an unbearable level.

He removed his hand. Her skirt whooshed down her legs.

"Don't stop!" she gasped, glancing over her shoulder.

"Oh, I'm just getting started." He winked.

Paper crinkled. Fabric rustled. He gathered her skirt at her waist, baring her to his view. She arched like an eager tart, lifting her bottom, widening her stance. *God*, it felt so wicked to be bent over the billiard table.

He grasped her hip. Her breaths stuttered in anticipation as his cock nudged the entrance to her body. As soon as the broad head made the breech, she pushed back, eager for more. Eager for his hard thrusts. Eager to come on his cock.

He held her steady. "Wait. Until I'm all the way in."

"But—?"

"You're so tight, I don't want to hurt you," he murmured, eyebrows lowered with concern.

Frustrated, she shook her head, but held still. He rocked, pushing slowly, easing in, stretching her delicate flesh. She trembled, impatient and needy, wanting it all. *Now.* Her eyelids fluttered. Her swollen clit throbbed, sending heavy pulses throughout her body. Her climax so close . . .

A knock sounded on the door.

Gideon snapped his head up. He froze, buried almost hilt deep inside of Bella, her innermost muscles gripping his cock like a fist.

"Lady Stirling?" came her butler's voice, muffled by the thick door.

"Fuck," he cursed under his breath. The interruption could not possibly have come at a worse time.

"Oh no!" Dread soaked her whispered exclamation.

He stepped back, flipped her skirts down over her delectable bottom and turned her around. "Bella?" he whispered urgently as he whipped off the French letter. Suppressing a wince, he shoved his hard cock into his breeches. Her face was pale, her eyes wide, her breaths coming in shallow, quick pants. "You have to open the door. Now."

She closed her eyes. The long column of her neck worked as she swallowed. Then she nodded. Her lashes swept up, the cool composure in place. Smoothing a hand over her hair, she walked serenely to the door.

His hands shook as he buttoned his breeches. He grabbed Bella's discarded cue stick and the ivory ball, leaned over the table and set up a shot.

She opened the door revealing her haughty butler. "Yes, McGreevy?" she asked, her shoulders ramrod straight and her tone all bored condescension.

"You have a caller. Mrs. Tavisham."

"See her to the drawing room."

"Yes, your ladyship." McGreevy's gaze flittered to Gideon. His thin nostrils flared.

Gideon lifted one eyebrow then took aim. The ivory cue ball whizzed across the green felt, connecting sharply with the red ball and sending it into the corner pocket.

The butler turned on his heel. His footsteps echoed and faded as he walked down the hall.

Bella closed the door, turned, and sagged against it. Eyes closed, she pressed a hand over her mouth.

He dropped the stick and rushed to her. "Are you all right?" He made to rub her shoulders, but with a harsh jerk, she shrugged him off.

"Don't touch me. You'll make it worse."

"Oh, Bella. I'm sorry. I-I promise, I'll make it up to you." His hands hovered over her thin shoulders. He wanted to touch her, to take her in his arms, to feather light kisses over her tightened brow, to soothe away her distress.

"I'll hold you to it." Her mouth twisted in a grimace. "I need to come so bad it hurts."

I know how you feel.

She glanced down his body, her gaze settling on his groin. His cock strained against the placket of his breeches. He had tried to will it down, but the effort had not yet produced the desired result. The scent of sex hung heavy in the air, a signal his body refused to ignore. There was no way her butler could have mistaken the scent for anything but.

"How did you get that in there?"

He gave a self-deprecating chuckle. "It was not pleasant. If it's any consolation, it aches something terrible."

She *harrumphed.* "Good."

"I had no idea you had such an evil side. Should I be worried?" he teased, needing to lighten her mood.

Her lips twitched with a hint of a smile. "No. Never." She took a deep breath and stepped from the door. "I shouldn't be long."

He tipped his head and reached around her to open the door, careful not to even brush her skirt with his forearm. Admiring the smooth sway of her hips, he watched her glide down the hall. He had seen her do it so many times, yet it still amazed him how quickly she could don the cool aristocratic mask. Just looking at her one would never know that minutes ago she had been writhing on his cock, her lush derrière lifted high, begging for more.

Gideon closed the door, blocking out the view. Closing his eyes, he clenched his jaw, willing away his erection. He had not been exaggerating—it ached something terrible. His ballocks were drawn up so tight it was beyond painful. And damn it, he had forgotten to lock the door when they entered the billiard room. Luckily, Bella had well-trained servants.

Frowning, he glanced about the room. He did not want to wait here, that was for sure. Without Bella by his side, he felt distinctly uncomfortable in the manor house, like an unwelcome guest who refused to leave.

He opened the door. Bella and her neighbor were in the drawing room, and judging by the way her soft melodic voice drifted down the hall, he guessed the door was open. He would have to slip out the back. The drawing room windows faced the side of the house, so they would not spot him walking through the back garden.

He stepped from the billiard room and was about to turn toward the kitchen when Bella's words caught his attention.

"You are too kind. Won't you stay for tea?"

He and Bella were supposed to have tea together and now she was offering his place to another. *I shouldn't be long*, he mouthed silently, suddenly sullen and grumpy. How quickly they forget. His shoulders slumped. He should be used to it by now, and he shouldn't be so disappointed—it was only tea. But . . .

He let out a dejected sigh. There was nothing he could do about it. When it was convenient, when she wanted him again, she'd seek him out.

He returned to the cottage and grabbed the *Times* off the dining table. After sprawling on the couch, he snapped open the paper. But the news did not hold his interest. With a weary sigh, he set the paper aside, located his deck of cards, sat at the dining table, and tried to focus on a game of patience.

Three games lost and zero won turned his mood even darker. He was about to swipe the cards from the table, let them scatter about the floor, announce defeat, when a knock sounded at the door. He pushed back from the table and went to see what the servant wanted.

"Bella."

She stood on his doorstep, smiling brightly. "Hello, Gideon. Aren't you going to invite me in?"

"Oh. Yes. Sorry," he mumbled. He stepped aside, allowing her to pass. Her appearance should have chased away the dark cloud hanging over his head, but strangely it did not. "To what do I owe the pleasure of this visit?"

She lingered by the armchair, trailing her fingers over the high back. He remained at the door. "I came to see you."

No. You want me to make you come. He tipped his head. "Thank you."

She studied him. "Gideon, are you all right?"

"Did your neighbor return home already?"

"Yes. She came by to deliver the Rose du Roi."

"Ah. Your delayed gift. Has it recovered from its journey from France?"

"Yes. I had one of the servants take the rose to the hothouse." She furrowed her brow. "Gideon, are you all right?"

"Why wouldn't I be? You're here." He pushed from the door and sauntered to her. "I seem to recall I made you a promise recently," he said, lowering his voice to a level he knew she liked.

"Well, yes, you did." She tipped her chin down. A blush colored her high cheekbones. "But I'll call it in later. I stopped by to ask if you wanted to come see my new rose."

He blinked.

She cocked her head, her beautiful face twisted in puzzlement. "Why do you look so surprised?"

He gathered his wits before she could stumble over the answer. "I'm merely pleased." And he was pleased, ridiculously so. He was certain he was grinning like an idiot. "Does your rose have any blooms yet? Or is it too young?"

She gazed up at him, eyes soft and shining with an emotion he could not place. But whatever it was, it made his stomach do an odd little flip. Then she surprised him further by lifting up onto her toes and pressing a light kiss to his lips, scrambling his wits anew.

"Come along. You can see for yourself," she said as she grabbed his hand, hanging limp at his side.

Still dazed, he allowed her to lead him from the cottage, no longer caring in the slightest that she had given his tea to another.

Thirteen

THE late May afternoon sun was high in the sky, bringing a strong hint of summer. It was so warm outside many of the hothouse windows had been opened to allow a fresh breeze to pass through. With scissors in one hand and a wicker basket at her feet, Bella carefully set to pruning another bush. Chinas did not require or want much in the form of pruning, but the bushes still needed some attention to keep them at their healthiest. With a snip of her scissors a spindly, weak offshoot was removed and dropped into the basket at her feet.

There were servants to see to the task, but she had found long ago that she enjoyed doing it herself. It was peaceful in the hothouse and it gave her something to do to while away the usually long, lonely days.

But today she was not alone. Nor had she been for the past ten days. With a glance to her left, her gaze fell on Gideon. As had become his habit when she was working in the hothouse, he was sprawled on the wooden bench situated along the dirt path, perusing the latest copy of the *Times*. One booted foot was on the ground, the other bent up on the bench, an elbow resting on his knee.

She had the distinct impression he enjoyed their lazy afternoons just as much as she did. It was so very easy to be with him. There were no inhibitions—she could just be herself. There was no fear he would think less of her if she behaved like an ill-bred tart. In fact, he encouraged her wicked side. But it was more than that. With Gideon came not only searing passion, but also a sense of comfort the likes of which she had not felt in years, like a warm, sun-filled blanket.

A soft sigh escaped her lips. He must have heard her for he looked up. A smile curved his lips. She gave him one in return, and then turned back to her roses.

She had wondered since she first laid eyes on him how he had come to be in his current profession. And as she had gotten to know him, as she had been fortunate enough to spend time with him, that curiosity had grown. In addition to being a perfect gentleman and a highly skilled and attentive lover, he was also an intelligent man. Surely someone of his caliber could have easily found a more respectable form of employment. And he did not strike her as inherently lazy. Gideon could have been a man of Quality—a lesser son. But somehow she thought he must be of common birth. Still, there were other avenues available to him, other means of employment, even if he did not wish to be a servant. Gideon as a footman? No—she could not imagine that.

It had not escaped her notice that he had a tendency to be closed-lipped about himself. Any time she had begun to ask him anything personal he steered the conversation so deftly elsewhere it would be several minutes later before she realized what he avoided.

But they were better acquainted now—she could feel the bond between them. Hoping it was strong enough, hoping he felt comfortable enough with her, she asked as casually as she could, her attention trained on the red bloom before her, "Gideon, how did you come to be a . . . companion? Why this?"

The only sound was the faint buzz of bees flittering from one bloom to the next.

Her shoulders tightened. She swallowed hard. "Pardon. You needn't answer if you don't wish. It's not at all well-done of me to pry," she said, fearful she had just committed a grave mistake and wishing she had not allowed her curiosity to get the better of her.

There was a rustle of paper as he set the *Times* down. After a long pause, he spoke, his voice casual with a shrug behind it. "I entered the family business. Seemed the thing to do."

She glanced over her shoulder at him, doubly shocked he answered and by his response. "Your parents know what you do? They condone it?"

"I assume my mother's aware," he said. "She left to live with a paramour years before, but she kept in contact with some of the other women. My father . . . his opinion matters not as I've never met the man."

"You don't know who your father is?"

"No. One of Christina's paramours, no doubt."

"Christina?"

"My mother," he clarified. "Though I seldom think of her as such. She's more the woman who happened to give birth to me. Christina was not made for children. Too high-strung, too pampered, to give much thought to anyone but herself. But I don't hold it against her. It's just who she is."

He was a bastard—the result of one of his mother's gentlemen. Bella had never met a by-blow before, but somehow Gideon was not what she would have expected. Since he had answered her first question, she decided to try a second one. "How does one become a . . ."

"A companion to ladies?" he finished for her.

She nodded.

"I grew up in a brothel," he said. "Well, I lived with an old aunt until I was seven, but I was not a calm seven and she was getting on in years. So after that I went to live with Christina, which was kind of her. She could have simply abandoned me, and fortunately, the owner of the brothel allowed me to stay. I kept out of the way and worked to earn my keep. Odd jobs, fetching things for the other women, tending the fires, and helping in the kitchen. And when I was old enough, I changed jobs. Couldn't fetch sweets for the women my whole life."

He made it sound so ordinary, as if his upbringing had been commonplace. "When?"

"When what?"

"Did you change positions?"

"Oh." His eyebrows pulled together as he thought for a moment. "About seventeen."

He had been but a boy. Outrage pounded through her veins. How could his mother have allowed that? He should have been in the schoolroom or at boarding school, not earning his living pleasuring women. He should have been chasing after girls his own age, not being hired by adult females. And what sort of person would employ a boy for work such as that?

Gideon must have read the indignation on her face, for he shook his head indulgently. The corners of his mouth pulled with a bemused smile. "It wasn't as horrible as you may think. Given my other options, my current line of work is much preferred."

"But surely there were other avenues available. A man such as yourself? You could do anything you put your mind to."

He gave her an odd look, one she could not define. "You don't approve?"

"Well, it's just . . ." Had she insulted him again? Discomposed, she looked down to the basket at her feet, then back up to him, gathering her courage. "I am very fortunate to have the pleasure of your company. I am infinitely glad to have met you and very grateful to Madame Marceau to have had her send you to me. It's not that I don't want you to be here, rather that there is more to you than this. Don't you wish for something more?"

His eyes widened. He dropped his foot from the bench to the gravel path and tugged at his jacket sleeve. "Of course I do. I-I want . . ."

Not meeting her eyes, he shook his head, his voice tailing off. But she was desperate to learn what it was this man wanted out of life.

What was important to *him*. The rigid set of his shoulders warned she had reached a point where he did not want to venture further. Yet she needed to know. "What do you want, Gideon?" she asked gently.

He looked to the paper lying beside his hip and toyed with a crisp corner. Just when she had given up on the answer, he spoke. "A wife. A family. But first, I need money. A whole lot of it."

"Whatever for?"

"What woman in her right mind would have me without it?"

I would. Her heart clenched at the defeat in his gruff tone.

"When I have enough, I'll buy a property in the country. One with a respectable income. And hopefully, it and my bank account will garner me a wife." He crossed one booted ankle over his knee and met her gaze. Every trace of discomposure was gone, as if it had never been there. "Who is Madame Marceau?"

It took a moment for her mind to adjust to the abrupt change in topic, but she recognized it for what it was—he did not want to discuss his future any longer. "My cousin. The lady who made the initial arrangements."

He nodded sagely. "Wondered who she was. Why would a lady's cousin arrange for a man such as myself?"

"She . . ." Bella's cheeks burned but she resisted the urge to glance away. "She believed I was in need of a flirtation. She is French; therefore, a flirtation cures all."

Gideon raised one dark eyebrow. "What was I to cure?"

"Madame Marceau believed I was getting much too maudlin."

"And are you cured?" The teasing lilt was gone. He asked as though he truly cared about the answer.

Bella tipped her chin, hiding under the wide brim of her straw hat. "When I'm with you, I am," she admitted.

Another spindly branch was quickly selected and clipped from the bush then dropped to the basket at her feet. She waited for him to ask why she had been maudlin. Waited for him to ask about Stirling. But the question she did not want to answer never came. Whether it was because he did not care or because he sensed her reluctance, she did not know. She only knew she was grateful for the silence, whatever the cause.

At length, she heard the rustle of paper as he picked up the *Times* and went back to perusing the news. It was many minutes later when her pulse finally slowed, when the tremble disappeared from her hands, when the tightness left her throat and she was again able to relax and enjoy just being with him. But it was not the same feeling she had but a half hour ago.

The questions she asked and the answers she received reminded her anew he would leave soon and go to another. Bless another with his presence, with his charm, with exquisite pleasure. She did not want him to go, but she knew better than to ask him to stay. As he had once pointed out, there was no place for him with her. He wanted a wife someday, and that woman could never be her.

The last lonely five years had not been her penance at all for failing her older brother. This was. This knowing she could never have more of Gideon than this—these short visits, these glimpses of what she had thrown away years ago.

But it had been worth it. If not Stirling, then some other like him. She would have never found with a husband selected by Phillip what she found with Gideon. This was unique. This was different. This was what she was never destined to have.

She would not ask Gideon to stay, and she did not know if she could even write to him again.

A **parting** fuck or one last tumble. It didn't matter to Gideon what it was called. He was simply grateful Bella had found a way to arrange it this morning.

Crouched over her, he paused at the end of a downstroke. He needed to give her one last orgasm. With a hand braced on the bed, he wrapped his other arm around her. "Hold on," he whispered in her ear. The slim arms wrapped around his neck tightened. Her lean thighs cradling his hips, he pushed up onto his knees, bringing her with him, the contact of their bodies unbroken. Capturing her lips, he settled back on his heels and grasped the neat indent of her waist. Tongue twining with hers, he flexed his hips.

Bella twisted her head, breaking the kiss. "Gideon," she moaned.

She tried to rock against him, increase the pace. With a light yet firm hold, he held her steady and pushed in deeper into the tight depths of her body. Her eyes drifted closed and she relaxed into his slow, steady thrusts. The three orgasms he'd already given her this morning must have taken the edge off her impatience. Fingers tangled in his hair, she allowed him to set the pace, to bring the climax to her.

He slid one hand up her back. Hand splayed between her shoulder blades, he nuzzled her neck. Arching, she threw back her head, offering herself up to him. He pressed a light kiss to the delicate hollow of her throat and dragged his lips down her flushed chest. Her skin was so smooth, like the finest silk. He flicked his tongue over her nipple then opened his mouth and suckled on the hard bud.

The fingers tangled in his hair tightened. Her little breathy moans began to crescendo. "Gideon," she gasped, arching her hips, writhing against him in a seductive rhythm.

Her clit rubbed maddeningly against his groin. He tried to keep the pace slow, to draw out the moment. To keep her suspended on the brink of orgasm, desperate and needing him.

But it was no use. The climax he had managed to keep at bay teased the base of his spine, quickening his thrusts. Sweat beaded his brow. His heart hammered in his chest.

Her body tightened around his cock. He grunted, deep and low from his gut. "Come for me, Bella. Now," he said, beyond desperate not to come before she did.

Her spine went taut. Eyes closed and lips parted, she gasped.

Abruptly, he pulled her close and slanted his mouth over hers, capturing her screams of ecstasy.

The orgasm raced up his cock. He kissed her fiercely as he came, his groan lost in the hot recesses of her mouth.

Bella sagged against him, pliant and sated in his arms. Forehead resting on his shoulder, her labored breaths brushed across his chest. He combed his fingers through her hair, gently smoothing the tousled locks. She had the most beautiful hair. So long it covered her back, the ends grazing the firm swell of her backside.

A light knock sounded on the dressing room door. "Lady Stirling?" came a muffled voice.

Bella sighed. "Yes, Maisie?"

"The carriage is ready."

Gideon winced.

"Thank you, Maisie." Bella leaned back.

He forced an easy smile the moment before her gaze met his. "I should be going."

Her lashes swept down. She nodded.

Reluctantly, he lifted her off him and set her on the bed. He swung his legs over the side of the bed. His joints ached from having his legs folded under him. Christ, he was getting old. He resisted the urge to rub his thighs and instead removed the sheath. Bending, he picked up the wax paper wrapper from the floor, folded it over the used sheath, and tossed it into the nearby waste bin.

He grabbed his trousers from the floor and stepped into them. Standing, he pulled them up and buttoned the placket. A small hand grabbed his arse.

Startled, he glanced over his shoulder.

"Couldn't resist," she said, smirking. Lounged on her side, pale blonde hair tumbled over her slim shoulder and alabaster skin flushed from four orgasms, she was the picture of temptation.

Turning, he leaned down, cupped her check, and kissed her. Hot and quick, pulling back before temptation got the better of him.

"Your carriage awaits," he murmured, needing to remind himself it was time to leave.

The smile on her lips faded. "Yes, it does," she said, with a little lift of her shoulder. Rolling onto her back, she arched and stretched her arms overhead.

Gideon turned from the tantalizing image and walked about the room, locating his clothes and getting dressed.

"We never finished breakfast," she said.

He pulled his shirt over his head and tucked the tails into his trousers. Last night she had invited him to breakfast before he left for London. Their very first breakfast together. But when he'd arrived at the manor house and her lady's maid had shown him to the informal sitting room adjoining the bedchamber, he had known Bella had had plans for the morning that did not include food. Plans he wholeheartedly approved. "Correction. We didn't start breakfast. If I recall correctly, the silver covers were not even removed from the dishes. If you're hungry I can bring the tray in for you. The food is likely still warm. Or I can order up another tray."

"No, thank you. I'm not particularly hungry at the moment." Bella sat up and flicked her hair behind her shoulders. She glanced about the room. The late morning sun streamed through the windows. The crisp golden light caressed her bare skin. "Do you see my chemise on the floor?"

"Yes. Why?" He tied his cravat in a simple knot and pulled on his gray pin-striped waistcoat.

She rolled her eyes. "I need to get dressed. See you to the carriage."

He shook his head. "Stay in bed. Laze the morning away. I can see myself out."

Her lush lips pulled into a straight line, her gaze testing. Then she flopped back down on the bed. "All right. I must admit, I am a bit tired."

He chuckled as he buttoned his navy jacket. "I wonder why?"

She rolled onto her side and rested her cheek in her palm. "Smug man. You know exactly why."

He tipped his head and tugged on the end of his jacket to straighten it. He was dressed. He should leave now, but there was one last thing he needed to see to.

Taking a deep breath, he reached into his jacket pocket. He walked to the side of the bed. "Here."

Her brow furrowed as she looked at the proffered note. She held out her hand and he pressed the folded note into her palm.

"My address." He swallowed past the lump in his throat. "If you wish to contact me, simply send a note to that address."

She held his gaze. There was something in the violet depths which caused his chest to tighten.

"Do you understand, Bella?" Hell, it wasn't all that difficult, and Bella certainly was not a simpleton. Why did he need her reassurance?

Ducking her chin to her chest, she nodded. "Yes," she whispered.

He lifted his hand from hers. Her fingers closed over the note. "Thank you, my lady. I had a very enjoyable fortnight."

The corners of her mouth curved in a soft smile. She peered up at him from under her lashes. "As did I."

Gideon sketched a short bow, turned on his heel, and walked out of the room. He closed the bedchamber door, leaned against it, and tipped back his head.

He had practically begged her to hire him again. What was wrong with him? It was always left in their hands with no expectations either way. But with Bella, with Bella . . .

Frustrated, he dragged his hands through his hair, not able to explain it to himself. He pushed from the door, left the sitting room, and went down to the front door.

He found the traveling carriage waiting for him at the foot of the stone steps. The four chestnut horses in the traces shifted impatiently, their harness jangling. One tossed his head. Another stamped a hoof. The silver banding on his trunk glinted in the sunlight. One of Bella's servants had collected it from Garden House and strapped it to the back of the carriage.

All was ready.

A footman leapt down from the driver's bench and opened the door as Gideon approached.

Awfully eager to get me back to London, aren't they?

Never one to be rude to a client's servants, he tipped his head to the footman and sat on the black leather bench.

The door closed. The carriage shifted as the footman got back onto the driver's bench. There was a snap of leather and the carriage lurched forward.

Paper swooshed to the floor. He looked to his feet. The *Times*? He let out a *harrumph*. It meant nothing. Efficient servants, nothing more.

He refolded the paper and set it beside him. He crossed one ankle over his knee then shifting, stretched out both legs as much as he could in the confines of the carriage. Bella had not asked him to stay. He should be relieved, so why wasn't he? And why had it been so hard to leave that house?

After being at a woman's beck and call for more than a handful of days, he usually looked forward to returning to his comfortable bachelor apartment, where he could relax and do as he pleased without thought to what they wanted to do. Yet today, he found London was not where he wanted to be.

He glanced to the sky. Large white clouds were scattered among the blue. A fresh breeze blew into the carriage, ruffling his hair. It was a perfect afternoon for a stroll about the gardens, or for lounging on a bench reading the *Times* and watching Bella tend to her flowers.

And it struck him. It wasn't her body he would miss, but simply her. Bella.

Lady Stirling. He squeezed his eyes shut and did his best to ignore the pain in his chest.

Her ladyship.

Not his. Never his.

She was a lady and he only played the part of a gentleman. No, it was more than playing, and he was well aware of it. He could vividly remember the moment when that need had seized hold. Eight years old and watching from around the corner of the receiving room, he wanted to be like those men who came to Rubicon's. With his cast-off clothes and hands dirtied from piling coals onto the grates, he envied the polished gentlemen as they moved among the beauties. Status and wealth radiated from their perfectly tailored clothes and their confident bearing. Their well-bred blood gave them a security he had never known.

As he had grown older, he recognized the folly of his boyhood dream. Those nameless lords did not live perfect lives. He knew there were some who did not know their true father, but unlike him, they at least had a man who claimed the title.

Yet still, he had made himself into the image of a gentleman. Spent hours upon hours teaching himself everything a tutor had never taught him. He frequented their tailors, lived in one of their apartments, and lost his money at their gaming tables. The veneer was perfect but it could not change what he was inside. A bastard son of a whore. A prostitute. Only wanted by Lady Stirling for the pleasures he could offer and for nothing more.

Gideon pinched the bridge of his nose in an effort to regain his composure. The fortnight had ended. The appointment was over. Nothing would come from dwelling on it. He needed to let it go, push Lady Stirling from his mind. Push the memories of her, that indefinable feeling of simply being with her aside and focus on returning to London, whether that was where he wanted to be or not.

His own wishes were, as always, irrelevant.

Fourteen

ONE month later Gideon was still struggling to push Lady Stirling from his mind. Seated in a comfortable leather armchair, elbow resting on the edge of the chess table, he absently turned a black pawn over and over between his fingers.

With a soft click, the black queen fell to the board in defeat.

"You made it much too easy that time. You needn't let me win. I promise not to pout."

Gideon looked up and focused on the voice's owner. "You shouldn't make promises you can't keep." The smooth words flowed off his tongue without conscious thought.

A light chuckle tickled Helen's lips as she nodded, conceding the point. She did pout, just a bit, whenever he beat her at chess. But he had not let her win this time. In fact, he could not even recall the game.

He glanced back down to the black-and-white checkered board. There were black pieces scattered about, so he must have participated. Not very well though. He had left her with a clear opening, his queen completely undefended.

"Your mind is elsewhere, is it not?"

There was no censure in her query, yet he felt exposed to have been so obvious. "No. Never. I am with you."

"You needn't lie to me, Gideon. You should know that by now. There is no need to flatter me."

He did know that. Still, it was pride that pushed him to reassure her. But he held back.

They had a standing appointment, he and Helen. She was one of the few he visited at regular intervals. Since Helen, Lady Knolwood, the widowed marchioness, was currently in Town, it had been but a quick drive to her stately townhome versus the three-hour carriage ride to her Hertfordshire country estate.

Gideon liked Helen. He had known her for years. Theirs was an easy friendship, though how he could define it as "easy" when he had no others to compare it to he was not quite certain. Maybe it was because she sought his companionship more than anything these days. It had long ago stopped being about sex. More often than not, they simply talked, played chess or a hand of cards, or had a pleasant meal. Every now and then she would make her wishes known. Some subtle hint she wanted more from him than his conversation skills. But that had become few and far between.

Not that it had ever been a bother. Though well into her forties, Helen retained a youthful beauty and her figure was what it had been a decade ago. The gray scattered in with her strawberry blonde hair was only noticeable when the light hit it at just the right angle, and her heart-shaped face held only a few faint lines from the ready smiles that brightened her sky blue eyes.

Even if she hadn't been a beauty that would not have put him off. He had found long ago he had a certain knack for looking beyond the surface and seeing the beauty within. He liked women—there was no way he couldn't in his line of work. But it was more than a passing appreciation of what made them different than him, a man. He *truly* liked women—their little quirks, those unexpected eccentricities that made them who they were.

But tonight he was rather hoping it would not end in her bedchamber. Strangely, he found himself without any will to bed her, or to even press his lips to hers. Maybe that was why he had been such a monk of late. On some level, perhaps he had known—

"Does she know how lucky she is?"

Gideon pulled his thoughts back to the woman seated across the chess table. "Pardon?"

"She who has your heart. Does she know how fortunate she is to have secured that which, I am certain, many a lady would commit murder for?"

Every muscle in his body tensed. He held his breath, fearing the next words out of her mouth, but helpless to stop them.

"I do so hope she is worthy."

"Helen, I assure you, I do not know what you're speaking of," he said, unable to mask the defensive note in his voice.

She gave him a little look, one that said he was fooling no one, least of all her. "It's all right, Gideon. I'm happy for you, truly I am. I was the one who started you off in this life and I feared, for a while there, that because of it you had hardened your heart and would refuse to give it up. I am quite relieved to find you have entrusted it to another."

Helen had been his first, though at the time she had not known it. It had been years later when they were teasing each other one night that he let it slip. She had been taken aback, and even more shocked when he revealed his age.

If I'd have known, I would have never asked for you. I thought you worked there.

I did, just in a different capacity.

I would have never guessed it had been your first time.

My first lady, but not my first time.

The three years before his first appointment had been spent in various beds at Rubicon's. An adolescent male in a whorehouse? It would have been unthinkable for him to reach the age of seventeen a virgin. He'd have never turned any of them down at that age. He had been in heaven—countless beauties willing to show him all sorts of interesting things. They had been quite the adventure-packed formative years.

"Who is she?" Helen asked, dragging his thoughts back to the present.

Gideon turned his head. One lady was never mentioned to another. But more than that, he could not bring himself to answer, for Helen had it spot-on. And it shook him, rattling at the core of how he defined himself as a man. Unreachable, in control, and one who knew better than to form an attachment to any client, no matter how intriguing the lady. He had seen enough of Rubicon's girls reduced to tears when a favorite client chose another, and had long ago vowed to never make that mistake himself. Never let them in.

He had not recognized that feeling in the pit of his stomach for what it was until Helen pointed out the truth.

He had let one in.

Now faced with it, he did not want to examine it for there was no hope.

"Oh, Gideon. I'm sorry. She's one of your clients, married to another, is she not?"

The genuine compassion in her tone was not comforting in the slightest. Gripping the black pawn tightly in one fist, he stared blindly into the fire burning down to embers in the nearby fireplace.

"Is he elderly, her husband?"

"I don't know," he replied stiffly. Bella's husband was the last person he wanted to think about.

"Does she know?"

"Know what?" He glanced uneasily at Helen from the corner of his eye.

"What you've given her?" she asked gently.

How could Bella, when he hadn't known himself until mere moments ago? Still as a statue, he again averted his gaze and focused on keeping his breaths slow and even, forcing the ragged note away.

"When will you see her again?"

"I don't know. I don't know if she plans to hire me again." Every morning he awoke with a glimmer of hope of receiving a letter from Bella, and every afternoon he was disappointed. It had been a month. A very long month of disappointing afternoons.

Helen let out an exasperated sigh. "Gideon. If you care for her, you should go see her. Or at least write to her."

Eyes flaring at the absurdity of her request, he glared at Helen. "No. I can't."

"Why not?"

"It's not done. I can't . . . show up at her front door without an invitation." He would not do it. Would not arrive on her doorstep like a lovelorn fool. Would not dare to step that far above his place. Could not survive the distinct possibility of rejection.

"Yes, you can. It's not uncommon for married ladies to have male callers, or to indulge in discreet affairs. If nothing else, find out if her husband is elderly or in poor heath. Perhaps she'll be as fortunate as I, and her husband will pass away, leaving her free and with his fortune."

Ever the practical Helen. He looked back to the fire, unwilling to even tease himself with the hope Bella could someday be his. Even if she were not married, a woman like her would never choose a man like him.

"Gideon, you have to stop thinking of her as a client and start thinking of her as the woman you love. Fight for her, or at least do something. Don't continue down this path you're on. If ever there was a man deserving of happiness, it is you. Give yourself a chance, for you will regret it forever if you do not."

Biting the inside of his cheek, he squeezed his eyes shut, determined not to completely lose his composure in front of Helen. He wanted to press the heels of his palms to his eyes, to scream against the force tearing at his chest. But he could do nothing but endure it, and hope that with time it would fade.

There was a rustle of fabric as she got to her feet. "Thank you, my friend. This is where we part and where I wish you luck, for you will need it," she said sagely.

He stood and dropped a kiss on the back of her proffered hand. "Thank you, Helen," he said, hoarse from the tide of emotion crashing inside of him.

"If ever you should feel the need, I would welcome a letter from you. And you must drop me a note if you win your lady."

THAT evening Bella lingered in the hothouse for as long as she dared before the darkness of night pushed her toward the bright manor house, toward the safety of her rooms. She walked through the garden and opened the back door just enough to peek her head around it. The kitchen was empty. She let out a relieved breath and, careful not to make a sound, stepped into the house and closed the door behind her.

She crept through the kitchen. *Why had he returned today?* The loneliness and isolation were much preferred to this feeling of being on edge. She never felt comfortable around him, even when he was being amicable. This waiting, this constant suspense, it was tiring, yet she never slept well when he was at Bowhill. It wouldn't be for days after he left until her guard would finally fully drop.

And why had he brought "them" with him? Stirling was bad enough, but to have his latest band of followers in her house? Those disreputable souls, soaked in vice, did not inhabit the edges of polite society but some place far beyond. They were loud, crude, and forever inebriated. And they were not merry drunks either.

The loud riot, the squeals of the local tavern wenches, and the bellows of laughter signaled they had taken up in her drawing room. It would be safer to take the back servants' stairs to her rooms. She pivoted on her heel and strode back down the hall. With a quick glance over her shoulder, she turned a corner and bumped into a solid object. Instinctively she reached out to regain her balance, but snatched her hands back at the feel of slick silk and cool metal buttons.

"What have we here?"

A large hand grasped her waist, halting her attempt at a hasty retreat. His dark, half-lidded eyes sparkled with malicious intent.

"Release me," she said in her haughtiest voice, icicles stuck to the words.

"You aren't one of the locals, that's for sure. So you must be the wife. Stirling said you were a prime piece, and he wasn't exaggerating."

Her pulse raced in her ears. She lifted her hands and made to push him away, but could not bring herself to touch him. "Release me."

The man leaned close. A chuck of his black forelock fell over one eye. A lecherous smile curved his lips. "I think not. Now that I've caught you, I'll be keeping you."

She averted her face. "You will do no such thing. Release me this instant!"

"Where is the hospitality? Don't you want to properly welcome one of your guests?"

That hand on her waist glided upward and curved inward, the large fingers spreading, reaching toward her breast. Her skin crawled in revulsion. "You are no guest of mine and you are *not* welcome."

His dark eyes narrowed into hard slits. The teasing hint was gone. Before she could brace herself, he pushed her roughly against the wall, knocking the breath from her chest.

"Isabella."

The harsh whip of her name quickened the pulse racing in her veins. Stifling dread descended, a thick heavy blanket that almost brought her to her knees. She had managed to avoid him all day and now—

"You will give Lord Ripon your apologies," Stirling said as he advanced on her. The swiftness of his stride blew his tousled auburn hair away from his face. His passably handsome features were contoured with fury. He wasn't but a decade older than her twenty-four, but years of vice and dissipation had aged him. The buttons on his scarlet waistcoat strained under the force of his well-fed belly.

Every time she saw him she swore he was taller and broader than the last. Her husband was not a man many men provoked and for good reason.

Gathering her teetering courage, she squared her shoulders. She had done nothing wrong, save try to stop a man from mauling her. "I will do no such thing."

Her head snapped sharply to the right, connecting hard with the wall behind her. Sparks danced before her eyes. Pain shot from her left eye and radiated through her entire skull.

"Apologize," Stirling growled.

Lord Ripon's cruel chuckle barely made it through the pistol fire-like buzz filling her ears. She moved to shake her head but it made the blinding pain worse.

"Apologize."

She hated the words, but the pain would only intensify if she did not heed his command. He would not allow her to disobey him, especially not in front of one of his fellows. She could feel her eye swelling shut, skin stretching under the agonizing throb. Clasping her hands, she dug her fingernails into the delicate bones and veins on the backs to resist the urge to press her palm to her eye. Her arms shook under the strain. The pain was incredible and having to stand before Stirling and Lord Ripon, Stirling's features harsh with the threat of more and Ripon's satisfied and gloating, intensified it to unbearable levels.

Swallowing the tears clogging her throat, she tipped her chin in submission. "Lord Ripon, you have my apologies. You are ever welcome in Lord Stirling's home." The words were stilted and slow with the effort required to give them voice.

She caught Ripon's answering smug nod from of the corner of her right eye. Her humiliation was complete.

"Ripon!" A drunken male voice shouted from the drawing room.

"Pleasant wife you got there, Stirling." Lord Ripon turned and strode down the hall, leaving her alone with her husband.

Hot, whisky-soaked breath fanned her face as he leaned close. He loomed over her, more than thrice her size, as broad as a barn, and seemed to take up the entire hall. She shrank back against the wall. Every muscle instinctively drew tighter in preparation, her chest struggling under the force of her panic-laden pants.

"Remember your place. If you should ever speak to one of my acquaintances like that again, you will deeply regret it."

Then he was gone, his heavy footfalls fading down the hall. The instant his broad back disappeared into the drawing room, her spine collapsed on a great silent sob. Crouched on the floor, she buried her face in her hands. Her tears were like fire, searing her bruised eye. But she could not make the tears stop. They just kept coming, as if from a bottomless well.

Why does he hate me so much? After five years, she should be used to this. It was not the first time he had blackened her eye or humiliated her in front of others. Yet . . .

The image of a handsome face with a kind smile and fathomless whisky brown eyes materialized behind the lids of her closed eyes. *Oh, God, I miss you.* She clenched her jaw to keep the words inside, trembling against the onslaught of pure longing, pure need to be with him. Every day she missed him, and every day she cherished the memories of him. Yet today, right now, she needed him more than ever.

The sound of footsteps in the marble-floored entrance hall reached her ears. On a hitched breath, she bolted upright, darted around the corner, and slipped through a small door. She closed the door behind her, cloaking the narrow servants' stairs in darkness. With one hand on the wall to guide her way, she rushed up the steps, head bowed and left hand still pressed to her eye.

She collided with an unexpected object and stumbled back. A hand grabbed her wrist, righting her. Instinctively, she ducked her head from the flare of candlelight.

"Lady Stirling?"

Bella took a moment to steady her breaths before speaking. "Pardon, Mrs. Cooley."

She waited for her housekeeper to release her wrist, but the older woman's grip merely shifted until it resembled a comforting hold.

"Are you all right, your ladyship?"

"Yes."

Mrs. Cooley sighed. "No. You are the furthest thing from all right."

It was one thing to have Stirling hit her in front of his friends, but quite another to have her housekeeper, a woman Bella had to face every day, see her like this—shaking with fear, tears streaming down her cheeks. She tugged. Mrs. Cooley let go of her wrist, turned, and went up the stairs.

Bella stood still for a moment. But down the stairs led back to Stirling, so she reluctantly followed her housekeeper. The golden light from Mrs. Cooley's candle threw shadows on the walls. When they reached the second floor, Mrs. Cooley uncharacteristically poked her head around the door before opening it fully.

She motioned to Bella. "Come along. Shall I have Maisie sent to you?" she asked, once again the efficient housekeeper.

"No." Bella quickly stepped into the empty hall. She slipped into her bedchamber, her knees buckling the instant she turned the lock on the door.

ONE month later, Gideon stared out a carriage window at a tall black door. The half moon window above it was dark, as were the windows flanking the door and those on the second and third floors. But he knew the townhouse was not empty. There was one person inside. A woman to be exact, and she was likely growing very impatient by now.

He prided himself on punctuality, on arriving at the specified time. Yet ten o'clock had come and gone before he had left his apartment. Thus the reason why he sat in this carriage. It would have taken thirty minutes to walk to Lady Devlin's and, no matter how much he was avoiding it, it really would not do to arrive after eleven.

Pulling out his pocket watch, he held the face up to the window to catch the light from a nearby streetlamp. Ten minutes to eleven. He sighed. He could not put it off any longer. In any case, if he stalled much longer, his jacket would pick up the smell of this old rented carriage, and dust and mold were two scents a lady would not welcome into her bedchamber.

"Ye gettin' out or not?"

"Yes," Gideon said defensively. He exited the carriage and paid the impatient driver. With a snap of leather lines, the driver left Gideon standing next to a streetlamp. Once the carriage was out of sight, he walked up the front stone steps, turned the knob, and opened the black door. After locking the door, he gave himself a moment to get oriented to the dark house.

"Third floor," he said, recalling his notes from his appointment book.

When he reached the second floor landing, he paused to let out a contemptuous snort. One would think he was climbing the steps to the hangman's noose. It would be midnight when he reached Lady Devlin's bedchamber if he kept up this pace.

More to prove a point to himself than anything, he bounded up the next flight of stairs. Yet he paused at the door at the end of the short hall and stared at the shiny brass knob.

"Enough," he muttered, completely disgusted with himself. This inner resistance would disappear if he could just get this one appointment behind him. Then he could go on, as he always had. For this was what he did. This was what he was. And he needed to work if he had any hope in hell of ever leaving all of this behind some day.

He closed his eyes and righted himself to his current task.

Lady Devlin. Five foot one. Lush, petite brunette. *Not so bad, could be worse*, he thought with an apathetic shrug.

He knocked once and opened the door.

Damn.

His stomach sank. So much for any hope of easing into it. The many lit candles stationed about the room illuminated Lady Devlin in all her nude glory sprawled on the large four-poster bed.

"Gideon," she exclaimed as she hopped off the bed. She rushed across the room. "Naughty man. You kept me waiting."

She did not wait for a response but threw her arms around him. Avoiding her parted lips, he pressed his mouth to her neck. He tried to close his mind, shut it down and react purely on male instinct, but everything was wrong. The scent of lilacs filled his nostrils. Full breasts pressed too low against his chest. Breathy mewling noises filled his ears. The skin under his tongue tasted of salt and scent.

Small hands reached eagerly for the falls on his trousers. Somehow he resisted the impulse to jerk away and instead adroitly, smoothly, took her hands in his. He absently tickled her palms with the tips of his fingers as he debated where to place her hands. He did not even want her to touch him. Pulling her arms behind her back, he held them there as he nuzzled the small cove behind her ear.

Seemingly excited by the hint of bondage, she pressed those mountainous breasts against him again. "Yes," she sighed.

Maybe he should tie her to the bed. But then what would he do with her? His mind refused to cooperate. All he could think about was getting away from her. And his body—he'd had a strong inkling the moment he stepped into this bedchamber that *it* was not going to cooperate.

She took a step back, moving toward the large bed that dominated the room, but he kept his feet firmly rooted to the floor. There was no way in hell he was getting in that bed. He should not have come to this house tonight. He should have stayed on his self-imposed celibate path.

The many notes he had received these past weeks had been ignored, left to pile on his dining table. None of them bore the distinctive flowing feminine script he had been waiting for. But even if his clients did not complain about his silence, Rubicon would soon. He hadn't paid her in months. And in order to fill his long, lonely days, to divert his mind from the reason why he did not want to work, he had been frequenting the gaming tables.

The memory of last night's loss washed over him, and it did not help his current predicament. He could not believe he had sunk so low as to play roulette. It was common knowledge the odds were heavily stacked in favor of the house. Yet still, he had thrown those chips onto the green baize and numbly watched as the croupier snatched them up.

He had absolutely no will to bed this woman, and it wasn't just her. He had been as limp as an impotent old man since he returned to London, without even a trace of a morning erection.

Gideon felt her squirm to take another step back and he tried, truly he did, to summon up something, some hint of desire. Anything. The lurid images swam before his mind's eye.

A woman on her knees, her rouged mouth on his cock, her raven tresses skimming her derrière. Two beauties on a bed, their lithe limbs twined together, hands playing at each other's quims, an open invitation in their half-lidded eyes for him to join them. A lush harem houri on her hands and knees, her perfectly rounded backside lifted high, begging to be rammed to the hilt.

But there was nothing. Not even a twitch. He had never been so flaccid in all his life.

His cock had never let him down before. It was the most reliable part of him. He did not even have to think on it—he just got hard whenever he needed to. It never occurred to him before this night that his most trusted of body parts would let him down. He felt like a musician who suddenly could not play a note. A soloist standing before the orchestra without his violin. It shook him to the core, rattling loose every bit of confidence he had in himself. His entire adult life had been built around that one body part, and now—

"Oh, Gideon." She lifted up onto her toes and tried to capture his mouth with hers.

Tightening his grip slightly on her wrists, he bent her upper body back, keeping those questing lips away from his own. She threw back her head and he sprinkled a necklace of light, nipping kisses on her exposed neck, moving his attentions to her other ear.

Sweat pricked between his shoulder blades. His cravat felt like a damn noose. He needed to get out of this room. She would only allow him to nuzzle her neck for so long before she started voicing demands.

The seconds ticked down in his head. Urgency pressed in on him. For the life of him he could not figure out how to leave without delivering the deepest of insults. He did not want to hurt her feelings, but there was no way he could go through with it tonight. No matter how hard he tried to will it, his body simply would not cooperate.

And it felt so wrong to be here, the taste of betrayal thick in his throat. How was he to get out of this room, this house? He wracked his seized brain. Pretending as though he had another engagement was not an option. Lady Devlin had been on his calendar for months. Lord Devlin had planned an excursion to the country after Parliament closed for the summer and Lady Devlin had decided to indulge in her husband's absence. She had even managed to get all the servants out of the house.

Maybe he could plead a headache, or feign sickness? He certainly felt ill. Each mewl from her lips made his stomach churn as though it was filled with live eels.

Yes, that was it. Dinner was not sitting well. And the thought of him ensconced in the washroom puking his guts out should douse her passions, if nothing else.

Fifteen

THE next day Gideon paced the length of Rubicon's office as he waited for his employer to make an appearance. Ignoring the well-stocked liquor cabinet, he kept his strides determined and his thoughts focused on his errand. He could no longer avoid the inevitable. But strangely, it was not an errand that brought dread, rather something that resembled relief.

After a very long ten minutes, the door hidden in the paneled wall swung open. Rubicon glided into the room and took her place behind the teakwood desk. Her blonde hair was pulled up in its usual deliberately tousled coif and her face was painted in the standard madam's mask. He must have interrupted her at her toilette, for the figure-hugging scarlet gown had been replaced with a laced-edged pink silk wrapper.

"Good afternoon, Rosedale. How convenient you came to call. I haven't heard from you in so long I was beginning to grow a bit concerned."

He ignored her not-so-subtle reminder that he had not paid her in months and walked to the desk, dropping a slim black leather book onto it. "I have come to give you my resignation. You may contact my clients and if they are amenable, send someone else in my place."

Her expression did not change as she picked up his appointment book, which contained the names and addresses of every woman he had visited in the last decade, less Bella. There was a little *swoosh* of paper as she flipped the pages. At length, she closed it. "Have a seat."

"No, thank you. I prefer to stand."

"Sit."

He opened his mouth to argue then closed it and sat down. It was the last command of hers he would ever obey.

The edges of her lips curved in satisfaction. Her gaze dropped to the leather volume. "I never knew you were so organized, Rosedale. It is a rare trait in this business." She tapped her finger against her chin. He could almost hear her mind whirling. Her kohl-rimmed eyes met his, and the hard gleam put him immediately on his guard. "I do not accept your resignation."

He blinked. "Pardon?"

"You are much too valuable to me. You will go to Hampshire tomorrow and leave her ladyship with a very big smile on her face."

"Rubicon, you do not understand. I will not work for you ever again."

"No, Gideon, it is you who does not understand," she said. "I will not release you. I will not allow you to pimp yourself out on your own, or to go to some other establishment and deny me my rightful profits. You will remain in my employ."

Stupid, greedy woman. She thought he was trying to make a go on his own. "I quit. Completely. I have no intention of ever bedding a woman for monetary gain again."

"Oh, so you've developed a conscience, have you?" she asked archly.

"I have developed a severe dislike for my line of work."

"You'll just have to learn to like it again."

Frustrated at her insistence, he shook his head. "I will never like it again as I will never do it again."

"Whether you like it or not is of little concern to me. You will adhere to my wishes."

"I can't," he said coldly, taking perverse satisfaction in his response. She could push him at women all she liked. It would not bring her even one shilling.

Rubicon cocked her head, as if his words caught at something in her greedy brain. She was silent for a moment. "Can't or won't?"

"Both. I am of no use to you anymore. Ask Lady Devlin if you doubt."

She picked up the appointment book, flipped a few pages, and studied it. The slow, knowing smile that spread across her face made him distinctly uncomfortable. "Couldn't get it up? I assume you displayed the appropriate level of tact and didn't blame it on the lady."

"It had absolutely nothing to do with Lady Devlin. It could have been anyone." Well, not anyone. There was one, but he would likely never get to see her again. Two months had passed and she had not written to him.

"Not to worry, Rosedale." Rubicon waved a hand, casually dismissing his life-altering problems. "This happens to all my men at least once. Overuse. Overstimulation. A rest is all you need. I shall send Albert to handle your appointments for the next month and you shall stay in Town and recover. After a month of no women, of not touching your cock for anything but the necessary, you'll be so hard up even a three hundred-pound matron won't put you off."

His lip curled in distaste. "Rubicon, it has nothing to do with a need for rest. I simply *cannot* anymore. Nothing will work. I've tried. Believe me. I am completely useless to you." And he had tried. Done everything he could think of, even taken himself in hand. But it had all been in vain. He could not deny it. He was ruined, broken, no longer "simply perfect." And would never be again.

Her eyes narrowed to hard slits. Flattening her palms on the desk, she half rose out of the chair. Her breasts threatened to spill from the deep V-neck of the thin wrapper. "It's that Scottish bitch, isn't it? The one who requested your company for the space of a fortnight. She's gotten to you, hasn't she?"

Rage surged, hot and thick. Gideon bit the inside of his cheek in an effort to hold back the unwise retort and gripped the arms of the chair to keep his hands from flying out to strangle Rubicon. How dare she refer to Bella like that?

"You fool," she spat. "Did she profess her undying love for you? Did you actually believe her? You are a prostitute, Rosedale. Nothing to her, or to any of them, but a servant. In fact, you're less than a servant. You're merely a means to an orgasm."

Somehow he kept from flinching at the hard truth in her cruelly slung words. He knew it already. He did *not* need Rubicon to remind him of the reason why he couldn't even bring himself to write to Bella. At length, he felt calm enough to respond. "I will no longer work for you," he said flatly. "Nothing you say will change that fact."

"You owe me," she said, any vestige of composure now long gone. "If it wasn't for me, you would be nothing." Her gaze raked the length of him. Her rouged mouth thinned in disgust. "I've clearly spoiled you. I let you move out of this house. I indulged your pride and allowed you to refuse paying clients simply because they were men. And this is how you repay me? I was the one who convinced Christina to bring you here. Your mother didn't want anything to do with you, but I saw your potential. I let you live here, clothed you, fed you, and never once had you whipped even when you left your sooty little handprints on the walls. If it weren't for me, your mother would have left you to rot in the street. And this is how you repay me?"

Gideon bristled at the reminder. "I am well aware of that. But any debt I owed you is long since paid. I've been working for you in one form or another since I was seven."

"No, it is not paid until I deem it so," she said. "Do you know how many offers I turned down for you when you were a boy? I kept the lechers away from you, saved you until you were older. Gave you the luxury of learning in my girls' beds for years before I hired you out. You haven't come close to paying me back yet."

"What?" he asked, with a confused shake of his head.

Her cold, mocking laughter grated down his spine. "Did you actually believe they swived you because they wanted to? None of my girls spread their legs without my consent. Your education was my doing, Rosedale. I ordered them all to fuck you, to teach you how to please a woman. I molded you into the perfect instrument of pleasure. I made you, and you *will* work for me until such time as I release you."

He dragged a shaky hand through his hair. "But I am of no use to you anymore."

She raised one blonde eyebrow, her lips quirking at the desperation in his tone. "I can find a use for you. Even a eunuch has his uses in a whorehouse."

His gut tightened in trepidation, but he squared his shoulders, held his ground. "No, Rubicon. I refuse."

She ignored him, as if he hadn't spoken. "In fact, I have the ideal use for you. And if you even think of refusing me, you will find yourself on the prison hulk *Justitia*, arrested for sodomy."

"What? I-I have never—" he sputtered, too outraged to finish the sentence.

"You are a prostitute, Rosedale, and the purpose of male prostitutes is to be used by other men. No one will believe you've worked this long without bending over at least once. You may try to deny it. You may even try to cast me in the role of vindictive madam. But it will do you no good. No one will believe you. I have many friends, and the captain is a special favorite. Very useful man to have on one's side. He has a particular pleasure and I am one of the few who can provide it. If you try to refuse me, you will find yourself in the bowels of his ship where even the guards rarely go. A man such as yourself? Ah, they will fight over you, Rosedale. So handsome, so pretty. They'll never leave you alone. And I won't let them kill you. You will waste away down there, until disease takes you. You will beg to go ashore to the Warren for hard labor, but you will never again see the light of day. So the choice is yours. Either work for me, or work on the *Justitia*. You can't escape me, Rosedale. Wherever you go, I will find you."

He had known she was a ruthless woman, one not to be crossed, but had never expected this. She had a network of informants. Her reach was far. As for her threat . . . it was neither idle nor empty. He had no doubt she would see it through.

No one could live in London without knowing of the converted old ships of the line anchored on the Thames at Woolwich. They were worse than Newgate, than any prison on land. He had heard the tales often enough and knew what would await him. Gideon was certainly no coward, but even the hardest of criminals blanched at the prospect of serving time on a prison hulk. The lowest level, prisoners kept in irons, the overcrowed conditions, the hatches screwed down tight each night—chaos and darkness would reign. And she would ensure he never set foot on land again.

He had no choice. None at all. His kind rarely did.

His shoulders slumped in resignation. He hung his head. His will, his pride, gone.

"What will you have me do?" he asked hollowly.

A gloating smile spread across her face. "You will take Timothy's place tonight. He is currently . . . recovering. But don't worry. I will have someone watching the room lest matters get out of hand again. I wouldn't want anything to happen to you. I charged quite a pretty price for Timothy. For you I can charge even more. And your little problem won't be a hindrance. Timothy rarely got to fuck them. His clients' interests lay elsewhere."

THE heels of her slippers clicked on the stone floor as the woman walked slowly around him admiring the result of her handiwork.

Careful not to make eye contact, Gideon kept his face blank and stared straight ahead at the gray stone wall.

He had never been in this room before. He knew it existed, but even when he had worked here as a boy, he never had cause to enter it. It was tucked below, away from the other rooms in the house. The wooden door was thick to muffle the sounds from within. There were no windows, only sconces placed at regular intervals along the bare walls. A bed stood against one wall. The leather lines tied to the wrought iron frame lay stretched on the sheet waiting for their next victim. A massive cabinet dominated another wall and was filled with everything the room's occupants might need. A straight-back wooden chair stood by the door. That was it. The room was very spartan and definitely not a pleasant place to find oneself.

The slow clicks stopped as she paused before him. A very pleased smile curved her lips, her eyes alight with satisfaction. Dark, almost black hair hung in a straight sheet down her back. The creamy swells of her breasts spilled from the black lace corset tied so tightly it pulled her body into a severe hourglass. The triangle of hair between her thighs was just as dark as that on her head, and framed by black ribbons tied from the bottom of the corset to the tops of black silk stockings.

The end result should have produced at least a nudge of desire. But he was as unaffected by her as he had been by every other woman since he had left Scotland. It was a rather good thing, for the black leather breeches she had him don were so tight they were almost cutting off his circulation. A hard cock in these breeches would have been most uncomfortable.

He had always done his best to avoid the likes of her. His tastes did not run toward bondage or sadism. Pain was never needed to incite his passions, and he refused to inflict it on others. His gift was in giving pleasure.

But this had nothing to do with pleasure. It was about control and domination. Her desire to inflict her will upon him, to vent her frustrations.

She would leave here tonight and go back to her townhouse, slip back into the rigid rules of society, bow to her husband's wishes and to the dictates of propriety. None of her vaunted acquaintances would ever guess that beneath the ladylike demeanor was this.

Without a word she resumed her circuit, her gaze sweeping possessively up and down his body, which was bare except for those damn breeches. A small hand grabbed his arse. He flinched, powerless to do anything to stop her as she groped him at will. She squeezed hard, almost pinching, and then smoothed her palm in slow circles.

"Very nice," she purred, warm breath fanning his bare shoulder.

He winced. The chains locked around his wrists stringing his arms out and up to the ceiling rattled harshly at the startled jerk of his body as she brought a riding crop down smartly on his backside.

Bloody hell. She knew how to wield that thing. She had quite the snap in her wrist and the leather breeches did nothing to dampen the blow. He could feel the line across his arse stinging and smarting.

Tapping the end of her crop against her palm, she came around to stand before him again. A very smug smile curved her rouged mouth. The unholy gleam in her pale blue eyes did not bode well for him. "Did you like that?"

His gaze snapped to hers.

"I did not give you permission to look at me," she admonished.

Gideon obediently averted his gaze to the stone floor.

"Answer me. Did you like that?"

This was it. This was all he was good for anymore—to serve as a pampered lady's whipping boy.

He knew his role. He knew the answer she wanted to hear. And he wiped his mind clean of every thought, every wish, every need and of all emotion. Until there was nothing left inside.

Bowing his head, he closed his eyes and said in a toneless voice, "Yes, mistress."

Sixteen

THE door clicked shut as she left the room. Gideon stood there, completely numb, for what felt like an eternity. Head bowed and eyes closed, he waited.

His ears registered a door opening, the shuffle of footsteps, and the scrape of a chair being dragged across the stone floor. Thick, callused fingers brushed his wrist. With a click, the lock opened and his arm dropped like a dead weight to his side. A moment later the other arm was freed. Fiery pain snapped along his muscles as he rotated his shoulders. His fingers started to tingle, like needles pricking the skin, as blood flowed anew.

"Do you need anything?" a male voice asked gruffly.

Gideon did not look at the voice's owner. He couldn't. He just shook his bowed head.

And the footsteps retreated, the door closed, leaving him alone.

He would not do that again, could not go through that again. She had toyed with him for well over an hour, alternating between whipping his arse and taunting him, like a cat torturing a mouse. Every one of her questions had been answered with the same two words—*yes, mistress*. After she'd grown bored of him, she had pressed her back against the wall and pleasured herself, the whole while asking him if he wanted her.

He had stood there, chained, his backside stinging and burning, as she came. The flush of arousal that had tinged the creamy swells of her breasts and the soft pants from between her parted lips had no effect on him. He had just waited until she was done.

The pulse that had stayed strangely even the past hour started to pound through his veins. His breaths turned short and ragged. His muscles trembled.

God, he felt so wrong. He could not even stand himself. He wasn't a man, but something much less.

There is more to you than this.

On a low, pained groan, he clenched his jaw and squeezed his eyes shut tight. He took a great gulp of air and clung tightly to her words. The words Bella had spoken with such conviction, with such certainty. They fortified him, giving him the strength to peel off those breeches, put on his clothes, and leave that room.

Regardless of what Rubicon believed, he wasn't completely without acceptable options. There was one left. One he had previously refused to even consider.

After slipping unnoticed out the back door of Rubicon's, he traveled the short distance to his apartment on foot and quickly stuffed a few things into a leather saddlebag. He opened the top drawer of his dresser, pushed aside the neatly folded cravats, and pulled out a plain wooden box. He lifted the lid, set aside the bundle on top, and stared at the box's contents.

The small fortune's worth of gold sovereigns and pound notes had never felt like enough. Not when it needed to blind a woman to what he was and where he had come from. For the past decade women had been paying him, and he had been saving their money to buy himself a wife. He chuckled, oddly amused at the irony.

But when he looked into that wooden box, it now felt like too much. At the moment, he did not feel like he was worth more than a farthing. He felt like the cheapest of whores—those poor souls who let themselves be used for a bottle of gin. But Rubicon believed him to be worth quite a bit. He could only hope he had enough to placate her greed.

He stuffed the box in his saddlebag and grabbed the bundle on the dresser, but before pocketing it he unwrapped it. It wasn't the fold of pound notes inside that made his heart clench, but the paper wrapper itself.

With a shaky fingertip he traced the aristocratic curve of her cheekbone, the lush lips pulled in the faintest of smiles and the graceful length of her lean arm. His throat tightened, his body trembling with longing. He was a hack of an artist and had not done her beauty justice, but his soul remembered the look in her eyes he had tried to capture. That look had made him feel like a king among men. Only Bella had ever looked at him like that.

He loved her. *Christ*, he loved her and he could not possibly go on without at least seeing her. And the only way to see her was to give up on his boyhood dream, to give up all he had. There would be no house in the country, no family to call his own in his future. He'd be left with nothing save his love for Bella, and that was all that mattered anymore.

After carefully refolding the sketch over the pound notes, he slipped it into his coat pocket. He left, not pausing to give a last glance to his cherished apartment before closing the front door.

Fifteen minutes later he was opening the door to Rubicon's office.

Slamming her glass of gin onto her desk, she stood from her chair. "Where have you been? I have another client who has been waiting for half an hour. Get your arse back down to the dungeon." She pointed a hard finger at the closed door behind him.

Unfazed by Rubicon's anger, he stopped in front of her desk. "She'll be waiting an awfully long time if she wants me. I quit."

"We have been through this once already, Rosedale. Have you developed a preference for men? Do you wish to be raped? If not, then I suggest you take off that fine coat of yours and get your pretty arse back down to the dungeon."

Ignoring her, he pulled the wooden box from his saddlebag. The distinctive clink of coins as he dropped the box onto her desk caught her attention.

"You claim I owe you. So, I'm paying you back. The choice is yours," he said coldly, relishing the opportunity to throw her words back at her. "You can either accept this or nothing, for I shall never work for you again. Go ahead, throw me in the *Justitia*. No one will pay for me down there."

Shaking with fury, she glared at him and he stared right back, daring her to doubt his conviction. Her eyes widened as she opened the lid of the box, but she quickly masked her shock. "I'm not sure if this is enough," she said, sounding like a peeved adolescent.

Standing tall, he clasped his hands behind his back and lifted his chin. "It's enough. The deed to my apartment, along with the key, is in there as well."

She poked a finger into the box, investigating his offer. "I suspected you were tucking some money away, but . . . This is everything?" she said, her tone both a question and an awed statement.

"Everything," he lied. "If you accept it there will be no going back. No claim I still owe you even one penny." There was honor, even among thieves and whores. Rubicon may be a vindictive greedy bitch, but he had never known her to go back on a deal.

For a long moment, she was silent. She must have sensed this was his best and final offer, her last opportunity to ever receive a shilling from him for she nodded curtly. Her greed won out, just as he hoped.

"Good-bye, Rosedale."

Without even the courtesy of a parting nod to the woman who had kept him off the street, he left and headed for the nearest livery. He rented the swiftest horse, threw himself into the saddle, and tore down the lamplit streets of London. His horse's hooves thundered on the dirt roads.

There was no relief at finally being free of Rubicon. Only an all-consuming need to reach Bella. She was the only thought in his head. She would welcome him, he reassured himself over and over again, as he kept his heels pressed to the mare's sides. He could not go back to what he had been and could not go on without her. She would cleanse his soul, fill his heart, make him feel like a man again. Make him whole.

He traveled relentlessly, stopping only to change horses. Not stopping to rest and only stopping to eat when his body felt as though it was going to shut down. His backside was past numb—he severely doubted he'd ever have feeling in it again. But he refused to hire a carriage. It wasn't fast enough. He could not reach Bella fast enough.

What he would say to her, what he hoped to accomplish . . . that he did not know. He only knew that he needed to see her again—a few hours, a few moments, anything.

BELLA squinted against the afternoon sun as she looked out her bedroom window. Her roses were in full bloom, the back garden a wash of pink, red, and white. The roses needed her and she needed them. The only time she approached calm these days was when she was with them. Yet she hadn't been to the hothouse or the garden in over a week. The hot August days had been luring her guests outdoors for lawn games and various other drunken revelries, and she did not dare leave her rooms for fear of crossing one of their paths again.

Why hadn't they left yet? Moreover, why hadn't *he* left yet? Stirling had never stayed this long before. Usually it was just a brief stopover on his way to another of his estates in Scotland, or on his way back to England or Edinburgh. A few days, a week at best. A month was unprecedented. Hopefully he had not decided to take up residence. If he had . . .

A scowl marred her brow. Irritation seeped into her near-constant anxiety. He didn't even care for this property. Bowhill meant so little to him he had conceded to Phillip and included it in the marriage settlement. Yet her husband had decided to torment her and spend this particular summer here, at what could someday become her house, that is, if he went to his grave before she went to hers.

A knock sounded on her dressing room door. She tensed.

"Lady Stirling?" came her maid's voice through the narrow door.

Bella unlocked the door and opened it. "Yes, Maisie?"

"Lord Stirling wishes to see you in his study," she said, ginger eyebrows lowered and shoulders hunched, clearly reluctant to be the bearer of bad news.

A tight knot twisted Bella's stomach. Keeping her spine straight, she nodded. The maid left. Bella checked her reflection in the mirror above her vanity. The old bruise now long gone, her face was pale, her cheeks slightly more hollow than usual. Her simple morning dress would have to do as she did not dare take the time to change.

After unlocking the doors to her bedchamber and sitting room, she crept down the steps, her senses attuned for any sign of his guests.

The study door loomed at the end of the hall. As she neared it, she told herself perhaps he simply wanted to inform her of his imminent departure. It was wishful thinking, as he never kept her abreast of his plans, but she clung tightly to the thread of hope.

Her arm shook as she lifted it to knock on the door.

"Enter."

Willing the anxiety in check, she took a deep breath and entered the room.

Stirling sat behind the walnut desk, his attention on an account ledger. A full glass of amber whisky was on one of the untidy piles of paper at his elbow. Mr. Leighton's filing system, or lack thereof, never seemed to upset Stirling. Her husband granted Bowhill's aging secretary limitless largess while she received none.

She stopped two paces from the desk. As she waited for him to acknowledge her presence, her glance slid over his broad shoulder. Her heart skipped a beat.

His portrait was swung against the wall exposing the open safe.

She felt the color leech from her face.

Stirling looked up from the account ledger. "Ah, wife. You are my wife, aren't you? I've been at Bowhill for a month and only recall seeing my wife once."

His reproachful gaze swept up and down her body. She lifted her chin and tried to hide the way her knees trembled.

He sneered. "Haughty cold bitch. That's you." He leaned back in his chair and threw back half the contents of his glass. The man consumed whisky as if it were water. "I've had enough of your temper tantrums. You have been quite negligent in your duties as hostess. You will be at dinner tonight. I expect you to be polite and gracious, and not at all your usual self. You will charm our guests, leave them panting in your wake. Leave them believing I am the luckiest of men to have you for a wife."

She wanted to say no. Presiding over his table, pretending as if he were not a monster . . . She could not do it. The effort required to hold back the word pulled her brow and tightened her mouth.

"Yes, my dear? You have something you wish to say?"

He gave her the opening to at least voice the word, but she did not take it. Yet she couldn't remain silent either. "Where are your guests this afternoon?" The house was quiet—too quiet. And she had not seen them from her window.

"They went out for a ride."

Foxed men on horseback. She could only hope a few of them lost their way, or cracked a skull taking a jump. It would be particularly pleasing if Lord Ripon was one of the unfortunates. Then she wouldn't have to see his gloating, leering face across the dining table.

Stirling picked up his pen and went back to studying the account ledger. Through sheer force of will, she kept her gaze from straying to the open wall safe and waited. Waited with baited breath, nerves strung tight with suspense. And just when relief began to wash over her, just when she was about to turn and leave the room, his deep voice broke the taut silence.

"You're an expensive one to keep. That pathetic dowry I got off your brother doesn't even begin to cover you. Over five hundred pounds gone since I last visited. Your modiste should be kissing my boots. Since you now have ample gowns to choose from, I expect you to dazzle my guests." He didn't look at her as he flicked his fingers in her direction. "Something revealing. Ripon liked your tits."

The way he spoke, as if she were an object, a pet to parade in front of his friends. She had endured *his* temper tantrums, his tirades, his neglect and abuse for years! And had never once complained, but this . . . this . . .

The hate welled up. Hot and thick. Every trace of fear vanished. Her hands balled into fists and she asked the question that had plagued her for five years. "Why did you marry me?"

Startled, he glanced up.

"Why? You clearly hate me. You've never shown the slightest interest. As you so eloquently pointed out, there wasn't a fortune attached to my name. You never even danced with me when I had my coming-out. So why did you marry me?"

Lip curling, he averted his gaze. "Because everyone wanted you, at least until you proved yourself a whore. But that, dear wife, was the ultimate appeal. A woman who looked like you yet would fuck a stable boy? You were a guaranteed good ride. You were supposed to fix—" He clenched his jaw, cutting off the words.

Bella gaped at him as it dawned on her. She was supposed to have been his cure. He hated her because she had not cured his impotency. It made perfect sense. She hadn't felt hate from him on the day of their wedding. It had made its first appearance that night.

"But you're a haughty, cold bitch, both in bed and out. And yes, I hate you."

Any trace of compassion she started to feel for him disappeared. "I didn't buy any gowns," she said calmly.

He looked taken aback at the abrupt change in topic. She reveled in the confusion on his ugly face. A little triumphant grin pulled her lips.

"The five hundred pounds," she said. "I didn't buy any gowns with it. I hired a man, one who could do what you cannot. I freely gave him what you could not take. He was amazing, both in bed and out, and I love him. And yes, I hate you."

As soon as the words left her lips she went utterly still. Her voice echoed strangely in her ears. The courage slid out of her body, leaving her weak. Did she actually say that?

Stirling did not move. For a seemingly endless moment, neither of them moved. She knew she had made a grave mistake, a mistake she would pay dearly for, yet her feet were locked to the floor.

A flush rose up his neck. His eyes narrowed. A low rumbling growl filled the study.

On a strangled cry, she turned and ran. Out of the study, down the hall. Holding her skirt high to free her legs, she used her other hand on the banister to pull her upward as she sprinted up the stairs. The heavy footsteps behind her sent her pulse racing to panicked levels. She wrenched open her sitting room door and slammed it shut. Gasping for breath, she fumbled desperately in her pocket for the key, but her hands shook too hard to cooperate.

The brass key was finally in hand when the door flew open, knocking her to the ground. The back of her head smacked the hard wooden floor, sending her senses reeling.

"You whore!"

A large hand grabbed her upper arm, wrenching it almost out of the socket. He yanked her roughly to her feet. She caught a glimpse of eyes wild with fury before being thrown against the wall. Her shoulder blade connected painfully with the sharp corner of a picture frame. Instinctively, her arms flew up to cover her face.

She tried not to cry, not to plead for mercy, as he rained blow after vicious blow on her. Her ears rang from the deafening force of his screams.

"You fucking whore!"

The moment before the pain overwhelmed her, one strangely coherent thought flickered in her mind. Either his fists were a lot harder than she remembered, or he must be hitting her with something. It felt like a candlestick. Probably the silver one that had been on the small console table right inside the door.

Pity that, she had been rather fond of it.

THE sight of the manor house pulled a great sigh of relief from Gideon's chest. Praying Bella's husband was not in residence, he pulled the sweating horse to a stop and landed on his feet. He grunted, knees buckling for an instant before he willed them to work. After looping the reins over the wrought iron rail, he marched up the stone steps and knocked on the front door.

It was late but hopefully not too late for Bella to be in bed. He hastily buttoned his coat and swatted at his sleeves, sending up little puffs of dust from the road. Christ, he must look a sight. He hadn't shaved or bathed since he left London. Perhaps he should have stopped and cleaned himself up before—

The door swung open, revealing Bella's dour-faced butler. After a quick look at Gideon the man flared his thin nostrils.

Gideon squared his shoulders. "I am here to call on Lady Stirling."

"Lady Stirling is not at home."

His eyes flared. Panic seeped into his voice as he asked, "Where is she?"

"Lady Stirling is not at home to callers," the man clarified, looking down his hooked nose at Gideon.

He shook his head. Why hadn't he caught on? The butler had not meant she was not physically at home but that she wasn't receiving. "Tell her Mr. Rosedale is here to see her."

"Lady Stirling is not at home." The butler moved to shut the door.

Gideon put his foot in the jamb and placed a hand on the door to keep it open. "Tell her," he demanded desperately.

Half hidden by the partially closed door, the butler turned his head. Gideon heard a low female voice, not Bella's. A grimace pulled the butler's thin mouth. Then he nodded once and opened the door, fully revealing Bella's housekeeper. The capable, efficient air was gone. Her face was taut with unease. The tension pouring out of the open door pricked the hairs on the nape of Gideon's neck.

"You are here." There was a hint of astonishment in her statement.

"Where is she?"

Gideon's forceful demand pushed the woman back a step. But the butler held firm, the unflappable guardian of Bowhill.

"Is Lord Stirling here?" Gideon asked, fearing the possible answer.

"No," she said with a short shake of her head.

Alarm tightened his gut. "Has he been here?"

The gray eyes heavy with regret, with sadness, answered his question.

Gideon pushed the butler roughly aside, clearing a path for him to sprint into the house and up the stairs.

"Mr. Rosedale?" Mrs. Cooley's voice echoed in the hall, her quick footsteps behind him.

"Bella," he called as he approached her door. The knob turned but the door wouldn't open. He threw his shoulder into the door but it held. Bella must have blocked it. Dread skittered lightning quick through his veins. He rattled the knob in frustration. "Bella!"

"Mr. Rosedale. Do stop." The censure in the housekeeper's slightly out of breath voice turned him from Bella's door. "It won't do any good. I've already unlocked the doors but she won't answer."

"Did you tell him?" Every muscle drew tight in trepidation. If he had brought the earl's wrath down on Bella . . . He swallowed hard.

Affronted, she lifted her chin. A sneer twisted her mouth. "That Lady Stirling has had a male caller at Bowhill who is not her cousin? No."

There was a brief, very brief moment of relief before the possible true cause of the blocked door set in.

Why had he never asked Bella about her husband? She had told him she had been maudlin, had given him the opening, but he hadn't taken it. It had been too ingrained in him not to take it.

Forcing aside the question of what had pushed Bella to employ a chair in addition to a lock, he studied the door. It was big, imposing, and thick. Too thick. But not all the doors in this house were constructed like this one.

"Mr. Rosedale?"

Gideon ignored the housekeeper and disappeared inside the earl's unlocked sitting room. Beneath the scent of lemons and wax, of newly polished floorboards, was the distinct odor of a man. The room had been recently inhabited. Instinctively he held his breath as he passed through the bedchamber and into the dressing room. He turned the knob on the door but to no avail.

But this door was narrower and felt to be constructed of thinner wood. He knocked on the door first and called softly, giving Bella time to realize it was he. To open the door.

He received no response.

His muscles vibrating with panic, he took a step back and threw his shoulder into the door. The wood creaked but held. He took another step back and kicked under the knob with all the strength in his body.

The door flew open under the onslaught. Under the sound of wood splintering was the clank of metal. The room was dark, the curtains drawn tight.

"Bella, it's Gideon. Don't be frightened." Breaths sawing in and out, he lit the candle on her vanity. The flare of golden candlelight illuminated a figure curled on the massive bed. He rushed to her side, put one knee on the mattress, and brushed the tangled pale blonde hair from her face. "Bella-Bella," he whispered, the tone heavy with anguish.

Violet eyes snapped open. "Gideon?" She spoke his name as if she feared he was a ghost.

"Yes, Bella. I'm here." He made to take her in his arms, but she recoiled like an injured animal. "*Shh*," he crooned.

"It hurts," she confessed in a childlike whisper.

"What hurts?"

"Everything. Everywhere."

"Can you stand?"

"I don't want to."

"Please, Bella. Let me help you. I need to see you."

At length, she nodded and allowed him to help her off the bed. Careful and slow, he unbuttoned her dress. It slipped from her arms, fluttering in a violet wave to the floor, revealing a familiar white zephyr silk chemise. The lace-edged hem skimmed her calves.

When he made to undo the tiny buttons on the bodice of her chemise, she started again. He crooned lightly, begging her to trust him. His fingers brushed the smooth warm skin of her chest as he undid the row of buttons. She mutely lifted her arms and he pulled the garment over her head, dropping it to the floor.

She stood bare before him, trembling like a blade of grass in the breeze. The single lit candle did not provide an extraordinary amount of light, but the rays that reached the bedside were plenty enough. Dark bruises on her torso and outer thighs stood out in stark contrast from the patches of pale ivory skin. She was much thinner than he remembered. The firm breasts had lost some of their fullness. The jut of her collarbone was more pronounced and her lean hips had lost their gentle curve.

"You have not been eating well," he commented, his voice detached.

She tipped her chin down in a gesture of patent submission. "He makes me nervous."

The dark smudges under the worried violet eyes probably matched his own. But there wasn't a single mark on her beautiful face. He glanced to her forearms and found the answer. The backs of them were heavily bruised from taking the intended blows.

He reached out to turn her around but stopped, hands hovering an inch from her thin shoulders, afraid to touch her for fear of hurting her. "Turn around," he said softly.

She gave a little nod and obeyed.

He swept the heavy sheet of pale blonde hair over her shoulder and the sight of her back made him suck in a swift breath. "What did he hit you with?"

"A candlestick." She rolled one shoulder uncomfortably, the sharp plane of her shoulder blade working with the motion.

"Why? Why would he do this to you?"

"I told him about you. I shouldn't have said it, but I couldn't stop the words."

She confirmed his worse fear. This was his fault. He struggled to catch his breath. "When did he do this to you?" he asked, thankful she could not see his face.

"Yesterday afternoon. I heard them leave shortly after."

"Them?"

"Stirling and his acquaintances."

"Will he return?"

Bella shook her head. "He probably won't be back for many months. I don't know why he stayed as long as he did. He's usually only in residence for a day or two, a week at most."

Two strides brought him around before her and he embraced her as gently as he could, as though she were made of the thinnest, most fragile porcelain. She burrowed into him, hiding her face. Shivers wracked her body.

"Where are your nightgowns?"

"In the dresser," she mumbled into his chest.

He reluctantly released her and strode across the room, but a glint of metal stopped him short. Stooping down, he picked up a silver letter opener from the floor near the vanity. He stared at it a moment, then his gaze moved slowly, hesitantly up to the dressing room doorframe. Straightening, he leaned in closer.

There was a small gouge in the molding, flush with where the door would be when it was closed. He glanced back to the letter opener in his hand. The tip was blunted. With a shaky breath, he set the letter opener on the vanity and closed the dressing room door the best he could. But his kick had misaligned the hinges, leaving the door ajar.

Mindful of the naked woman standing a few paces behind him, he went to the dresser. He selected the softest nightgown from the neat stack in the middle drawer. Then he helped her to put it on and climb into bed. But he didn't join her.

"Where are you going?" she called to his retreating back.

"I'll be gone for only a moment. I need to speak to your housekeeper."

"Why do you need to speak to Mrs. Cooley?" There was a fearful suspicion in her tone.

He paused at the door to her sitting room and looked over his shoulder. "The whole household is worried about you. I'll be right back; I promise."

After seeing Bella, he had a clear understanding of the terror that had driven her to lock and block every entrance leading to her rooms. But that gouge in the doorframe . . . it wasn't fresh. That letter opener had been put into service many times. It was an easy trick, one he had used as an adolescent when he had need of uninterrupted privacy. Jam the end of an object, in his case a knife, in the frame of a closed door. The length of the knife prevented the door from swinging open. Required little strength yet highly effective.

As he removed the straight-back chair from under the sitting room doorknob and made to put it back in front of her desk, he noticed another object out of place. A candlestick lay on the floor a few paces from the desk. It was sleek and long, clearly more an object of art than practicality. He picked it up, the weight of it heavy in his palm.

The candlestick clutched tight in one hand, he opened the door. He found Mrs. Cooley waiting in the hall, an odd mixture of censure and anxiety on her face.

"Is she—?"

Gideon nodded curtly. "Fetch a doctor. I want him here now."

Mrs. Cooley's eyes flared at the sharp, commanding tone laced with fraying fury, but she did not nod in agreement. "How is Lady Stirling?"

"Black-and-blue. Fetch a doctor. *Now.*"

"Is anything broken?"

Amazed at the woman's line of questions, he gave his head a half shake. "I do not believe so, but that does not mean she is not injured. Fetch the damn doctor."

She shook her head again.

"Why not?"

"The local doctor and his lordship are acquainted."

"And? If my presence is a worry, I will make myself scarce."

"No, it's not that. If his lordship had wanted the doctor fetched, he'd have done it himself."

"Do you honestly think a man would call for a doctor after he has beaten his wife?" Gideon asked, incredulous.

"This is not London. The doctor is well-known in the village. Her ladyship would be humiliated if word got out. And the doctor may mention it to his lordship, and that would only incite his fury anew."

Gideon willed away the outraged anger. He was powerless in this household, his place undefined, but certainly below that of the vaunted housekeeper. Unless Bella requested the doctor herself, and he highly doubted she would, the man would not be making an appearance. "Do you have anything medicinal in the house? Laudanum, anything to ease her pain?"

"Only spirits. Her ladyship refuses to keep laudanum in the house. His lordship has a fondness for it."

Brilliant. In addition to being an abuser of women, Bella's husband was also an addict. No wonder she had been maudlin. "Warm some brandy and have it delivered to Lady Stirling's room immediately. And take this." He thrust out the candlestick.

"Whyever for?"

"Just take it. I don't care what you do with it. Lady Stirling is never to lay eyes on it again."

With something that resembled a nod, Mrs. Cooley snatched the candlestick and left to do his bidding.

Gideon stood alone in the hall for a long moment, battling with the need to take Bella away from here, to keep her safe with him always. But he had nothing to his name, no means to support her. And he was a whore, even if a retired one at that.

A sense of utter powerlessness threatened to overwhelm him. Squeezing his eyes shut, he fought the prick of tears.

When he felt he had regained some semblance of composure, he returned to Bella.

FOR the first time in many weeks, Bella awoke with a feeling of peace and tranquility. A dull ache rode every inch of her body, but she felt safe. She opened her eyes to find a very handsome gentleman lying beside her. Gideon was sprawled on his stomach, one arm bent under his head, the other slung across her waist.

Awakening next to a man was a singularly wonderful and unique experience. The heat radiating from his body warmed the surrounding sheets. The mattress shifted the tiniest bit with each of his deep, rhythmic breaths.

She did not remember asking him to stay. In fact, she didn't recall much after she had finished the glass of brandy he'd insisted she drink. Had he intended to stay the night? He must not have, for he was still mostly dressed. The only concession to comfort he had given himself was the removal of his cravat and coat. She slowly stretched out a leg and located his calf. Her bare toe skimmed over soft wool. He had also removed his boots. How thoughtful.

Sleep relaxed his face, giving the classic angles and planes a younger, more vulnerable smoothness. She lightly trailed her fingertips along his jaw, the few days' worth of dark beard bristly beneath her fingers. She had never seen him anything but clean-shaven, and the effect made him less the polished gentleman and more the rugged man. But it could not distract from his beauty. If anything, it added to it.

Her fingertips whispered up to brush the silken curve of his eyelashes, the thin skin beneath darkened with fatigue. He had been quite the sight last night when he'd burst through her dressing room door. The lamplight illuminating a man who had looked as though he had just traveled to the ends of the earth.

Dark lashes fluttered and swept up to reveal soft, drowsy eyes. "Good morning." His voice was raspy from sleep.

"Good morning," she said with a smile.

"How are you feeling?"

"Much better, now that you're here."

Dark lashes swept closed. A deep breath, with an ever so faint hitch, expanded his chest.

"How did you know to come?"

"I didn't. I needed to see you," he replied hoarsely, eyes still closed, eyebrows pulling together.

She snuggled closer to him. "And what a sight I am."

He rolled onto his side and fit her gently next to his body. The press of bruised flesh against his hard long body should have been painful, but it wasn't. It was immensely comforting, his presence a balm that cured all her ills.

She brushed her cheek against the soft silk of his waistcoat, soaking up the masculine scent of him. "I missed you."

"As I did you." Soft lips nuzzled her neck, his bearded jaw a bristly scrape against the sensitive skin. A strong gentle hand coasted up and down her side then paused on her hip. His body drew tight. "Did he hurt you?"

Bella tipped her head back to meet his gaze, her eyes questioning.

"Did he force himself on you?"

"No."

Dark eyebrows lowered and whisky brown eyes sharpened, testing her answer.

"No. I thought you understood. He . . . can't. He's, oh, I don't recall the term." Discomforted, she dropped her gaze and traced one of the fabric-covered buttons on his light gray waistcoat. "He used to try when we were first married but it never ended well." A jagged shudder skipped down her spine. "He hates me. Absolutely loathes me because of it. He can be polite and charming when the situation demands it, but he is a cruel man at heart."

Seemingly satisfied, Gideon went back to nuzzling her neck. His lips whispered across her cheek to find her mouth. How she loved his kisses—they made everything rosy. He kissed her softly, his lips brushing lightly. A comfort kiss. And suddenly the kiss shifted, his mouth slanting over hers, his tongue possessing the hot cavern of her mouth.

He had kissed her like this once before, and then she hadn't been able to identify the element that had made it different. But now she could, for it took up the entire kiss, hiding under nothing else, layered with no other intention.

This kiss was Gideon, honest and pure. Just him.

Just when she lost herself in that kiss, forgot everything but the feel of his body pressed against her, the urgent tremor in his limbs that matched hers, he broke the kiss. She moaned the loss. Determined to get him back, she gripped his skull and rocked against the hard arch of his arousal straining beneath the placket of his breeches.

"Bella-Bella," he whispered.

She reluctantly opened her eyes.

"Good morning," he said with a wide smile, lips wet from their kisses. The crests of his cheekbones were flushed lightly. His eyes sparkled with happiness.

Before she could form a reply, he asked, "Are you hungry?"

"Famished," she sighed, sagging into him.

"Good. I'll see to breakfast." He got off the bed.

Breakfast? She hadn't been referring to food. Bella put out an arm and made to sit up. An ache seized her entire body. Suppressing a grunt of pain, she dropped back down onto the pillows. As she waited for him to return, she realized maybe she was a bit hungry.

Seventeen

SPANNING from floor to ceiling, the shelves filled the length of one wall. Rows upon rows of books, all lined up like neat little soldiers. Yet not one of the books had ever been the slightest bit of help. The Earls of Mayburn before him had chosen to fill their London study with books on history, literature, art, poetry, and philosophy. Phillip had come across a few on the erotic arts. He had read them, of course. What man wouldn't? Yet he had rather hoped at the time his father had not been the earl who added those particular books to the library.

But what the impressive library did not hold was one single book on how to pull the earldom out from beneath the crippling pile of debt he had inherited at the age of twenty. Apparently all the other Earls of Mayburn had not deemed such a book fitting for their library. At the moment though, Phillip could use a bit of advice for he was fresh out of ideas.

Staring down at the account ledger, he rested his elbows on his desk and held his head in his hands. No matter how hard he willed it, the numbers did not change. He was still in dun territory. At least he had been able to make some progress over the last five and a half years, though most of it had come courtesy of his resourceful little brother.

When Julien had won a frigate in a card game four years ago, Phillip had pressed him to promptly sell the ship. Instead, Julien named himself captain, pulled together a crew, which happened to include a stowaway in the form of their sister Kitty, and sailed out of the London Docks, insisting he would return with far more than the ship was worth. That first voyage had not been as profitable as either of them had hoped, but Phillip couldn't deny that Julien had been right. And he also couldn't deny that it rankled a bit that Julien's ship was the only decent investment in the Mayburn earldom.

He dragged his hands through his hair. Julien better get back soon, and he best not return empty-handed like he had the last time he'd stopped over in London. Though Julien hadn't left empty-handed, at least that was what Phillip assumed given Kitty and her new husband had vanished the same night Julien departed. Phillip let out an exasperated sigh. He had more pressing matters on his mind than errant siblings, like an account ledger which refused to cooperate.

Olivia's finishing school would demand payment by the end of the month and it would not do to be late again. Phillip could only hope the expense was worth it and by this time next year his littlest sister would have succeeded where the other two had failed. It was cruel of him to expect so much of her, but there wasn't much to be done about it. The earldom needed an obscenely large influx of money, the size of which could only be had by an extremely advantageous marriage.

Phillip picked up an ivory cup and took a long sip. The coffee was hot and rich, exactly the way he liked it, but it did little to revive his exhausted brain. The morning rains had turned the roads from Norfolk into a muddy mess. It had taken him all day to travel from Mayburn Hall to London. He should have gone straight to bed, but the bills and correspondences that had piled on his desk in his absence would not take care of themselves. At least it was August and the House of Lords had recessed for the summer, giving him one less thing to worry about.

Trying to ease the tight knot at the base of his neck, he rolled his shoulders. Then he turned his attention back to the ledger. A moment later a light scratch on the door pulled him from the family's finances.

"Enter," Phillip said.

The door opened, revealing his elderly butler, Denton. "You have a caller, milord."

Phillip picked up his pocket watch from the desk. Past midnight. Debt collectors rarely came at this hour. Well, the unsavory ones did. But unless a debt had changed hands without his knowledge, there would be no cause for their kind to be calling at the door of Mayburn House.

He looked to Denton and raised his eyebrows in expectation.

"A young man, and judging by the brogue, he hails from Scotland," Denton said.

"I will see him." Suppressing a weary sigh, he closed the ledger and pushed it to the corner of the desk. He had just unrolled his shirtsleeves when the door opened again.

A sturdy young man with a wild shock of untamed red hair entered the study. The man looked more exhausted than Phillip felt. Mud flecked his boots and tan trousers. The lightweight jacket over the equally mud-flecked shirt was dusty and travel worn. The young man stopped inside the door and, wringing his hat in his hands, gave Phillip a nervous nod. "Good evening, milord."

"Come. Sit." Phillip motioned to the two maroon leather armchairs facing his desk.

The young man hesitated before crossing the room and dropping into the chair not already occupied by Phillip's discarded coat. "Thank you, milord."

"What can I do for you?"

"I've been sent to give ye this." The man wrestled with a pocket of his jacket and eventually produced what looked to have once been a folded note.

Phillip took the proffered missive. *The Earl of Mayburn, Mayburn House, London* was scrawled neatly across the paper in unfamiliar script. He pulled a letter opener from the top drawer of his desk and used it to break the seal. His eyes swept quickly over the written words. The knot in his neck tightened. "Who sent you?"

"Mrs. Cooley, Lady Stirling's housekeeper."

"Your name?"

"Seamus MacKenzie, milord," the man said with a deferential nod.

Reaching behind him, Phillip grabbed the bell pull. Within a moment his butler was at the door again. "Take Mr. MacKenzie to the kitchen and see he has a decent meal. If he so desires, he is welcome to stay the night in the servants' quarters. Then have my bag packed. I depart for Scotland tonight."

Denton gave a short nod.

"Thank you for your haste, Mr. MacKenzie. If you have need of anything, Denton can see to it."

"Thank you, milord," Seamus mumbled. He nodded again and took his leave.

His mind fixed on Isabella's housekeeper's note, Phillip stood and rounded his desk. He stopped short beside the armchair the young man had occupied. He bent down to retrieve a crumpled sheet of paper. "Mr. MacKenzie."

The man turned at the open door. His eyes widened at the sight of the paper in Phillip's outstretched hand. "Oh, sorry, milord." He scurried across the room.

The instant before Seamus's dirt-smudged fingertips touched the note, Phillip snatched it back. "Who is Mr. Rosedale?"

Hand outstretched, Seamus froze. He gave his head a short, nervous shake.

"How can you not know? Were you not to deliver this note?"

"Don't need to no more."

It did not escape Phillip's notice that the young man had ignored his first question. "Why not?"

"I was only to deliver that one if you were not here."

He glanced back at the note. There wasn't an address. Just the name, *Mr. Rosedale*, scrawled in the same script as his own letter. "Who is Mr. Rosedale?" he asked again.

Seamus's uncomfortable wince was answer enough for Phillip.

Damn Isabella. Would the girl never change her ways? "Where were you to deliver this?"

Seamus backed up a few quick steps at the flush of anger making its way up to Phillip's forehead.

"Where?" he demanded.

"Don't recall the exact address," Seamus mumbled, cowering before him.

He glared at Seamus, using his height, his broad frame, and the weight of his title to his full advantage.

The intimidation tactic worked. The young man swallowed uncomfortably and dropped his gaze to his mud-flecked boots. "To the house with the two red doors on Curzon Street."

Phillip kept his expression from changing as the bottom dropped out of his stomach. After a short pause, he spoke, his voice once again calm. "Denton will see you to the kitchen."

Clearly relieved, the man nodded and quickly left the study. Phillip ripped open the seal and read the note. It was similar to his own—a request that he was needed immediately at Bowhill Park.

As Phillip pondered the note, he heard the slam of a door then footfalls in the marble-floored entrance hall. He looked up to see Julien striding toward him.

"Evening, old man," his younger brother said with a wry grin. "No need to look so grave. Kitty and that husband of hers are back in London, disembarked this afternoon, and the two of them are disgustingly besotted with each other. Positively nauseating.

You can thank me properly over a glass of French brandy. I have an entire case of the wonderful spirit being unloaded from my carriage as I speak. A gift for the earl," Julien added with a grand bow.

"I am relieved to hear you have returned with our sister and Lord Templeton," Phillip said. "The dowager viscountess was most distressed at the unexpected disappearance of her son and her new daughter-in-law. I had to placate her with a tale of a wedding holiday I had given the newlyweds as a gift."

"Wedding holiday? That's a unique way of looking at it. I will have to inform Templeton when I call on Kitty. He's sure to find it most amusing."

Phillip shook his head, not in the mood to ask his brother what he meant. For to ask would mean answers, and he had long ago found it was better to be kept in the dark where it concerned Julien and his precious frigate, the *Mistress Mine.*

Julien dropped down onto the brown leather couch and crossed a booted ankle over his knee. Passing a lazy hand through his sandy blond hair, he tipped back his head. A very satisfied smile curved his lips. "God, I love London."

Phillip rolled his eyes. "Is that the first thing you do once you get off that ship of yours?"

"Of course," Julien scoffed. "I was gone for almost two months."

Two months—an inconceivable amount of time for his brother to go without a woman. But to Phillip, two months were the same as a day, and were the same as a year. The passage of time did not matter when one's mind was forever fixed on the family's never-dwindling debts. "I thought you had one in every port?"

"I do, but there wasn't time. Busy," Julien replied with a casual shrug. He took a deep breath and bellowed, "Denton!" He shot Phillip an annoyed frown when the man did not immediately materialize at the open door to the study. "Where's that butler of yours? The man is always sulking about but disappears when you need him most. That brandy will turn rancid by the time he gets around to having it unloaded."

"Julien, it's good to see you, too. But I haven't time for a drink and neither do you. I need your help."

Julien's blue green eyes sharpened at Phillip's serious tone. The latent after-sex haze vanished as if it had never been there. "With what?"

Those in London might take Julien as a wastrel, an indolent second son who fluttered in and out of Town on a whim, and spent his evenings at the card tables and his nights with the Season's most coveted ladybirds. They could not see past the ruse, or more so, past Julien laughing at them all as he had a jolly good time filling his pockets with their coins and winning their ladies. But Phillip knew him better. At the core of Julien was rock solid, unswayable loyalty. He knew that no matter what, Julien would always be there when he needed him, and the boy had proved it time and time again. Brothers did not turn their backs on each other.

"We need to find out who Mr. Rosedale is, and how he's associated with Isabella. And we haven't much time. We leave for Scotland tonight." He handed Mr. Rosedale's letter to his brother, who quickly read it.

Julien shot to his feet, stance strong and expression determined. Even in black evening attire and a brilliant pink silk waistcoat, Phillip could well imagine him on the deck of the *Mistress Mine* shouting orders to his crew.

"We'll go to the docks. I need to stop at the ship and inform the crew I will be unavailable. In the meantime, Fodder, my first mate, can pull up some information on Mr. Rosedale. The man's mighty quick. Within an hour he'll be able to tell us the name of Mr. Rosedale's wet nurse. Do you know where this was to be delivered?"

"Curzon Street. The house with the twin red doors."

"I know that house."

Phillip could not help but take satisfaction at the shock on his brother's face as he said gravely, "So do I."

BELLA'S days with Gideon were a stark and very welcome contrast to those of the last two months. He was infinitely careful with her, infinitely patient. He refused to allow her to leave her bedchamber for the first few days and very rarely allowed her to leave the bed. But she wasn't bored. The loneliness and anxiety were gone. Gideon was always by her side. Bella forgot about Stirling, forgot she was a married woman, forgot she had an older brother who would not at all approve of her houseguest, and lost herself in being with Gideon.

The only thing she found vexing was he kept pushing food on her. Two light meals a day and an afternoon tea were quite enough for her. But he was continually calling down to the kitchen for something or other to tempt her. The small table by the dressing room door held a silver tray heaped with dishes and bowls that were perpetually filled. And the door—it had yet to be repaired since Gideon refused to have a carpenter hammering and creating a racket.

She did her best to be patient with him, to politely refuse when he insisted, though she came close to snapping at him when he wouldn't put that bowl of fruit down.

"Just one bite, Bella. The strawberries are perfectly in season. Fresh and ripe and sweet."

"Gideon, I'm not hungry. We had breakfast less than an hour ago."

But he would not stop and the pleading look in his eyes, as if her refusal was hurting his feelings, made her snatch the berry and pop it into her mouth. The kiss he gave her—the taste of Gideon mixed with sweet, succulent strawberry. Now that was delicious.

Finally judging her strong enough to venture beyond the sitting room door, the next day he decided she could leave her bedchamber, though the outdoors was strictly prohibited and he even carried her down the stairs cradled in his strong arms like a small child.

They had dinner in the dining room, just as they used to. The only difference being she was clad in an alabaster dressing gown over her white nightgown, versus the appropriate attire for an evening meal. She hadn't even bound her hair because Gideon seemed to have developed a fondness for running his fingers though it.

After an early dinner they retired to the drawing room, he seated on the settee, she curled up beside him. There were very few words between them for none were needed. His arm was slung protectively around her shoulder, absently toying with a lock of her hair. She rested her cheek against his chest. The strong steady beat of his heart lulled her into a sort of semiwakefulness.

The sun slowly set. Its warm amber rays gently receded until all that lit the room was the faint glow of a single candle. A cool summer night's breeze floated in from an open window.

"Are you tired?"

"No." She could lay here with him for hours, but was not the least bit tired since she'd done nothing all day save walk a few steps and lift her fork to her mouth.

"What would you like to do?"

At his open question, she grinned mischievously.

He covered her hand with his, halting the upward glide along his thigh. "Not that. Not yet," he said, indulgent but firm.

Pouting, she pursed her lips. "Anything that doesn't involve going back to my bedchamber."

He chuckled softly, his chest vibrating against her cheek. "How about a game of chess?"

"That would be lovely. But you shall have to teach me, as I've never learned how to play."

"*Umm*, my lady Bella. The things I will teach you."

His sinfully rich voice pulled a purr from deep in her throat. She clung tightly to him as he gathered her in his arms and carried her the short distance to the chess table. He settled her in a chair, and as he set up the pieces, he explained the game. It didn't sound all that difficult, but her assumption was quickly proved wrong.

"Bella, sweet, a rook doesn't move that way. Over and up," Gideon said, his warm fingertips on hers as he corrected her play.

"But I wanted it to be there."

"That's the intriguing part of chess. Each piece conforms to its own set of rules. The challenge is getting them where you want them, constraints and all." Leaning one elbow on the table, chin in his palm, Gideon pondered the board. The candlelight played happily on the perfect angles and planes of his face.

"You are taking an awfully long time to decide."

He chuckled lightly. "Ever my impatient Bella."

The way he said *my*—how she would love to be his. Those endearments had been popping out of his mouth of late. He had referred to her as "Bella-Bella" for quite some time; a name owned by him. But since he had broken through her dressing room door, his vocabulary had broadened to include *sweet*, *angel*, *my dear*, *my Bella*. She liked the *my* ones best.

In fact, his words were not the only things that were different. Gideon was different. The veneer of the skillful lover was gone, leaving just the man, Gideon as he truly was. It was a side to him she had longed to see. That feeling of pretense, of manipulation, but not of her, of him manipulating himself to please her, was gone. When his gaze fell on her, it was not because he was gauging her reaction and calculating his response, but because he simply wanted to look at her.

At length, he lifted his free hand from the table, fingertips hovering over a rook before settling on a black knight. A notched *V* pulled between his dark eyebrows.

"Are you trying to figure out how to let me win?"

Startled whisky brown eyes snapped to hers.

Daring him to try and deny it, she arched her eyebrows. "You may capture my queen. I promise not to hold it against you."

"But where's the challenge in that? The game would be over in a matter of minutes."

Bella huffed in mock offense. "Are you telling me I'm easy, Mr. Rosedale?"

His lips quirked. "You, easy? Never." He moved the knight. "Let's see what you do with that. The door is open. Can you find it to walk through it?"

He was setting up a play for her again in an effort to teach her the game. She studied the board, struggling to remember how all the pieces moved and searching for that open door, when she heard the sound of horses' hooves on gravel.

She froze, her chest excruciatingly tight. It was suddenly very difficult to draw breath.

The slam of a door interrupted Gideon's concerned "Bella?"

His head snapped to his right, attention on the drawing room door, at the sound of strong, agitated male voices.

She hadn't heard it in years, but she knew the owner of one of those voices. The door to the drawing room burst open and Bella received no pleasure at learning she had guessed correctly. *Oh, dear Lord.* Why had he come, and now, of all times?

Gideon got to his feet and positioned himself in front of her, his stance defensive.

Her brother, the Earl of Mayburn, strode across the room, another gentleman on his heels. Phillip's short, medium brown hair was windtousled, his face flushed with anger. "Mr. Rosedale, I presume," he bit out through clenched teeth.

Gideon nodded once.

"Step away from Lady Stirling."

"Phillip," Bella protested. She stood beside Gideon and took his warm hand in hers. She felt him try to pull his arm away, but she held tight, needing his strength. "How dare you come into my home and behave so rudely toward my guest."

The man on Phillip's heels stopped next to her older brother. She peered into the man's face. The years had matured his features and broadened his frame, but even with the days-old dark blond beard and tanned face, she recognized him. "Jules?"

"Good evening, dearest sister. I must say, you sure know how to pick them."

The cutting tone pushed her a step closer to Gideon. Where Phillip was projecting severe irritation and displeasure, Jules, her mischievous, hotheaded little brother, was radiating venom the likes of which she had never seen before. Stirling's wrath was blunt and primitive compared to Jules's razor-sharp tongue and pinpoint precise malice.

Shoulder to shoulder, her two brothers loomed before her, an intimidating duo in long dark greatcoats with matching narrowed blue green eyes. Too dissimilar in personality, she had never known them to work as a pair. The fact they were seeing eye to eye tonight did not bode well.

"I assume Stirling is not in residence," Phillip said.

"As a matter of fact, you just missed him. He retired early tonight." Phillip's face blanked at her sarcastic comment. Good. He deserved a bit of shock. "Of course he's not here, Phillip."

"I should be pleased to find you're displaying a bit more discretion this time. But I'm not pleased. Not in the slightest. I wonder why?"

Did Phillip expect some sort of answer? The muscle ticking along his strong jaw was a resounding no. That horrible sense of guilt washed over her. It felt so familiar settling easily on her shoulders as though it had never left. But an apology would not be attempted this time. She would not repent for what she had found with Gideon, for what Phillip had tried to deny her.

"Take her to her room. Mr. Rosedale and I need to have a discussion," Phillip said in a coldly ominous tone.

Jules nodded once and walked toward her.

"No. You have no right to order me about." Holding her ground, she glared at Phillip. But Gideon shifted, pulling his arm forward, pushing her at Jules. Gideon's hand went lax and her gaze shot desperately to his, but he would not look at her. His impassive eyes were fixed on Phillip.

He was a stranger to her at that moment. It shook her enough so that when Jules took her free hand and pulled her away from Gideon, she did not resist.

YOU have the advantage over me, sir."

"You will address me as 'your lordship.' I am the Earl of Mayburn, Lady Stirling's brother, and you are not welcome in this house. Do not come here again. Do not attempt to contact Lady Stirling. Your services"—he spat the word—"are no longer needed."

His face blank, Gideon nodded. Mayburn knew. There was no point in trying to hide it. Protesting would only bring more shame onto Bella.

The last few days had been heaven. A tranquil paradise. A glimpse of true happiness. He had known it couldn't last, but he hadn't expected to be torn from Bella so soon. With great effort, he resisted the urge to howl with misery. "You will take care of her?"

He didn't think it was possible, but somehow it was. The man's response was to glower harder at him. It hadn't been wise to ask anything of the earl, but he had to be certain the man would take care of Bella. He didn't want to leave her alone. It was too soon. She was still too weak, too bruised, too frail.

Gideon reached into a pocket of his navy jacket, pulled out a paper-wrapped bundle, and held it out to Mayburn. "If you could return this to Lady Stirling. It belongs to her. I had meant to return it to her . . ." He trailed off, averting his eyes. The way the man was looking at him, as if he were gutter trash.

He felt the bundle leave his hand.

It was done.

Those pound notes had been ever in his pocket, with him, since he left London. Many a time he had been on the verge of pulling them out and returning them to Bella. But he had resisted, not willing to risk upsetting her in any way. Not wanting to remind her of what he had once been to her. No—what he *was* to her.

There was no place for him here. There never had been. Bella's brothers had arrived. They would take care of her now, and they could protect her far better than he.

He should at least be thankful that he'd been left with this brother to deal with. For they were definitely brothers. They possessed the same cold blue green eyes and the same commanding presence—that innate indicator of good breeding, of Quality, of superiority. The other one, the younger one, the one who'd taken Bella from him, had a dangerous lethal edge. One that bespoke death, of having inflicted it without remorse. If Gideon had been left with that brother to deal with, he would have highly doubted his ability to walk out of this room.

As it was, walking away from Bella was almost worse than death. In fact, at this moment, he rather thought he would prefer death, even welcome it.

There was a light rap on the door.

"Enter." The earl's command cut through the taut silence.

"Your lordship, the mount is ready."

Mayburn didn't turn to the servant. "Good day, Mr. Rosedale."

Gideon walked solemnly past Mayburn and out of the drawing room he had once shared with Bella, the earl on his heels, intent on ensuring he left the house, no doubt. The butler stood at his usual spot guarding the entrance to Bowhill. The older man's dour face held a satisfying, superior smirk.

By sheer force of will he resisted the urge to glance over his shoulder, up the stairs, and instead, without pausing, walked out the front door and to the waiting horse.

He took the reins from the groom, flipped them over the horse's head, threw himself into the saddle, and left Bowhill. Left Bella's brother standing on the top stone stair, the fold of pound notes, his wages from Bella, clutched in one large fist.

A prostitute, Bella? What were you thinking? To dally with the servants is one thing, but to actually hire a man? I can't believe you paid him. Does Stirling know where your pin money is going?"

Bella flinched. Not because of the cruelly muttered words, but because Jules's long strides were devouring the hallway and with each stride she received a tug on her arm, the one that felt as though it hadn't fully settled back in its socket. She struggled to keep up with him as he pulled her to her rooms, growing weaker with each step, hurting more with each step.

As the distance from Gideon grew, that cloak of comfort, the one that gave her the strength to stand up to her brothers, lifted. She ached in places she had not ached for days. The impact of each step reverberated up her spine, smacking each half-healed bruise on her back.

By the time Jules reached her sitting room, every inch of her hurt. He slammed the door shut, released her hand, and swung around to face her. She shrank back against the door from the disdain pulling his mouth.

"Do you have any idea the trouble Phillip went through to find Stirling for you?" he said. "But an earl's not good enough for you. No—they're *too* good for you, aren't they, Bella? You like to pull them from the gutters, the lower the better. Phillip could have saved himself the expense of your dowry and just let that groom have you. As if he doesn't have enough problems to deal with that he's got to drop everything and hightail it to Scotland. Is this how you repay Phillip for all he's done for you?"

She shook her head as he battered her with his words. The impacts hit harder than Stirling's fists ever had.

Jules stood over her, hands clenched at his sides. "We traveled straight here, not stopping except to change horses, worried out of our minds. And we find you having a quiet evening with your whore. Christ, you're barely dressed. You look like you just crawled out of bed. Was he worth it, Bella? Did you get your money's worth?" he sneered.

She pulled her dressing gown tight around her stomach, acutely aware of her state of undress. "No, Jules. I didn't . . . didn't pay him to come to Bowhill," she sputtered, finally finding her voice.

"Oh, that's rich," he said, all mocking condescension. "Try your lies on someone else. I know what he is."

"No, it's not like that. I didn't even send for him this time. You don't understand. He cares for me."

"All he cares about is your money. He doesn't care about you, and if you believed him, then you're a fool."

"No." She glared up at him. Jules had gone too far. She would not allow her *little* brother to speak of Gideon that way. "He needed to see me. You don't understand. I love him. Gideon cares for me. He needs me like I need—"

The words stopped in her throat. Bella started, her eyes going wide. The sound of gravel under horses' hooves grated on every inch of her skin, as though those hooves were traveling over her. Breath held, she strained to hear. That was the distant sound of one horse galloping.

Only one.

"No! He can't. Phillip can't!" She whirled around and threw open the sitting room door with such force it banged against the wall. She heard Jules protest behind her. A hand pulled at the back of her dressing gown. Twisting her shoulders, she let her arms fall behind her as she escaped the garment, eluding her brother. Halfway down the stairs, she felt that hand again, but her pace was no match for the comfortable well-worn cotton. With a loud rip of fabric, she broke free of Jules again, her gaze fixed on the lone broad silhouette of Phillip framed by the open front door.

Beyond desperate, she flew through the entrance hall, through the open door, but was caught by strong arms. "Gideon!"

"Isabella, stop it," Phillip commanded.

"No. No. You can't. Phillip, I need . . . Gideon!" she cried, struggling against her bonds.

"Isabella, he's gone. He will never come back."

The panic at the threat of losing Gideon had numbed her to everything but reaching him. But at Phillip's implacable words, the whole-body ache returned with such startling force it overwhelmed her nerves, swamped her senses. Using her last reserve of strength, she wrestled free of the iron-band arms encircling her sore back and crumpled to her knees.

"No, no, no," she wailed, over and over again.

Phillip had sent him away, just as he had sent everyone away from her. The physical pain was nothing, a mere pinprick, compared to the knowledge she would never see Gideon again.

DAMN it, Phillip. Don't just stand there. Do something," Julien said, with a faint pant in his voice.

"Me? You were to keep her in her room."

"I tried. She's quicker than Kitty. It's those long legs of hers." Julien scowled, clearly indignant at being bested by a female.

The two men glared at each other, daring each other. But Phillip was locked to the spot. A part of him refused to aid her. She deserved this anguish. She had brought it on herself. He had merely been cleaning up after her, yet again. But Isabella was a woman. His sister. And the sound of her wails, soaked in misery, pulled heavily at his chest.

He was still amazed he had the presence of mind to grab hold of her. The sight of her running toward him, her white nightgown and pale blonde hair streaming behind her—for a moment he had feared she was a ghost.

Julien cursed under his breath. Then he dropped to his knees. "Bella," he whispered. Her long hair covered her bowed head and back like a silvery blanket. He gathered the heavy mass in one hand, pulling the ends up from the stone landing and uncovering her face. He sucked in a swift breath. "What the bloody hell?"

Both men stared, aghast, at her prone form. A large tear in her nightgown exposed the frail lines of her back. The light from the lanterns on either side of the door illuminated a grotesque assortment of long, thick bruises mixed with fat impacts.

"Rosedale's a dead man," Julien seethed.

"No. It wasn't him," Phillip said, quick to keep his brother's wrath from landing on the wrong target. He curled his hand into a fist, gripping the fold of wrapped pound notes tightly. He had only glanced at the image sketched on the paper before Bella had come down the stairs, yet he knew the artist would have never hurt his sister.

A mighty torrent of rage roiled up from his belly, but knowing he needed to keep a clear head, he fought it down. He dropped to his haunches on the other side of her. "Isabella? Who did this to you?" He was succeeding in keeping the rage contained for he was able to suppress the urge to rip someone, anyone, limb from limb. But he had failed at his attempt at a gentle, nonthreatening question.

She shook her bowed head. Her wails had died down, the intensity gone, but still she whimpered over and over again, "No, no, no."

"The note."

At Julien's words, his attention snapped from their sister.

"This was why the housekeeper sent for you."

Annoyed by the obvious, Phillip nodded once. "Get Rosedale."

"Pardon?"

"Bring him back. Now. I don't care how you do it. Just get him here."

"Why?"

"We'll get nothing from her, but Rosedale knows what happened." The man's request had seemed odd, out of place at the time. But this was what he had been referring to. This was why Rosedale had needed to ensure someone would take care of Isabella in his stead. "Go, Julien. Now. Before he gets too far. I'll see to Isabella."

His brother's response was to get to his feet and sprint in the direction of the stables.

Eighteen

AFTER about a mile, Gideon judged himself a satisfactory distance from the earl and pulled the mare to a walk. His right pocket now empty, he had less than five pounds left to see him wherever he was headed. He needed to conserve the mare's strength, for he hadn't the coin to exchange her for a fresh horse if he wore her out.

In fact, those notes and spare coins in his pocket were all he had left to his name. He had nothing.

Impotent frustration welled up inside of him. An angry force that made him want to scream, shout, bellow at the injustice of it all. His jaw locked, he clenched the reins tight. *Goddamn Rubicon!* If that bitch would have just accepted his resignation, he'd have a small fortune at his disposal. Something, anything, to show for himself. Not that it would have helped. He was still a son of a whore. If he had been anything but a bastard retired prostitute, he would have stayed at Bella's side and stood up to her brothers. Given them a piece of his mind for allowing her to wed a monster like Stirling. Cold-blooded, greedy aristocrats. Willingly sold their kin for a title without thought to the consequences.

But what had he done? Given her over to her brothers and walked out the door. There had been no other option available to him. Nothing, because he was nothing.

The mare picked up her head, ears swiveling back toward the sound of an approaching horse. With a nudge of his leg, the mare moved off to the side of the dark road. The approaching horse skidded to a halt next to him, kicking up dust and dirt.

"Rosedale."

Just his luck. It was the other brother. The one Bella had called Jules.

Gideon's response was a mute turn of his head.

The man's narrowed eyes caught the moonlight, making them stand out in the shadows of his face. "Come with me."

Not trusting himself to speak, he turned from the man and nudged the mare forward, but pulled up at the unmistakable sound of a pistol being cocked. Judging by the volume, it was aimed right at his head.

"I am in no mood to argue with you. Turn around and return to the manor house," the man said in a chillingly flat voice. After a brief pause he continued, whatever patience he had been displaying coming to an abrupt halt. "Now," he snarled. "Do not tempt me. I *will* shoot you. I'd rather Bella blame me for your death than return empty-handed, proving you are not the man she believes you to be."

It was not the promise of a bullet, but the prospect of Bella that brought Gideon's hand to his hip, quickly turning the mare. With a kick of his heels, he prodded the horse into a ground-covering gallop.

Bella's brother surprisingly said not a word on the short ride back to Bowhill. But that could have something to do with the fact that Gideon had yet to say one word to the man. Maybe "Jules" had finally picked up the hint. Or it could simply be that they were traveling too fast for conversation to be practical.

Gideon pulled the horse to a halt at the foot of the front steps, leapt off, and tossed the reins to a waiting groom. He stopped one pace inside the house, eyes sweeping, ears straining, heart beating rapidly—and spotted Mrs. Cooley hovering in the hall by the drawing room. He pinned her with a hard questioning stare.

Her gaze flickered over his shoulder before landing once more on him. "Lord Mayburn took her ladyship to her rooms to rest."

With a short nod of thanks, Gideon headed for Bella. The sound of her voice flittered down the second floor hall. Though he could not make out the words, the heartache and desolation in the weak protests pulled him, picking up his pace.

He passed through the sitting room and stopped inside her bedchamber. Closing his eyes, he soaked up just being in the same room with her again. He took a slow deep breath, her presence filling the emptiness inside of him. Then he opened his eyes and opened his ears again.

"No, Phillip. No!"

Mayburn stood over her, clearly trying to keep her on the bed. "Calm yourself. It will be all right."

Half sprawled on the bed, she struggled against her brother's caging arms. "No, it won't. It never will be again. Please. I need him back. I need . . . *Gideon*!" The last word was ripped from her soul as her wide violet eyes met his over Mayburn's broad shoulder.

Gideon was before her in an instant. Bella rose up onto her knees and flung herself at him, face pressed against his chest. He wrapped his arms gingerly around her frail body. His gaze left Bella long enough to flicker to the earl standing beside him. He took in the grave face and nodded.

Mayburn turned from the bed.

All of Gideon's attention, every nerve in his body, focused on Bella. "Shh, Bella-Bella. Don't cry," he crooned over and over again, until her soft sobs eased and her body went lax in his arms.

He laid her gently on the bed and dropped to his knees so he could be on eye level with her. Crooning to her all the while, he gently combed the silken strands away from her face, revealing the long spiky-wet sweep of her downcast lashes and tearstained cheeks. At length her breathing turned deep and even, and thinking sleep had overtaken her, he moved to get to his feet but was stopped by an urgent hand on his wrist.

Wet lashes framed large, pleading eyes. "Why did you leave me?"

"Bella, I—" He swallowed, tried to speak again, stopped, then forced the words. "Your brothers are here. They can take better care of you than I."

She gave a short, callous huff. "I haven't seen either of them in five years. Haven't heard from either of them in just as long. That's how much I mean to them. How much they care about me."

"They're your family, Bella." The admonishment was gentle and soft, yet held a hint of intense longing. To have a chance to see Bella, he had freely given up any hope of having a family to call his own. Yet still, that longing had not gone away.

She gave that sardonic huff again, the one steeped in pain. "They are a poor substitute for you."

His breaths turned shaky at her words. He bowed his head. *I love you.* He wanted to tell her so badly it hurt, but the words would not leave his throat. Instead he pressed a chaste kiss on her forehead and got to his feet.

"Gideon, don't leave me. Not again." Tears pooled anew in her eyes.

"No. No. I'm not leaving the house. I just need to have a word with your brothers."

Desperation weighed heavily on her face. "Don't let them send you from me. Don't. No matter what they say. No matter what they do." At his silence, she pushed up onto an elbow and gripped his wrist harshly. "Don't. Don't let them. Promise, Gideon. Return to me."

"I promise," he said solemnly, hoping beyond hope he wasn't making a vow he would not be able to keep.

Her whole body relaxed and she slumped back onto the pillows. He covered her with a light blanket from the foot of the bed, doused the candle on the bedside table, and left the room.

He found Mrs. Cooley at the bottom of the stairs.

"Lord Mayburn is in his lordship's study," she informed him.

Her face was implacable, yet her gray eyes saw right through him. She may have suspected before but the scene Bella's brothers had put on this evening confirmed the truth. In less than a day the entire household would know he was not Lady Stirling's relation, nor that he was merely her ladyship's gentleman caller. Experience had taught him what to expect from this point forward from the Bowhill servants. They would be subtle, but the message would be clear.

Squaring his shoulders, he went to Stirling's study. Without bothering to knock, he opened the thick oak door for the first time. Over the past few days, he had purposely not entered this room. A study was a man's sanctuary, and this one was Bella's husband's. The room wasn't as large as he had imagined, but rather the size of Bella's sitting room. Judging from the many shelves of books lining the walls, it appeared to serve as both an office and a library. And it was surprisingly disorganized. The books weren't in neat tidy rows on the shelves and papers were heaped on the desk.

Mayburn and his brother looked out of place in this room that had the air of a dotty old man. They stood behind the desk at the rear of the room. By the agitated stance of the younger, Gideon had clearly interrupted an argument.

The earl shot his brother a warning glance, and then looked to Gideon. "Have a seat," Mayburn said calmly, indicating a chair in front of the desk with a flick of his hand.

Gideon did as instructed, settling in for the interrogation he knew was forthcoming. It was not a comfortable situation to find one's self in, but he wasn't worried. After all, he had been called back to the house and not left for dead on the side of the road.

The other brother moved to stand at the side of the desk, the better to pierce Gideon with that cold mutinous stare.

Arms crossed over his chest, Mayburn contemplated Gideon. "I know my brother well enough to know that the niceties often elude him at times like these. Therefore, an introduction is in order. This is Mr. Julien Riley, Lady Stirling's younger brother. You will be relieved to hear there are only two of us brothers, so you needn't worry about a third making an appearance."

"Two are more than enough, thank you."

Mayburn raised an eyebrow at Gideon's glib comment and sat in the chair behind the desk. Gideon had not noticed it before, for Mayburn had been standing in front of it, but the portrait on the wall now had his undivided attention. He was vaguely aware his breathing became harsh and uneven as he stared at the portrait of a man in his prime with auburn hair and dark blue eyes.

If that was who Gideon thought it was—

"Mr. Rosedale?"

Gideon's gaze snapped to Mayburn. "Who is that man?"

The earl looked taken aback at the abrupt question then glanced over his shoulder. "Lord Stirling. I take it you have never met?"

Gideon shook his head. "When was that portrait commissioned?"

"I haven't the faintest notion, but it looks to have been commissioned within the last few years."

Clenching his jaw, Gideon closed his eyes. A part of him had hoped Bella's husband was elderly. A frail old man on death's doorstep. The bruises that covered her back had proved the frail part quite wrong. But old? He had clung to that hope. An old man would have used a weapon against a woman. But the man in the portrait was powerful enough to never need the aid of a heavy silver candlestick to inflict pain on another. Yet he had done so.

Rage the likes of which Gideon had never known pounded swift and fierce through his veins. His muscles shook with the force of it.

"Rosedale."

Gideon's eyes snapped open. "What?"

Mayburn's polite contained demeanor teetered on the brink of collapsing. The muscles in his arms bulged beneath the well-tailored black jacket. The blue green eyes were not cold like Riley's but burning with malicious intent. "Who hurt my sister?"

"Him," Gideon snarled.

Mayburn glanced quickly over his shoulder again. His dark eyebrows met. "Lord Stirling?" he asked, as if fearing the answer.

"Yes."

A look of pure horror spread across Mayburn's strong face, speaking louder than words—the man knew nothing of Stirling's abuse of Bella. His shoulders sagged with the weight of his shock. "When?"

"Five days ago."

"Why?"

Gideon shook his head. "You need to pose your questions to Lady Stirling."

The shock vanished in a blink of an eye. Mayburn's face darkened with rage. He placed his hands flat on the desk and leaned forward in a clear effort to intimidate Gideon. "I will get nothing from her and you know it. You will tell me everything or you will not walk out of this room. I want to know why my sister looks like she's been run over by a carriage."

Gideon debated how much to reveal. "Lord Stirling took exception to something Bella said."

A muscle along Mayburn's jaw ticked at Gideon's use of his sister's given name. "What did she say to him?"

Gideon swallowed hard before admitting the truth. "Bella told him about me."

"Why would she do that?" Mayburn's demand reflected Gideon's own disbelief.

"I don't know." He cursed himself for not asking her what had possessed her to tell her husband she had a paid lover. She had to have known Stirling's reaction would be severe.

"Has he hurt her before?"

"Yes."

Mayburn passed a shaky hand over his jaw. "How often? How many times?"

"Only once that I know for certain, but I suspect many more. According to Bella, he hates her."

Riley advanced a menacing step. "You knew, and you allowed him to hurt her?"

"I did not know, not until a few days ago," Gideon shot back. "However, I am not the one who ignored her for five years."

Both men flinched, as if Gideon had struck them.

Riley was the first to recover. His entire body vibrated with barely suppressed rage. "You know nothing—!"

Mayburn held up a quick hand to stay him. Riley glared at his brother. Riley looked as though he was going to argue, but instead broke eye contact on a low, short growl. Then he pierced Gideon with that hard stare, as if the silent argument and his defeat had been Gideon's fault.

The earl turned his attention back to Gideon. "Has she had other lovers?"

"No."

"How can you be certain?"

"Oh, I'm certain," Gideon replied darkly.

Mayburn scoffed in disbelief. "*If* that is true, then why in God's name did he hate her?"

"Because he cannot bed his wife."

The earl's jaw dropped. His face was wiped clean of all emotion. "He is impotent?"

"Great choice, Phillip," muttered Riley in scalding derision, his arms crossed over his chest.

Mayburn ignored his brother. "How can you be certain?"

"For the same reason why I am certain she did not have any other lovers."

The earl's brow furrowed, then his eyes flared as he caught what Gideon did not explicitly state. "That cannot be. She was not an innocent when she married Stirling."

"Yes, she was. I have experienced the proof," he said with grave conviction. Mayburn stared at him, refusing to believe the truth. But Gideon wasn't done yet. "Stirling's impotency is not a recent phenomenon. According to Bella, past attempts not only didn't meet with success, but also did not end well."

He knew exactly the moment when Mayburn believed him. It was probably the instant when the image clarified in his mind of a virginal Bella in bed with her brute of a husband, as the man vainly forced himself on her then vented his frustrations. It was the same image that had tormented Gideon when Bella had confessed the truth of her marriage. The same image that still tormented him.

"Phillip—?" Riley's voice broke through the silence.

With his eyes closed, Mayburn shook his head, a clear dismissal of any question his brother wanted to pose. He raked both hands through his hair, and when next he opened his eyes, he had regained some semblance of composure. "How long have you been associated with Lady Stirling?"

"Since April of this year."

"And how did you make her acquaintance?"

"A woman came to London and"—Gideon lifted his chin—"hired me for her ladyship."

"What woman?" At Gideon's silence, Mayburn said, "Who?"

At his continued silence, Mayburn demanded through clenched teeth, "Who? Who hired you to fuck my sister?"

Somehow Gideon kept from flinching. "Madame Marceau."

"Esmé?" Riley said in incredulous disbelief. "Why the hell would she have hired a man for Bella?"

Gideon directed his answer to the earl. "She believed Bella was getting too maudlin. That she was in need of a flirtation."

"Esmé's answer for everything," Riley muttered in disgust.

Mayburn raised a weary eyebrow at the comment.

Riley's gaze slanted to meet his brother's. "I'll have a word with her." His words were barely audible, but the conviction was crystal clear.

Mayburn nodded once. "Is Madame Marceau aware Stirling beat her?"

Gideon thought for a moment. "No. I don't believe so. Her solution would not have been fitting. In fact, when Lord Stirling was informed about me, Bella's situation only got worse."

"Is Madame Marceau aware Stirling is impotent?"

"I don't know."

Mayburn was silent for a long moment. A very long moment. The silence stretched thin. Then his eyebrows pulled. "Mrs. Cooley sent two notes to London. One addressed to myself and one addressed to you. I know you did not receive yours as it is in my possession. Therefore, how did you know to come to Scotland? Did Lady Stirling send for you?"

That housekeeper had sent him a note? The woman must have been near panic to have been that desperate for someone to help Bella. "No. Lord Stirling was in residence and had been for quite some time. Bella would not have sent for me as she didn't know when he would choose to depart. I came on my own."

"Why?"

Gideon certainly wasn't going to answer that question, least of all to Bella's brother.

At length, Mayburn shrugged, as if realizing the question had been foolish to ask. "You have told me what I needed to know. You may take your leave."

Gideon did not heed the earl's command. He remained seated, uncertain if the man was trying to get him to break his word to Bella and leave not only the study, but the house.

Mayburn gave a short exasperated sigh. "You are welcome to stay, if it pleases Lady Stirling." The earl winced at the innuendo in his own words, while his brother snorted on a roll of his eyes.

Gideon got to his feet and left the study but stopped at the top of the stairs. As he debated his destination, a maid approached.

"The blue room has been readied for you."

The destination settled for him, he nodded and followed the girl down the hall in the opposite direction of Bella.

She gave him a cool assessing glance from the corner of her eye as she opened the door. Word had gotten out, and quickly. Any deference she had once paid him as a guest of the lady of the manor was now gone.

Gideon shut the door and doused the candle beside the bed. In the darkness, he pulled off his clothes and slipped under the cool sheets. He should be used to sleeping alone—he'd done it all his life and deliberately at that. But the last few nights with Bella had erased the familiarity. He had grown very fond of falling asleep with her slender body pressed gently against his, and now he felt like a child denied his favorite toy to snuggle up with.

He rolled over, punched the fluffy goose-down pillow, then settled in and tried to get to sleep.

BELLA rapped lightly on the door and turned the knob. She had already checked all the other guest rooms. This one was her last hope. "Gideon?" she called softly into the dark room.

Please, let him be here. Please, Phillip could not have sent him away again. Mrs. Cooley had reported no loud arguments. But with Phillip, volume was not always needed to inflict his will on others.

"Bella?"

The anxiety vanished, leaving behind a distinct note of indignation. She closed the door and flew to the bedside. A dark figure sat up and turned to her.

"You promised," she admonished.

The moonlight seeping between the partially closed curtains was enough for her to see the sigh that slumped his broad bare shoulders. "I didn't leave the house."

"You promised to return to me."

"Bella, I can't share your bed when your brothers are here."

"Nonsense. This is not their house. You promised," she said, sounding hurt to her own ears.

He sighed again and lifted the sheet. "Come here."

She hesitated half a second, but it was long enough for him to speak again.

"Please, Bella."

The soft plea had her dressing gown and nightgown on the floor in an instant, and then she was crawling into the bed, into Gideon's waiting arms. The lingering ache disappeared the moment his arms wrapped around her.

With her hands on his jaw, she pulled his lips down to meet hers. Pleasure, desire, rapture instantly saturated every nerve in her being. Bare skin rubbed deliciously against bare skin as she moved against him. She felt him trying to contain the kiss, but she would not be denied. She wrapped her limbs around his body. Clinging desperately to him, she trailed eager kisses down the line of his jaw and mouthed his neck, her tongue caressing his rapidly beating pulse.

"Make love to me," she whispered against the smooth taut skin.

"No. Not yet. I don't want to hurt you."

"Yes."

"Bella—"

She hitched up her hips and slid down until the hard arch of his manhood met the soft folds of her sex. "Yes."

Every trace of resistance, every trace of refusal, left him. His kiss was harsh, demanding, unyielding, and she loved it, drank it up, met him hot stroke for hot stroke of his tongue.

A large hand skimmed lightly down her back, over the swell of her bottom, and between her thighs to play at the apex of her pleasure. Seeking more, she writhed against him as his long fingers dipped into the wet, aching cove of her body.

And then she was on her back; he crouched over her, his strong arms bracketing her shoulders. The hard satiny length of his cock pressed against her inner thigh. She hooked a leg over his hip, pulling him closer. "Now," she said into his mouth.

But instead of complying, he reached over the side of the bed.

Realizing at once what he was after, she grabbed his upper arm. "No."

"Yes, Bella."

"No. I just want you. Just us." She heard the soft shift of fabric and the crackle of paper. His hard bicep flexed with his movements.

"Bella, I won't take you without it."

She brought her hands up to cup his face. "Just once." She had never needed him like this before. It was more than lust, more than a wish for shared pleasure. She had almost lost him forever.

He gave a short shake of his head. "I can't. Don't ask it of me. Not tonight," he said intently, his breaths coming hard and harsh, his body drawn tight above her.

"Gideon—"

"Either agree or nothing. Your choice."

"But—"

"I don't want to argue with you. Please, not now. Not this night. Don't push me. Don't ask—" His throat worked under her fingertips. Even in the darkness she could make out his strained features.

The last time they had had this clash of wills he had been prepared to walk away from her. She could not risk that happening. Yet she sensed in the rapid beat of his heart and in the faint quiver seizing his muscles that he was almost at the point of giving in. Just a few more words from her would take him past that point, giving her what she wanted.

But he did not want it. He would be acting against his conscious will. She trailed her fingertips past the taut cords of his neck to settle on his hard shoulders. The skin wasn't its usual velvety warm but hot with the threat of sweat.

"All right," she conceded on a nod.

He tipped his chin. His deep exhale tickled her nipples. He shifted enough to reach between their bodies and tie the sheath on securely. Then his lips met hers, the thank-you clear in the kiss for a fleeting moment before passion took hold.

The hard muscles surrounding her gathered, as if to change positions. She clung tightly to him, her nails scoring his back. "No. Here."

"Bella," he said harshly in her ear. "I don't want to hurt you. You shouldn't be on your back."

"But—"

With her leg still hooked over his hip, he rolled them onto their sides, cutting off her protests. He reached down, positioned himself at her core, and with a thrust of his hips, slowly glided into her. A groan rumbled the back of his throat. She threw back her head, reveling in that first stroke. The tightness of her body, the inherent resistance to the intrusion, the way every inch of him felt like ten.

When he was only halfway in, he pulled out and began a rhythm of short, compact, slow nudges. She could tell he was holding back, could tell he was determined to be careful. And it frustrated her. She'd waited days for him to agree to make love to her and she did not want careful. She did not want slow. She wanted hard and fast. Wanted to feel him slam against her. Needed every inch of him, body and soul.

Determined, persistent, demanding, she rocked her entire body in counterpoint to those careful thrusts. A warm hand settled on her hip, trying to force her to accede to his pace. She shook her head. "More."

"Bella—"

"More."

"Angel, please. Don't." The request was torn from his throat.

"More," she gasped, thrusting her hips into his with all the strength in her body.

Beyond impatient, beyond frustrated, she brought a hand to his shoulder and pushed him onto his back, the contact of their bodies unbroken. She planted both palms on his sweat-slicked chest and sat up on a low, drunken moan as she sank completely down onto him, fully to the hilt. Exquisite pleasure swamped her senses and for a moment, she could do nothing more but sit there impaled on his cock, her body trembling against the onslaught of sensation.

With a hard abrupt thrust, he flexed his hips, pushing somehow incredibly deeper. Her eyes flared then rolled back on a rapturous groan as an orgasm crashed over her. Swaying slightly, she struggled to catch her breath. It was almost too much.

"Is that what you wanted?" he asked with a distinctly feral edge.

"Yes," she moaned. Rocking her hips, she chased the next orgasm teasing her senses. Her clit rubbed maddeningly against his groin. "More." She could feel it getting closer, each thrust pulling it faster toward her.

He levered his upper body up and the second his hot mouth captured one hard nipple, she came. Fingers gripping his skull, she clutched his head to her chest and ground her hips hard against him, seeking even more.

He pulled free of her grasp. "Enough, Bella," he gasped, hot breath chilling her wet nipple, drawing it tighter.

"No. More." She never wanted this to end. Never wanted to be parted from him again.

"Bella, I can't hold back . . . Oh, *God.*"

All pretense of gentleness vanished. He grasped her hips, quickening the pace. Each thrust was punctuated by a raspy masculine grunt. He tipped his chin up, seeking her lips. She wrapped her arms around him, the muscles of his back rippling beneath her hands, and kissed him passionately as the orgasmic shudders gripped his body.

He dropped his forehead to her chest. His lungs heaved like bellows. "Oh, Bella," he sighed, amazement heavy in the low tone.

She couldn't help but smile. She had actually made him, Gideon, lose control.

Nineteen

I'LL start in the stables." Julien pushed from the dining room table. His expression determined, he stood and gave his black jacket a sharp tug to straighten it.

Perhaps it hadn't been the wisest decision to unleash his brother on Isabella's household, but there was nothing to be done for it. Phillip was pressed for time and he still had a couple of errands to see to this morning. Errands he shouldn't put off any longer, no matter how much he dreaded one in particular. "If you could, please try not to upset the servants."

Julien rolled his eyes. "I'm not going to threaten them with bodily harm. Just ask a few questions."

"Try to be civilized. That's all I ask. We're Isabella's guests and it would not be well-done of us to terrorize her servants."

"Shall I follow your example from last night?"

Phillip clenched his jaw. He didn't need to be reminded of his sins. He had all of last night to recount the ways he'd failed Isabella. Behaving like a domineering ass was just one of the many. "Just go to the stables, Julien."

With what was undeniably a condescending bow, Julien turned on his heel and left the room.

Arrogant whelp. Phillip shook his head, then took a large swallow of coffee and set his empty cup on the white linen tablecloth. A footman approached, a silver pot held at the ready. With a flick of his fingers, he waved the footman away. The last three cups hadn't helped in the slightest, so another would do no good.

Resting his elbows on the table, he rubbed his eyes. Christ, he hadn't gotten a wink of sleep in well over twenty-four hours. Exhaustion pulled heavily on his mind but it couldn't silence the words that resounded in his head.

She is your responsibility. And you failed her.

He was the eldest. It was his responsibility to take care of his brothers and sisters. And he could not have done worse by Isabella if he had tried.

Yet she hadn't once complained or protested. Even when he'd stormed into her home and assumed the worst, she had not railed at him for marrying her to a man who beat her. Her only concern had been for Rosedale. For the man she obviously loved, who loved her in return.

Sometime during the long, sleepless predawn hours, he had come to a decision. It went against all he had been taught and against the rules of polite society, but he didn't much care. All that mattered was that he find a way, however small, to make it up to her.

He pushed from the table. He could delay his errands no longer. Since he needed an answer from one before seeing to the other, he set off for the guest bedchamber down the hall from his own.

SHAFTS of morning sunlight pierced the gaps in the heavy curtains. Completely content, Gideon sighed as he absently rubbed a lock of pale blonde hair between his fingers. Through heavy-lidded eyes, he gazed at the beautiful woman who shared his bed. Her back rose and fell in the rhythmic pattern of one in a deep sleep. Even sprawled half on top of him, the innate elegance of her long limbs could not be denied.

Nor could he deny the strength in those long limbs as they had been wrapped tight around him last night.

He should have been gentler. Hell, he should not have even given in to her. He should have waited longer, until she fully healed. But the combination of two months of abstinence and a demanding, impatient Bella . . .

He let out a low grunt. He had never come like that before—the orgasm rushing upon him, too swift, too fierce to be denied. His cock swelled, pressing against the smooth skin of Bella's upper thigh. The idea of waking her was tempting indeed, but he resisted. After last night, she needed her rest. So he closed his eyes, content to fall back asleep with her warm body draped over his.

There was only a very brief knock in prelude to the sound of Mayburn's strong voice. "Get up, man. I need—Oh!"

Jolted awake, Gideon yanked the blankets up to cover Bella's naked body. Apparently the light knock and the sound of her brother's voice weren't enough to wake her, but Gideon's movement was enough.

She lifted her head from his shoulder, her eyes half-lidded. "Good morning," she said drowsily.

She must have read something on his face, for she twisted around and sucked in a startled breath. On a little squeak, she dove under the blanket, huddling close to him.

Gideon draped one arm protectively over Bella's back and stared at Mayburn, daring him to take issue with Bella's presence in his bed. He was not about to apologize for making love to Bella. In any case, she had come to him.

"Is he still there?" a meek little voice asked from beneath the blue blanket.

Gideon couldn't help it. He chuckled. "Yes, Bella. Though it looks like you scared him more than he scared you."

Mayburn snorted, the jest bringing him to his senses. "Sorry, Isabella. I didn't know . . ." He shook his head. Then his voice returned to its normal strong tone. "Rosedale, I need to speak with you."

Gideon lifted one eyebrow.

"Alone. I will await you in the hall. And put some clothes on." Mayburn stalked out of the room and shut the door.

It took a bit of doing to disengage from Bella, and three promises on his part to return promptly before she would consent to let him out of the bed. He pulled on the trousers he had left in a heap on the floor and quickly buttoned them. Pulling his wrinkled shirt over his head, he walked to the door.

Hand on the knob, he looked over his shoulder. Clutching the blanket tight to her chest, she sat on the bed. Her pale blonde hair was loose and disheveled around her shoulders, her eyes wide with uncertainty. And he gave her one more "I promise" before slipping out the door.

The hall was empty save for Mayburn, who stood a few steps to the left of the room. Gideon stopped before him and waited for the earl to speak.

Mayburn dragged a hand through his hair. "We shall pretend that did not happen," he muttered.

"Define *that*," Gideon said hesitantly.

"I did not just see my sister naked. That makes two of them. Here's hoping the third doesn't follow in the others' footsteps."

Gideon shrugged. He didn't know what to say. He had not known Bella had sisters.

The discomfort disappeared from Mayburn's face, leaving a stern frown in its wake. "There is something I need to ask you and I expect an honest answer."

Gideon bristled at the condescending tone. He squared his shoulders. "You may ask all you like. Whether I chose to answer is another matter."

The earl did not react to Gideon's snide comment. "Are you still in the employ of Madam Rubicon?" he asked, voice pitched low.

Gideon tried, truly he did, not to get rattled by Mayburn's question.

The man clearly had had him investigated. No wonder Mayburn had been so livid when he had come to the house. Gideon could understand the man's need to verify his employment status. He was still amazed Mayburn had allowed a known prostitute to remain at his sister's home last night. Yet he could not help but feel exposed by the blunt reminder of his past.

"No." At Mayburn's hard glare, Gideon clarified, "It is true I had been employed by Madam Rubicon for a number of years. However, I have since resigned."

Mayburn crossed his arms over his chest. The way the earl studied him reminded Gideon vividly of the way Madame Marceau had appraised him many months ago in Rubicon's office. As in that instance, he had to fight to keep his chin up and not to shift his weight.

After a long moment, Mayburn nodded. "Riley and I are leaving for London this morning."

"So soon?" The man was an earl. Still, to be so busy he could not spend even twenty-four hours with a sister he had not seen in years? A sister who had recently been severely beaten by her husband?

"Yes. I was unexpectedly called away," Mayburn said. "There are business matters that require my attention and Riley has his own business to attend to. I am leaving Isabella in your care. Bring her to London immediately if Stirling returns. She knows the way to Mayburn House. If I am not there when you arrive, inquire with the butler. He'll know my whereabouts."

"But—"

Mayburn continued as if Gideon had not spoken. "I have already informed the household that Lady Stirling has been placed in your care. You have my authority to act as you see fit. You are to keep her safe, at all costs."

"But Stirling is still her husband," he pointed out.

Mayburn tipped his head. "And I expect Isabella to remain safe while in your care. No harm is to come to her. I don't care what you have to do. She is to be protected. Do you understand?" His blue green eyes bored into Gideon's.

"Yes," he replied, stunned. It sounded as if the Earl of Mayburn trusted him.

"According to Mrs. Cooley, Stirling rarely visits. He shouldn't be due back until after the new year."

Gideon nodded again.

"Until then, you are to focus all your efforts into Isabella's recovery. What did the doctor advise? Shouldn't she limit her physical activity?"

He resisted the urge to roll his eyes at the underlying meaning in Mayburn's words, and instead admitted, "The doctor has not seen her."

"What?"

"I tried, but Mrs. Cooley advised heavily against it. Nothing was broken. Bella was just very badly bruised." The excuse sounded pathetic even to his own ears.

"What possible reason could that housekeeper have?"

"Many and varied," Gideon said. "The doctor and Stirling are acquainted. Bella would have been humiliated if word got out. If Stirling had wanted a doctor, he would have called for the man himself—"

"That's absurd."

His shoulders slumped. "Yes, I know. But short of going into the village and knocking on every door in an attempt to locate the man, he would not be making a call."

Mayburn glowered, bringing to mind the image of an extremely displeased feudal lord. "If you feel a doctor should see Isabella, call for him. I will have a word with Mrs. Cooley. She will get the man here, if need be."

Gideon nodded. He was relieved, but a bit emasculated to have his station in this household so thoroughly revealed.

"Good. I expect a note if any problem should arise."

"Yes," Gideon droned. He felt as if he were being put in charge of a group of young children for the day and getting his orders on how to care for them properly.

"I need to speak with Isabella before I leave."

"Alone?"

"Alone."

"Tell her I went down to the kitchen to get her some breakfast." At the odd look on Mayburn's face, he added, "I promised her about four times that I'd return. Immediately."

Mayburn snorted. One corner of his mouth pulled in a rueful grin.

He left the earl knocking on the door and went to fetch some food for Bella. She was still much too thin. He had tried everything he could think of and everything the kitchen staff suggested, but she didn't seem to have a preference for much.

As he went down the stairs on bare feet, he debated the merits of various dishes to tempt her. Definitely some eggs. Sausages? Maybe. Kippers? No. But yes on the fruit. She seemed to like that.

He came upon Riley in the entrance hall by the front door. Hands on his hips and stance wide, it was obvious Riley was not having a pleasant chat with the unfortunate young footman.

"Are you certain?" Riley questioned.

"Yes, sir."

Riley scowled at the footman. The piercing gaze quickly left the servant, took in Gideon's disheveled appearance, then snapped up to meet his eyes. Gideon tipped his head in greeting but said not a word. As he made his way down the hall, he could feel those blue green eyes scorching a hole through the back of his neck.

Yes, it was a good thing the brothers were leaving today. He did not much care for that one.

THERE was a soft knock on the door followed by a low, hesitant, "Isabella?"

"Yes, Phillip."

"Are you dressed?"

Sitting in the center of the bed and huddled in the blue blanket that retained the scent of Gideon's warm body, she couldn't bring herself to admit the truth.

Phillip must have suspected though. "Can you, please?"

Bella reluctantly discarded the blanket, scooted off the bed, and pulled on her nightgown and dressing gown. She kicked Gideon's boots, waistcoat, and jacket under the bed; shook out the blanket to cover the rumpled sheets; and, running her fingers through her hair, tamed the tousled locks as best she could.

She sat in the armchair by the window. "Phillip, you can come in."

The door slowly opened. Eyes shut, he took one step into the room then opened one eye. At finding her dressed, he opened the other eye.

With effort, she straightened her spine and tipped her head to the chair next to hers.

He sat down. "Julien and I are leaving shortly. I have notified the household that you are in Mr. Rosedale's care. You are to follow his instructions."

Bella nodded. With his medium brown hair, strong features, and powerful build, the sight of him alone was a heavy reminder of their father. But when he spoke to her in that paternalistic tone, she could have sworn he was the man himself.

"If Stirling returns, you are to let Mr. Rosedale deal with him. He has been instructed to bring you to London immediately. If anything should happen or if Mr. Rosedale is removed from you, I want you to come straight to London, to Mayburn House."

She maintained her serene expression and nodded again, effectively hiding the apprehension his dire words sparked.

Phillip's mouth tightened. His brow furrowed. Somehow she managed to sit perfectly still, to not even reclasp the hands folded demurely on her lap.

"Why did you never write?" His tone was soft, probing, almost injured. "Why did you never say anything? If you didn't want to tell me, you could at least have told Esmé."

"What good would it have done?"

He leaned toward her. "Isabella, he was hurting you."

"He is my husband," she stated calmly, careful to keep any censure or accusation out of her tone.

Still, Phillip looked as if she had slapped him across the face. His throat worked soundlessly. But when next he spoke, she had the distinct impression the words were not those that had lodged in his throat. "Kitty has married."

"She has? Liv didn't mention it in her last letter." Bella was a bit piqued at the omission. While Kitty's letters were infrequent due to her travels with Jules, Liv was a diligent correspondent and Bella counted on her to keep her apprised of events related to their family.

"It was a rather hasty informal affair much like your own. There wasn't time to fetch Olivia from school so she could attend. Likely her next letter will include the news."

Kitty, the unconventional girl who grew up in Jules's shadow, had needed a quick wedding? Hopefully Liv would relay the details. "And who is the chosen gentleman?"

A wince pulled his mouth. "Lord Templeton."

Bella tipped her head in approval. She remembered the rugged, imposing gentleman from years ago. She'd have never thought to match the two up, but Lord Templeton was a viscount, and though not fabulously wealthy, a well-respected one at least.

"From what Julien reports, they are quite happy together."

She was relieved to hear that—Jules would know if Kitty was truly happy. "I shall write to them and extend my congratulations."

They sat in silence, strangers who had run out of polite topics to discuss. A cool morning breeze ruffled the curtains. The distinct scent of roses wafted into the room.

She stared at her clasped hands. Once they had been quite close. Kitty had Jules and she'd had Phillip. They had understood each other, understood their roles, and had a similar desire to be the people their parents had wanted them to be. But the bond they once shared had been crushed by her own hand. Every shred of trust he had in her was long shattered. Phillip had become the man he had wanted to be. He was the very image of their father, a living replica of the man they lost six years ago. Whereas she . . . she had let him down. He had to come up to Scotland and have the full extent of her continued fall into disgrace revealed to him.

"How are you faring?" Phillip asked, breaking the silence. "If you need anything, tell Mr. Rosedale."

She glanced up. "I am quite well, thank you, and I will notify Mr. Rosedale if I require anything."

It was Phillip's turn to nod. He reached into an inside pocket of his dark green jacket and held out a poorly wrapped bundle. A thick fold of pound notes was visible beneath the paper wrapping.

Bella looked blankly at the offering. Why was he giving her this? Did he believe Stirling denied her pin money?

"Mr. Rosedale asked that I return this to you."

She froze. The quick beats of her heart filled her ears. How had Phillip gotten ahold of it? "No. I don't want it. It belongs to Mr. Rosedale."

He thrust the bundle at her. "Isabella, take it."

"No." She leaned back, keeping her distance. It was one thing to have Jules accuse her. Quite another to have the proof so harshly and plainly before her, and to have it come from Phillip.

"What would you have me do with it?"

"Return it to him. I do not want it," she said, her voice strengthening in intensity.

"Isabella," he admonished. "I will do no such thing."

"Why not?"

"Because he does not want it." Incredulous, Phillip stared at her. "I thought you cared for him. Do you have any idea the insult you would be delivering if I were to return this at your request? I will not do it."

Frustrated at his insistence, she snatched the bundle from his hand.

The weight of it felt wrong. Brow furrowing, she thumbed through the stack.

Phillip frowned. "He didn't spend it, if that's what you think. I suspect his employer has the other half. You will never see it."

"Half?"

"Yes. That's how it usually works," he said wearily.

"But there's more than two hundred and fifty pounds here, unless . . ."

"Unless what?"

She shook her head. "Nothing. I miscounted." Quickly, she refolded the paper over the pound notes. She was not certain if Phillip was aware Gideon had been hired twice to come to Bowhill. If he wasn't, then she did not want to inform him Gideon had returned his wages from both occasions.

And he had returned them. Without even knowing the sum Esmé had parted with, she was certain she held exactly half of what she and Esmé had paid for Gideon. The significance of the paper wrapping did not escape her notice. It was worn and wrinkled, the pencil marks slightly smudged, but even half covered by the pound notes she recognized the artist's hand.

Bella wasn't sure which meant more to her—the fact he returned the money, or that he had kept the sketch for so long.

Phillip shifted, dropping his gaze then resolutely meeting hers again. "Isabella, you're my sister. I never meant to see you harmed."

"I know, Phillip," she said softly. While he had been upset with her at the time, and rightly so, she had never been so foolish as to believe Phillip had married her to Stirling with full knowledge of his true character.

He slumped heavily in the chair and ran a hand through his hair. "I never should have had you wed Stirling. You didn't even know the man. I'm sorry. I had no idea he would . . ."

The obvious pain on his face tore at her chest. Stirling was not Phillip's fault. She had inflicted him on herself. She would not apologize for Gideon. That she would never do. But she did still owe Phillip an apology of her own.

"I'm sorry, Phillip. I-I'm sorry I let you down all those years ago. I shouldn't have been so reckless. I should have tried harder. I should have expended an effort to bring a gentleman to heel. If I would have then . . ." Closing her eyes, she shook her head, trying to find the words. "Kitty and Liv write to me. They are never so blunt, but it's obvious you're still struggling. I can't help but feel if I wouldn't have failed you when you needed me most then—"

"Isabella."

She looked up and took a swift breath at the mingled horror and disbelief on his face.

"No," he said harshly. "The state of my finances is not your fault. Nor is it your responsibility. Don't think it. Ever." He leaned forward and grasped her hand firmly. His gaze bored into hers. "It is I who failed you. I should have been more understanding. I shouldn't have tossed you out onto the marriage mart mere months after we lost Mother and Father. Hell, the least I could have done was send you a note within the last five years. Let you know that I . . . that I still—"

Eyes clamping shut, his face contorted on a wince. He released her hand and pressed his palms to his temples. Dragging his hands down his face, he took a deep breath. The tension slipped out of his broad shoulders. He met her gaze: his steady, hers wary. "I want you to be happy, Isabella. Don't worry about me. You do what will make you happy. And whatever that is, I will always be your brother."

She bit the inside of her cheek to keep the calm façade in place and nodded. There had been a time when she had been certain he would never call himself her brother again.

He stood on a weary sigh and tugged on the end of his jacket to straighten it. "Take care of yourself."

"I will."

He turned and left the room on heavy footsteps.

"I still love you, too, Phillip," she whispered as he closed the door quietly behind him.

Do you know where you're going?" Phillip asked of his brother, who sat sprawled in the maroon leather armchair facing his desk. After an arduous journey back to London, the two men had cleaned up, and then met in the study to start in on the French brandy.

"A maid overheard Stirling mention he was headed to Rome," Julien said. "One of his cronies has a villa outside the city where they plan to spend the winter. Christ, he had a whole group of them up at Bella's house. Judging by what the servants reported, they were a raucous, unpleasant bunch. Emptied the wine cellar and all. Bella's housekeeper said she was still working on righting the house."

If Julien thought Stirling's friends raucous and unpleasant, then that was saying a lot. "Will you take the ship or go overland?"

Julien passed a hand over his jaw. How could he stand to go so many days without shaving? The sight of the scruffy, dark blond beard made Phillip's neck itch.

"It'd be best to go via sea," Julien said. "Couldn't discover anything as to their travel route, but by the time I reach Rome they should be well settled in."

"When are you leaving?"

"As soon as I can get the crew back on the *Mistress Mine*. Rounding them up will be a chore. May require a day or two. The crew hasn't even had a week of shore leave yet and most of them scatter the instant I give the word. And I'll stop over in France, see if I can locate Esmé. I still can't believe she hired a man for Bella. What was she thinking? If she thought Bella unwell, she should have mentioned it to you or me. I saw her over the winter and she said not a word."

"I don't know why she didn't mention it," Phillip said. "But you know her better than I. Just don't be too hard on her. She was trying to help Isabella, in her own way."

Julien snorted his disgust, clearly at odds with their cousin's methods. Phillip didn't condone them either. But ever conscious of how quickly Julien's temper could escalate when he believed one of his own had been wronged, Phillip felt the need to add a few calming words of wisdom. They might fall on deaf ears, but at least he made the effort.

He swirled the remains of his brandy, watching the amber liquid catch the nearby candlelight. At length he posed the question that had been weighing heavy on his mind for the past few days. "Julien, is Kitty truly happy with Templeton?"

"Of course she's happy. I already told you. It's nauseating to be in her presence. A more lovesick pair I have yet to encounter."

"He would never hurt her, would he?" Phillip asked carefully.

"No. Never laid a hand on her, and she's given him ample reason to do so. She ran that man ragged. Even made me feel sorry for him at times—but not too sorry. He rather deserved it for daring to trifle with our sister. He is a good man though, has her best interests at heart. And he positively adores her. Got to, to put up with Kitty. She can be quite a handful."

"Good to hear," Phillip said, immensely relieved. At least he had managed to get it right once.

With a thud, Julien dropped the foot that had been crossed over his knee onto the floor. His eyes narrowed. "I'm assuming you did not know what sort of man Stirling was when you tied Bella to him?"

"No, I didn't," Phillip said with forced calm. "Though I'll admit, I didn't know the man very well. He was simply the only peer I could find who was willing to take her."

Julien *harrumphed*. "Could have expended some effort to have him investigated."

To be scolded by his younger brother was not a pleasant experience. Resisting the urge to drop his gaze, he squared his shoulders and glared at Julien. "Yes, I could have. And I normally would have, but at the time the possibility never entered my head that he could be an impotent abuser of women." He purposefully left out the "he had seemed like a nice enough chap" comment. "And I had to act quickly. For Christ's sake, after finding her with that damn groom I feared she could have been with child."

"Well, we now know *that* wasn't a possibility." Sarcasm dripped off Julien's words. "And you couldn't have chosen more poorly if you tried. An impotent husband for a woman like Bella? That's a punishment if I ever heard of one."

The barb hit sharply home. "Enough, Julien. I feel bad enough as it is. I don't need you to make it worse."

"Good. You should feel bad. She's our *sister*."

The fierce protectiveness radiating from Julien's hard words rankled far more than it should have. "Yes, she is. *Our* sister. Convenient how that fact slipped your mind for five years."

"I've been occupied earning the money that pays for your damn servants."

"'Earning' money, that's an interesting way to put it. I thought the correct term was *smuggling*."

"At least it's something. What the hell have you done? Besides ignore our sister."

"Everything!" Phillip shot back. Though they felt like trivial, inconsequential matters compared to Isabella's well-being. "You have no concept of what it takes to manage an earldom, and you never bothered to learn. You were too occupied swiving anything in a skirt."

Julien flinched, as if Phillip had actually hit a raw nerve. But in the blink of an eye, he recovered. "Bugger you, Phillip. You're the earl. You chose Stirling. I trusted your decision." His sandy blond forelock fell over eyes blazing with anger. Gripping the arms of the leather chair, he looked ready to launch himself at Phillip. To take out all his pent-up rage on a brother whose decision had ultimately caused harm to their sister.

Phillip made not a move. Merely stared blankly at Julien. There was no defense to be had against the truth. Frankly, he was surprised it hadn't come to this point sooner. "Go ahead. Hit me. I certainly deserve it."

For a moment, Phillip thought Julien *would* hit him. But after a few tense seconds of silence, he leaned back and loosened his grip on the chair. Apparently he had a better leash on his temper than Phillip gave him credit for.

"What are you planning to do about Rosedale?" Julien's tone held only a shadow of its previous animosity.

"Nothing."

"Nothing?" His brother gapped at him. "You're going to allow a prostitute to live with our sister?"

"Former prostitute," Phillip clarified. "Rosedale is no longer employed by Madam Rubicon. He resigned."

Julien snorted. Clearly his brother thought that detail to be of little significance.

"He cares for her. And more importantly, she cares for him. She deserves a spot of happiness in her life after all she's been though. I will not stand in the way. Neither will you," Phillip said firmly.

Julien looked as if he was going to argue, then he tipped his head, submitting to Phillip's will.

In an effort to ease the guilt gnawing viciously at his gut, Phillip took a long swallow of brandy. Gripping the crystal glass tightly, he stared at the sliver of amber liquid coating the bottom. "I never before realized how much power a man has over his wife." His voice was low as he spoke the thoughts plaguing his mind. "It's disturbing and completely unnecessary." He glanced up to Julien. "Do you realize Stirling practically owns her? I'm an earl, her brother, and still there's not much I can do for her. If I thought it would help, I'd try to get her a divorce. But I doubt Stirling would be agreeable. He'd fight it. What man would want his marriage nullified due to impotence? And if he wanted to be rid of her, he'd have done so himself by now. Instead, he keeps her up at that house, rarely visits, and when he does, he beats her."

Phillip dragged a hand though his hair in frustration. He had hated leaving her, but he had too many responsibilities in London and at Mayburn Hall to let either place go unattended for any length of time. He felt like he was being drawn on the rack, pulled in opposing directions. But at least he had not left her alone. He was confident he had gotten through to Rosedale. Isabella would be kept safe under her devoted beau's watchful eye in Scotland.

"Well, that problem will soon be solved." Julien got to his feet and set his empty glass on the desk. "I better start rounding up the crew."

"Be careful in Rome." Phillip refilled his own glass of brandy.

The remark got him a smug, devilish smirk. "Of course. When have you known me to be anything but?"

Twenty

GIDEON glanced out the dining room window. It was early October. Autumn had arrived in full force. The Scottish winds held a definite bite of winter and often kept Bella and him indoors. The last rays of the setting sun picked up the deep ambers and golden yellows of the leaves on the trees in the distance. Scotland was beautiful in the autumn, but it could not compete with the woman seated on his left who was currently moving neatly cut squares of lamb around her plate with the tines of her fork.

Relocating her food was a sure sign she was not going to eat another bite. He had stopped arguing with her. It was a battle he rarely won, and in any case, she had regained some weight. Her figure was back to being lean and willowy, no longer on the verge of being labeled *gaunt* or *frail.* The last of her bruises had faded to nothingness weeks ago. He should know, as he had ample opportunities to examine every inch of her soft alabaster skin.

His cock began to swell, as thoughts of Bella's lithe naked body slammed into his mind. Closing his eyes, he willed the erection down.

An hour or two wasn't an unreasonable amount of time to wait to indulge his desires.

Reaching for the glass of wine, he downed the remaining Bordeaux in one swallow. It certainly couldn't hurt to speed the evening along.

"Are you finished with dinner?" He knew the answer, but it was always best not to assume where a woman was concerned.

Her hand stilled in the process of pushing a square of lamb toward the barely touched mound of peas. She looked up from her plate. "Yes."

He flicked his fingers. The footman stationed along the wall jumped into action, clearing the table of plates and silverware. "Do you have a preference for our afterdinner activity tonight?"

Bella's lashes swept down. Slow and sensual, a thoroughly wicked grin curved her mouth. "Yes, I do. But I'm almost finished with the embroidery on the pillowcase I plan to send Liv. I should take care of that first or it won't get done tonight."

Quickly revising his earlier timetable, he pushed back from the table. That grin said Bella would have her embroidery completed in significantly less than an hour. He stood and glanced to the footman. "Have tea and a glass of scotch delivered to her ladyship's sitting room."

Loaded down with the remnants of their dinner, the footman tipped his head and left the dining room.

Gideon pulled out Bella's chair and held out a hand, helping her to her feet. She looked as regal as a queen in the deep amethyst silk gown. The vibrant color was the perfect complement to her fair complexion. His glance fell to her chest and his fingers itched with the need to tug on the low neckline. It wouldn't take much to free her luscious breasts, and then he could take the weight of them in his hands and lift them high to suck on the hard tips.

"Have I told you yet how beautiful you look tonight?" Gideon asked, as they walked out of the dining room.

"Yes, you have. Twice in fact, if I recall correctly." She lifted her skirt with her free hand as they ascended the stairs. "Thank you, and you look rather handsome yourself this evening."

He stopped at the top of the stairs and gave her his best indignant expression. "Rather?"

She turned to face him, stepping so close her breasts brushed his stark white waistcoat. Placing a hand on his shoulder, she lifted up onto her toes. "Very handsome," she whispered and pressed her lips lightly to his.

Her fingers drifted down his chest to brush the placket of his trousers before taking hold of his hand. The light contact made his cock twitch with impatience. He resisted the urge to pull her against him and kiss her soundly. The servants knew he and Bella shared a bed, but it would not be well-done to engage in a tryst in the hallway.

Hand in hand, he followed her into the sitting room. Her naughty fingertips caressed his palm as she released his hand. She disappeared into her bedchamber to gather her embroidery hoop and thread. He stopped before the tall narrow bookcase next to her writing desk. *What to read this evening?* He needed something to take his mind off Bella's luscious breasts for the next half hour or so.

A maid entered the room carrying a silver tray laden with an ivory tea service and a crystal glass half filled with pale amber liquid. The teacup rattled on its saucer as she set the tray on the table beside the settee.

"For you, sir," the maid said.

He glanced to his right to find the maid beside him. "Thank you." He took the proffered glass.

Smiling slightly, she gave Gideon an abbreviated curtsey. The maid busied herself lighting the fire in the small hearth then left the room, closing the door behind her.

With the glass in one hand, he skimmed a fingertip over the leather spines of the books. Ever since Mayburn had left the servants had treated him, well, not quite like a lord, but definitely not like someone below their ranks and with distinctly more deference than a mere guest. It had taken him a few weeks to stop bracing for the usual resentment and grow accustomed to his new status in the household. And it was a rather nice feeling to be looked upon as a man and not as an object worthy of scorn.

After making a selection, he settled in the floral chintz armchair, crossed one leg, resting his ankle on his knee, and opened the thick leather-bound book.

Bella gave him a soft smile as she walked back into the sitting room. She poured a cup of tea and sat on the settee. The crisp scent of Earl Grey made its way to his nose. With a flick of her wrist, she arranged her skirt about her legs and then set to work. Her long swan's neck was bowed in concentration, her fine eyebrows pinched together the tiniest bit.

The logs in the hearth crackled. It was so quiet in the room he could hear the sound of the needle and thread pushing through the taut linen as Bella embroidered. He took a sip of scotch and savored the pleasing burn down his throat. With a soft click, he set the glass on the end table and flipped a page in the book.

The minutes slipped peacefully by, one seamlessly into another. Every now and then there would be a little snip as Bella used her small scissors to cut a thread.

"Finished. I do hope she likes it."

Gideon looked up. "I'm sure she will. It's a gift from her sister, and a beautiful gift at that."

She brought the ivory cup to her lips. "How can you say that when you haven't even seen it?" she said, setting the cup on its saucer.

He shrugged. "I just know, but you could show me if you like." He let the book fall to his lap and beckoned her with one finger.

Her little chuckle was music to his ears and never failed to make him smile. She removed the pillowcase from the embroidery hoop and crossed the short distance to stand before him.

He ran a finger over one of the expertly embroidered red roses.

"Chinas. My favorite, and beautifully done. As I said, I am certain Liv will like it."

She tipped her chin. A faint blush colored her high cheekbones. "Thank you. But even if it were atrocious, I believe you'd still tell me it was beautiful."

"Of course," he said with a wink.

She rolled her eyes and snatched back the pillowcase. "I'm going to retire for the evening. Are you coming?"

"In a minute. Just want to finish this section."

Peering down at the book, she titled her head to read the words upside down. "Rose propagation? Why would you read that? You don't grow roses."

"No. But you do."

The smile she bestowed on him made his heart thump against his ribs. It was the same smile she had given him after he sketched her many months ago. But this time, the need to pull back, to retreat from what he saw reflected in her eyes was absent. If anything, he now longed for more.

She cupped his jaw. Her warm fingertips rested lightly on his neck. "You are the dearest of men," she whispered. She brushed her thumb across his lips. He flicked out his tongue, tasting her skin.

She took a swift breath then turned in a *swoosh* of silk. "One minute." Her back straight and her head held high, she disappeared into the bedchamber.

He laughed as he turned his attention back to the book. *One minute.* He better read quickly.

After he finished the chapter on grafting techniques, he replaced the book on the shelf. He went into Bella's bedchamber, closed the door quietly behind him, and turned the lock. Leaning back against the door, he absently worked the knot on his cravat.

She was seated at the vanity, bare ankles crossed and tucked to one side under the stool. The thin straps of her chemise framed the delicate planes of her ivory shoulder blades. The amethyst gown, crossed with a pair of white silk stockings, draped the back of a nearby chair.

Her young lady's maid, Maisie, moved around her pulling the pins from Bella's hair and releasing the glorious length from the confines of its tight knot.

He loved to watch Bella undress in the evening. He knew the ritual by heart. The maid and her lady working in harmony. The mirror above the vanity reflected Bella's beautiful face. Her eyes closed, her expression relaxed, yet her back was still ramrod straight.

These were the moments he treasured above all. When he could believe, truly believe, she was his. That she was not another man's wife. That he belonged here, in this room, watching her undress night after night. That this was his life, their life. The life they should have together.

He squeezed his eyes shut, his heart pleading, his soul begging. He knew it could not be forever, but for one night, just one night, he wanted the fantasy to be true. He wanted Bella to be his.

A sense of rightness washed over him. *He* loved her. Loved her with all of his heart, all of his soul. He would do anything for her. Had given up everything for her. She should be his. She was *meant* to be his.

A shiver of anticipation raced up his spine. The blood surging through his veins felt different. It was lighter, yet mixed with excitement. With the prospect of what was to come. A grin curved his lips. He began unbuttoning his coat. As his gaze fixed once again on Bella, his grin turned positively sinful.

Maisie finished brushing Bella's hair. Long pale blonde tresses hung straight down her back, tickling the top of her white chemise-clad derrière. He flexed his hands then shrugged off his coat.

"Good evening, Mr. Rosedale." The maid gathered the amethyst gown in her arms. She turned toward him, took a step, and halted in her tracks. Her eyes flared. A crimson blush stained her round cheeks. She yanked her attention from his groin, her gaze darting about the room as if uncertain where to look.

He chuckled, a low, amused rumble. The girl was accustomed to his presence in Bella's bedchamber, but on previous occasions he hadn't been fully hard, his cock straining beneath black wool trousers. Apparently he had embarrassed her. Too bad. He was not up to the task of hiding his desires until she left the room tonight.

"Shall I take your coat, sir?" the maid said in a tiny voice, refusing to look at him.

He pushed from the door and held out his black coat. "Yes. Thank you."

She darted forward and grabbed his coat. Her gaze flickered again to his groin before she turned on her heel and scurried out the dressing room door.

"Hello, Gideon." Still seated on the stool, her back to him, Bella tapped her fingernail on the porcelain clock on the corner of her vanity. "You took longer than a minute."

He smirked. *Cheeky little thing.* Strides long and predatory, he crossed the room. He said not a word as he stopped behind her. Sweeping her silken hair over one shoulder, he pressed his lips to her exposed neck. On an indrawn breath, she tilted her head, granting him access.

He alternated between nipping and kissing the long column of her neck. The plunging bodice of her chemise revealed the valley between her breasts. He let out a short grunt. The need to slide his cock in that valley, to feel the firm mounds cushion his hard length, to come on her nipples, coat them with his seed, gripped hold. Quick and ruthless. An unbidden urge he could almost not suppress. But he fought it back, fought it down. Not that way. And not yet.

Bella squirmed, her breaths coming short and quick. One hand skimmed down her side to the sleek indent of her trim waist, while the other glided over her shoulder to lift a firm breast and test the weight of it in his palm. Locating her nipple beneath the chemise, he rolled the hardened tip and delivered a sharp pinch.

She moaned his name. "Gideon."

"Come to bed," he whispered in her ear, lust drumming thick and hot through his veins.

"Yes, yes," she breathed.

He leaned fully over her and gathered her in his arms. He tossed her gently onto the four-poster bed they had shared for the past two months. She landed with a small gasp, her hair fanning the pillow. She levered up onto her elbows and gazed at him with hungry violet eyes. The lace-edged hem of her chemise rode high about her hips, exposing the long length of her legs. Hard nipples strained against the thin white fabric.

He stood beside the bed, struck motionless. In awe of her. "God, you're beautiful." So beautiful she took his breath away.

She arched, rubbing a bare foot along her calf, clearly reveling in her sensuality, tempting him to join her.

It was a siren's call he had no will, no desire, to resist. He attacked the buttons on his waistcoat, yanked if off, and whipped his shirt over his head. With a hard tug on the placket, his trousers were undone. They fell to his feet.

Her gaze fixed on his erection. A wicked smile curved her lips. He was acutely aware of the heavy weight bobbing between his thighs as he crawled to her on all fours.

Crouched over her, he met her hotly passionate gaze. He stayed still as a statue, letting the attraction between them coil tighter and tighter. A tangible force. It swirled over his skin like a teasing brush of silk. He could feel it licking his ballocks. His cock so hard it arched up to brush his stomach.

He abruptly rocked back onto his knees and grabbed hold of the plunging bodice with both hands. Tore it down the center, exposing her breasts, her stomach, the pale blonde triangle between her thighs. Her eyes flared then fluttered closed on a moan of approval as he dropped down to feast on her breasts.

He kneaded one while plying the other with his mouth. Sucking on the hard tip, delivering teasing little nips, lapping with his tongue. She arched beneath him, fingers tangling in his hair, holding him tight. Demanding more.

He gave it to her. Dragged his mouth down her chest, down her stomach. Paused only long enough to swirl his tongue around the crease of her navel. A quick spasm wracked her limbs, her stomach muscles twitching. A breathless chuckle broke the rhythm of her short pants.

Lips pressed against her lower belly, he grinned. *God*, he loved the sound of her high, tinkling laugh. Then he spread her thighs wide. Wide enough to accommodate his shoulders. Crouched on his knees and bowed over her body, he looked up. She was spread out decadently before him. Her hands fisted in the rose coverlet. Tendrils of pale blonde hair graced her shoulders. Her eyes were heavy-lidded, glazed with desire. The violet depths glittered with passion, for him.

Using his thumbs, he parted her sex, baring her to his view. Pink folds glistened with the proof of her desire. The sweet musky scent of her arousal was almost his undoing. Lust clawed at his gut. His cock hardened even further, the skin stretched so taut it added a heady tease of pain to the lust spiking every nerve in his body. But he didn't give in to the demands of his desire.

He dropped his head and allowed his breath to fan her clit.

Her entire body tensed in anticipation. "Please," she whimpered.

He licked a slow path on either side of her clit, savoring the taste of her. Sweeter than honey and with a spicy hint, like that of a well-aged brandy. Raw need swamped his brain as he drank of her body. Lapped at her soaked entrance. Slipped his tongue into her wet depths. Paid tribute to every delicate fold of her sex, while deftly avoiding her clit.

Feet planted on the bed, she thrust her hips, alternately pushing on his head and pulling on his hair. "Please, please, please," she chanted, over and over again.

He splayed one hand on her lower belly, holding her hips still, and captured her wrists with the other. He continued his sensual onslaught, his senses fully attuned to her body. Waiting.

Her little breathy mewls began to crescendo. Her thighs gripped his shoulders with surprising force. One light flick of his tongue over her clit and she would come. *Perfect.* He lifted his mouth from her sex, left her dripping wet and poised for climax, and crawled swiftly up her body, spreading her legs with his knees.

Her arms wrapped about his neck. Her calves hooked around to rest against the backs of his thighs. Her lips parted and wanting his kiss. Her hips lifted, eager for him.

Braced above her, he paused. His cock aimed right at her core. Scalding heat bathed the head, sent flames roaring through him. Instinct screamed to lunge into her, to pound his cock relentlessly into her welcoming body. But he held back. He needed to be certain she wanted him, bare, without the protection of a sheath. He needed her permission.

"Do you want me?" His voice was so hoarse he almost didn't recognize it as his own.

Her brow furrowed. She glanced down between their bodies. She gasped. Met his intent gaze. "Yes. Please, Gideon. I want you." Her words were a beg, a plea, a vow all in one.

Closing his eyes, he hung his head against the rush of raw gratitude. Unexpected tears pricked his eyes. His muscles shook as he struggled to draw air into his lungs.

Soft hands skimmed the length of his heaving sides. Her touch patient, calming, accepting. Then a small hand grabbed his arse, fingers digging into the crease. She levered up and nipped at his lower lip.

"Take me," she said, thick with passion.

Lust slashed through him. Seized him. For the first time in his life, he willingly turned himself over to it. Let it have him completely. He let out a feral growl and claimed her lips, his mouth slanting harshly over hers, the kiss hot and demanding.

He broke the kiss, grabbed her luscious bottom in both hands and slid into her on one long stroke, settling to the hilt.

Holy Mother of God. His jaw dropped. Heat, pure liquid heat surrounded his cock, gripping him tight. Bella remained still beneath him, as if she understood one move from her, one little lift of her hips, would shatter his control. Breathing heavily, he gave himself a moment to absorb the decadent sensation, allowing his body time to accustom itself to the unprecedented event.

When he regained a thread of control, he slowly pulled out, savoring the slick glide, the way her body tugged on his cock as if never wanting him to leave. Holding her awed half-lidded gaze, he slammed sharply home.

Body arched like a bow and head thrown back, she let out a high screech of delight. He swooped down and kissed her fiercely, passionately, possessively, laying claim to her as he began an unyielding rhythm.

Her first orgasm almost pulled his own out of him. It was right there, gripping his ballocks, demanding to be released. Somehow he managed to hold back, to hold off, determined to wring ever more out of her, unwilling to allow this night to come to an end so soon.

With a hand at the small of her back, he pulled them up onto their knees. Hands spanning her waist, he held her tight against him as he flexed his hips, thrusting deeper, harder. She writhed against him, hard nipples scorching his chest, nails scoring his back, her kisses devouring him. Pushing him onward. Driving him forward. Past the point of any semblance of control or rational thought, until his passion matched hers.

It was sex like Gideon had never experienced before. The lines separating them blurred. He felt each tremor, every quake that shook her body as if it were his own. Every mewl, every rapturous moan from her lips pulled an answering growl from his throat. He turned her, flipped her, rolled her this way and that. Moving over her, under her, behind her, like a man possessed, unable to get enough. Until the blankets were twisted and hung off the bed, until the pillows were thrown to the floor, until his skin and hers was slicked with sweat, until he could barely catch his breath, until he couldn't hold back anymore, until he didn't want to hold back anymore.

Until her next orgasm sparked his own.

His climax surged through him. A white-hot wave, thick and

fierce, more powerful than anything he had ever experienced. He threw back his head and roared as he came, buried deep inside her.

With the orgasmic shudders wracking his body, she wrapped her arms around his neck, pulled his lips down to meet hers, and kissed him with such intensity, such stark blinding bare emotion that he could feel her love in that kiss.

And his kiss matched hers.

EYES half-lidded and mind fogged with sleep, Gideon rolled onto his side and propped his head up on a bent arm. In the darkness, he could just make out Bella sprawled on her stomach. The sheets tangled around her legs, her hair half covering her back.

Dawn had yet to break. After last night he would have thought himself so drained and sated he'd have slept well into the morning. Yet he had awoken a few minutes ago with a pressing need to look at her, be with her, verify last night had not been a dream. He wanted to wake up beside her for the rest of his days. Never wake up alone again. This was why he had staunchly avoided sleeping beside any other woman. The intimacy of this moment could not fail to soften even the most hardened of hearts.

He had had the pleasure of waking beside Bella every morning for the past two months. Yet this morning it was different. As if it was their first morning together.

An urge to capture this, capture her, seized hold. Her face softened with sleep. Lush lips slightly parted. The long sweep of her downcast lashes. The graceful lines of her back.

Careful not to disturb her, he got out of bed, donned the trousers he left on the floor last night, and padded over to the hearth on bare feet. The fire had burned down to faintly glowing embers, but he needed a bit more light. He crouched to grab a log from the metal rack. It crackled and popped as he tossed it onto the fire.

After unlocking the bedroom door, he went into the dark sitting room. He passed the desk to throw open the curtain. The sky outside the window was deepest midnight. The crescent-shaped moon provided little light but it was enough—his eyes having adjusted to the darkness.

He went back to the desk. In the first drawer he opened he found a neat stack of stationery. With a couple of sheets of paper held in one hand, he opened the top drawer. A pencil rolled into view. He pulled it out and scowled at the dull tip.

His fingertips encountered folded paper edges as he reached into the drawer. Searching, he pushed them out of the way. Realizing he'd never find a small penknife in the dark drawer, he lit the candle on the desk. Blinking against the flare of light, he looked back to the open drawer. His brow furrowed at the name "Esmé" written in flowing feminine script across a folded piece of paper.

Esmé—her cousin, Madame Marceau. Fingertips hovering over the note, Gideon glanced guiltily to the open bedchamber door. He shouldn't read it. He'd be invading her privacy. If she found out, oh, she would not be pleased. But . . .

Curiosity made his fingers close over the note. Bella had only mentioned her cousin once and Gideon had only met her one time. He was curious what the letter would reveal about a woman who would hire a prostitute for a cousin.

Just one peek, he promised himself.

The sound of crinkling paper echoed in the room, a remonstration Gideon ignored as he opened the letter.

Why does he hate me so much?

The hastily scrawled words jumped from the page. Gideon blinked, his eyes going wide. Cold dread invaded his gut. His hands started to shake as he forced himself to read from the beginning.

August 10, 1814
Esmé—

When will you come to visit again? You haven't been to see me in ages. I miss our conversations. I miss our walks. Though I know you've no real interest in my roses, you are so kind to listen to me prattle on. I miss being with someone who does not hate me. Why does he hate me so? He returned today. I try to avoid him, but he seems to take perverse pleasure in seeking me out, in finding fault with me. He accuses me of being cold, frigid, and many other things I cannot put on paper. All the while his eyes blaze with loathing. I hate the way I tremble in his presence. I believe he likes to watch me cower before him. Why would he do that? I almost wish he would get it over with so he can leave. Please, Esmé, please come to see me. I don't like it when he is here. I detest this waiting. I know he will not leave without leaving his marks on me and it's summer. I don't want to have to ask Maisie to pull my long sleeved dresses from the attic.

—Isabella

Gideon stared at the letter. His heart pounded deafeningly in his ears. Then he dropped the note and wrenched the drawer fully open. There were more—he'd felt them. Frantic, he pulled out over a dozen neatly folded notes. All bore the name "Esmé"—no address, just the name, indicating she had never sent them.

No longer trusting his knees not to buckle, he sat in Bella's straight-back desk chair and began reading. One was so blurred by watermarks, the handwriting almost illegible, he could only make out some of the words.

Esmé—

I'm scared. He's still here and he hasn't left. Yet, what more could he wish to do to me? . . . It hurts to breathe and . . . Why does he hate me? I don't . . .

By sheer force of will, he resisted the urge to crumple the note in his fist. He set it with great purpose on the desk and picked up another. They were all the same. Pleas for help. Pleas to know why Stirling hated her so very much.

He felt her terror in each quickly scrawled word. Felt her fear in each disjointed sentence. Resting his elbows on the desk, he dropped his head in his hands. His entire body trembled. He never felt so helpless in all his life. Five years she had lived in fear. He had seen the results of Stirling's rage. Seen the broken woman the man left in his wake after every visit.

He wanted to protect her forever. To never have her feel pain again. Yet he had not a shilling to his name. No home to call his own. No means of employment. He had nothing but himself, and that wasn't much.

Pressing the heels of his palms to his eyes, he shook his head. Mayburn had instructed him to take Bella to London if Stirling returned. *What the hell am I waiting for?* For Stirling to return? And the man would return eventually, Mayburn had told him as much. Stirling rarely visited Bowhill, but he did visit. Gideon should have taken Bella to London weeks ago. Kept her far out of harm's way. But he hadn't. He had selfishly ignored the whispered warnings, those little nudges on the back of his mind. For he could not live with her at her brother's house. These days they had shared, their wonderful autumn, it would be no more. To keep her safe, he would have to turn her over into another's care. Her brother was an earl—far more able to fend off any claims by Stirling that the man could do as he pleased with his own wife.

A harsh wince pulled his mouth. *Damn it.* She was still that man's wife. No matter how much he did not want it to be true, he could not dispute that fact.

She belonged to another. A vicious pain tore at his chest. He squeezed his eyes shut against the urge to howl with misery. *No, no, no!* She should be his. *He* loved her. He would never harm her. A wretched groan, one of purest agony, erupted from his soul.

He sagged back in the chair on a shaky sigh and stared unseeing at the notes for many long minutes. One by one, he carefully folded them along their creases, gathered them up, and put them back in their hiding place. Tucked in the very far corner of the drawer, its white corner just visible, was another note. It wasn't addressed to Esmé, but to Lady Stirling at Bowhill Park.

Fearing what he would find, he opened it.

Isabella—

If my timing proves correct, then Bowhill Park will receive a guest on the afternoon of your receipt of this letter. Mr. Gideon Rosedale will be situated at Garden House. He is prepared to remain at Bowhill for the fortnight. Please be so kind as to inform your housekeeper of the imminent arrival of your dear cousin. I promised to find you one who would suit, and I do believe this one will suit.

Regardless of how displeased you may be with me, I do hope you at least invite your guest to dinner before dispensing with him. If not for yourself, then do it for me, because I love you and only wish for your happiness. S'il vous plaît, take a holiday from your penance.

—Esmé

It took two passes before the meaning sank in.

"Oh." The exclamation came out on an awed exhale as he saw their first fortnight in a whole new light. Every glance, every word from her lips, it all had a new meaning. And those terms of hers . . . his lips quirked. The fact a virgin had hired him always stood out as odd. But Bella had not hired him. Well, not the first time. Madame Marceau had acted on her own. It had been the Frenchwoman's idea to send Gideon as a gift.

It should rankle, it should abrade his pride, to have been given as a gift. To be chosen like one would choose a necklace or a bauble. A shiny trinket to brighten a lady's day. But it didn't. He cocked his head, searching for any hint of wounded male pride. Nothing. In fact, he was pleased.

He chuckled, the sound low and tired, as he tucked the note back in its hiding place. He picked up the pencil and tapped the end against the desk. His hand stilled and he nodded slowly. Two more days. He'd give himself two more days, then he would take Bella to London.

Twenty-One

THE soft scratch of pencil on paper roused Bella from sleep. Eyes closed, she rolled onto her back and stretched. A smile pulled her lips. She felt decadent. Divine. Last night had been amazing.

He was amazing.

Gideon had taken her, possessed her, claimed her as he had never done before. By giving himself so completely, by trusting her enough to let go of every bit of control, he had made her his own. He had imprinted himself on her heart and on her soul. She didn't think it possible to love him more, but she did.

A soft sigh escaped her lips. She reached out and encountered cool sheets. Rolling onto her side, she opened her eyes. Gideon had moved the Egyptian armchair near the bed. Clad only in black trousers, he was sprawled in the chair. The drapes on the windows flanking the bed were pulled back, letting in the morning sun. A large leather-bound volume was propped on his thighs. The quick, deft movements of his hand indicated he was sketching.

She levered up onto an elbow and tucked her hair behind her ear. "Good morning."

His hand stilled and he glanced up. The corners of his mouth lifted, but didn't quite form a smile. "Good morning."

She rubbed the sleep from her eyes and studied him. He had turned his attention back to the sketch. A crease notched the space between his dark eyebrows. Lines bracketed his mouth. Even the set of his shoulders seemed tight.

She pursed her lips. He looked entirely too serious. It was too early in the morning for him to be working so hard.

The impatient side of her loved their nights. Frenzied, hard, and fast. Orgasm after orgasm until she couldn't take anymore. But over the past few weeks Gideon had showed her the beauty of mornings. Languid and lazy, her impatience dulled by sleep, when she could fully appreciate the erotic sensation of skin rubbing against skin.

A slow wave of lust washed over her. Pressing her thighs together, she bit her lip on a low moan. Her hungry gaze wandered over his body. His sable hair was tousled, his jaw darkened with his morning beard. The golden light of dawn bathed his broad chest and well-muscled arms, giving the honey-kissed tone of his skin a rich inviting glow. Loose black trousers, the hems of which grazed the tops of his bare feet, concealed the power of his long legs.

Passion ignited, a flame that burst from her belly, wrapping her in sensual heat. Her body begged to feel the velvety warmth of his skin pressed full against hers. But she did not beckon him, did not lure him to her, did not demand he take her. A need to please him seized hold. To repay him for all the pleasure, for everything he had given her.

She sat up and threw her legs over the side of the bed.

At the sound of the mattress shifting, he lifted his head. A scowl marred his brow. "No, don't get out of bed."

She walked the short distance to stand before him. "The last time you said I could move, that you had the image in your head."

Her hair fell over her shoulder as she bent at the waist. He made to tilt the book up, shield his work. With a shake of her head, she placed a hand on the sketch, holding it down.

The extent of his talent once again took her breath away. "It's beautiful."

"It's not done," he grumped.

"You'll have time to finish it later." She pulled the book and sketch from him and, letting her hips sway, walked to the bedside table to set the items down. When she turned from the table, the mulish frown had vanished from his lips. Her skin tingled from the force of his passion-soaked gaze. Except for the long hair covering her breasts, she was bared to his view.

The pencil fell from his grip, clattering to the wooden floor. Bracing his hands on the arms of the chair, he moved to rise. Soft wool brushed her outer thighs as she stepped to stand between his legs. The light smattering of dark hair tickled her fingers as she placed a hand on his chest, the muscles hard, the skin hot from more than the heat of autumn's morning sun. A jolt shot up her arm.

He gazed up at her in question then relaxed back into the chair.

Cupping his bristly jaw, she pressed her lips to his. His mouth opened and she swept her tongue inside, delighting in the taste of him. He kneaded her hips. She shifted her weight, loving the feel of his hands on her bare skin.

But before she lost herself in his kiss, she pulled back.

His hands shifted. Long fingers rested just under the swells of her buttocks. He tugged. "Come here." His voice was a low rumbling command.

Bella gave him a coy shake of her head and swirled one fingertip over a flat copper nipple. It hardened beneath her touch. She marveled anew as she ran her hand over the defined ridges of his abdomen. The man was put together perfectly. He didn't spend long hours in the saddle or swimming in one of the many ponds on the property. His body was a gift from God.

Well, their nights could have something to do with keeping him in such sublime shape.

She glanced to his lap and licked her lips. "I believe one of us is overdressed."

He chuckled. He captured a lock of her pale blonde hair and moved it aside, revealing her breast. Her nipple hardened under his gaze. "Perhaps," he said, his lips quirking.

Lifting his hips, he started to unbutton his trousers.

She laid a hand over his. "Allow me," she said, using one of his phrases.

His brow furrowed then he tipped his head. He removed his hands, resting his elbows on the arms of the chair.

One by one, she undid the metal buttons. The last one proved difficult, but with a determined tug, it released. His stomach muscles contracted as she reached inside to gently pull out his erection. She had at first thought to remove his trousers, but the sight of him sprawled decadently in the chair, legs spread, the placket open and draping his upper thigh, magnificent cock standing at attention . . . No, the trousers would stay exactly where they were.

Dropping to her knees, she took hold of his thick length and bent toward the broad head.

His hand settled on her shoulder, effortlessly holding her in place. "No. You don't have to do that."

Startled at the quick reprimand, she looked up. She was under the assumption men liked this particular sensual act, but the tension gripping every line of his body, from the tight line of his mouth to the rigid set of his shoulders, made doubt settle in her mind. "But I want to give you pleasure."

He stared back at her, his gaze heavy with what was almost guilt. His chest rose and fell on a shuddering breath. "You do. More than any man should be allowed."

"Oh, Gideon." Heart clenching, she scrambled up onto the chair and straddled his hips. His arousal bumped her inner thigh. She threw her arms around his neck and kissed him, telling him what was in her heart. But now was not the time to voice the words. Now was the time to show him.

She nipped at his ear. "Then allow me to give you more."

Dragging openmouthed kisses down his chest, she moved back

to her previous position. Her knees protested against the hard wooden floor, but she didn't give any heed to her own needs. For once, she focused solely on him, intent on bringing a smile to his lips.

Taking hold of him again, she feathered her fingertips over the impressive length. Without the French letter, she had been able to intimately feel every detail of his cock last night. Her insides fluttered at the memory.

She swept her hair behind her shoulder, bowed her head and paused, lips poised over the crown. A drop of fluid leaked from the small slit.

"May I?"

His cock twitched. "Please," he said, hoarse with need.

She allowed instinct to guide her. Pressing her hand flat against his groin and holding him steady with her forefinger and thumb, she started at the base. With the tip of her tongue, she followed the path of the prominent vein. When she reached the top, she opened her mouth wide and took him inside.

On a deep groan, he tipped his head back, exposing the taut cords of his strong neck. Eyes closed and lips parted, his expression was one of sensual agony. He never looked so handsome, so starkly masculine.

"Oh, God, Bella. *Yes.*"

His low grunts urged her on, telling her what pleased him. She bobbed up and down, taking as much as she was able. Pausing every now and then to lavish the head with attention. She reveled in the hot glide of his cock in and out of her mouth. The thin skin felt like wet silk on her suddenly highly sensitized lips.

She could tell he was trying to remain still, yet his hips thrust up and down, tiny uncontrolled movements in rhythm with her attentions. Determined to shatter his control, she suckled on the head of his cock while pumping the ironlike length with a tight fist. Biceps bulging, he held tight to the chair arms and let out a growl.

She purred in response. The heady masculine scent of him filled her every breath. The salty tang of pre-come teased her tongue. Desire spiraled low in her belly, sending tendrils of fire to lick every nerve in her body.

Was this how he felt when he plied her sex with his clever, agile mouth? Submitting oneself wholly to another's pleasure. Devoted to another's needs. There was such pleasure to be found in giving. Her clit throbbed, making her head light. The folds of her sex felt slick with arousal. An orgasm was one touch away. She resisted the urge to reach between her legs and instead channeled all of the lust saturating her senses into pleasing him.

His short thrusts lengthened. His cock bumped the back of her throat and she instinctively relaxed into his strokes, letting him fuck her mouth at will. Hand wrapped tight around the rigid length, she continued to stroke him. The scent of male sweat pushed her lust even higher. With her other hand, she reached down to cup his bollocks.

Abruptly, he pushed her away. "No more. I'm going to—" He clenched his jaw, cutting off the words.

She glanced down to the head slick and flushed with need. "Allow me," she said, leaning forward, but the large hand on her shoulder kept her in place.

"No. I want . . ." The sound of his heavy breaths filled the room. "I want . . . I—" His gaze met hers. His eyes narrowed into thin slits. His lips twisted into a feral grin. "I want to come on your tits," he growled.

She arched her back, his wicked demand calling to her inner tart. "Yes," she said on a throat-scraping purr.

He loosened his hold on her shoulder but didn't let go. With both hands, she pumped his cock, long firm strokes from the base to the tip. Her hands slid easily over his skin slicked from her mouth. He swelled, hardening even further, until there was absolutely no give to the thick length. His entire body drew tight. She leaned forward, aiming his cock at her breasts.

He tipped back his head. "Oh fuck," he roared, shooting hot seed onto her chest, hips thrusting in rhythm to the heavy pulses seizing his cock.

He let out a heavy shoulder-slumping sigh and sagged, chin dropping to his chest. His eyes were heavy-lidded, his expression one of utter exhaustion. Then he sucked in a swift breath, his body jerking, as she swirled the blunt head over one hard nipple coated in his seed.

"No, no, no." He pushed her back. "Too much, too sensitive," he gasped.

She curled her toes and arched, pleased to her bones she had reduced him to such a state. Arousal still rode over every inch of her skin, but the pressing need for satisfaction had shifted, enveloping her in a heavy veil of sublime decadence.

Releasing his cock, she leaned back and grabbed his shirt from the floor. After wiping away the proof of his explosive climax, she tossed the shirt aside and crawled up onto the chair.

Snuggling close to him, Bella curled up like an elegant kitten on his lap. Arms draped loosely about his shoulders, silken cheek pressed to his sweat-slicked chest. Her warm breath tickled the smattering of dark hair.

Gideon's chest rose and fell with each labored breath. Surely she could hear his heart pounding against his ribs. His limbs felt too heavy to move. With effort, he wrapped his arms around her.

She had, quite simply, blown him away. His mind reeled from the force of his orgasm. A thick haze of sated lust seized his wits. He hadn't been sucked off in ages. It was a luxury rarely bestowed on him and one he never contemplated asking for. Well, *never* was no longer entirely correct. The chains he placed on his desires had been shattered. He could well see himself asking a thing or two of Bella in the future.

Christ, she'd not only sucked his cock but he had come all over her luscious tits. He lolled his head back and let out a low tired chuckle. *What has become of me?* His lips twisted in a wry grin.

Love. He was in love.

He sighed and pressed a kiss on the top of her head. He wanted to lay her on the bed, make love to her all day and into the night. Gorge himself on her, while savoring every moment until he had to tell her he was taking her to London. He had a feeling she wouldn't be pleased, but he would find a way to make her understand. He couldn't keep her here just to appease his own selfish needs. She was much too precious to him.

Bella shifted closer and nuzzled his chest. The soft drag of her lips made his spent cock twitch with life. Her fingers played lazily in the short, sweat-damp hair at the nape of his neck. Arousal curled slowly down his spine.

"I love you." She spoke so quietly, the words holding the barest hint of sound, yet it was as if she spoke directly to his heart.

He held his breath, and for a moment he could do nothing but listen to the echo of her soft melodic voice ringing in his head. He thought he had felt it last night, but he didn't dare tease himself with the hope of someday hearing the words from her lips. Yet she had said them.

Clutching her tightly, he bowed his head over hers and struggled to draw air into his lungs. "Bella—" Completely overcome with emotion, he squeezed his eyes shut and gritted his teeth. His entire body trembled. He never believed he would find someone who could truly love him. "Bella, I—" The word lodged in his throat, refusing to leave.

Her hand skimmed down to rest on his chest, directly over his heart. "It's all right, Gideon." Her quiet voice held a lifetime's worth of patience.

Frustrated, he shook his head and opened his mouth again.

The distant sound of a door slamming broke his concentration. He lifted his head. The rumble of a deep male voice reached his ears.

Bella went utterly still. "S-S-Stir—"

Dread slammed into him. "Oh shit. Get up, get up, Bella." He didn't wait for her to move but lifted her off him and set her on her feet.

Within a second, his trousers were buttoned. He leaned down to reach for his shirt then stopped. Not that one. He'd have to find another. Grabbing the hand hanging limp at her side, he pulled Bella toward the dresser and pulled open a drawer. *Fuck!* Why the hell hadn't he taken her to London already?

He snatched a chemise from the drawer. "Bella, put this on. We need to leave."

She made not a move, but stood still as a statue next to him. All the color had leeched out of her face. Trembles wracked her body. Her teeth began to chatter. She looked as though she had just emerged from the icy cold Thames in January.

Her terror struck at his heart, knifed through him. "Angel, put this on," he said with a calm he did not feel in the slightest.

She blinked then gave him a jerky nod.

"But Lord Stirling—" came a young female voice from out in the hall.

"Maisie," Bella whispered, identifying her maid's voice. With shaking hands, she pulled the chemise over her head, tugged it down, and flipped her hair out from under it.

"Get out of my way, gel," answered an agitated male voice, which held a hint of a Scottish accent.

Bella's gaze met his, her violet eyes wide with a panic that made dread knot and tangle in his stomach. Disheveled pale blonde hair draped her narrow shoulders. The thin white chemise did little to hide her lithe, fragile frame. "Gideon?" she said in a weak little whisper.

"Don't worry. I won't let him hurt you," he vowed, tucking a strand of her hair behind her ear.

He would do everything he was physically capable of to keep Stirling away from her, but that didn't mean it would be enough. Bella had told Stirling about him. When Stirling found him with

Bella, it was a distinct possibility the man would summon the magistrate, have Gideon arrested for prostitution. He wouldn't be able to protect her in a prison cell, and the law could easily forgive Stirling for killing his wife, a woman who had hired a prostitute, in a fit of rage.

Grabbing her waist, he pulled her to him. He clutched her tightly and slanted his mouth over hers, needing to experience her kiss, to feel her love. She clung to him, her tongue tangling desperately with his, as if she too knew this might be their last chance.

At the sound of the sitting room door slamming against a wall, he tore his lips from hers. His head snapped around to stare at the bedchamber doorknob. *Damn.* He'd forgotten to lock it.

Thump. Thump. Thump. Coming ever nearer, the sound of heavy footfalls reverberated through the closed door.

He glanced frantically behind him. He should have shoved Bella into the dressing room, not paused to cover her naked body. For Christ's sake, there were plenty of dresses in the dressing room. But it was too late.

Forcing his arms to release their hold around her waist, he turned, positioning himself in front of her. "I won't let him hurt you," he repeated, muscles drawing tight in preparation.

Soft lips brushed his bare shoulder blade. "I know."

The bedchamber door banged harshly against the wall.

"Isabella, are you hiding from me again?" Bella's husband stopped one step into the room. His eyes flared, his mouth curving in what could only be described as gloating satisfaction. "How did I know this was what I would find? My dear wife has called for her whore."

Taking hold of Gideon's hand, Bella moved to stand beside him. "He is not a—"

Gideon tightened his grip, cutting off her words. Startled, she glanced up to him. He gave his head a tiny shake. Now was not the time to debate such an insignificant point. They had a much larger problem to deal with.

Stirling's cruel chuckle raised the hairs on Gideon's nape. "The slut accedes to her whore's wishes. How pleasant. Does she do everything you ask, I wonder?"

Gideon clenched his jaw against the unwise retort and met Stirling's hard, deep blue gaze. The man was huge. Taller and more powerful than Mayburn. Built like a pugilist who had gone slightly to seed. The sight should have instilled a bit of intimidation into Gideon. But it did not.

This man had hurt Bella. Frightened her. Scared her. Terrified her. Gideon squared his shoulders, widened his stance. *Never again.*

With a smirk, Stirling sauntered into the room. "You have spoiled my winter in Rome, Isabella. I made it all the way down to Florence before I had to turn around. Couldn't abide the thought of my dear wife fornicating under my roof."

As Stirling spoke, Gideon splayed his hand, but Bella held tight. Her shoulder grazed his biceps as she shrank closer to him.

"Let go," Gideon muttered, tracking her husband as the man slowly advanced on them.

For a split second, he feared she'd refuse his command. Then the small hand released, delicate fingertips caressing his palm. He flexed and clenched his hands at his sides, testing his fists.

Stirling's arrogant gaze swept the room, taking in Gideon's discarded clothes and Bella's torn chemise clinging to the edge of the disheveled bed, before settling on Gideon. "How much did this one set me back? He looks mighty expensive. Did you call for him the moment I left, or did you wait until your pretty bruises healed?"

A bolt of fury shot through Gideon. The muscles in his right arm vibrated with the need to give Stirling a few pretty bruises of his own.

The earl stopped a couple of paces in front of Gideon and wrinkled his nose. "Bloody hell, it smells like sex in here."

"How would you know?" a surprisingly strong voice asked from the vicinity of Gideon's shoulder.

He resisted the urge to close his eyes on a groan. Why the hell did she have to goad him?

Stirling's gaze snapped to Bella. A deep scarlet flush rose quickly up his neck. His eyes narrowed into hard slits, his face contorting with fury. The arrogant, mocking earl vanished to be replaced with a monster.

Gideon shoved Bella behind him at the same instant Stirling screamed, "You fucking bitch!"

Teeth bared, Stirling lunged for Bella. Gideon jabbed his left arm, fist connecting with flesh and bone. With a deafening roar, Stirling's boulder-sized fist redirected in midswing.

"Gideon!" Bella shrieked.

His head snapped back. The impact of Stirling's blow reverberated across his skull. Right fist at the ready, he swung blindly at the spot where Stirling's chin had been.

His knuckles grazed a bristly jaw, the miss throwing him slightly off balance. Stirling swung again. Gideon managed to knock the thick arm aside and threw another punch. Stirling met him blow for blow, and then some.

He hadn't fought since he'd been a boy, scrapping in the back alleys with the pickpockets. Rage surged though his veins, but his reflexes were rusty. Hitting Stirling was like hitting a goddamn brick wall, and the man's massive size did not slow him down in the slightest.

The air was knocked from his lungs by a well-placed punch to the gut. Staggering back, Gideon doubled over, gasping for breath.

"No!" Bella latched onto Stirling's arm, which was poised to deliver another punch.

Pure horror gripped him. "Bella. No. Get out of here." Gideon lunged for Stirling.

Swinging his other arm, the earl turned. A pained cry rent the air.

Deep savage crimson clouded Gideon's vision. Fury erupted, overflowed at the sight of Bella sprawled on the floor.

"You bastard!" Grabbing a fistful of auburn hair, he jerked Stirling's head back and slammed his other fist into the side of the man's head.

Stirling let out a roar and twisted violently, breaking free of Gideon's hold. Stirling's arm shot out, fist connecting with Gideon's jaw, knocking him against the wall. Rage, thick and hot, the likes of which he had never known before pervaded every inch of his being, blinding him to the pain. With a feral growl, Gideon dropped his head and rushed Stirling, wrapping his arms around the thick waist, pushing the man out of the bedchamber and away from Bella.

Twenty-Two

BELLA pushed up onto her hands and knees. Her head swam. She shook her head to clear it then groaned as a heavy ache seized the back of her skull. Pushing her hair from her face, she looked up. Her vision blurred then focused. The open sitting room door framed Gideon as he grabbed her straight-back desk chair and swung it in a determined arc.

There was a loud crack of wood followed by an angry bellow, like that of an irate bear.

Fists at the ready, Gideon darted out of her view.

"Oh, my dear Lord, they are going to kill each other," she said in a horrified whisper. Bella scrambled to her feet. A wave of dizziness threatened to send her back to her knees. She clutched one of the bedposts. Gritting her teeth, she forced her mind to clear.

The prospect of Stirling's death meant nothing to her. But Gideon's . . . She refused to think about it. Couldn't think about it.

Heart in her throat, she ran from her room then skidded to a halt. Her eyes flared at the wreckage the men had left in their wake. The remnants of her chair littered the sitting room floor. The tall, narrow bookcase had been pulled down, books and papers scattered everywhere. The gilt-framed painting of roses in full bloom hung at a sharp angle on the wall.

The unmistakable thumps of fists impacting with bone and flesh drew her attention to the hall. The two men were locked in combat. Fighting like rabid animals, enraged beyond rational thought. Gideon's fists flew almost too fast for her to make them out. A constant stream of obscenities poured from his mouth, uninterrupted by Stirling's answering blows.

"Bloody cocksucker!"

Barefooted and bare chested, Gideon took every one of Stirling's hits as though he couldn't feel them. The muscles in Gideon's back bunched and flexed with each swing. His biceps bulged. A fine sheen of sweat coated his skin.

"Fucking bastard." Gideon punctuated his curse with a jab to Stirling's jaw.

She had never seen Stirling take a punch. Blood smeared his nose and his once neatly tied cravat was completely askew, but her husband appeared to be faring just fine. Alarmingly fine.

Panic and dizziness threatened to overwhelm her. Knees shaking, Bella gripped the sitting room doorframe, determined to stay on her feet.

She gasped as Stirling's fist connected with Gideon's abdomen. Gideon grabbed Stirling by the ears, jerked forward, and smacked his forehead against her husband's. Bella's hand flew to her mouth to stifle a shocked scream. As Stirling staggered back a step, Gideon locked his hands and swung both fists together aiming for Stirling's neck.

Stirling crashed against the wall. Arm raised and fist clenched, Gideon lunged forward. "Useless prick!"

With an all mighty bellow, Stirling grabbed Gideon, using Gideon's momentum to hurl him into the closed door opposite her sitting room.

She jumped at the deafening crack of wood followed by a hard thump. Dodging the mess on the floor, she raced into the hall. The door to Stirling's rooms was open, the wooden frame cracked.

Gideon got to his feet just in time to block Stirling's blow. But he wasn't fast enough to block the second. He let out a grunt and gave his head a sharp shake, backing up. Relentless, Stirling advanced. His olive green jacket stretched taut over his broad back as he rained blow after blow on Gideon, driving him against the wall. Gideon valiantly tried to fight back but his once lightning-fast punches weren't as quick. Before her eyes, his reactions slowed. His face was still a mask of undeniable rage but beneath it she saw desperation.

It was clear he could sense his impending defeat.

She knew in her bones Stirling wouldn't stop until Gideon's broken body fell to the floor, never to rise again.

Her breaths sharp and fast, she glanced frantically about the room. An empty crystal vase on the fireplace mantle. A neat row of thick leather-bound books on a shelf. A brass lamp on an end table beside the maroon leather armchair. Nothing here would be enough to stop Stirling. But—

Turning on her heel, she darted from the room. Her feet barely kept up with her as she ran down the stairs. Grabbing hold of the banister, she turned right at the bottom of the staircase, ignoring the cluster of worried servants in the entrance hall. The door to Stirling's study was slammed against the wall. She rushed across the darkened room and rounded the desk. Praying Stirling hadn't decided to lock it when last he visited, she swung the portrait and turned the handle. The square steel door opened.

Thuds sounded overhead, vibrating through the floorboards in Stirling's room. Hastily pushing aside documents and stacks of pound notes, she froze as her fingers encountered cool metal.

I left it loaded, Isabella. Though I doubt you'd even know which end the bullet comes out of.

Stirling's words from years ago echoed in her head. He had showed her the dueling pistol when he had first deposited her at Bowhill—his only thought to her safety while he left her at the remote estate for months on end.

"It's the end I'm going to point at you," she muttered, grabbing the pistol. She had grown up with Jules and Kitty, after all. She had even partaken in one of their little competitions, though her shots had gone far wide while her siblings had argued over which of theirs was closest to the mark.

But her current target was significantly larger than the scrap of paper Jules had tacked to the trunk of the old oak tree.

Leaving the safe open, she ran from the study. Conscious of the lingering servants and the pistol in her hand, she took the narrow servants' stairs and skidded to a halt at Stirling's sitting room.

Her heart caught in her chest. Gideon was sprawled in a heap on the floor amidst the splintered remains of a broken end table. Bruises and scrapes marred the perfection of his sweat-slicked back.

"Get up, whore," Stirling snarled, standing over him.

Struggling, Gideon pushed up to his feet, his muscles shaking with the effort, his head bowed in fatigue. Before he could straighten, Stirling punched him in the jaw. Gideon crashed against the wall and crumbled to the floor.

"You dare touch my wife? Dare touch something of mine?" Stirling drew back a leg, as if to kick Gideon in the stomach.

Holding the pistol with both hands, she brought her arms up. "Stop."

Stirling stilled. He looked over his shoulder. Tension gripped his broad shoulders for the briefest moment, then a sardonic grin tipped his lips. "Ah, my dear wife comes to the aid of her fallen whore. Quite admirable of you, but also very unwise."

Swiping his forearm across his bloodied mouth, he turned. Completely at his ease, he sauntered toward her. "Do you think to shoot me? Your husband?" He shook his head, all mocking condescension. "No. You won't."

"Yes. I will." The urge to flee, to run, pressed heavily on her. It took all of her willpower to keep her feet rooted to the floor, to stand her ground, as he slowly advanced.

"You can't."

"Yes, I can. I will," she said, desperate to convince herself.

When the barrel of the pistol pressed against his waistcoat, he stopped. "Prove it."

She swallowed hard and locked her elbows. All she needed to do was pull the trigger and all of this would end. All she needed to do was kill her husband. A living, breathing man. Gritting her teeth, she closed her eyes. Her finger trembled against the smooth curve of the metal trigger.

Stirling let out a sigh, like that of an annoyed parent. "Whatever am I going to do with you, Isabella? Clearly you have not learned your lesson."

The pistol was wrenched from her hands. Instinctively, she flung her arms up to cover her face; eyes still closed tight.

A feral roar filled the room. She opened her eyes, peeking between her forearms, to see Stirling turn.

"Don't touch her!" Gideon screamed, swinging a leg from the broken end table at Stirling's head.

Ducking, Bella scurried aside. Stirling crashed into the wall, exactly in the spot where she had been standing.

Eyes narrowed and mouth twisted in a furious grimace, Gideon attacked Stirling as if he hadn't just been beaten within an inch of his life. Avoiding a blow, Stirling dropped down and grabbed Gideon's leg, pulling him to the ground. Rolling, twisting and kicking, the two men wrestled for dominance. They knocked into furniture, sending objects crashing to the floor, until Stirling straddled Gideon, both large hands wrapped around his neck. With one hand, Gideon aimed punch after punch at Stirling's elbows, attempting to break the man's hold, while with his other, he tried to pry Stirling's fingers from his throat.

"No!" Beyond desperate for him to stop, she launched herself at Stirling's back. Pulled his hair, scratched his face.

"Get off, bitch." Stirling grabbed her arm and flung her as though she weighed nothing.

Landing hard on her shoulder, she scrambled to her feet. The pistol. Where had it gone? It was the only way to stop Stirling, for he would never let Gideon up alive. She cursed herself for not having done it earlier. This time, she would not hesitate. Wreckage covered the floor. The pistol could be anywhere. Panting heavily, she tried to calm her pulse, force the panic aside and focus.

A deafening blast smacked her eardrums.

For a split second, everything stopped.

Then Stirling slumped over Gideon.

She stared blankly at her husband's prone form. The broad back was eerily still, the olive green jacket marred by a singed hole between his shoulder blades.

"*Bon matin*, Isabella."

Whirling around, she nearly jumped out of her skin at the sound of a familiar voice.

Her cousin walked casually into the sitting room. A few strands of her dark hair had escaped their pins but other than that, and the dueling pistol held lightly in one gloved hand, she looked as if she were merely paying an afternoon call. She arched one elegant eyebrow. "Though it doesn't appear as if you've had a very pleasant morning. Are you all right, my dear?"

"Yes, I'm—Esmé? What—?" Bella's mind seized with shock. What was she doing here?

Bella heard the *thumps* of rapid, slightly off-rhythm footsteps in the hall. "Madame?" Porter said, concern heavy in his tone, as he appeared in the open doorway, his stance strong, ready to do battle. His astute gray gaze swept over the room, the straight line of his shoulders sagging the tiniest bit when it stopped on Esmé. He quickly shut the door. "Madame," he said, his hand outstretched, his tone once again that of a proper servant.

With a tip of her head, Esmé gave him the pistol and he slipped it into his coat pocket.

A low groan came from the vicinity of Stirling. Bella tensed, fearing Esmé's shot hadn't been enough. With another groan, Gideon shoved Stirling's body off of him.

"Damn, he's heavy," Gideon muttered as he got to his feet.

"Oh, Gideon." The most profound relief washed over her. Bella rushed to him and threw her arms around his waist, burying her face against his sweat-slicked chest. The strong beats of his heart made tears prick at her eyes. "I thought I was going to lose you."

He held her tight. "Never. You will never lose me," he whispered hoarsely, pressing his lips to the top of her head.

She leaned back to look up into his face. "You're bleeding." She pulled her arms from around his waist and feathered her fingertips over the cut on his temple.

"It's nothing." Yet he stood still, arms wrapped around her and head bowed, allowing her to fuss over him.

"Your poor jaw, and your nose, and your brow." She graced each bruised feature with the lightest of touches. "And he cut your lip," she admonished, running her fingertip over his bottom lip.

"Doesn't hurt," he said with a shrug of one shoulder. His gaze slid over the top of her head then he stiffened.

"Good morning, Mr. Rosedale," Esmé said.

Esmé. Bella had momentarily forgotten about her. Taking hold of Gideon's hand, she turned to her cousin, suddenly quite conscious of the fact she wore only a plain white chemise.

"Good morning," Gideon said, in a measured tone. "You are Bella's cousin, Madame Marceau, are you not? Thank you for your most timely arrival."

Esmé's lips curved in a knowing smirk, her violet eyes glinting with a hint of the usual impish gleam. "My timing is always impeccable. Though Julien won't be pleased, that's for certain. He planned to do it himself."

She gaped at Esmé. "Jules?"

"Yes. He stopped by to pay me a call on his way to Rome. Didn't say too much. Porter didn't give him much of a chance. He didn't care for Julien's tone," Esmé added, though the explanation was unnecessary as Porter's heavy scowl spoke for itself. "Those brothers of yours . . ." Letting out a little sigh, she shook her head. "After Julien and his broken nose left, I came straight up to Scotland to see you. Given that, I'm a bit taken aback to find Stirling here. Julien had been certain Stirling was planning to winter in Rome." She paused. "I wish you had seen fit to confide in me. I would have had Stirling taken care of for you long ago."

Bella took a breath, a mixture of apology and explanation on her tongue, but Esmé held up a hand.

"I understand what drove you to stay silent. I just wish you hadn't. You needn't have suffered so." Then her attention shifted to Gideon and the heavy note left her voice. "What month is it, Mr. Rosedale?"

"October," Gideon said, clearly confused by the question.

Esmé tapped a fingertip to her lips. "Last I checked there was considerably more than a fortnight between April and October. Yet, here you are."

Bella tensed at the steel behind Esmé's casually spoken words. She sensed Gideon stiffen as well, his grip on her hand tightening.

"Did you have a nice holiday, Isabella?"

Her face twisted in confusion before Esmé's meaning struck home. *S'il vous plaît, take a holiday from your penance.* It seemed ages ago when she had received her letter. A smile flittered on her lips. "Yes, very much so."

"Good to hear." Esmé winked. Then the teasing glint left her eyes. "Now, about Stirling, we'll need to—"

A knock on the door interrupted her.

"Mr. Porter?" came her housekeeper's worried voice. "Did you find Lady Stirling and Madame Marceau? Are they all right? That noise, was it a gunshot?"

"Yes, yes, and no, Mrs. Cooley," Porter replied. "Please have Lady Stirling's traveling coach readied."

There was a short pause. "Yes, Mr. Porter."

"You're leaving?" Bella asked Esmé the moment Mrs. Cooley's footsteps faded down the hall.

"Oh no, my dear. I just arrived." Esmé said.

"He's leaving." Porter tipped his head toward the large body on the floor.

"Where is he going?"

"You needn't concern yourself, Isabella." At her look of obvious confusion, Esmé rolled her eyes. "Do you want the authorities to investigate his death? They will ask questions you won't want to answer. Stirling had clearly been in a rather serious fight prior to his death. You don't have a bruise on you and neither do I or Porter, yet Mr. Rosedale does."

"Only because he took Stirling's punches in my place," she said in staunch defense of the man she loved. "Stirling was going to kill him."

Esmé waved a dismissive hand. "It doesn't matter. Stirling was a peer and your husband. The local magistrate may not accept your word that Stirling beat you, and even then, well, they may not care. The only other witnesses to the events of this morning are myself, who happens to be a woman, and Mr. Rosedale, who happens to be a male prostitute. While I—"

"Not anymore," Gideon interrupted. "I resigned months ago."

Esmé lifted her eyebrows and tipped her head. "I am pleased to hear that, but it won't matter. It doesn't change the fact Isabella has a lover living with her at Bowhill. As I was saying, I am more than willing to tell the magistrate that I shot Stirling. But I'm not English or Scottish. I'm French, and the war hasn't been over for that long. The situation could become dreadfully messy. Therefore it's best Stirling disappear for a bit, and you, too, as well, Mr. Rosedale."

"No," Bella and Gideon said in unison.

"I'm not leaving her," Gideon said resolutely. Then he closed his eyes on a heavy sigh. "But I will continue to make myself scarce when callers come to Bowhill. Except for the servants, no one will know I am here."

The resignation in his tone, the pain on his face . . . it tore at her heart. How he must have felt every time a caller had come to the door. He had not said a word though, had simply made himself scarce. And it struck her—he had done it so easily, so effortlessly, because he had been doing it all his life, since he had been a child in that brothel. Staying out of sight every time his mother had callers.

Esmé nodded. "Isabella, you will receive word within a month or so that Stirling's body has been found. And when you do, please be sufficiently shocked at the dreadful news of your husband's untimely death."

"What about the servants? They may talk," Gideon said.

Esmé's face hardened with conviction. "Their silence will be secured. Stirling was never here."

"McGreevy won't stay silent," Bella pointed out. "He's worked for Stirling's family for too long, and he has never cared for me."

"Well, I have never cared for him," Esmé said, a scowl marring her features. "That butler won't say a word. In fact, I believe it's time to pension him off." She looked to Porter, who still stood guarding the door. "If you would."

"Yes, madame." He crossed the room and dropped to his haunches beside Stirling. He laid a hand on the man's chest and another on his thick neck. "He's dead."

"Of course he's dead. I shot the unpleasant man, and I never miss." Esmé flicked her fingers in Gideon's direction. "Mr. Rosedale, give Porter a hand. We need to get him down to the carriage."

Gideon began to move toward Stirling then stopped. He glanced down at their joined hands. "Bella." His gaze met hers. "You can let go."

"No." Ducking her chin, she bit her bottom lip. She couldn't explain it and she knew it was irrational, but she did not want to let go of his hand. She didn't want to lose the warmth of his palm, the strength of his grip.

With a light touch, he lifted her chin. "It will be all right. I'll be right back. I promise," he said softly.

She gazed into his eyes. She loved him so much it hurt. "I'm sorry," she said, whisper-soft, only loud enough to reach his ears. "I didn't mean to make you feel as though I was ashamed of you. As though you were something I needed to hide. I was just so afraid Stir—"

He cupped her cheek. His thumb settled over her lips, cutting off her words. "Bella, it's all right. I understand." He pressed a kiss to her forehead. "Why don't you get dressed and I'll meet you in your bedchamber in a few moments."

Trying to keep the tears at bay, she took a deep breath. He was so patient it made her want to weep. "All right."

"I promise," he said again when she released his hand.

She left him crouched beside Stirling. She found her maid sweeping the litter from the sitting room floor. Mrs. Cooley had been efficient as ever. The gilt-framed painting on the wall had already been straightened, the bookshelf righted, and another chair placed before her desk.

"Maisie, you can leave that for now."

The broom clattered to the floor as Maisie looked up in shock. "Lady Stirling, you're all right. Oh, I was so afraid he had hurt you again."

Bella shook her head. "Mr. Rosedale took the brunt of it for me."

"He is a wonderful man, Mr. Rosedale." A dreamy little smile played across the maid's lips. Then Maisie regained herself, bending to pick up the broom and lean the wooden handle against the desk. "Shall I help you dress?"

"No, that won't be necessary."

With a short curtsey, Maisie left the room. Bella entered her bedchamber but she didn't go into her dressing room. Instead, she sat on the edge of her newly tidied bed and waited for Gideon to return to her.

She was free of her husband. Free of the man who hated her. And she felt not a drop of grief over his death. Esmé though . . . She shook her head, unable to reconcile her old image of her with the determined woman she'd left Gideon with. Years ago, before Stirling and before her ill-fated Season in London, when she lived at Mayburn Hall with her siblings, Jules had once whispered to her—*It wasn't an accident. Esmé's husband didn't shoot himself while cleaning his pistol.* Had Jules been right? Bella didn't much care if he was. Esmé had arrived at Bowhill at a most opportune time. She had killed Bella's husband, thus saving Gideon's life. Bella owed her cousin a great deal.

It seemed wrong she would have to pretend to be married to Stirling for a bit longer, but in her heart she hadn't been his wife for quite some time.

Her heart belonged to another.

She glanced to the clock on her vanity and let out a frustrated breath. Another who was taking an awfully long time to return to her.

Bella was smoothing her chemise over her knees when Gideon entered the room, closing the door behind him.

"Madame Marceau is settling into the yellow bedchamber, and Porter said he'd be back by nightfall," Gideon said as he walked across the room.

She sucked in a horrified breath. She had been so focused on his handsome face earlier that she failed to notice what Stirling had done to the rest of him. Her body ached in sympathy, yet he seemed completely unaffected. Deep purple bruises marred his honey gold skin. On his ribs, his shoulders, his chest. Around his neck she could make out the distinct imprint of Stirling's thick fingers. A shudder gripped her at the reminder of how close she had come to losing him.

She hopped off the bed and took hold of his forearm. "Gideon, you need to rest." She glanced up to his face. Fresh blood smeared his temple. "And you're still bleeding." She tugged on his arm. "Lie down. I'll clean it for you."

He resisted her efforts to get him onto the bed. "Bella, I'm fine." He gently removed her hand from his forearm. "Sit. Please. I need to talk with you."

His serious expression gave her pause. With a nod, she complied.

He turned from the bed. The muscles in his back flexed, strong shoulder blades working under bruised and freshly scraped skin, as he dragged both hands through his hair. On a heavy sigh, he turned back to her, his eyes downcast. He shoved his hands in his trouser pockets then pulled them out. A wince flickered across his brow. He opened his mouth then closed it, pursing his lips in annoyance. His gaze shifted up to meet hers before dropping to the floor. "Will you marry me?"

She blinked in shock. Of all the things he could have been working up to say, she would have never guessed a marriage proposal.

Gideon shook his head, his shoulders hunching. "My apologies. Forget I asked. I shouldn't have presumed—"

She jumped off the bed and pressed her fingertips to his lips, silencing him. "Yes, yes," she said quickly, needing to erase the doubt and pain clouding his whisky brown eyes. "I will marry you."

"Really?"

"I would be honored to be your wife, Gideon." She chuckled, unable to contain the all-encompassing joy washing her senses.

But no echo of her radiant smile graced his lips. Mouth drawn in a firm line, he nodded curtly. "Sit. Please." His hands were infinitely gentle as he guided her back onto the bed. "I need you to understand the implications. And if you change your mind, I will understand."

Taking a step back, he clasped his hands behind his back. "If you marry me we cannot live in London. We cannot mix in Society. No matter where we live, there is always the possibility we may run into someone who recognizes me. You must be prepared for that. Society will look on you differently if they learn what you married. I can offer you very little, Bella. Only my name, and you will be a mere Mrs. and no longer Lady Stirling."

"I thought you wanted to marry me? Yet it sounds as if you are trying to persuade me otherwise."

The serious façade began to crack, letting her glimpse the vulnerable man within. "I do want to marry you, Bella. I want to be able to call you my own, more than you could possibly imagine. But you must understand what you are agreeing to. I don't want you to regret a decision made in haste."

She nodded. He was concerned for her, but he need not be. She had never been more certain of herself in her life. Phillip had told her to do what would make her happy, and becoming Gideon's wife would make her beyond happy. Yet she remained silent, letting Gideon continue, allowing him to reassure himself she understood.

"I-I don't yet know where we will live." His gaze shifted to a spot over her shoulder. A barely perceptible flush colored his cheeks. "I-I honestly have nothing, Bella. Not even a halfpence to my name. But I will find a way to support you. I'm not good for much, but somehow I will find a respectable means of employment, one that will not reflect poorly on you."

"Gideon," she said, tilting her head, "how can you be penniless?" She winced as soon as the words left her mouth. She shouldn't ask, but the question came out before she could stop it. The state of his bank account didn't matter, not in the slightest, yet he had worked for a decade. Where had it gone?

"I'm not irresponsible, if that's what you think," he grumbled. "I had saved a small fortune over the years, but I-I traded it all. Everything. Even my apartment."

"Why?"

"For you. For a chance to see you again. My employer was not pleased to learn of my resignation. It was the only way to convince her to accept it."

Her jaw dropped at the significance of what he had done. *A wife. A family. But first, I need money. A whole lot of it.* That was what he had told her months ago when she'd asked him what he wanted out of life. And he had given it all up. For her. For simply a *chance* to see her.

"Oh, Gideon." Stifling the sob welling up in her throat, she bit her lower lip and tried to rein in her emotions. "You needn't worry about where we will live. This house is mine. Phillip arranged it in the marriage settlement. The property isn't part of the earldom, but came to Stirling through his mother. Upon Stirling's death, it reverts to me. And it will become yours once we are married. You will have a property in the country, one that generates a decent income, just as you wanted."

He gave her a weary lift of his lips. "That's all well and good, but it doesn't make up for the fact I come to you with nothing."

She stood and took his hands in hers, squeezing them tight. "All I want is you. You feed every part of my soul, with comfort and kindness and searing passion. You give me everything that is important in life. Everything I need. Titles and wealth mean very little to me. I would gladly trade it all to become Mrs. Rosedale."

Abruptly, he pulled their joined hands behind her back, jerking her toward him. He slanted his mouth over hers, silencing her gasp of surprise. The kiss began fierce and desperate, his tongue twining with hers, as if he couldn't get enough. Then it shifted, softened. He dragged his lips across her cheek. Gooseflesh pricked her skin as he nuzzled her ear.

"I love you, Bella."

His whispered words unleashed the tears she had tried to keep at bay. And they were not quiet ladylike tears, but big, loud, sobbing ones. She ducked her chin, embarrassed by her overwrought emotions.

"Oh, Bella. Don't cry. Please, don't." There was a chuckle in his soft croon.

"I'm sorry," she said between great pulling sobs. "It is just that it has been so long since I've heard those words."

His arms tightened around her, pressing her closer to the warm expanse of his chest. "Bella-Bella," he whispered in her ear. "You shall never again have to go another day without hearing them. I promise you."

She didn't think it was humanly possible, but somehow she cried even harder. She hadn't realized how much she had missed them. They were three small words, but hearing them from Gideon had the power to erase the long years of famine.

With tears of joy streaming down her cheeks, she cupped his jaw and pulled him down for a kiss. And she started the kiss with those three treasured words whispered hoarsely against his lips. "I love you."

Epilogue

COINS clinked as Gideon grabbed the black bag from the vault then closed the square steel door. March had come, which meant it was time to pay the household servants their quarterly wages. With a flick of his wrist, he swung the picture frame to cover the vault. He had lost the battle over what would replace Stirling's old portrait, a portrait Bella had taken great delight in burning in the fireplace. In his opinion, his simple pencil sketch looked entirely out of place in the heavy gilt frame, not to mention hanging in a position of prominence in the masculine study. But his wife had insisted something from his hand should grace the space. And who was he to deny her what she wanted?

His lips twisted in a rueful grin. He settled in the leather chair behind the desk, set down the bag of coins, and opened the account ledger. In an effort to make himself useful, he had taken over management of the estate and Bella's ancient part-time secretary had been more than willing to be pensioned off. The man was a disorganized nightmare with almost illegible handwriting, which fully explained why this room had been the only room in the house that hadn't been as neat as a pin.

Bella strode into the study. The door snapped shut behind her. "Gideon."

He set down his pencil. "Good afternoon, Mrs. Rosedale," he said with wide smile. God, how he loved to call her that. He had wanted to marry her the moment she agreed to be his wife. The moment she agreed to be his forever. But he had to wait until after the government official had notified Bella of Stirling's death, and then had to wait an additional four long months to avoid throwing any suspicion onto her first husband's "unfortunate" death at the hands of unknown highwaymen on an infrequently traveled road outside of Carlisle.

Lips thinned, she stopped in front of the desk and flicked an envelope at him. It bounced off his chest then landed on the account ledger. "Who is Lady Knolwood?" Her violet eyes flashed with a strain of jealousy only women were capable of producing.

"She is an old acquaintance," he said calmly.

"What sort of acquaintance?"

Gideon leaned back in the chair, pushed away from the desk, and beckoned her. "Bella, sweet, come here."

She did not move an inch. "Was she one of your—"

He let out a low sigh at the pain, the heartache that kept her from voicing that last word. Gideon had thought nothing of it when he had tossed the note to Helen onto the silver tray with the rest of the day's outgoing post. He had no intention of hiding the letter from Bella, but he should have known she would see it and question it. She had been in her sitting room for the past hour corresponding with her sisters. She was a woman—there was no way she would set her letters on the tray and not notice her husband was corresponding with another lady. And especially when he was that husband.

"You have no cause to get so worked up. Come here."

Her fine eyebrows met in uncertainty. "Was she—?"

"Bella, my love. Please, don't. Come here."

Her hands clenched into fists at her sides. She stared hard at him, needing the answer.

So he gave it to her. "Yes, she was. But it's not what you think. Open it, read it, if you will. I've known Lady Knolwood for years. She's the only friend I have and she simply asked that I drop her a note if I ever won my lady. And so I did. I couldn't resist the urge to tell her you married me." He had no one else with whom to share the most important news of his life. There was no one else who cared to know.

Her eyes flared. "You spoke to her about me? Did you—?" Her ragged, uneven breaths caught in her throat.

"Oh, Bella." He got to his feet and rounded the desk. "No. No. I played chess with her. That was it. I was so caught up in you I lost quite horribly. Pathetic," he added with a disgusted shake of his head. "I've known Lady Knolwood for a decade. It stopped being about 'that' years ago. She knew though, even before I did, that you had captured my heart. She wished me luck and asked me to let her know if I won you. That's all, Bella."

He wrapped his arms around her and held her tense, lithe body close. But she did not hug him back. "Bella, love, my lips have not touched another woman's since I first laid eyes on you. I can't be with anyone else. I don't want to be with anyone but you. Honestly, Bella. You have no idea how much it shook me when I realized . . ." He gave a short, sardonic snort. "I was a male prostitute who couldn't get it up. Nothing. Not even a twitch. Why do you think I came to see you? I needed to be with you. Only you. I couldn't stomach the thought of another woman. I didn't even want them to get close to me, let alone touch me. All my body, my heart, my soul wanted was you."

She tipped her face up to gaze into his eyes.

He nurtured the flicker of hope in the violet depths. "You never have cause to be jealous. Never have reason to even let the notion pass through your beautiful head. You have ruined me, Bella. Completely. But being ruined is a good thing. It's wonderful. I much prefer it to all else because it means I love you. Only you."

Her lower lip trembled.

"I haven't said them yet today, have I?" He had never spoken those words to anyone but Bella. They were hers. In the morning he awoke and told a sleepy Bella he loved her. In the afternoon over tea he told her he loved her. In the evening, with her in his arms, he told her he loved her. It was as if there was a glut that had built deep inside of him over the years and needed to get out.

She shook her head, looking as though she would burst into tears at any moment. She was right there, at the precipice.

"I love you, Mrs. Rosedale," he said softly. "And you are the only woman who has ever heard those words from my lips."

A pleased little amazed smile curved her mouth. "I love you," she whispered.

Countless women had said those words to him in the heat of the moment. But they had not truly loved him, simply what he could do to them. But Bella, she did love him.

Her long lashes swept down on a soft sigh of contentment. "There is something else you haven't done yet today."

She peered up at him and his body reacted instantly to the hunger, the passion, burning in her eyes. His hands coasted down to cup her firm backside. He pressed her close, hard, so she could feel what she did to him, even through the layers of muslin skirts and wool trousers.

Bella's eyelids fluttered as she arched into him, kneading his shoulders. "Yes. Now," she breathed.

He could not hold back the grin—his impatient Bella. With her, all it took was the knowledge he was ready to rut and her senses would focus on nothing else.

He nuzzled the small space behind her ear. "Come upstairs with me."

"No. Here. Now."

"But—?" His attention flickered to the unlocked study door.

"You're my husband. You're allowed to ravish me in the study." She pulled at the waistband of his trousers as she stepped back, bringing him with her. With a little hop, she perched on the edge of the desk. Her long legs wrapped around the backs of his thighs, pulling him in as she freed his swollen cock. "*Now,*" she said, desire thick in her voice.

"Of course, Mrs. Rosedale," he drawled as his hands drifted up from her knees, gathering her skirt. "Don't I always give you what you need?"